Secrets & Curses of Exile

Shay Taylor

WESTWIND PUBLISHING LLC

For my husband, who gave me the courage to chase my dreams.

Contents

Contents

SEA OF VOID
AKECIA
KIZAR
FALGON
CERITHIA
EXILE
CRIMSON
FORBIDDEN WOOD
ELLORYON
SEA OF VOID
ISLANDS OF DEATH

Chapter I

We were all going to die.

That was the truth that was slowly suffocating all of us fae in Exile. The weight of our impending demise threatened to crush me with a sense of responsibility. The urgency to break us all out of our isolation was becoming harder to ignore. It's the reason why I was risking everything. It would give all of us here a fighting chance for a longer life. Even if that life was a shitty one, we still deserved it. I felt the little glimmer of hope in my chest expand. Maybe we would all escape this isolation one day and live with the rest of the fae.

I had to believe that, or I would go mad. The only way to keep pushing forward was to think that something good would be coming our way. Until that happened though, I would risk everything to save those trapped in this insufferable prison that we called Exile.

"It will be fine, Sybil," I assured her as I gathered my bow and arrows. "I've done this a dozen times already, and I'm still alive."

Sybil's hard blue eyes silently reprimanded me. She and I both knew how dangerous this was, but I couldn't lose her, too. We had already lost too many friends and family members. Her loud sigh let me know exactly how she felt about what we were doing. I was tired of having this disagreement every time I planned to cross the boundary.

"Just because things went well the last few times doesn't mean this time will go so smoothly, Thea," she bit out.

"There will always be a chance of something bad happening, Sybil, but I won't stand by and watch you waste away." Her skin was pale, and she was losing too much weight. We were running low on food, but everyone else was too. She was too sick for me to not go. I didn't have any choice but to cross the shadow boundary and steal her some medicine.

My fingers picked at the loose string of my cloak as worry consumed me, worry that we'd wake up one day to find all of the prisoners of Exile eating each other just to stay alive. I *needed* to do something. There was no way I would sit here while we all died, just because the king of Crimson thought we were monsters. He was the monster, locking us away to die.

"I'm crossing the boundary and getting us supplies," I said with finality. I hoped my tone would make her stop arguing with me. She couldn't keep me from going, no matter what she said or did. Sybil may be several hundred years older than me, but I was not a child. I had to be over two hundred years old now, not that I could really remember. In fact, I had no memory of my life before waking up in Exile, but whoever I was, I was far from being a child.

"I just worry about you," she whispered. "You have a big heart, Thea, but you also carry too much anger within it. Sometimes you do not think things through. It's as if you *hope* the Crimson guards will find you, so you can let out this rage you hold."

I sighed and rolled my eyes. She was right, but I was too stubborn to admit that to her. I tied a dark green cloak over my shoulders, my only defense against the cool night air, as I thought of a response that would satisfy her.

"I've thought this through, and I'm going. This is not fueled by anger or rage, but by the fact that I can't lose you." Sighing heavily, I continued. "If I lose you, I don't have anyone else but the twins. So please, just stop trying to make me stay."

Sybil was the only reason I didn't feel completely alone, like I still had a purpose and a family. She managed a weak smile as she lay on her tiny mattress on the floor. Her blue eyes filled with a look I couldn't quite place, but it was one that comforted me. She held her hand out for me, and I crossed her room to grasp it in mine, my footsteps heavy on the floor. A shiver ran through me as I realized how much colder she had gotten, even since yesterday.

I gave her a small, reassuring smile to hide my concern. "I'll start a fire before I go." It wouldn't take much heat to warm our simple home. It was barely large enough for the two of us to be living in, but we made it work.

"Please be quick and safe," she pleaded.

"I'll be back soon," I promised as I squeezed her hand once more before walking over to the small metal bin that served as a makeshift fireplace. I tossed a few pieces of firewood into it and lit the kindling underneath. My eyes watched the flames move over the wood before the popping sounds let me know it would stay lit. The smell of burning wood filled Sybil's room as I glanced over my shoulder once more. Her small body was curled up tightly to hold in her own heat, looking for warmth as she drifted to sleep.

Stepping out of her room, I headed for the front door and slipped my bow string across my back. My chest tightened as I let myself look at the small, suffocating space we called our home. The hallway that separated our two bedrooms was narrow, and I felt like the walls were closing in on me as I turned slightly to fit between them. As I stepped out of the hall, the inadequate kitchen didn't help this feeling of suffocating. It barely had enough room for cupboards and a small sink.

I made sure the front door shut all the way before turning my attention toward the Forbidden Wood. To avoid stares from the other fae that lived here, I slipped on my oversized hood. I glanced around at the many bodies lying in the street dead, waiting for morning light to be buried. Tears sprang to my eyes before I averted them. It never got easier seeing the destruction that came from the king of Crimson's cruelty, but it was a harsh reminder that I couldn't save them all and that if I didn't act, Sybil or I could very well be next.

Forcing my mind not to wander into dark thoughts, I focused on the edge of the meadow ahead of me. Darkness would trap my mind, blocking out reason and tricking me into doing what it really wanted. And it was so hard to control those thoughts once they started. Killing those responsible for our entrapment, while I'm sure it would make me feel better, it would only agitate Sybil further.

I got little relief, however, as my attention caught on a young mom holding her child, begging for food. My stomach churned with dread, as I knew there was a high chance that they would both die soon. I darted my gaze away from her quickly. Her desperate pleading echoed in my mind as I tried to shake the thoughts away.

I glanced over my shoulder as I stepped into the meadow that separated our shambled homes from the shadow boundary. The field had started dying in recent months, but to a stranger, it would have looked as if it died a long time ago. Only dry grass and dirt remained, and the crunching of dead weeds echoed in the silence of the night. The loudness made me scan the dozens of makeshift homes behind me to confirm that no one had followed me.

Only once had I been followed, but it was enough to make sure it didn't happen again. The fewer fae that knew what I was up to, the better. I couldn't risk anyone knowing I could cross over without dying. The shadow boundary's sole purpose was to keep us in Exile and kill whoever tried to escape.

I looked out at it as I approached, my body tense, knowing I would feel its discomfort shortly. The thin wall was dark, inky, and seemed endless. As I stared, there was a slight shimmer across it, reflecting the magic that was held inside of it. The boundary was as thin as a blade, but making it across that threshold was painful and hard.

The field of decaying plants ended abruptly, cut off by a forest of dead trees that no longer had leaves or bark on them. The smell of rotting vegetation clung to the stale air, making it difficult to breathe. When I reached the edge of the trees, I tossed one last glance over my shoulder.

The woods on this side of the meadow were eerie. There were no birds that sang or animals to run through them. They had all disappeared. My lungs took in the dry air of Exile one last time before I took the small step through the barrier that was meant to keep me in.

My body automatically curled in on itself as the agony of the border's magic seemed to punch right through my stomach. My lungs struggled to exhale the breath I was holding as I fell to my hands and knees. A searing pain coursed over and through me, undoubtedly trying to kill me for stepping through the barrier.

The agony paralyzed my muscles for what felt like an eternity, but slowly, it subsided. I pulled myself up on shaky legs and leaned against a nearby tree, breathing deeply to help ease my aching chest. The crisp, clean air on this side of the shadow boundary always soothed my tense muscles. I closed my eyes and listened to the birds chirping and the animals moving. It was easy to forget how much I missed those noises until I heard them again.

I wished Sybil could experience this, but I knew that she would die crossing, just like everyone else who tried. All except me, that is. Something I only figured out when I had tried to end my suffering one night. I didn't understand *how* I could cross, but I would take this small victory and use it to my advantage.

Once I felt recovered enough to continue, I set off. Following a tiny trail that animals had created over time, I headed in the direction of a neighboring town. It was dark and everyone would be sleeping, so it was the safest time to steal things. My eyes slowly adjusted to the moonlight, and I took a moment to stare at the thick forest, admiring how peaceful it was. Exile was nothing like this. It was always hotter than the rest of the realm was, and there was nothing peaceful about it—no pleasant smells or sounds to be found anywhere.

The Forbidden Wood was a neutral territory in the realm of Elloryon. No one regulated the land, and no one had authority over it. It was a perfect place to hide prisoners so no one would stumble upon them. Not that anyone was looking for us. From what Sybil had told me, the land was bordered by the kingdoms of Crimson and Cerithia, two of the five kingdoms in Elloryon. According to her, monsters lurked in these woods. Creatures so vile that nobody wanted the land for themselves. Most fae refused to even enter the Forbidden Wood in fear they would be slaughtered. Most fae except me, that is.

The town I was headed for wasn't far from the boundary, but darkness had fallen hours ago, making it difficult to navigate the fallen trees of the forest. Far off, the city of Crimson, backed by an immense castle, illuminated the dark sky.

Crimson's castle loomed in the distance with a sense of mystery surrounding it. Its exquisite beauty was so majestic that it made it hard to look at anything else. My eyes always drifted to it because of its impressive height and beauty. It sat on top of a green hill, as if guarding the city beneath it. It was crafted of black stone that seemed to exude power amidst the lush green landscape. My eyes gazed at the dark red lights that illuminated the outside of the keep, and despite my feelings about the king of Crimson, it was truly a sight to behold at night.

Curiosity about the city flitted through my mind, but I would never dare to go there. It was too close to the Crimson King, and that was a risk even I wouldn't take. It was a shame that my favorite view belonged to the man who was to blame for imprisoning elite magic holders in Exile. It was too pretty for a monster like him to live there.

So, I would stick to these small, nameless towns where I could steal necessities on a rotating system. However, there was always a fear of being recognized by the citizens as a prisoner, even when I hid my elite magic mark. Although I wasn't sure they would be able to tell just by looking at me. These towns were small enough in size that my stealing was noticeable, so I tried to not steal from the same town twice in a row. After all, I didn't need any unnecessary attention drawn to me.

The snap of a stick made me freeze in place. My eyes shifted to the direction of the sound, but I saw nothing other than the darkness that was there.

Then a light blue glow caught my eye. It moved silently in the shadows of the woods, floating a few inches off the ground. It didn't matter how many times I had seen this creature lurking; it always mesmerized me. The soft light it emulated glowed brightly around it.

The blue flame was shaped like a fae would be, but it didn't have any distinguishable features. It wisped in the wind, which was how I came up with its name, Wisp.

As if it sensed me looking at it, it stopped and turned to me. Curious, I hazarded a step towards it. The wisp moved slowly, leading me farther from the trail I had been following. In all the times I had seen it before, it had never let me get too close to it. On some trips out of Exile, it wouldn't even show itself. But I sensed it lurking by all the time, like it was waiting for me, watching me. The creature was not something to trust, but it had yet to lead me astray. There were others like it around too, each one slightly different, but I couldn't quite place my finger on how I was able to tell them apart.

Cautiously, I walked forward, gripping my bow with a loaded arrow in my hand. My numb fingers rested on the string as the wind blew freezing gusts around me. Monsters always lurked in the forests of Elloryon; everybody knew that. I myself had learned this lesson the hard way, and it almost cost me my life. But things were different now; no other creatures ever seemed to be lurking around Exile except the wisps, but I couldn't let my guard down.

It was difficult to avoid the broken limbs and chunks of fallen trees that littered the forest floor as I crept silently. After I moved far from the trail, I heard something behind me let out a loud breath. I dropped down into the bushes at the base of a large pine tree and waited for whatever created that noise to step into the moonlight.

A dark figure stood on the trail, but it was too tall and thin to be a fae. My breath caught in my throat as the creature sniffed the air, almost as if it smelled me nearby. Suddenly, the monster turned towards me, its eyes glowing a faint red. The noise it bellowed curdled my blood.

It took one long step toward me, but I didn't dare move.

Then it took another, and another.

My heart pounded so loudly that I thought all the monsters in the woods would find me.

Suddenly, Wisp moved quickly to distract the creature from my direction. The monster's eyes instantly snapped to the wisp, just as mesmerized by it as I was. Thankfully, it started following the floating blue orb as if in a trance. As I watched, the flame of the wisp flickered farther into the woods away from me, taking the dangers of the monster with it.

This was not the first time this orb had saved me, and I was sure it wouldn't be the last. There was no reason I could think of for the wisp to help me, but I was thankful for it.

The lights of the town I was planning to steal supplies from glowed faintly through the thick trees. Mentally, I ran through my list of needs. The first thing I required was medication for Sybil. That was my main purpose for coming here. Once I had that, I could gather more things, like food and clothing.

The town was nearly dark when I finally reached the edge of the Forbidden Woods. Waiting at the tree line, my eyes scanned for any fae that might still be lingering on the streets. Seeing nothing, I slowly made my way to the merchant section of the town, where the wind blew the apothecary sign and made the chains it hung from creak in the eerie silence as it rocked back and forth, almost as if it were beckoning me to come closer. Taking a deep breath, I darted from the woods and sprinted across the dirt roadway.

Quietly, I tried the latch, but the doors of the apothecary were bolted shut with thick metal bars.

Shit.

It wasn't that I couldn't break through the bars; I could do that easily. What I was worried about was summoning my elite magic to do it, which would leave me open to being discovered. I knew that I didn't have a choice though and began slowly heating the door. My fire magic was a welcome reprieve from the numbing cold. Sybil had stressed to me that our elite magic should not be used unless it was absolutely necessary. If anyone saw it being used, they would know I had escaped from Exile.

I still remember the way Sybil comforted me after coming back from getting us supplies the first time. I had been so terrified because my fire magic exploded out of me without warning. She had been so worried that someone saw my magic, exposing my secret. That was when Sybil explained to me that elite magic was different from regular magic. Regular magic was not held by all fae. And those that had it were severely limited in its powers. Those that did have magic all had similar talents, usually manipulating elements, controlling nature, or conjuring objects. However, they could sustain their abilities for very short periods of time. Elite magic, though, was more powerful. Wielders of this type of magic were constantly in danger of being discriminated against. After all, if power couldn't be controlled, it was to be feared.

I stared at my reflection in the window of the door. My dark braid had loose strands falling from it. My normally dark green eyes burned red now with the use of my elite magic. I shattered the glass; the noise echoed in the dead silence of the night, pulling me from my thoughts. I reached through the doors and lifted the bar that was in place, then hurried into the small shop. It was dark inside and smelled of herbs and dust. I scanned the shelves and saw that they were lined with things I didn't need. I had to find valuable medicine, and those were always kept safely in the back of the shop. Not knowing exactly what was wrong with Sybil made this harder, but any valuable medications I brought back seemed to help her symptoms for a short time. She had wielded elite healing magic before the king had exiled us, which meant she didn't need herbs and medicines to heal others. The way she described it, the magic flowed from her and fixed injuries. Once she had been thrown into Exile, though, she not only became a prisoner but was stripped of her abilities as well.

I slowly made my way to the special medicines tucked in the back room and immediately saw what I came for. After rummaging on the shelves for as long as I dared, herbs and vials filled my small leather bag to the top. Once I was satisfied that I wouldn't be able to fit any more in, I snuck back out. Lingering for long in one spot was dangerous, and the next items would be trickier to steal.

Once back outside, I hurried towards the first house and rejoiced internally when I discovered the door was unlocked. I was sure the Crimson King had told everyone that with us locked up, they were safe. The monsters couldn't hurt them.

It made stealing a lot easier for me. I quietly hurried into the kitchen, flicking my hand so the flame from my magic illuminated the room. Grabbing a bag that lay on the table, I filled it with flour, yeast, eggs, milk, and anything else I could find that would benefit us.

Stars above, I wish there was a way I could carry more, but this would last us for a long time. Smothering the flame, I headed out of that house and into the next. Tonight, I will push the limit of what I would carry. Crossing the boundary was not something I could do too often. My luck would run out eventually, so I would use it all up today if I needed to.

I took what food items I found from their home, too. These fae could afford it, I told myself. This town was full of nice homes, which made taking from them all the easier. These were the king's followers, the fae that had stood aside as he ransacked every town and village looking for marks of elite magic so he could banish us, so he could make us the villains in his story.

My fingers curled into fists, like they did every time I thought of the king of Crimson. Killing him was my top priority, if I ever had a chance to do it. If he were killed, then maybe everyone in Exile would be freed. All the other fae in the kingdom of Crimson might not like us, but I was sure there would be refuge in other kingdoms. We would all be better off with him dead.

After filling another bag of food, I began to leave. My feet slowed as I headed for the door, though. A child's blanket had caught my eye, and I took it for the mother with the starving child. Once outside, I strapped the bags across my back and shoulders. There was no way to carry more, even if I wanted to. Slipping from the town, I moved back towards where I had emerged from the Forbidden Wood.

It only took a few short minutes for my hands and back to begin to ache from carrying so much weight. However, I managed to make it most of the way back to Exile before taking a break. Once I was close to my destination, I set down my supplies and leaned against a tree for a moment.

As I gathered my breath, my eyes wandered to the full treetops and the stars above them. They were beautiful, but they made me sad. The fae locked in Exile had forgotten the small details of the realm, such as stars and moonlight, birds singing, and creeks flowing. It was the little things that I appreciated the most when I came back to this side. While taking in the skyline one last time, my eyes drifted back to the dark, brooding castle in the distance. Something seemed to tug deep in my chest every time I glanced at it, something I couldn't explain.

For the second time that night, a snapping twig close by broke me out of my thoughts. I thought I heard a faint breath somewhere close to me, but the noise seemed to float through the silent woods, making it difficult to know where it came from. My mind flashed to the slender figure that had been stalking me earlier. Maybe the monster was back. Peeking around the tree, I sighed in relief when I saw that it was just a fae. He wasn't trying to be quiet, so I assumed he didn't know I was there. Moments later, though, more deep voices whispered out in the distant darkness. They were getting closer to me.

Gripping my bow, I loaded one of my hand-carved arrows onto the string. I glanced around the tree once more and noticed he was wearing the red uniform of a Crimson guardsman. He was staring at the ground, following something. I cursed myself when I realized it was likely my footprints or the drag marks from my heavy bag of stolen supplies. The guard knew I was somewhere out here, and if I continued, my tracks would lead him right to Exile.

Suddenly, he looked up and stared directly at me. His mouth opened to yell for help, but I was quicker than he was. Quickly, my arrow flicked off the string and stuck directly into the guard's chest. His mouth opened and closed in surprise, before his eyes glazed over, and he fell to the forest floor, dead. My feet moved towards the guard to retrieve my arrow.

When I reached him, I pulled it from his chest and wiped the blood on his tunic. His thick, red wool uniform held the Crimson King's family crest in gold stitching directly over his heart. I smiled; it had made for the perfect target. The darkness that lived deep in my chest tried surging forward now that danger was present, but I wouldn't allow it. I could handle a few guards without the help of my darkness taking over.

My breath stilled as I listened for the others that would be coming once they realized one of their own was missing. Darting my eyes to the dead man at my feet, I waited for the guilt to wash over me, but it never came. I seemed to always be immune to that when it came to killing, as if I was made for it. Perhaps I was a monster for killing him, but I had to be in order to save Sybil and others in Exile.

I loaded another arrow and pointed it in the direction of the twigs that I heard snapping in the forest around me, steadying my hands as best as I could.

I inhaled one long breath of frosted air into my lungs as I released my bowstring. My eyes closed, and I strained to listen for the deep thump of my arrow burying itself into the chest of another guard. Once that undeniable sound echoed in the silence, I grabbed another arrow. When chaos broke out among the last few men walking through the Forbidden Wood, I smiled to myself.

"Retreat!" one of the men yelled.

Moonlight illuminated the woods just enough that the silhouette of my next target was easy to spot. His back was towards me as he tried to run back to the king.

Coward.

I only needed one of them to survive. I wanted them to tell the story of the villain in the woods who killed the king's guardsmen without mercy. I had overheard stories once, when I snuck into a town before darkness had fallen a long time ago. They spoke of a mercenary that lived in the woods that couldn't be seen, a defender without mercy.

The king's fae were appalled and disgusted by acts of rebellion, but it only made my work more satisfying. I would be a voice to those the Crimson King tried to silence, even if he had no idea who I represented.

My hands worked quickly as I darted through the thicket of trees towards the other guardsmen. Once I spotted them, I let another arrow fly, and one of the men crumpled to the forest floor. I ripped it from his back as I passed, needing to preserve my shots. I calmed my puffy breaths as I lined the next arrow with the last man I would kill tonight. The thrum of my bowstring releasing made the man turn at the last moment. It was enough time for my arrow to hit his heart.

Dark blood soaked his red uniform around the shot as he fell to his knees. The only man left stopped and turned, staring into the dark where he thought I was. The light of the moon illuminated the stiffness in his body as he stood paralyzed with fear. The guard was waiting for the shot he thought would be coming for him, but I only watched in the darkness, waiting for him to leave so I could gather my precious arrows. Each one took so much time to craft, and I couldn't afford to leave them behind.

After a long silent moment, the man turned and fled back towards the Crimson kingdom. Once his footsteps had faded into the distance, I hurried to pick up my arrows.

A hand wrapped around my ankle as I started to pull the arrow from the chest of the last man I shot. His eyes peered up at me in a quiet pleading to end his suffering.

Blood flew from his mouth as a cough racked his body. He whispered something unintelligible, and I knelt closer to hear him. He took a deep, labored breath and tried to speak again.

"A man who hides in the shadows is a coward," he grunted up towards me.

I pulled my hood back, smiling at the pure shock contorting the guard's face as he realized I was a woman. I flicked my fire magic into the palm of my hand so he would die knowing who I represented.

"Your king banished us to the shadows, and for that, he and all of his men will die for it." I sneered as I twisted the arrow in his chest before yanking it out completely.

"Thea..."

"What did you say?"

My mind was playing tricks on me. How would he know my name? There was no way that's what he said. All the adrenaline pumping through me must have been making me hear things. The guard's eyes watched me as he struggled to breathe. His mouth opened and closed as he tried to say something else. I leaned my ear down to his mouth. Damn it, say something.

The last gargled breath he took let me know I would never know if I heard him correctly.

But even as I tried to convince myself, the tingling on the base of my neck told me I had heard him correctly. My eyes darted around me as paranoia settled in my chest. I needed to get out of there.

I turned back to where I had rested and found my bags of supplies. My lungs burned with the coldness of the air on this side of the shadow boundary, but my back was dampened in sweat from chasing the guards.

I paused to admire the moon cresting over the treetops for one more second before continuing my trek back into the starless night of Exile. None of the children in Exile had ever seen the stars or moon, a thought that sent anger and sadness flowing through me. The children there were robbed of life because the king was a power-hungry coward.

Taking in one last lung full of cold, crisp air, I stepped through the boundary. The familiar pain raced through my body, and I fell to my hands and knees. A painful sob escaped me as I braced myself on the hot, dry ground. My body fought to catch its breath, but the stale air did little to comfort my lungs.

I wanted desperately to crawl back through the shadow boundary and breathe the clean air again. Collapsing on my back, I stared into the starless night and begged the gods above to end our suffering. I couldn't keep doing this. One of these times, the guards would kill me, and then Sybil would die too. Something needed to change.

I groaned in helplessness at the pain I was feeling, which seemed unending. But my muscles slowly unclenched as it lessened its grip on me. After resting for a moment, I stood with the little energy I had left and made my way through the meadow and toward the shambled buildings. It was dark and most fae should be sleeping, so I was hopeful that no one would notice me with these supplies. If anybody did, they would kill me without a second thought. Not caring where the supplies had come from.

I dragged my bags through the side trails to avoid any part of town that fae may have been walking. My eyes were fixated on the dark green door that marked mine and Sybil's home, and I welcomed the feeling of comfort that settled in my chest when I saw it. The color resonated with me and was the reason I had picked this home.

Hurrying in, I slammed the door shut and locked it, feeling paranoid that I was being followed. It was a ridicu-lous thought. When I turned, Sybil was standing in the doorway of the hall watching me.

"By the gods, Thea. You're covered in blood."

She moved quickly to help me.

"It's not mine, Sybil," I reassured her. She recoiled in disgust as she took in my blood-stained clothes, her face contorting with judgment as she crossed her arms tightly across her chest, creating a barrier between us. Her eyes frosted over as she glanced up at me.

Sybil detested violence. That was where we were different. My body hummed when danger was near. It liked the rush of it and feeling the power of my magic pulsing with adrenaline. Sybil's reactions always made me wonder if there was something wrong with me finding satisfaction in killing guards.

"How many?"

"How many what?" I moved towards the small living area to hide our supplies. Our shelves filled quickly with the new things I had gathered.

"How many men did you hurt?"

"I killed four," I sighed and waited for her to yell at me. When she didn't, I pressed on. "One guard lived. Besides, they were the king's guardsmen, and they were following me. I didn't have a choice."

"You can't go again." She spoke as if she were my mother, but she wasn't. No one would stop me. What would she say if I told her that I had run into two different creatures and one of them helped me? Or that the dying guard had muttered my name? Uneasiness curdled my stomach, and

I tried to convince myself that it couldn't have been what he said.

"When we run out of medicine and supplies, I'll go back out." I didn't want to argue with her, but she seemed to forget what would happen if I didn't go. I did this for us, so we would survive together.

"I worry that you are looking for a fight, Thea. You want to find trouble so you can take out your anger on someone or something, but it will not change our fate."

"If I can do anything to help change our fate, then I will try. We don't deserve to die in this prison." Sybil scanned all the supplies I had managed to carry and backed up from me as the metallic scent of blood filled the space.

"We all lost someone or something, Thea." She stepped back deliberately, putting space between us. "Our homes, our families, our magic." Tears formed in her eyes and spilled down her cheeks as she remembered all the things she had lost. I wasn't even allowed that small amount of comfort because I had no memories. At least she had things to remember, unlike me.

No one here understood how unworthy of love or happiness I felt. Most days I wasn't sure if fighting for our freedom was even worth it because every time I tried to make connections with others, I noticed their distance, as if they viewed me as the monster here. How can I believe that anyone outside of Exile missed me, especially when I couldn't remember?

We were all suffering, but I was the only one who couldn't remember my life before this damn prison. My memory was either damaged or gone. My teeth clenched tightly. It wasn't fair. I didn't understand why I couldn't remember, but there was no point in trying to understand any of this madness. The more I thought of our circumstances, the more my face heated. Everyone here was lonely, but at least they remembered what love and belonging were like at some point. Loneliness gnawed at my soul like an unrelenting ache.

"Our families abandoned us as soon as the king called us monsters," I spat back at her. "You said so yourself that they all let us suffer, but they continue to live their lives as if we aren't slowly dying and being forgotten. And for what? Because we have elite magic, and the king thought we would rebel against him!" Every word I spoke was laced with the betrayal that we experienced every day here.

Sybil frowned at me, and her eyes filled with disappointment and sadness. The weight of the guilt that hit me immediately crushed my anger. Avoiding her gaze, I stared at the floor and blinked rapidly to keep my tears at bay. She was upset with me, and I couldn't bear to see disappointment in her eyes. Everyone here had a loved one or family that just stepped aside and let the king and his guardsmen exile us here. No one cared about us. They all thought we were monsters, so I wanted to prove to them with every fiber in my body that I was their worst nightmare.

They should all be punished.

"I'm tired. I'll mix up medicine in the morning." Sybil excused herself to her room, and I didn't let out my breath until her door shut. The overwhelming feeling of remorse seeped into my bones for all the times I had lashed out at Sybil and others in anger. I pushed everyone away, especially those that cared for me.

The realization hit me hard that perhaps it wasn't others who viewed me as a monster. Maybe it was how I viewed myself.

I sank to the floor for a long moment, trying to control my hurt and anger. Like always, my overwhelming emotions triggered my magic, and it simmered under my skin now, begging to be released. Shoving myself off the floor, I went to my room and hoped the silence would help.

I closed my eyes and leaned my head against the door. Exhaustion was nothing new to me since living in Exile. Every day took a toll on all of us. We were being suffocated, and there was nothing we could do. We would have to accept this fate eventually, but until then, I would fight with everything I had.

I slipped off the blood-stained clothes and washed my-self while getting ready for bed. My eyes stared at the small bed made from old clothes that didn't fit anymore. Even without knowing what my life had been like outside of Exile, I could see from the towns I stole from that we were living in complete squalor here.

I hated this place. I hated this house that was too small, the air that was too hot and sticky, and I hated that I couldn't remember if my life had been better than this before.

Chapter 2

My dreams had never given me much insight into my past, but each nightmare only made me hope that one-night things would change. That my dreams would reveal something that had been forgotten about my past.

I was back once again in the dark hallway. The large, wooden door awaited me at the end, a sinister red glow coming through the crack at the bottom. It was familiar. I wasn't sure if it was because I had dreamt of it for as long as I could remember or if it was a memory from my lost past. Dread filled my chest as I stared at the golden handle of the door, like it held all the answers to my past. But what if those answers only showed a life worse than the one I had in Exile?

I reached out to open the door but paused when a swirling red, black, and orange tattoo began crawling up my arm. These had never shown up before. My fingers traced the markings on my skin, and they glowed brightly at my touch for a moment. I focused back on the door in front of me and gently tried to push it open. As in all the other dreams though, it didn't move at all.

I paused when a small noise sounded behind me. I wasn't scared though, because I already knew who it was. Slowly, I turned, and the man I expected was standing in shadows, watching me silently. Most of his features were hidden in the darkness, but his golden eyes were always shining brightly enough to be seen. He was here almost every dream, too, but I didn't feel any sort of threat from him. He never spoke either, never revealed anything about himself. I was too worried that if I said a word to him, he would disappear. Despite this, there seemed to be a comfortable silence between us. I simply gazed at his golden eyes, glowing out at me from the dark. The tension in my muscles always eased the longer I watched him, which was a rare comfort.

Suddenly, screaming from behind the door ripped my gaze from the man.

"Thea!" the voices pleaded from the opposite side of the door.

The urge to help whoever it was overtook me, and desperately, I yanked on the door. But it didn't budge; it never did. Flames appeared and engulfed the door, the smoke making my eyes water. The door handle instantly heated, and I pulled my hand away in pain. The roaring of the fire filled my ears as their frantic pleading became louder from the other side.

But I couldn't save them; I never could.

I bolted up in my bed. My hazy eyes flew to the door, checking for flames or smoke, but I was in my room in Exile. I took a deep breath, calming myself, then I chuckled at the irony of feeling relief that I was happy to be in Exile for once.

Falling back onto my lumpy bed, I stared at the moss and mud that we had used to make the roof. It was cracking under the constant heat of this place and would need to be replaced at some point. I didn't know exactly how long we had lived here, but this house was certainly due for some work.

There were things I kept secret from Sybil. One of them was that I couldn't remember periods of time while living here. Other fae would tell stories, but I couldn't recall past events like they could. It was like I hadn't been here for as long as them. Sometimes, I woke up in a fog of confusion and couldn't remember anything from the past few days. Sybil never said I had gone missing, so I knew something had to be wrong with me. Especially if I couldn't keep all of my memories from Exile, much less my time before I came here.

From what others had said, we all appeared in Exile at the same time. My brain just couldn't remember like theirs could. It was crazy to think that I was missing time in Exile, so I said nothing. But deep down, I felt there was something very wrong with me.

I guess it didn't really matter how long we lived here though, because not once did it comfort me like a home should. Not that I had something to compare it to. The only happy memories I had were of Sybil teaching me new things or the twins showing me how to fight or shoot a bow.

Sybil's loud movements in the kitchen had me slipping out of bed and putting on my clothes so we could work together on making bread.

Even though our home was small, I was thankful for the privacy it offered. Most males lived in community houses with little privacy, opting to let the females and children have the small homes. Our house was bland and had no personal or warm touches besides the dried herbs Sybil displayed.

There was nothing frivolous about Exile.

I had lived alone at first, but Sybil moved in a short time after. I had found her barely breathing in the street and brought her back here with me. I shook my head to clear the memory of her near-lifeless face.

"Good morning, Thea. I've already made bread." The aroma floated through our house, the comforting smell mingling with the obvious tension between us. She gave me her usual happy smile, but I was cautious that it wasn't genuine. Guilt still gnawed at my insides because I had been cruel to her.

"Smells great." I picked up a piece of warm bread and nibbled on it. My stomach clenched almost in protest at the food. It wasn't used to getting enough to eat. "Thanks."

She nodded and sat on her stool, staring at me. I wanted to avoid a conversation with her. After all, we had never agreed on how to view the world. We didn't see eye to eye on hardly anything, really.

"I'm sorry for being upset with you," she started. My hand froze midway to my mouth with my next bite of bread. How was she apologizing so easily? We had fought countless times before without her ever acknowledging that my violence might be necessary for survival. "You are the reason we are both still alive. If you must kill to do it, then so be it." The sudden shift in her views startled me. My stomach churned with hunger, but also with the oddness of Sybil validating my violence.

"I'm sorry for saying your family abandoned you. It was a low blow and uncalled for."

"Sometimes, I wonder what would have happened if I had chosen differently," she whispered, more to herself than to me. "I should have fled like my husband begged me to. Then my life wouldn't have ended like this." She waved her hand around our cramped kitchen for effect.

"But you always said our families abandoned us. Yours wanted to protect you?" My eyes narrowed on her. She had never said this before.

"There are things that you don't remember, Thea. But I made a decision that was bigger than my own wants and needs. I did it for the realm of Elloryon."

Her eyes were fixated on the herbs and vials I had brought her last night. She didn't say anything for a long moment, and I thought that we were done with this conversation.

"Maybe one day, somehow, we will be rescued from Exile and find our place in society again. That is the thought that keeps me going, Thea. Hopefully, my family will be waiting for me when I'm freed, and they will forgive me for not listening to them."

Confusion swarmed my mind, and a heaviness settled on my heart. Sybil had never revealed any of this before. *Everyone* here made it sound like their families had abandoned them and turned them into the Crimson King the moment they could. Why had she led me to believe that the world hated us?

"So, your family didn't abandon you?" I questioned. Her eyes found mine, and worry flickered across her face. Doubt stormed inside of me, casting a shadow over everything she had ever told me.

"It's complicated," she frowned and turned from me to end the questioning.

"Why would you choose to come to Exile if you had a different option?" Her body became rigid at my questioning. My fingers dug into the skin of my palms as my fists clenched tightly. What else had she not been truthful about? My heart raced with this news. Sybil wasn't abandoned by her family; she chose to come here. Had I chosen to come here too? Uneasiness swarmed in my stomach; something was wrong about all of this. It contradicted all of her stories from before.

"There are decisions we make because it is what's needed. We don't always have the luxury of doing what we want." Her eyes focused on a spot over my shoulder. "If you had your memories, I'm sure you'd agree with me."

"There is no reason I can think of that would make me choose this hell over my family."

Her eyes frosted over as she spoke, making me shiver even though the air was warm. "You would if it meant saving them," she said quietly. "You would give up anything for those you loved, even your own happiness."

All I could think at that moment was that we would never be saved, we would never find our places in society, and elite magic would die out once and for all. The king would never allow us to exist in this realm again just because an elitist had tried to kill him.

Or at least that is what I had been told when I woke up in Exile without any memory of myself, my past, or the realm of Elloryon. I couldn't trust that anything I had been told was true. My skin prickled at the realization of how easily I could be manipulated by others. My lack of memory could be used to others' advantage, and that was terrifying.

"Enough sad talk. Tell me how using your magic was." Sybil's gloomy expression was replaced by intrigue. A war raged inside of me. Did I continue with this conversation and risk losing Sybil's companionship, or should I let it go?

"Honestly, I don't even know how to describe it, Sybil. It feels comforting and so much stronger each time I use it. It's like every time I leave Exile, it grows bigger inside of me."

Her eyes widened at this bit of information, but then she smiled softly as if remembering a fond memory.

"What I would give to have my magic coursing through my veins again," she chuckled. "You know I met my husband when he came to me for healing."

Sybil rarely talked about her family. All she had told me was that she was married and had a couple of daughters and a son. She had not passed down the elite magic in her blood to her children and thanked the gods every day she didn't give them her mark.

My hand instinctively rubbed the mark of elite magic behind my ear. I was lucky that mine wasn't as visible. Sybil's was on the back of her hand in the shape of some sort of black flower. Everyone's mark was different. Mine was a half moon with four stars that lined the crest of it, but all of our marks glowed slightly, making them different than tattoos.

"What was wrong with him?"

"He shot himself in the foot with an arrow on accident." Sybil's burst of laughter made me smile. We didn't experience sounds of happiness here very often.

A woman's scream from outside jolted us back to reality. I grabbed my viper-handled dagger and stood in front of Sybil. We didn't hear anything again, and I cautiously opened the front door to assess if I could help.

A woman around my age lay on the ground next to a man, who I assumed was her husband. He was dead and had been moved into the streets with others who had died so they could be buried.

Grief surged through my veins at the sounds of her overwhelming anguish. I longed to be able to do something to take away her pain. Powerlessness filled me as I watched her body tremble with loud sobs. Her hands clenched her husband as if it would bring him back to her.

We couldn't keep living like this. We would all be dead by next year. The woman wrapped herself around the man and cried into his lifeless chest even harder. I wish we had our magic still. Sybil would be able to save everyone from sickness, but the king had made sure to take the biggest parts of us—our families and our magic.

We might as well have been born humans. We were weak without our magic abilities. We would become extinct like they had hundreds of years ago.

Other fae walked by her, not saying or doing anything to ease her suffering. No words of comfort, no helping her or making sure she wasn't alone. She was on her own in her grief.

That thought compelled me to step forward. I didn't want this woman to feel what I did every day I was stuck in this prison. Sybil pulled me back before I was able to take another step.

"Let her grieve, Thea."

I nodded as I watched the woman, still pleading with the man to open his eyes. Hatred and sorrow thundered inside my chest. I couldn't do this. I went inside and grabbed my bow and arrows before slipping on my cloak.

"Thea."

"I'll be back," I muttered as I headed towards the meadow. I crossed the field to the farthest part of it, wanting to be far away from the shitty town we were forced to call home.

Once my makeshift targets came into view, I stopped and loaded an arrow onto my bowstring, just trying to take my mind off of everything. I had spent the first few years here perfecting both my offensive and defensive skills. Mainly because there was nothing else to do, but also because I wanted to be ready for when I had an opportunity to save us or kill the king of Crimson. Needing to vent my frustration on something, I envisioned the targets to be the king and his disgusting line of heirs, not that I had the faintest idea what they looked like. That part didn't matter though. They all deserved to die. All the fae living outside of the shadow boundary deserved to be punished for allowing the king to dole out such a cruel fate, simply because our magic made us more powerful.

My arrows hit the center of the target every time. Each was a small victory, making it a little easier to breathe again.

But something deep in my chest still stirred with uncertainty. Would I ever have a chance to at least fight for us?

Gods above, I would give up anything to kill the king.

The crunch of dead grass behind me alerted me to the fact that someone was coming. I turned quickly and drew my arrow, prepared to defend myself.

"Gods, Thea!" The boys dove down as if I would shoot them. I lowered my bow in relief as the twins straightened and smiled at me. They were at least fifty years older than me, but when they smiled, they looked young. They were the same in every way except where their elite magic marks were on their skin. Kaz's blackbird elite mark was on his forearm, and Kai's identical mark was on his neck. They never talked about their magic, but I had overheard them mention shifting once.

"Sybil sent you," I muttered. I had just wanted time to think alone.

"She gets worried about you when you're angry and left to your own thoughts."

I knew this, but I still wanted to be alone.

"Where have you been lately, Thea? We haven't seen you much," Kaz frowned at me. His blonde hair was a lot longer than I had remembered. It had been longer since I had last seen them than I thought. His dark eyes held my stare, waiting for a truthful answer. My eyes drifted over them.

"Taking care of Sybil. She hasn't been doing well," I sighed.

Kai was the one frowning now. He had always been the more caring of the two. Kaz's heart hardened when his girlfriend exposed their hiding place and turned him and Kai over to the king's guardsmen. I was certain there was more to that story, but he would never talk about it when asked.

"She said you crossed again." Kaz stared at me like an annoyed older brother. Although I wasn't sure what having a brother was like, I had seen children in Exile give this same expression to their annoying younger siblings. "It's too dangerous."

"I don't need a lecture from you too. I'm going to continue to cross over to keep us alive. I got enough food this time to make you fresh bread, and Sybil has to have medicine. Would it kill any of you to thank me for keeping us alive?"

"We are thankful, but we're terrified for your safety. What if it's a test, Thea? What if the king finds out and all of us are punished for it? You shouldn't be able to go through the boundary. I don't know how you figured out you could, but it's not a blessing. It's a curse!"

I didn't acknowledge him, as guilt soured my stomach.

I had stolen a cart of food from one of the towns before and brought it back. No one knew where it came from, but because of it, chaos ensued. Fae were beating and killing each other for the supplies. Having learned my lesson from that terrible event, I never did it again.

Kaz, Kai, and Sybil were the only ones that had any idea I could cross the boundary, and it would stay that way. If the others found out, they would demand more than I would ever be able to deliver. They would become dependent on me, and I could barely care for the four of us as it was.

"Thea, you're too impulsive. Your lack of regard for yourself will kill you," Kai chimed in. Great. He was right, but I didn't care. My eyes narrowed on him as my anger simmered under my skin, drawing my magic forth. Feeling it so close to surfacing was its own form of torture. I wondered if others in Exile felt that, too.

"So what?" I huffed. "If I died, it would be an improvement from this hell."

Kaz and Kai didn't say anything in response. They cared for me, even though I never asked them too. In reality, they had found out that I could cross the boundary completely by accident. They had been leaving the Forbidden Wood as I came back through one night and had witnessed me emerging back into Exile. Sybil, though, was clever. She had asked too many questions about where I found herbs and was never satisfied with my answers. Eventually, I felt like I needed to tell her, if only to keep her trust. Once my secret was revealed, I had expected them to tell others, but they hadn't.

Deep in my heart though, I still felt like I couldn't trust any of them completely. Especially now, with what Sybil had revealed to me earlier. Our recent conversation replayed in my mind. Something about what she said made me doubt how we all ended up here.

Was my ability to trust completely broken now? Would I always doubt other faes true intentions? Not having a memory of my own made me rely on others for information, and I hated it. It caused a constant unease that weighed heavily on me, draining me of energy because I was always on edge and overthinking. My shoulders slumped when I realized how tired I truly was.

"Thea, we don't want you to get hurt, or even worse, killed. We just want you to think about your decisions," Kaz sighed. The weight of his words settled over me with his genuine concern for my well-being.

"Why does everyone assume that I don't think before I do something? If I don't go, we will all die. If I can prevent that, then I will." I raised my bow, pulling the string of it against my cheek forcefully. My magic tried to claw its way out but was reduced to just sitting under my skin, like an itch I couldn't scratch. "You will not tell me what I can and can't do."

I released the string, and my shot hit the dead center of the farthest target. I walked away from them to gather my arrows, but they followed.

"Sybil wanted to make sure you'd come back before the town meeting, so we can make some food," Kai muttered.

I nodded as I grabbed the shafts and pulled them from my imaginary victims. I never missed a town meeting, even though it was torture to go. Tonight's meeting would likely be just another reminder of our gloomy future.

"Let's practice throwing daggers first," Kai offered when he saw how upset I was. "We've been slacking on helping you learn different weapon skills."

Kaz and Kai had taught me all the combat knowledge that I knew. It was Kaz who taught me how to shoot my bow after I brought it from across the boundary, but both of them had helped me carve new arrows for it. They had said I was a natural fighter, and, to be honest, all the fighting and weapons skills they taught me felt natural. Maybe I had a background in these things.

I set my bow down and pulled out my viper-handled dagger. Kaz grabbed one of my targets and moved it closer.

"Do you remember the stance from the last time we practiced?"

I nodded and took the stance, making sure I widened my feet like he had drilled into my head. Lifting the dagger with a firm grip, I waited for his instruction.

"Good. Now feel the weight of the dagger. Balance it within your fingers. Remember to twist your hips the same time you release it," Kai instructed. I listened to him and focused on the target before twisting and releasing it, just as he had said.

The dagger hit just outside of the bullseye.

"Again. You can do better than that." Kaz went and got my dagger for me. They made me practice until I was begging to be done. They were perfectionists if nothing else.

"Your throwing has definitely improved." Kaz chuckled as he clamped his hand on my shoulder. "You just need to be confident, like you are with your bow."

"Well, I can still take both of you down in hand-to-hand combat," I muttered before laughing softly.

"Honestly, Thea, I think you might be able to fight both of us at the same time and still kick our asses," Kai laughed. "Actually, that might be a great lesson for next time."

"Great," I spoke sarcastically. I was thankful for their willingness to teach me fighting and weaponry skills.

As the twins and I walked in silence towards home, my eyes glanced to where the woman had held her dead husband in the street. My footsteps faltered as I saw that she lay still across his chest, gripping onto him, but now she was dead as well. The knife she had used on herself lay in her bloodied hand. Another one I couldn't save in time, but at least they were together now.

When I walked in to the house, baked bread sat everywhere on the counters. Sybil smiled and handed us each a loaf. I took mine and wrapped it in the baby blanket I had found last night before grabbing a thing of milk.

"I'll be right back."

I headed out the door and down the side trail next to our small house. The woman with the child lived in the house next to ours. Hopefully, she was still there and hadn't been run off by others. I peeked in the window and saw her cradling her young child inside. I set the food and milk in front of the door and knocked before ducking behind a wall.

The woman answered the door, looking down at the gift I left for her. The sobs that escaped her made my hardened heart crack just a little. She hurried inside, and I crept back to the window. She already had a cup of milk and bread in front of her child. She wrapped the new blanket around him and smiled. I would continue to share our food with them. I would save them, too.

I hurried back to our house. Fae were scarce on the streets today. Either they were all dead or it was too hot to be out. The constant fighting and yelling in the streets got old. I would take the eerie silence over the blood-curdling screams anytime.

As I walked back in, Sybil, Kai, and Kaz were in a heated discussion that abruptly ended when I entered the room.

"What?" I asked, instantly suspicious.

"You can't save them all, Thea." Kaz frowned.

"Well, I got the food, so I will share it how I please. Besides, I will not let a child and his mother die because we were being greedy."

They all fell silent. I grabbed a piece of bread and ate it quietly. The small boy had been born with elite magic, but his mother was not. I had never seen the mark of the elite on her, which meant she had sacrificed a much easier life in order to come with her son.

It was more than any other family member had done for any of us. She deserved to live too. Who was I to decide that she was unworthy? If anything, she was more worthy than all of us because she *chose* to come. She had not abandoned her small child like so many others did.

Was it a decision that other family members were offered, and no one took?

I kept to myself for the rest of the afternoon while Sybil taught Kai and Kaz how to make medicines. While their presence in the house made it feel alive, and I would have loved it any other day, today I wish I lived alone. It was getting harder to hold my anger in. I worried constantly that I would snap at them or Sybil. Guilt would consume me if I hurt them in any way or if they turned on me.

A bell rang out through the town, signaling the start of the meeting. As we all walked in silence to the small-town center, I took mental note of the fae that were in attendance. Less than half of what we started with were here. Most fae attended the meetings, even though little information came from them. We had nothing else to do or look forward to in this hell, so at least it was something to look forward to.

Standing in the town center brought the stark realization that it was falling apart as quickly as we were. Homes that were once in decent shape would all crumble within the year because we didn't have the ability to provide upkeep. There were no roadways for carriages, but wide dirt paths carved by heavy foot traffic. Even the forest and meadows on the outskirts were filled with dead and decaying plants. It wasn't long ago that the grass and trees were colorful and full of life. Not even they could survive the harsh elements that the king had cursed us with. The change to Exile had been sudden and unexpected. I wondered if he thought we were all dead by now. It was hard to gauge how much time had passed, but it was likely several years.

Fallon, the oldest fae in Exile, took the center of our makeshift stage. He had assumed the role of organizing town meetings and deciding rulings of fae here. He was desperate to keep rules and laws in place to provide some safety and normalcy. It worked most of the time. Things had been uncertain when he first took over, but after he began executing those found guilty of high crimes like murder, fae quickly realized that he could bring some stability. He had made a spectacle about it, and the murder rates dropped significantly after that.

I admired his willingness to step into the role. No one else wanted to, and there was a high chance that we would have killed each other by now if he hadn't done it.

"Thank you all for attending." His voice carried through our silence. "I'm afraid I don't have much to say tonight. We are dwindling, our food sources are suddenly almost nonexistent, and we still have no plan on how to save ourselves." His shoulders slumped with exhaustion and defeat. "Our creek is drying up, and once that does, our main food and water source will be gone."

"Maybe a food cart will appear again?" Someone yelled from the crowd.

This caused a murmur of hope to erupt, but my chest tightened with dread. I could bring another cart, but what if they killed and beat each other again? Guilt crept in. I vowed to never do that again.

"We still don't understand where that came from," Fallon sighed. "It caused so much havoc the last time. I feel you all would kill one another for a slice of bread."

The fae fell silent in shame. It was true that they would likely kill one another again. Sybil's hand squeezed mine.

"Do we have any idea why all of our resources have suddenly dried up or died in the past months? We never had an issue in the seven years we've been here, then suddenly, this year it's all going to hell? Why?" someone called out to Fallon. Whispers sounded through the small crowd.

Seven years. We had been here that long, and I couldn't remember it all. Some small details were familiar from years prior, but mostly I could only remember the past several months. Why?

"We don't have answers to these questions. Perhaps we were on borrowed time, and that time is ending. We either need the gods to show us a way or pray for a merciful end,"

Fallon announced in defeat. If he had lost hope, then we were all doomed to die soon.

Silence fell once again. Fallon looked around at every fae that stood in front of him. Defeat was clear in everyone's eyes. They were worn down and tired. At this point, they were probably praying to the stars that death would come quickly. I was scared that some of them would take matters into their own hands and start jumping through the boundary.

"Let's make the most out of the time we have left." He gave us a soft smile, and the meeting was dismissed.

We all stood in a defeated silence before parting ways. Sybil, the twins, and I walked to the house without speaking. Kai was the one to finally disrupt the quiet.

"We're all going to die."

"You don't know that, Kai," Sybil sighed heavily into the small, quiet space. "There's always a chance for us."

"If there was a way, we would have figured it out by now," Kai spat back at her. He was the levelheaded twin most of the time, but he had a point. If there was a way to save everyone, wouldn't we have already thought of it? That had been the main goal when we first got here, but with each failed attempt we lost motivation. Eventually, the escape plans stopped altogether.

"Thea can track down supporters of elite magic and ask them to help," Kaz suggested.

"You know that would do nothing, Kaz." Sybil gave him a pointed look with an unspoken message within it.

"Perhaps kings from neighboring kingdoms would support us if they knew where we were."

"Kaz, it would be pointless," Sybil spoke more harshly this time as something unspoken passed between them again.

"Where would I find them? And besides, the other kingdoms aren't here because they stay out of each other's business. Why start a war over a small group of elite magic holders?" I sighed in irritation.

Kaz was confident when he spoke. "They would help."

"No, they wouldn't. If they wanted to help us, they would have already done it. They would have prevented this from happening in the first place, but they did not care."

He stood fuming in front of me.

"How would you know? You can't remember shit from before this prison. You sit here pissed off, but you don't even remember what it's like to be on the outside with family and friends. You don't know the emptiness that we feel—the loss of everything! You don't even know if there's anyone outside of that boundary that loves or misses you."

"Kaz!" Kai and Sybil both cried in shock.

I shut my mouth in an instant. That was a low blow. It was the thing that haunted me the most. Did I have a family or a mate out there that loved me or missed me? What if I didn't? What if they had turned on me and didn't care that I was stuck here?

It created a hollowness deep in my chest that made it difficult to move past sometimes. Maybe I would be just as alone out there as I was in here.

I shoved past him and headed into my room. I didn't want to think about life outside of this place because nothing but negative things ever came from it.

CHAPTER 3

The dreaded wooden door appeared in front of me. I had seen it hundreds of times in my dreams, but tonight it looked different. The detailed carvings were clearer, and I could see they held a large crest, one that I had never seen before. I examined it closely, trying to see if the symbols sparked a memory for me. My dreams could end abruptly, and I didn't want to waste my time. I reached for the handle, but his voice stopped me.

"Are you sure you want to open that?"

I turned into the darkness of the hallway and met his intoxicating golden eyes that were watching me thoughtfully. His voice was everything I expected it to be, smooth with a tinge of cold indifference. He hadn't spoken in the years I had been dreaming about him, and now he cared to chime in?

"Do you know what's behind that door?" I asked him, confused. He had been here since the beginning; didn't he want to know the answer to the screams behind the door?

"No," he sighed, "but neither do you. It's likely a trick."

"It's just a dream."

He reached out and held my wrist firmly in place so I couldn't open the door. My eyes traced the lines of the black tattoos on his hand as he kept me from moving.

"Dreams hold answers and memories for us, but that is not always a good thing."

"But sometimes it is." I pulled my wrist away and shoved the door open. I half expected it to not budge, as usual. Instead, though, it swung open with such ease that I almost fell through.

My eyes took in a stone fireplace roaring with life and two people standing near it. There was a tall man with dark hair and a woman with blonde hair. Both of them looked like nobles of some sort, with expensive light blue and gold clothing. With their backs turned toward me, they didn't notice as I moved closer.

"I can force Thea to do it." The man's voice was confident.

"Then tell her whatever you need to. Just get this done with," the woman said in a sharp whisper.

Suddenly, the door I was holding on to creaked, and both figures turned towards me. I shuffled backward in shock when I saw them. They had no faces. No eyes, no mouth, no nose, nothing. It was horrifying.

"Thea! Save us!" they started yelling, but this time their voices got louder and more haunting as it went. I covered my ears as they slowly crept towards me, their arms out in supplication, but it didn't drown out their pleas.

I want to wake up. I want to wake up.

I started backing out of the room, but in my haste to escape, my feet tangled in the rug, and I began to fall backwards. Before I hit the ground though, the mysterious man that waited in the shadows of my dreams wrapped his hand around me, catching me before yanking me out of the room and into the hallway while slamming the door shut. Both of us stumbled back onto the floor, but his hard body cushioned my fall. He let out a loud puff of air when I landed on him. I rolled off of him and on to the hard wooden floor. We lay next to each other for a moment, sprawled out and not saying anything.

"I told you some things are better left unknown," he said gruffly.

"Then why do I always have this same dream? And who are you anyway? You're always lurking about." I gave him a sidelong glance to see if anything about him was showing, but it wasn't. His oversized hood obscured everything, as always.

"A friend."

I scoffed in his general direction. I wasn't friends with dream stalkers. He chuckled softly as he stood up. The sound settled over me, and I found myself smiling back at him despite myself.

"It's time to wake up, little viper."

Before I could tell him not to call me that ridiculous nickname, though, the dream ended, and I was sitting up quickly in my own bed.

What in the hell was that? That is what I had waited all these years for? My mind tried to put together the pieces of what I had seen. Was this just a dream or was it a memory? The couple in the room were going to have me do something, but what was it? Why were their faces missing? And why were they plotting my demise in one moment and then begging for my help the next?

I needed to try to stay in the dream longer next time, even if it scared me. They couldn't actually hurt me, could they?

My mind shifted to the man who was always lurking. I had never seen his face, but he had called himself a friend. I didn't know what his intentions were, but I was not about to consider him a friend or anything of the sort. Even if I could remember the feel of his body under me as I fell on him...

I shook my head to clear it and focused on the world around me. As I stood up, I realized how quiet the house was. I couldn't hear Sybil moving about in the kitchen or anyone outside. I was never the first one up, and Sybil did not know the meaning of being quiet while I was still sleeping. Taking a hesitant step forward, I reached my door and cracked it open, knowing that something wasn't right.

I still didn't hear anything as I opened the door and headed to Sybil's room.

It was empty.

My heart pounded in my chest as I entered the shared living space. It was trashed like someone had ransacked it. Sybil's dried herbs were scattered all over the floor. Her broken vials crunched under my boots as I stepped forward to assess the damage. All the food I had gathered was thrown on the floor and ruined. Our furniture lay in broken heaps. This would have awoken me. Why hadn't I heard anything?

I looked for any sign of Sybil, but she wasn't there. Dread filled me as I slipped on my cloak and grabbed my dagger and bow. When I stepped out of the house, no one walked the path. There wasn't a fae anywhere in sight. Exile was dead silent, too silent, which had my stomach churning with uneasiness. I hurried up the dirt path and into the town center, where the stage was. My heavy breathing was all that was heard. Something was very wrong.

My chest tightened as I ran through Exile, not once seeing any sign of life. My legs were heavy as I got to the living quarters where Kai and Kaz lived. It was empty, too. How had hundreds of fae disappeared without a trace?

"Little viper." A voice startled me, and I turned, aiming my bow at the speaker. The golden-eyed man was standing in the shadows, and I couldn't make out anything about his face. He held up his hands to show me he wasn't a threat.

"How are you here?" I demanded.

"This is still a dream," he explained, but his tone was curious. "But something is odd about it. You brought me here with you instead of waking up." His golden eyes darted around nervously at the worn-down building we were standing in.

"I've never had a dream like this. Where is everyone?" I asked him.

"Where are we? I've never seen a town like this before."

Realization hit me in that moment that he may in fact be a real man. I had always thought that dream stalkers were made up—something to scare children into behaving well. Apparently, they were real things, and maybe this one had found my dreams and never left them.

"I didn't invite you to come with me."

"Well, I'm here, so you must have. I can't just join anyone's dreams, little viper."

Screaming from outside pulled my attention away from the man. I knew instinctively that it was Sybil, and I hurried out of the building. She was standing on the narrow path when I finally found her. Her back was turned toward me, and she was watching the town as it burned to the ground. Guards were throwing torches at every structure.

Except these guardsmen weren't in the Crimson kingdom's colors. They were dressed in all black. All of the guards were facing away from me, so I couldn't tell if they were familiar.

"Sybil!" I ran towards her, my feet sliding across the dirt under my feet when I stopped quickly. When she turned to me, she had a wound that was too deep on her chest for her to be up walking around or breathing. The blood from it had dripped all the way down her purple dress, so much so that there was a puddle on the ground below her.

Time slowed down as I watched her blood drip slowly. The noise it made filled the silence around us, echoing in my mind.

Drip. Drip. Drip.

"Sybil..." I paused. Her eyes were vacant, like she wasn't really there anymore. Their vibrant blue had been replaced by a cloudy white. "What's going on?"

"The end is almost near, Thea, and there is nothing you or anyone can do to stop it." Her face contorted into a freakish smile before vanishing into nothing after her message was delivered.

"Little viper!" His voice boomed so loudly behind me that I didn't have time to wonder where she had disappeared to. I turned to respond to him but never got a chance. As my eyes made contact with his, a spear erupted from my chest as a guardsman stabbed me through my heart with a hissing growl of disgust.

The shock of being stabbed jolted me awake. Sweat covered me and soaked my bed, causing the cloth to stick to me as I sat up groggily. What in the hell was wrong with me? My dreams had never been anything but the wooden door and wanting to get it open. Why were they changing?

I stilled my breathing and waited for Sybil to clank around in the kitchen. There was nothing but silence. Fearing the worst, I jumped out of bed and raced to find her. Before I could really think about it, my legs were moving me quickly through my door and into the shared living space.

"Good morning," Sybil said in greeting as she sat quietly by the fresh loaf of bread she must have made this morning. "You slept longer than normal." Her white eyebrow lifted in suspicion when she noticed how sweaty I was. The tightness in my chest disappeared when I met her vibrant blue eyes, not the milky white ones from my nightmare.

"I guess I was tired." I waited for her face to contort into the hideous smile from my dream, but Sybil's face remained its normal appearance.

Was I still dreaming? My eyes glanced at the darkened hallway behind me, but I didn't see the man anywhere.

"What's wrong? You look like you've seen a monster." Her worried eyes followed mine into the empty hallway. The man wasn't here, which had to mean this was real.

After reassuring myself that this wasn't a dream, I breathed a sigh of relief.

"Do you know much about dream stalkers?" I asked. Her eyes shifted to mine quickly and intently. Sybil's whole demeanor changed, and I couldn't quite place where her anxiety arose from.

"Dream stalkers can't join our dream while we're locked in this prison; so, if you have one, I would be cautious." Her typical friendly tone was gone and replaced with suspicion.

"Well, we aren't supposed to leave the boundary either, but I can. He says he's a friend." She scoffed and stood. Sybil had never been anything less than civil or content. Right now, though, she was clearly upset.

"Why would you invite a dream stalker into your dream? It's completely reckless, Thea, especially given where we live and who we are."

"That's the thing, though. I didn't invite him into any of my dreams. He just kind of appeared one night. Normally my dream repeats, but last night something changed, and when it did, he followed me into the next dream, without an invitation."

"Then that is not a dream stalker," she said. I didn't know how to process this news. Was this man a serious threat to me or a figment of my imagination?

"What is he then?" Fear coiled in my stomach.

She shrugged and turned away from me, effectively ending the conversation.

Sybil was lying to me. What was she hiding from me, and who the hell was the guy in my dream if not a dream stalker?

"Tell me what you know, Sybil," I demanded with irritation. I was upset that she wasn't being forthcoming with her information.

"I don't know anything, Thea. The man is probably just part of your imagination because you're lonely."

I didn't push the subject any further. If she wanted to withhold information from me, then I would not share information with her. This was exactly why I didn't trust others.

"The twins will be by in a little bit to eat some food," Sybil said with her back towards me. She was tense, but I wasn't sure what had upset her so much. Her voice held an icy edge to it. That was not something I had experienced from her before unless she was disapproving of my violence and anger.

"I'll be out." My response was curt as I stomped away from her.

I had no desire to be around Kaz after what he said to me last night, and Sybil's odd behavior made me want to disappear for the whole day.

"Fine," she snipped loudly enough that I would hear from my room.

Grabbing some bread, my weapons, and my cloak to help shield my skin from the scorching sun, I headed toward the creek. Sybil had never treated me like this before. Everyone was so on edge around me.

My thoughts disappeared as I arrived at the water's edge and realized the creek was hardly flowing anymore. We had running water in this a few days ago. How could everything suddenly be dying around us when we had been here for seven years without it happening? What was the cause for the loss of our resources?

Maybe the end was coming, I admitted to myself. Fishing was pointless now with the little flow of water, so I turned to head back to the house. It was too hot to be out here doing nothing. I would just stay in my room, away from Kaz and Sybil.

At some point, I knew I would need to make amends with them, but I also didn't think it was my fault. We all had imperfections, and tempers often were elevated due to stress, but Kaz was out of line and Sybil's behavior was definitely odd.

When I rounded the corner to head into the house, I froze. The front door was wide open, with a solid boot print right in the middle of it from somebody kicking it in.

What the hell?

I grabbed my viper-handled dagger and snuck in. Kaz and Kai weren't there, but Sybil's soft cries made me hurry.

When I rounded the hallway, a man was holding her down with his foot over her throat. His shoulders were so broad that he was turned completely to the side to fit. I watched as he pointed something at her.

A weapon.

Before the thought had even fully formed, I threw my dagger into his back. The man turned with a cry as the blade sank into his shoulder blade and stuck there. I instantly recognized him from town meetings. The sight of his eyes froze me in place. They were completely white, devoid of any color, just like Sybil's had been in my dream.

He charged at me, knocking us both into the wooden table that I had made for Sybil. All of her herbs and medicines fell to the floor as the table broke under our weight. The glass vials crunched under our boots as the man and I both struggled for the upper hand.

Out of nowhere, his hand struck out and backhanded me so hard that I fell to the floor on my back. Pain radiated from where he had hit me. Something sharp dug into my arm, and I cried out in agony. He reached down, twisting my long, dark braid around his hand to yank me up.

I kicked him hard in the knee, and he crumpled to the ground, wailing with discomfort. His white eyes tracked my movements as I went for a weapon.

The man swiped at me with a knife, barely missing me. Circling him as he kneeled on the ground, I ripped my dagger from his back, causing another eruption of strangled cries to release from him. His silver hair was damp with sweat as my fingers twisted it back far enough that I was able to rest my dagger on his throat. His pained sobs only called to the darkness that lived deep in my chest. I wanted to make *more* pain fall from his lips.

There was something uncontrollable about my darkness. It had a mind of its own, and if it wanted revenge, it would take it without consequence. Sybil's footsteps brought me to my senses though and stopped me from slicing his throat.

She stood frozen as she gaped at me. Her neck was marred and red from this asshole. The itch of my magic wanting to come forward still sat under my skin as my darkness sank itself into my mind. It craved his life for what he had wanted to do. It craved pain and hurt. It would make me feel better to have him lying dead on the floor.

The sensible side of me, though, was asking why he had attacked us. Food? No, it had to be something else. Something was wrong with his eyes. The raging of my darkness hindered my ability to form questions about his motives.

"Look away, Sybil," I ground out. I didn't want her to watch this. Sybil let out a small, distressed sound before doing as she was told. It was then that I noticed Kaz and Kai standing in the entryway of our home. How long had they been watching?

"How?" the man rasped. "You shouldn't be this strong still." I realized he was right. I still had considerable fae strength and speed here, when others had lost it completely. He'd lose it if he knew that I had the ability to cross the boundary, too.

Ignoring him, I asked, "Why did you come here?"

"I was sent," he groaned as I pressed my dagger into his flesh, producing a drop of blood.

"By who?"

"Just kill me because if you don't, they will when I don't return with you," he snapped.

"With pleasure." I slid my dagger through his neck with little effort. His gargled reply ended as soon as his corpse hit the floor. My darkness retreated back into the depths of my chest as I watched his blood pool below him.

As the haze of anger lifted, I realized that my rage had cost me answers. Answers that only that fae had, but now I would never know because I had been too consumed with vengeance. When I peered up, Sybil stood frozen in fear with Kaz and Kai. I was covered in blood, both mine and the man's, but that wasn't why they stared at me in shock.

"You're on fire," Kai sputtered. I furrowed my brows in confusion, but when I glanced down, my hand was engulfed in flames. I smothered it with a quick movement as my mind raced for understanding.

Magic didn't work here.

"It's never worked here," I said softly, shock beginning to set in.

"The rage must have set it off," Kaz suggested.

Inspecting my hand, I flicked my fingers, but only a small spark emitted. What was going on these past few days? Something was happening to me, and it didn't appear like it was a good change. This wasn't the first time I had been consumed with rage, but it had never caused my magic to ignite. It didn't make sense.

My foot crunched the broken vials as I stepped forward. "All of your medicine is gone." Frowning, I shoved the broken glass with my foot.

Sybil shook her head and frowned as she began to pick up the pieces, but her eyes followed me closely. Her hands trembled as she picked up the sharp shards. Kaz and Kai's dark eyes found mine in a questioning look.

They were scared of me.

I frowned at their behavior. "I won't hurt you."

"We've never seen you like that before. You enjoyed killing him," Kaz spoke accusatively at my actions.

"Would you have preferred if Sybil died? If you didn't want me to kill the man, then you could've stepped in." Grabbing the man's hand, I dragged him out to the street to join today's other dead fae. I just needed to get away from their watchful eyes because, honestly, I liked knowing that this man was dead.

Something inside of me was fucked up.

My eyes looked over the details of his face. His eyes had changed back to normal-colored brown instead of chilling white. I shook away the thoughts of why I didn't mind killing others. What was I like in my past to make me feel nothing for taking a life?

The king was probably right to lock me away because killing had never made me feel bad.

When I returned to the doorway of our home, I paused at the sound of harsh whispering. Worry gripped my heart when I realized it was me they were whispering about.

"Thea is going to put us all in jeopardy if she can't control her rage. Someone will notice her magic, and everything will fall apart," one of the twins whispered.

"She's unpredictable, and that is a problem. Did you catch sight of how fast and strong she still is?" The other twin whispered. "She's got to know there is something different about her by now. There is no way to explain her abilities. She will become more reckless and jeopardize the safety of everyone here."

I stayed frozen in uncertainty. *Should* they be scared of me? I would never hurt them, but I did agree with them that I was jeopardizing their safety. Part of me felt betrayed that they didn't trust me, but could I blame them? After all, my own guards were up too. Nothing was ever genuine or real to me if it came from someone else. Other's actions always had an ulterior motive, and I didn't understand why I thought like that all of the time.

Sybil had told me time and time again that I would end up alone or dead if I didn't learn to let others in. She told me my impulsivity and need for vengeance kept me stuck in my own lonely prison and would cause issues for me. It was beginning to feel like she was right.

It was just that everyone here *should* want revenge for what we were being put through, but I seemed to be the only one who wanted it. That fact alone kept me from letting my guard down. Keeping my distance and questioning others' intentions had served me well enough to still be alive. And sometimes, impulsive and vengeful actions were necessary. If I thought too much about why I did things in the heat of the moment, I would already be dead.

"Her behaviors are just like last time. It's getting close, but we need to just act normal. We aren't allowed to speak of it. So, let it run its course just like we do every time, and hopefully, this will be the time it works." Sybil sighed in a defeated tone.

They spoke about me as if something was wrong with me. If they knew something about me, then why would they keep it a secret? Doubt crept into my mind. Sybil's behavior had been so odd recently, and her stories were changing. Were they really my friends?

I walked in, not bothering to look at any of them as I rushed to my room. The door couldn't lock, but I wished it could because I couldn't tell if I was surrounded by friends or enemies.

Tonight, I would cross the boundary and steal more medicine to replace what had been lost today. Then, I would move out so I could be on my own. There was too much stress here, and I didn't need to worry if I was safe or not in my own home.

CHAPTER 4

I sighed heavily as the dark wooden door appeared in front of me. Couldn't I just have a dreamless sleep? This was the last thing I wanted to do right now. I sat down on the floor facing the door and crossed my legs. No noises or lights came from it, and I thanked the stars above for that. Hopefully, this would be a peaceful escape.

"Sleeping again so soon?" His deep voice reverberated in the space.

"Wonderful. You're here," I muttered. I turned so my back was against the wooden door and I could face him. His soft chuckle floated from the shadows, but his laughter cut off when he saw me.

"What happened to your face?" He hissed while moving closer to inspect me. For someone of his stature, he moved silently. He kneeled directly in front of me as his tattooed hands came up to hold my chin. He twisted my face gently to the side so he could inspect the bruises and cuts I had from my *fight with our intruder. My eyes closed as his fingers traced over my wounds before he skimmed them across the scar that started from my left eyebrow and ran over my eye to my cheek.*

His movements stopped when he realized he was touching me more than necessary. Why did he care what had happened to me?

"Some asshole broke into my house."

When he didn't say anything, I opened my eyes to watch what he was doing. I couldn't see his golden eyes anymore. But his hood was back slightly, and a few strands of his dark hair poked out by his forehead. This was the most I had ever seen of him.

"Is he going to be a problem again?" His voice was deep and angry.

"Not unless he comes back from the dead." My brow raised at the man in front of me. His body stiffened at my words.

"You killed him then?"

Would he leave if he knew I killed others? "Yes." I nodded and leaned my head back against the wooden door behind me. Part of me expected him to move away from me or say something like Sybil always had, but instead he spoke one simple, unexpected word to me.

"Good."

That brief acknowledgement validated me more than years with Sybil, or the twins ever had. I was used to others saying how I should feel bad or disgusted with hurting others, but this stranger seemed to not only understand but fully support my actions.

The man moved to sit next to me, his back resting on the wall. All of his clothing was black, including the cloak he always wore. That gave me no insight into who the hell he was. He lifted his knees up and rested his long arms over them. My eyes studied the dark tattoos on his hands to determine if there was anything about them that would give me any sort of clue as to who he was. They didn't, but my eyes traced the small designs, mesmerized by how big his hands were. He shifted slightly, and I inhaled his scent of forest and rain.

"Do you stare at everyone this intently, or should I be flattered?" he teased.

Rolling my eyes, I turned away from him, embarrassed that I had been caught admiring him.

"I can't see anything about you, so don't flatter yourself."

He paused for a long moment, as if trying to decide where to take this conversation.

"No trying to break in the door this time?"

"I just wanted to rest for a little bit in peace and quiet. I was tired after that guy broke in. The past few days have been... odd."

"Did I ruin your peace and quiet?"

His eyes were on me, but I didn't look. My hands tangled in my lap under his intense stare. His presence had never been worrisome for me, and I wondered if it was because I knew this was a dream. He couldn't hurt me here. Or maybe I just knew that he wasn't real at all, but somebody I made up in my lonely mind.

"It's kind of nice having company," I whispered truthfully. "Although I didn't think you'd be asleep right now, too."

"I'm not," he confessed as his head turned from me to rest back against the door. "You call into my mind whenever you fall asleep, and my mind follows you. Most of the time I am sleeping, but I was in a very important meeting this time."

My head whipped towards him.

"Why didn't you just not follow me? And what are you doing in the meeting? Taking a nap?"

"Trust me, I would prefer to be here with you. You saved me from a dreadfully boring day. As far as what happens to me, I just kind of blackout."

I couldn't see it, but I knew he was smiling. I smiled back at him, wishing he would show me his face. We both sat in silence. Normally I hated silence, but with him, it wasn't so *bad. Dread filled me when my thoughts wandered back to my waking life, and I remembered I would be going through the boundary later that night, but Sybil would need her medicine sooner rather than later.*

"I should go." I started to stand up, but his hand gripped my shoulder softly.

"Just sit with me for one more minute."

His voice was just above a whispering plea, and I sat back down without question. One more minute sounded nice.

I turned to look at him and was surprised to see that his golden eyes were looking at me. Something about his gaze made me feel exposed. I shifted with uncertainty.

"Do you stare at everybody, or should I be flattered?" I mocked his words from earlier.

"You should most definitely be flattered." His eyes crinkled like he was smiling. Something in his body tensed as he watched me, though. "Are you lonely?"

His question caught me off guard, but before I answered, he kept talking. "Sometimes, I think the only place I'm not completely alone is here, with you, in your dreams."

The way he barely whispered his words of loneliness, almost like a confession, had me speaking before I could filter my words.

"I only feel loneliness. Nothing makes it go away. Sometimes, I wonder if my existence in the realm matters to anyone."

"It matters to me." He gripped my hand tightly in his. We stayed there in silence for a long time. "Let's go, little viper."

He stood up, still holding my hand tightly in his, but before I could tell him that nickname was ridiculous, he was gone, and I was sitting up in my bed.

★★☽★★

I smiled as I glanced around my room, then stopped when I remembered what I was going to be doing. Facing Sybil and the twins was the last thing I wanted to do, but I needed to get it over with. My eyes burned with exhaustion. My mind drifted to the man from my dream sitting in his boring meeting and chuckled. I wondered who he was. Was he from another kingdom? Did he think I was real or just a figment of his imagination? What if he hated elite magic holders?

I took a long, calming breath before stepping into the hallway. When I walked out of the room, all three of them were there, and they all stared at me with worried looks. Kai caught sight of the bow and arrows I held.

"You can't go across the boundary. The intruder said he was here for you. You don't know if this was a trap to force you somewhere they can catch you."

"Don't worry about me. At least you'll be safe from me for the night," I spit the words out, dripping with venom, so they were aware that I heard them earlier.

"We care for you," Sybil pleaded.

"You're scared of me," I answered back. "You think I'm reckless, and you will be caught in the crossfire because of my actions. So don't worry, I'll keep my distance when I return."

I stalked out of the house and towards the boundary before another word was said. It seemed like every time I helped someone, they acted as if I was wrong to do so.

This time, I didn't bother pausing before jumping through the boundary. Once through, though, I immediately fell to my knees as the pain seared through my entire body. Thankfully, the forest ground was softer than usual, probably as a result of a passing rain shower. With each clean, crisp lungful of air I inhaled, more of my strength returned to me. The smell of rain hit me, making me pause briefly to enjoy it. I didn't bother taking in the pleasant sounds or the moon and stars. Standing on shaky legs, I rested against the tree for only a moment before starting off.

It was late into the night, so everyone would likely be sleeping. My first task was to find Sybil her medicines, and I would need a lot. I headed to a neighborhood west of the previous one I had stolen from. Hopefully, they had a fully stocked apothecary.

My chest tightened as I admired the dark black castle on the grassy hillside. It sat up there like it was watching every move I made. Why did it have to be so nice to look at?

The sight of the castle made my thoughts swarm. How could I fix our situation in Exile? How could I free everyone? My shoulders sagged when no ideas immediately came to mind. Our freedom weighed heavily on me because I was the only fae that could cross the boundary. The castle brooded in the distance, practically mocking me. Maybe I should just march right up there and kill the king. But would that shatter the border of Exile? There were too many unknowns to take a risk like that.

I lifted my face to the stars that twinkled brightly and closed my eyes in prayer. "Please, gods...or stars...whatever is in charge of our fates, give me a chance to free us. Anything, I will risk anything to save us."

The wind blew a gust of frigid air against my skin, making a shiver run through me. Opening my eyes, I stared at the castle, hoping for a sign. When nothing jumped out at me, I tore my gaze away and immediately spotted the apothecary sign. I sighed and headed towards it. I needed to put these thoughts to the side and focus on what I was doing. I would think of a plan for escape once I was safe back in Exile.

This apothecary wasn't as tightly secured as others I had stolen from. It took little effort for me to break in the door. I raided it quickly, fortunate that this town was larger than the last one I had visited, so the medicine had larger quantities to take. Once I was satisfied with how much I had, I headed to the nearest house to find some more food.

A soft blue glow of flame stopped me. Wisp was circling a hand cart next to the house. That would let me carry more supplies than I ever had before. I made quick but quiet work of gathering the rest of what I needed. This town was fancier compared to some of the others I had seen before. Houses lined the cobblestoned streets in per- fect rows. All of them had more than one story, all with green grassy lawns. They would be able to afford new food and a new hand cart.

Once I cleaned out the first house, I moved onto the next, and next, and the next. I grabbed fresh milk and took vegetables and fruit from their gardens too. I started to head to the next house but realized how full and heavy the cart was already. This would be plenty to last us.

Before I headed back to the woods, the blue glow of the wisp caught my attention again. It appeared in front of me but then slowly circled around me, making me turn back towards the house I had just walked past. Curiosity got the better of me when Wisp drifted to the door. I walked up to it and stared at a red envelope with the words "You've been selected" scribbled in perfect penmanship on the front. It held the king of Crimson's crest on it, which intrigued me. None of the other houses had this, so why did this one? I grabbed it off the door it had been pinned to and slid it into my pocket before returning to my cart.

I glanced around for the wisp, but it was gone. "Thanks," I whispered, just in case it was still lingering by. The walk back to the shadow boundary took longer than it normally did because not only was the cart incredibly heavy, but I had to cover my tracks with shrubs and branches so it couldn't be followed.

I finally arrived at the shadow boundary and paused for a moment to admire the sheer beauty of the forest and sky on this side.

My mind flashed to the man I killed earlier. Who had sent him after me? My eyes peered around to make sure I wasn't being followed. Did someone know my secret? I wasn't sure how they would know, but I would lay low for as long as possible. If someone was trying to find me, it meant they were living in Exile too. Otherwise, how had they made that fae attack us?

My eyes fixated on the black castle looming far in the distance once more before I took a long breath and stepped through the shadow boundary and back into my prison. As always, I fell to my knees and waited for the pain to subside.

"Thea, are you alright?" Kaz was moving toward me quickly. He kneeled down next to me and patted my back in comfort.

"What are you doing here?" I asked in short puffs.

"I can't sleep when you cross. Even though we're fighting, I still care that you return safely." He squeezed my shoulder as I sat back on my knees. "You're my family, and I know that we would all be dead without you. I'm sorry I made it seem as if I'm not grateful for you, because I truly am."

His words made tears fill my eyes. I didn't want to just forgive him so easily, but he and Kai were like brothers to me. I didn't want to lose them either.

"Let's get this home." He stood, pulling me up with him like I weighed nothing. He grabbed the cart and began walking.

We walked swiftly on the outskirts of town before sitting at the tree line with the cart of goods for a while to make sure no one was lurking. Once satisfied, we hurried to the front door. Sybil and Kai were in the shared living area waiting for us. I started shoving the supplies into the house with their help. As soon as that was done, I broke the cart into small pieces to burn in our stove.

They all stood around watching me. The tension was noticeable, and I was sure they wanted to talk to me, but I didn't stick around to find out what they had to say.

CHAPTER 5

"Were you sleeping this time, or just escaping another dreadful meeting?" I huffed at the shadows in the hallway. Golden eyes narrowed on me from under his black-as-night cloak.

"Are you flirting with me, little viper?"

I scoffed as a retort. "I don't even know how to flirt."

"I think you do. I think you know exactly how to flirt, little viper."

Sybil was right. I should be cautious of this man, but I just didn't feel threatened at all when he was around. It was an odd feeling to have.

He stepped towards me, but not enough to reveal anything about himself. The smell of rain and the forest once again flooded my nose as he moved closer, though. I turned from him so he wouldn't catch a glimpse of my smirk. My eyes met the dark wooden door, and my emotions overtook me.

I wanted to destroy it. I reached out for the handle, but he grabbed my wrist before I could pull on it.

"You're seriously going back in there? Do you not remember the creepy encounter you had last time?"

"Are you scared?" I taunted.

He scoffed.

To my surprise, the door opened when I shoved into it. This time, the man and woman were in a heated discussion, and I couldn't quite make out what they were saying. I stepped forward, and they both turned to me. I worried they could see me this time, but before I could do anything, somebody else walked past me and through the doorway I was standing in.

I gasped when I realized it was me.

My eyes followed a dream version of myself entering the room. My dark hair was in a thick braid, and I wore my green cloak, but I looked...different somehow.

A memory.

This was a memory.

The other me stopped in front of them. Again, they had no faces, but it was far less creepy from a distance. I knew the man in the shadows was in the room with me, but I didn't turn to figure out where he was.

"Where were you?" the faceless man hissed.

"Making sure everyone was prepared for the fight."

"*You will go with them,*" *the woman spat in my direction. I watched my face contort into confusion. Then my hands and jaw clenched tightly.*

"*Why would I go with them? That was not part of the plan.*"

"*You are the only one strong enough,*" *the man answered defeatedly.* "*One of us has to go to lead them, and you have the strongest magic, Thea.*"

My eyes watched the memory version of myself. It was clear I had been upset. Betrayal floated thick in the air between me and the man ordering me around. This was a memory; this was not a dream. But who were these two fae? And why couldn't I see their faces?

"*You will go, or you will be banished,*" *the man spoke again.*

I watched as these words hit the other me like a slap; her eyes lost focus for a brief moment before she straightened her back in anger. Storming from the room, I heard her mutter, "*Fine.*"

The man from the shadows stood next to me. He was silent for a long moment.

"*It's a memory,*" *he said.* "*Do you know what they're talking about?*"

"*No,*" *I sighed heavily and turned away from the face-less man and woman.* "*I haven't been able to remember anything about my past. It's one of the reasons I wanted to see what was behind this door. I thought it would give me answers to who I am."*

He didn't respond, but his body was rigid at the comment.

"My friend said I shouldn't trust you. Are you a spy or something?" I questioned him, hoping to catch him off guard. He wasn't fazed.

"Maybe I shouldn't trust you, little viper. Besides, I only remember you in dreams. When I wake up, I have no recollection of you or what happened."

"That's odd for a dream stalker," I accused. Part of me was disappointed he didn't think of me outside these dreams like I thought of him.

"I'm not a dream stalker."

"Then why are you here?"

"Because you called to me in my dreams, and I answered. You need me here."

"Sounds like something a dream stalker might say."

"You've met a lot of dream stalkers?" he asked sarcastically. "I told you I'm a friend."

It still didn't make sense, but maybe he really didn't know anything either. Neither of us had answers to this.

"Well, friend, why do you think you're here with me?"

He didn't answer at first, and I thought maybe he wouldn't at all. "Maybe the gods saw two lonely souls and didn't want either of them to be so alone anymore."

My heart raced at his words. His hand reached out and smoothed my braid over my shoulder. The touch was unexpected, like he couldn't help himself. Just as quickly as he touched me, though, he pulled back his hand. His golden eyes were now swirled with black, and I was so tangled in their beauty that I didn't register that he was upset.

"It's time to wake up, little viper. Something is wrong."

"What do-"

I was pulled out of my dream before I asked my question. Screaming consumed the normally silent night. Outside, fae were in utter chaos. Anxiety shot through me, and I jumped up from the bed and hurried to find Sybil. She and the twins had blocked the doors and huddled together in the small living space. Relief spread through me when I saw the twins here safely with us.

"What's happening?"

"There are strange men here. We don't know who they are, but they're killing anyone they come across and setting fire to buildings," Kaz explained between breaths, as if he had run over here.

"How are they here? There's a boundary."

"We don't know," Kai frowned. "Do you think the king sent them to deliver a message?"

It made sense, but the king had never done that before, so once again we had to ask ourselves why now? I could hear blood-curdling screams and headed for the door. Kaz gripped my hand and pulled me back. Fear laced his features as he held me close to him.

"No." He gripped my hand tightly. "We aren't going to lose you today. Stay here with us. If they come in, we will fight."

He was right. I didn't know what I was up against or who these men were. Squeezing his hand back, I nodded in agreement. Kaz and Kai both let out a breath, relieved that I wouldn't argue.

I grabbed weapons and made sure everyone was armed. We stood in the small space, ready to fight if we needed to. Smoke from burning buildings seeped through the crack of our door, making my eyes burn and my mouth feel parched, but no one tried to enter.

My heart beat erratically in my chest. I would never let them hurt Sybil or the twins. I would die for them if I needed to. The handle jiggled, and I pulled back my bowstring. I was ready, physically and mentally, to kill whoever stepped inside, but the jiggling abruptly stopped, and so did the screams of chaos. Uneasiness coiled deep inside of my stomach. Was everyone else dead? Why was it so quiet all of a sudden, and where did the bad guys go? I lowered my bow and arrow and listened closely. There were still fae crying outside, but the chaotic, terrified screams had evaporated into thin air.

"Are they gone?" I whispered.

"It has to be a trap, right?" Sybil asked. She could be right. They could be trying to lure out everyone who had locked themselves indoors.

"Let's wait a while before we check," I suggested. "It might be a trick to get us outside."

None of us spoke or made any noise. It was as if time stood still as blood-curdling screams rang through the air. The cries were dying down though, and smoke no longer seeped into our house. It had been hours since I woke up, and yet it only seemed like minutes had passed. Sybil seated herself at the table and busied herself by concocting medicines. The twins and I stayed alert, watching the only entrance into the home. The screaming still rang in my ears even though no one was screaming anymore. The desperate cries of fae being murdered would haunt me for a lifetime.

Why had the king done this now? Was it because I crossed the boundary, or did he know someone had used elite magic on the other side? Grief gnawed at me over the thought that this could be my fault.

Sybil cut bread for each of us, but I didn't touch mine. I couldn't stomach it right now. What would be waiting on the other side of the door when we opened it? Would there be anything or anyone left? An urgency filled my chest. I needed to know.

I hurried to the door and started moving things.

"Thea, we should wait until tomorrow," Kai pleaded.

"You guys can stay here, but I have to know who and what is left outside." Unlocking the door, I cracked it open. There was no noise or movement, so I slid out of the door quietly. To my surprise, Kaz, Kai, and Sybil followed.

What we were met with was a massacre. Almost half the town was burned down, and dead fae littered the pathways. My eyes didn't know where to look first. My chest tugged with sadness.

I walked forward and stopped when I spotted her. The woman and her young child lay in a small opening between the buildings. The boy lay in the blanket I had given her in secret. I rushed over to them and begged the gods above to let them be okay. Falling to my knees, I assessed both of them, but they were long gone.

No.

Tears threatened to escape when the wounds and blood came into view. It wasn't fair. They had deserved to live.

"Thea," Sybil sobbed quietly. I glanced up with tears in my eyes. Fae were starting to come out of their homes to witness for themselves what had happened. Horrified sobs escaped many of them. Some begged for their loved ones or friends to wake up. Numbness spread over me as I stared at the woman who sacrificed her happiness to follow her child here, and for what? To be murdered in an unprovoked attack?

A spark of rage ignited deep in my chest. Someone would pay for this. I locked eyes with Fallon as he appeared on the street, assessing the damage. It was the first time I saw absolute total fear consume his features. What had taken us years to build had been destroyed in mere minutes.

Time stood still as we realized the amount of destruction that occurred. Smoke lingered in the air, small fires still raged, and half our buildings were leveled. This was the only home I knew, and more than half of it was gone. We would never be able to recover what we lost today.

"Everyone!" Fallon yelled, standing on a piece of wood to gain extra height. "Did anyone notice who attacked us?"

No one spoke a word. Of course no one here saw it; we were all inside. Fallon looked as if he didn't know what to do or say, so I spoke up.

"Was anyone outside when they attacked?"

The fae shook their heads no.

"Whatever it was couldn't open our door but tried. I don't think they can enter homes. We should enforce a strict curfew until we know what we are dealing with. Every fae that was outdoors was slaughtered, so perhaps staying inside will help protect us. If there is a sighting of something unusual, we will go into lockdown. Fallon can sound the bell to notify everyone."

Fallon nodded in agreement. "I'll take the bell to my home for quick access."

"Now, let's give those we lost today proper burials," I shouted. Everyone got to work. I went to the woman and her small son. I would make sure they were properly buried.

Kai and Kaz helped me carry them to the edge of the forest near the boundary. No thoughts entered my mind as I dug a grave big enough for them to be together. My body was numb from any feeling. If I let myself acknowledge any emotions, I would explode, and I didn't know if I could control myself if that happened.

I made sure the child was nestled safely in his mother's arms, arranging them so they could rest peacefully together. After I shoveled the last bit of dirt on them, I sat there next to their grave and mourned them—these strangers whose names I didn't even know. Gone in the blink of an eye.

Sybil and the twins went to help others, but I couldn't force myself to leave them yet. This had to stop. The king had gone too far this time. We were defenseless and weak. Even by the king's standard, this was a disgusting act of power. He couldn't even kill us in the first place; he sent us into Exile instead.

A brief thought flitted through my mind that maybe this wasn't the king of Crimson's doing, but who else would have done it? I shook the foolish thoughts away. Of course, it was him. He hated us for simply existing.

After a long while, I stood up to head back home. I picked up my cloak from the ground next to the grave. The sound of something hitting the ground caused me to look back.

There on the dry dirt lay the red envelope I had stolen. Looking over my shoulder to make sure no one was watching, I picked it up. I had forgotten I hid the envelope in my cloak last night. I didn't know what would be in it, but I didn't want anyone to see I even had it.

My hands dirtied the fancy crimson-colored envelope as I fumbled to open it. The paper inside was also red and adorned with the crest of Crimson's king. My eyes scanned the page quickly.

Congratulations!

Your family has the honor of being randomly selected to participate in the Trials of the King's Guard for a special mission. The rules are as follows:

1. ***Only one member of your family can participate, so choose wisely.***

2. ***Your family may choose not to participate. If that is your wish, then you must find someone to take your place.***

3. ***A series of trials will be given to fifty participants that have all been randomly selected. These trials will give participants opportunities to demonstrate useful skills.***

4. ***The top ten performers will move on to the final task, which will be revealed once the finalists are announced.***

5. ***Whoever is selected must present themselves***

in the Crimson kingdom in two days' time from when you receive this letter. You must have this letter as proof you were invited.

Like previous years, the grand prize will be awarded to those that survive the final task, one wish granted by the King and his court. Nothing is off limits, except the Crimson Kingdom's crown. The wish will not be granted until the final task is completed.

Do not take this lightly, as no one has completed the final task.

My heart began to pound so loudly that I couldn't hear anything around me. I forced myself to read the page again and again to make sure I was not imagining things. "Nothing is off limits but the crown." That meant I could free everyone here for my wish. All I had to do was sneak into the king's secret guard and complete the mission.

The twins and Sybil were sitting in the small space eating bread when I barged into the house. I couldn't contain myself as I held up the letter. They stared at me like I had finally snapped and lost my mind.

"I found this when I was out last night and forgot about it until just now. It's an answer to save us all." A whirlwind of possibilities swirled within me as I clutched onto that precious piece of paper—a lifeline amidst despair.

Sybil took the letter and read it while Kai and Kaz read over her shoulder. Their eyes flickered over the words multiple times, like mine had. When they peered back up at me, though, my heart dropped. They were all frowning instead of sharing in my excitement. I grabbed the letter from them, worried they would burn it or something to prevent my participation.

"Thea, the chances of you winning are low," Sybil muttered. "You might be injured."

"We will all die if nothing happens. This is our only chance to escape this prison before we are all slaughtered."

Kaz and Kai were silent for a long moment, and I thought they would agree with Sybil.

"Thea's right," Kaz sighed in defeat. "It's our only chance."

I hugged him tightly against me. Finally, someone agreed with me on something. The small validation lifted the suffocating burden off my shoulders and eased the feeling of hopelessness. He gave me a hard hug back, which was unlike him.

"But what if you get caught? Maybe they'll know that you took this envelope," Kai questioned.

"It says the home was randomly selected. I doubt they will question if it was mine or not. It's not like they know every single fae living in the realm and where they are from. Besides, I can use my magic to escape if needed."

"It's a risk, but it is our only chance to leave Exile," Sybil nodded.

"I'll need to leave tonight to make it in time." I suddenly was unsure of leaving Sybil on her own. As if they sensed my hesitation, Kai and Kaz spoke at the same time.

"We will take care of her."

"I know."

"You boys should just move in here," she suggested.

"That would be for the best," I agreed. "Besides, I loaded up on supplies this last trip, so you should be alright for a long time. Hopefully, this won't take long."

They all nodded in agreement, but I saw the hesitation on their faces. Emotions bubbled up, but I needed to put on a brave face for all of us. This was the only way to save everyone. There was no other option. I took a slice of bread and ate it before gathering a small bag of my clothing and daggers. When I walked out of my room, I handed Kaz my bow and arrows. Maybe Kaz could use it here if anyone decided to attack them.

"You keep this safe for me until I come back."

"I will," he said, nodding. I hugged Kai before moving to Sybil. She had been like a mother to me, even though we hadn't viewed the world through the same lens. She hugged me back like it would be our last one, and a soft sob released from her throat. She was trying to be strong, but this was hard for all of us. This might be the last time I was ever with them.

"Take this." She slid a long chain she always wore off her neck. On the end was a small amulet that swirled with bright colors of orange, red, and yellow. It was stunning.

"Sybil, it's beautiful." I admired it as I took it in my hands. I had never seen the amulet at the end of the necklace before. As soon as I touched it, a pulse of power surged through me, catching me off guard. My eyes snapped up to hers. She couldn't give me this. How did she even do this?

"Sybil..."

"My magic is of no use here. I paid a witch to transfer part of my elite magic into the amulet before I came to Exile, in hopes that my family would keep it. I'm not sure how potent it will be, but I'm sure it will be helpful in healing."

I glanced at the small sphere that held elite magic, knowing she was right, but this was such a high honor to give. What if I didn't come back and she lost her magic forever? Then everyone here would die too.

"I'll give it back as soon as I free us all from Exile." I hugged her again. Her eyes sparkled with pride as her smile stretched from ear to ear, but beneath that joy, there was an underlying worry etched into her features. "I should go."

Turning, I walked for the door but paused one last time. I turned to them and captured their faces in my mind. My eyes drifted around the small house like I would miss it while I was gone. It had been the only home I had any memories of. The weight of saving everyone settled on my shoulders, but their confident looks made the pressure bearable.

"I'll see you soon," I promised. All three smiled like they believed that they would. Then I turned and headed for the Crimson kingdom to win freedom for all those who held elite magic.

CHAPTER 6

The Crimson Kingdom had always been off-limits to me when I snuck out of Exile. I had never allowed myself to be too close to the castle for fear of being recognized. My past was a mystery to me, and maybe no one else knew who I was either. I couldn't afford to risk everything on a maybe though. My name was the only thing I knew about myself. That made this whole trial ordeal even riskier for me.

Eyes glanced at me as I made my way up the red-stone roadways of the city nestled just below the castle. Fae watched me, but only for brief moments before turning away. I was wearing my green cloak over my head on the off chance I was recognized.

Anxiety filled my chest.

Not because of the tournament or possibly failing, but because I didn't know if I was walking into a trap. Would I even make it there? Surely, they would make a spectacle of my death if they knew my secret. With every step that took me closer to the castle, I imagined traps waiting to catch me and my lies.

I wasn't sure what would be waiting for me once I got there, but hopefully I would at least make it to the tournament without being killed. My feet froze as uncertainty gripped me.

Wisp swirled around me as if to encourage me. She had been waiting by the boundary as soon as I crossed, like she knew I would be coming through. The wisp had never given me bad guidance, so I continued. My footsteps were heavy with exhaustion from walking all night and most of the day to reach the castle.

The town that surrounded the castle was beautiful. Dark, crimson-colored flowers grew everywhere. The buildings all had stunning, stained windows that complimented the dark exteriors. More than all of that, though, were the fae dancing and smiling in the street. The sounds of life floated through the wind, and the smell of delicious food attacked my senses. Laughter echoed through the streets like mocking taunts, making guilt nearly cripple me. The twins and Sybil were living in complete squalor, while these fae were living completely different lives.

How can these fae be so happy under the rule of a monster like the king of Crimson? To them, he was the hero, and I was the villain. My thoughts ran through a million scenarios that may occur once in the castle for the draft. I knew as long as I kept my elite magic mark hidden, I should be fine, but I was worried about my ability to control it during the trials. If anyone saw my darkness, they would know what I was.

My heart beat with equal parts worry and anticipation.

The castle caught my eye when I gazed up to admire the beauty of the fae in the streets. It was black as night with giant red flags around it. It held a certain sense of power when you looked at it. It, too, had oversized windows with colorful stained glass windows. I wanted to despise it and curse at it, but I still appreciated its beauty. All those nights in the Forbidden Wood didn't do it justice. It was so beautiful, even more so up close where all the small details could be seen. The black of the stones contrasted so beautifully with the dark, crimson-colored flowers that vined their way up the sides. To the left of the main entrance was a vast garden with tall shrubs, thousands of flowers, and fountains of the same black stone.

As I got closer to the gate, it was apparent that I was late to the affair. A crowd of men just outside the castle doors in the courtyard was my focus as I approached. My survival instincts kicked in as I readied myself to go inside. Confidence would get me far. Losing wasn't an option.

The others would likely just wish to be rich or for land. I was playing for lives. When I walked closer, they turned to stare at me. My eyes were hidden by my hood, but I glanced around to size up my competition. All men from what I saw.

"Hey, little dove, you're in the wrong place," one of them shouted at me with an odd accent. I ignored him as I walked up to the king's guardsmen that were present. Instinctively, I wanted to grab my weapon at the sight of them. There was at least a dozen of them, all adorned in their signature red suits. They all stared at me, not saying a word until they parted for a man in all black.

I had never seen a black Crimson guardsman uniform, but it held the same golden crest over his heart. A perfect target for my arrows, I thought instinctually. His energy definitely gave off the fact that he was in charge. His confidence made me want to shrink away from him, but I would not show weakness here.

"You're late," he spoke sharply. His voice had me freezing to my spot because I would recognize his voice anywhere.

"There is no time stamped on the invitation," I argued. My eyes drifted over his chest and up to a face I wasn't expecting.

His dark hair was tousled, short stubble lined his strong jaw, and his mouth was pressed into a thin, unamused line. It was his eyes that had me sucking in a deep breath, though. Instinctively, I took a step back. They appeared green at first sight, but when he turned slightly into the sun, they were a deep, rich gold. He was both absolutely terrifying and incredibly beautiful. My eyes glanced over his tattooed hands, and I stood frozen.

This was not happening.

It couldn't be the man from my dreams. A chill ran down my spine, and I took another step away from him. His golden eyes narrowed on me and my deliberate movements.

His face filled with irritation, and I froze. I didn't breathe, fearful he would know it was me from that small sound. Would he know I was an elite magic holder? I had never used magic in my dreams, so at least that was a secret. Would I be punished for it here once he recognized who I was? My mind raced with what I should do. He had said he didn't remember me when he woke up from his dreams. That had to be the truth, or I was in trouble. I briefly wondered if this was just another dream.

"You're the last to arrive," he huffed as he took my invitation. His fingers brushed against mine, and I realized it was definitely not a dream. His eyes narrowed on me for a long moment before leaning down so only I would hear what he was about to say. Shit, did he know who I was? A heavy, unsettling feeling settled deep in my stomach.

"This is the one chance I'm giving you to turn around and go home."

I scoffed at him, denying that chance, and he stood up with a hint of a smirk on his handsome face.

"And miss the chance of winning? I'll stay."

His eyes gleamed with amusement as he whispered something to a guard on his right. The guard scurried away before the man in black gazed at me again.

"Well, you are not the first woman to compete, but maybe you'll be the first one to make the top ten."

He breezed past me towards the crowd of men that waited, and the scent of forest and rain attacked my senses once again. I took my spot with the men in the courtyard. Their eyes seared into me, but I gave them no satisfaction of looking back at them. The man in black's eyes flickered around at everyone before lingering on me for a long moment.

"Hood off," he demanded. My hands trembled as I slipped the hood off my head. His golden eyes lingered on me longer than necessary. Recognition wasn't anywhere on his features though, and relief filled me. I smoothed my dark braid over my shoulder before meeting his eyes again.

He held my stare as one of the other guardsmen spoke to him.

"It will be a shame to beat a pretty thing like you," someone spoke from behind me. I turned and saw a fae taller than the rest of us. He was muscular in a way that indicated that he was probably used to doing hard labor. His light hair was in a long braid down his back, and his face was riddled with scars.

"It will be an honor to beat you," I remarked. Several men laughed at the exchange, but the big, gruff male behind me glared. My eyes found the guardsman in all black when his voice boomed over everyone else talking.

"The king is not available, so I will be the one to welcome you all to the seventh year of the trials. There are fifty of you now, but in a short time only ten of you will be left standing. Once the top ten have been announced, you will then work as a team to retrieve a particular item. If the item is returned to the Crimson kingdom, all who survive will be granted a wish of their choosing. You may not ask for the crown, harm the royal family, or make yourself royalty. Otherwise, you may ask for whatever you like." His eyes glanced around all of us. I wondered what the king was hoping to retrieve. What was important enough that they had done this seven times?

"There are rules to the tournament, and anyone who goes rogue will be killed and dishonored. First rule: if you hold magic, you are not allowed to use it during the games unless given permission beforehand."

The men didn't seem to like that rule, and a disgruntled mutter spread like wildfire in the crowd. The rule suited me just fine.

"You can use it after the games if it will help you recover. Second, no killing each other between trials. The king will announce the trial the day you are to participate. You will all sleep at the castle and be fed there. You may form alliances with each other as you see fit, but there will be no tolerance for cheating. Any questions?"

"How many trials are within the game?" someone yelled from the back.

"It usually takes no more than four for the top ten to be announced. These trials will weed out the weak and identify those with a certain set of skills needed to pull off the last task. Many great warriors have come through this competition, but none have returned from the final task." His dark, golden eyes stared directly at me. "If you've noticed, there are no Cerithian men here. If you are working for them and we find out, I will personally rip your heart from your chest."

"Why not just send all of us on the task? Wouldn't it be better odds?" I asked. I wanted to ask about Cerithia, but I didn't want to draw too much attention to myself.

The guardsman watched me for a long moment before responding. "A large group will attract unwanted attention. A small group will be able to infiltrate where we need them to much more efficiently. We've tried sending a large group before, and it was a disaster."

No one else asked questions.

"My men and I will be standing guard to make sure rules are followed. If you have an issue, you will find me or one of my men. Now let's get you all to your sleeping quarters and fed. Tomorrow will be the first trial."

We all shuffled in behind the guards. If I was mesmerized by the outside of the castle, I was taken aback by the inside. It held the same dark beauty as outside, but the light from the stained-glass windows made it colorful. It was more whimsical than I thought the Crimson kingdom would allow. Tapestries and golden artwork graced the black stone of the walls. Beautiful flowers grew on vines that crept up them and held every shade of red imaginable. It was more amazing than I would have ever pictured in my mind.

I couldn't believe others lived like this. My mind flashed back to mine and Sybil's home. Thousands of our buildings could have fit in the castle.

My eyes drifted to the back of the man, all in black. There was no doubt that he was in charge. His walk was confident and exuded power. His black uniform stretched over his wide shoulders and showed how muscular his legs were. None of the other men wore any color but red. I turned away when he glanced back at me. Eventually we came to a stop in front of two plain, wooden doors.

"This will be your sleeping quarters. Down the hallway to the right is a second set of wooden doors. That is where you'll eat. Down the hallway to the left is another set of doors, which is the washroom."

The men piled into the sleeping quarters to pick out their beds. I hung back, not caring where I slept. As soon as the last male walked through the doors, I followed, but the man in black pulled me back out.

"You are not staying here."

"I'll be fine." I struggled to free my arm from his grip, but he held tight. He turned to me, so I was face to face with him. His look held a cold indifference when he stared at me. He didn't remember me from the dreams.

"No, you won't. It's a custom that women stay in their own room and have a private wash area. We've had issues in the past." My heartbeat was fast at how close he was to me. His golden eyes met my green ones with a demand that

I listen to him. Then his eyes briefly dropped to my lips before he pulled away and released my arm.

"You'll stay down here." He walked down the hallway, not even bothering to wait and see if I was following. We passed the washroom and dining hall before coming to a singular wooden door. The man opened it and led me inside. The room was simple, but still nicer than my house with Sybil.

A big bed covered in red linens sat in the middle of the large area. There was also a big window that I couldn't wait to look out, as well as a small desk and lamp. Another door in the room led to my own washroom, and I couldn't wait to shower when he left. As I took in the simple space, my eyes lingered on the bed. Had I ever slept in a normal bed? There was no doubt that it would be better than my lumpy, makeshift bed in Exile. He cleared his throat, and when I glanced at him, he raised an eyebrow at me. His tall, broad body filled the small space of the room.

"Is it to your liking?" The guard stared at me oddly.

"It will be fine." I set my bag down. "Thanks."

Giving me a curt nod, he headed for the door. He paused with his back to me and his hand gripping the door handle tightly.

"Lock this door when you are in here alone. Dinner will be served within the hour."

Then he was gone. Taking his advice, I locked the door, then removed my cloak and walked over to the window. My view overlooked the castle's private gardens, where fountains and statues lined the stone pathways. It was absolutely beautiful.

I turned and surveyed the room again. The bed called to me. I laid on it, and a smile crept on my face that hadn't been there in a long time. It was odd to look at the ceiling and not see cracking mud and moss like in Exile, but nothing in this room was falling apart. The thought made me feel filthy, and I headed for the bathroom. The shower relaxed me, but I cut it short when my stomach wouldn't stop growling.

I needed a good meal and a good night's sleep to do well tomorrow. I was sure they had already targeted me as weak because I was the only woman. Tomorrow needed to be a day I established myself as someone not to fuck with.

A knock on my door startled me.

"Dinner is served."

After braiding my hair, I headed to the dining hall, where most of the men had already taken seats. Ignoring their gawking stares, I filled my plate with a ridiculous amount of food. It all smelled wonderful. I was so used to bread and water, with the occasional vegetable if I could find any to steal. The smell of it all made my stomach clench tight with hunger. It had always been easier to just ignore the hunger because acknowledging it only made it worse.

I chose to sit at an empty table. The guards lined the outskirts of the room, including the man in all black. I wondered if they would stand guard the entire time. Slowly I ate my food, savoring the flavor and knowing that eating too quickly would make me sick. The men were loud, but I didn't mind. I was so used to pure silence or boisterous fighting in Exile that civilized chatter here was nice. I kept my face down and minded my own business, but that didn't save me for too long.

The burly man that had tried intimidating me earlier was walking around to each table and talking with them. I noticed men adding coins into a bag. What was that about? The man caught me looking and stared at me momentarily before laughing, which of course drew everyone's attention.

"Little dove, would you care to join the betting?"

It was easy to ignore him as I continued to eat my food. I told myself not to be bothered by him. He just wanted to get under my skin. Some of the other men started laughing, which caught my attention more. There was obviously something funny happening at my expense. The guard in black was watching the exchange with a hard-pressed face. He was not amused but didn't interfere.

"Yeah, I didn't think you would. Besides, you'd lose the bet anyway."

I rolled my eyes at his tactic to rile me up. He was acting like a big, ugly child. He sauntered up to my table when I didn't engage yet again.

"Listen here, you stupid bitch. I don't take kindly to being ignored, but I'm feeling generous today. I'll let you join the betting without having to pay in. If you win, you can have the whole pot."

I raised my eyebrow at him but gave him little else to go on.

"We have a little bet going. Who will be ranked the lowest after the first task?"

I knew I was likely the only person that was voted for, considering I was the only woman. His smug smile felt unpleasant and made my skin crawl. His whole demeanor radiated bad energy, and I just wanted him to quit pestering me. Still, I continued to eat without giving away my annoyance.

"You are the unanimous vote," he sneered, as if I would become upset at this information. Still, I said nothing. My eyes drifted to the tall guardsman in all black. He wasn't even watching us anymore. He talked to another man as if he were bored being here. The burly man turned to the room full of men.

"Seems here the bitch doesn't want to participate. Yeah, I wouldn't either if I knew I would be at the bottom of the ranking." This had the other men in an uproar of laughter. The guard's golden eyes moved from the burly man to me as I continued eating, his lip curling in disgust at the exchange. Just as the big, ugly man went to sit back down, I spoke up just to prove a point. I knew I should just let this go, but I couldn't.

"You know, a boy from back home always told me it was easy to spot the weakest fighter in a crowd." I shot the man a look of boredom. "It's always the one who is the loudest, the one who tries to intimidate and bully fear into others."

The man's face turned bright red with anger, and the laughter of the other men died out.

"I guess that would make *you* the weakest, since clearly you are compensating for your lack of confidence by trying to make *me* look weak." I took a bite as all the men stared at me like I was an idiot. Maybe I was. "I won't join your childish game, but just know that I will be ranked higher than you." I held up my cup to the room in a toast and smiled.

Their eyes darted around in surprise, stunned that I stood up for myself. The guard in black, though, held an amused smirk on his face as he watched all the horrified men glaring at me. The audacity I must have to speak up against this bully of a man.

"Watch your back, stupid whore," the man bellowed before he turned his back to me and headed to his table.

Once I was comfortably full, I stood up and headed back to my room. I was thankful that I didn't have to share a room with the men now. I was sure the big, ugly ogre of a man would try to smother me as I slept. Just as I turned the handle to my door, someone rushed up behind me. I pulled my dagger out of its sheath and held it to the throat of the guard in black. An amused smile spread across his face as he grabbed my wrist and slammed me back into the wall.

"Glad to see you have good instincts, considering you just insulted the man who is expected to rank first in the entire tournament."

Processing his words was difficult when he was so close to me. I had not thought much about what he looked like in my dreams until recently, but everything about him drew me in. Maybe it was due to him being around me for so long that I felt comfortable with him, or maybe it was something else entirely. Something about his presence made me less... tense, despite the powerless position I now found myself in.

His body molded to mine as he held me against the wall. His other hand squeezed my throat softly. His eyes swirled with gold and black, his fingers gripping me tighter as his gaze found mine. This man was nothing like my dreams, but I still found myself unable to resist him. He wasn't gentle or playful; he was cold, indifferent, and powerful.

"The man is repulsive," I argued weakly. "He will not rank in the top ten." The need to try and focus on something other than him overwhelmed me. Could he hear how hard my heart was beating from being this close?

His golden eyes traced over my face. I held my breath as his eyes lingered over my mouth. What did he see when he looked at me?

"I look forward to watching you in the trials since you seem so confident in yourself," he said, his voice softer than it had been, as if he were now distracted.

"Glad you'll be entertained while I fight for my life," I retorted.

A smug smirk curled on his lips.

"You signed up for this."

He had a point.

"May I go to bed, or are you planning on holding me here all night?"

He seemed to realize that he was pressed up against me and pushed away from me instantly, like I repulsed him. My body shivered at the loss of his body's warmth.

"Tell me your name." Not a question, but a demand.

"Thea." That was my only response as I closed the door on him. I locked it behind me and listened for him to walk away, ignoring the patter in my chest. The man was too handsome for his own good and too handsome to be a man who served my biggest enemy. *He was* the enemy, and I needed to remember that when he was near me.

CHAPTER 7

The guardsman who wore all black stood in the shadows in my room at the Crimson castle. I was lying on my bed as he looked around my room. His golden eyes paused when he spotted me.

"Come out of the shadows and show me your face," I demanded, acting braver than I felt because this was only a dream.

"No flirting this time, little viper?" he purred playfully. When I didn't answer he sighed, "No."

"I already know who you are."

His eyes held me in place as he thought about what his next move should be. With a defeated sigh, he stepped out of the shadows and lowered his hood. My suspicions were correct. It was the guardsman's handsome face staring back at me. Even though I had expected to see him, my chest squeezed at the sight of him. Disbelief mingled with fear within me as I struggled to find words amidst the chaos swirling inside my mind.

"Are you liking Crimson so far?"

"You're unpleasant in real life, you know." I sat up on the bed to watch him better. Choosing to ignore his question, I simply stared at him.

He didn't say anything either. His golden eyes pinned me like I was his prey, and my body reacted to the look immediately.

"I told you before that I don't remember you when I wake up. It's like these dreams never happen. Why would you expect to be treated differently than any of the other contestants?" His tone wasn't rude but more curious than anything.

"Hmm." I glanced at him. "I don't know if I believe that you don't remember me."

"Then don't," he snapped back.

"Do you wish you remembered me outside of your dreams?"

He turned his back towards me as he gazed out of my window. I watched him as he blatantly ignored my presence. When he finally turned back towards me, sadness had washed over his face, and his shoulders were sagging. His dark brows creased as he stared at me, probably wondering, as I was, how we could finally meet after having known each other for years. He had been in my dreams since I was exiled.

"Yes, I wish I remembered you," he answered. "It feels like I've known you for so long."

"I feel like I've known you forever. Maybe that's why I was a little disappointed you didn't recognize me today, in real life," I whispered my vulnerable thoughts to him.

"Why did you join the trials?"

"I need the wish."

His golden eyes glanced over me before frowning at my comment. "Little viper, what if you die in the trials?"

"Then I die for a good cause." I didn't miss a beat. "Why do you care? You don't remember our shared dreams in real life. You wouldn't miss me."

"Don't downplay your importance. You matter to me, and I would feel your absence every time I closed my eyes and you weren't there calling for me to find you. I would know something was missing, that you were missing, even if it was only in my dreams," he said, pacing back and forth across my small room. He sighed and pinched the bridge of his nose.

Over the years, I had wondered about this man and if there was a reason why he was always lurking in my dreams. At one point, I had even convinced myself that I had just made him up to help combat my loneliness. It hadn't oc-curred to me that I would ever meet him, but now that I *had seen him, I couldn't process that he was real. I sat in the middle of my bed as he paced once again. He was stressed out, but I didn't understand why.*

"I've seen you fight in your dreams. You'll do fine." He sounded like he was reassuring himself more than me.

"I'll be fine. Besides, if I die, then you won't have to miss your big, important meetings anymore," I joked, but he didn't laugh.

He swallowed hard as he stared at me.

"Don't joke about you dying," he whispered.

Before I could respond, a loud, clanging bell woke me from my dream. My eyes darted to the door when a loud commotion rattled it. The bell continued to ring out, and I got dressed quickly, leaving everything I owned in the room except my daggers. I assumed that this was part of the tournament.

As I slipped out the door, the other competitors were shuffling from their sleeping quarters and into the hall where the guards stood. I joined them just as the guard in black walked down the hallway with the most terrifying expression haunting his handsome face.

He was pissed.

His black eyes didn't spare me a glance as he stormed into the men's sleeping quarters. Peering around, I looked for answers as to how this was part of the tournament. Some of the men had the same confusion on their faces that I felt. The rest of them, though, didn't look confused at all. I couldn't think of any possible reason for him to be this irritated so early in the morning. The answer revealed itself a few moments later, thankfully.

Two guards emerged from the sleeping quarters carrying the body of a dead fae. Someone had died. No, someone had been killed. Blood stained the white linens he was wrapped in.

It was the first night, and someone had already broken the rules. The head guardsman came back out a moment later, and I took a step backward at the sight of him. His golden eyes were now solid black, and tendrils of shadows moved from him. They curled close to him in a menacing, angry cloud. He could control shadows.

"I will only ask once for the coward to step forward. Who killed Vatlin?" His voice was deeper and darker than I had ever heard before.

A soft murmur rippled through the crowd, but I couldn't pull my eyes from him, mesmerized by the way his shadows moved and tangled around his body.

Had I ever seen anything so terrifyingly beautiful? No.

His cold eyes turned to me with a sneer. I snapped my gaze away from him instantly, wondering if he noticed how much I was staring at him and how much I was admiring the sheer power of him in that moment. There was a commotion somewhere in the crowd behind me before a man was shoved from the group. The fae was young with red hair and freckles, which probably made him look younger than he was.

"You?" the guard said skeptically.

The boy remained silent. No way he killed a fae who was twice his size without making noise.

"No, sir."

"Then why are you in front of me?" His voice bellowed. "I'm not playing this game. I will start killing you one by one if the true killer doesn't come out now."

A faint murmur spread through the crowd, assessing the captain of the king's guard's threat. Whispers about the guard spread like fire, saying he would kill us all in less than a second. Others talked about how absolutely ruthless he was. I glanced at the men behind me, who were all avoiding making eye contact with him, like they were scared he would kill them with a look.

"It was Tagon!" someone yelled. A fight erupted immediately, shoving me into the black stone wall chin first.

Damn it.

Blood covered my hand as I tried to stop the bleeding, but my curiosity had me turning to watch how this played out. The crowd parted as the guardsman walked forward to the two fae fighting. One I assumed was Tagon, and the other was whomever called him out. Tagon was smaller than the fae who blamed him for the murder, but he was holding his own in the fight that had erupted. They stopped immediately when shadows erupted around all of us.

The force of the shadows knocked me back into the wall. Pain radiated down my back, but I didn't dare move my eyes from the head guardsman with shadow magic.

"Tagon, I presume?" he spoke softly, which only magnified the power he had.

"He's lying," he snapped defensively. His brown hair glistened with sweat from the fight. "Kael wants me dead because I'm competition."

The guard turned towards the other man.

"How do you know it was him?"

The man stared back without an answer at first. He looked around at everyone watching him closely. His body was tight with tension, and his eyes shifted around like he was trying to come up with a story.

"I saw him kill him."

The guardsman paced silently back and forth in front of the two men. His face did not shift from its cruel glare. Finally, he grabbed Tagon by the shirt and pulled him away from the other man, towards where I stood. He leaned down and whispered something to Tagon, who whispered a response back. The guard then walked back to Kael.

"How did he kill him?"

"With a knife," he answered quickly. "Sliced his throat."

Tagon stood close to me, watching the whole exchange. Whatever had been said between him and the guardsman caused him to look less tense.

Before anyone questioned the man further, the guard pulled his sword out and beheaded the fae. Everyone scurried back away from the gruesome scene as blood stained the floor below his lifeless body.

"Does anyone else need clarification on the rules of this tournament?" he bellowed. His voice filled and ricocheted off every hollow space in the hallway. No one spoke a word or even dared to breathe in that moment.

Tagon froze when the guardsman turned around. His black eyes shifted to me, and he noticed the blood coming from my chin but looked back to Tagon. He took a few steps to reach us. Tagon stiffened when the guardsman stopped in front of him.

"If it was you that killed the first fae, then you better pray to the stars above; I don't find out about it," the guard hissed.

"It wasn't me," Tagon assured him.

The guard had killed that man without knowing without a doubt if Tagon was the one lying. It was a power move. Even if the real killer was in our crowd, they were likely not to try that again. My eyes shifted behind Tagon as guards hauled the headless man up. His bloodied shoes hung from his lifeless feet and dragged across the ground as they took him away, leaving two distinct blood trails in their wake. Everyone returned to the sleeping quarters in silence.

A warm hand on my face startled me when the captain tilted my chin up so he could inspect my wound. I had been so focused on the dead fae, I hadn't seen him approach me. His touch was gentle, seeming out of place after the anger I witnessed from him.

"What happened?" he asked softly.

"I fell when the fight broke out. I'm fine."

I turned to head back to my room, but his shadows stopped me, holding me in place so he could get in front of me. His eyes were void of the blackness that consumed them only moments ago.

"Did I scare you?"

I shook my head. He was scary, but he didn't scare me. I was impressed more than anything.

"I've never seen shadow magic."

A cocky smile spread across his face. Smug prick.

"Impressive, isn't it?"

"Sure." I turned around, trying not to get distracted by him. He was already taking up my time when I slept. I didn't need him lurking when I was awake too.

"Today's the first trial," he spoke from beside me. "I'm looking forward to seeing what you can do, Thea."

My name rolled off his tongue like a wicked promise. I looked up at him and breathed heavily. His eyes examined my face as we walked back to my room. There was no reason he needed to follow me.

"What's your name?" I had been wondering about his name since the first night he was in my dream, but no name I had ever considered seemed to fit him.

"Not really any of your business."

He cocked his head to the side like he was studying me, like he was expecting a reaction from me, but I refused to give it to him. Normally I would let insecurity take over and shy away from his staring, but I needed to appear as confident as I could. His eyes finally glanced away, and he tilted his head like he heard someone behind us.

A guardsman in red suddenly appeared, startling me. How had he heard him coming? He muttered something and nodded curtly. He actually wasn't going to tell me his name. What an ass.

"Best of luck in the first trial, Thea. I hope you're here a bit longer." He gave me no smile or any emotion as he spoke. He simply said the words and walked away with the guard.

I headed down the hallway and had just reached my room when suddenly, the ground began to shake violently. I looked around in surprise as the walls of the castle began to crumble. The tapestries that adorned the walls fell with the rubble in piles of dust around me. Yelling from down the hall alerted me to the fact that this was real, and I wasn't simply imagining it.

I held tight to the door handle, trying to steady myself, but that didn't last very long. Before my eyes, the door slowly faded away into nothingness. Without anything to hold onto, I fell onto the hard ground. Lights began to flash so brightly that I couldn't see anything around me. All I could do was curl into a ball and wait for it all to stop. After what felt like forever but was probably only seconds, the sound quieted and the shaking stopped. My legs shook violently as I stood, and I covered my eyes from the still-blinding lights. The men made sounds of discomfort somewhere close to me.

This had to be the first trial.

The flashing lights finally ceased, and I opened my eyes to see a colosseum-like structure. The colosseum swept far and wide past us. It was filled with bystanders who were watching.

I stilled the moment I saw him. The king of Crimson appeared on a small balcony in the middle of the stands, dressed in dark red robes with gold accessories hanging off him. His black crown had many colored jewels in it, the largest being a stone the color of blood. He was tall with broad shoulders and dark hair.

To my shock, he looked less evil than I had pictured in my mind over the years.

The captain stood at his side, and even though I couldn't see his face completely, I knew his eyes were on me. My eyes shifted to a stunning woman with red hair who sat on the king's other side, along with three or four younger royals behind them. She was also wearing red and gold, the Crimson kingdom's colors.

"Good morning," His thick accent echoed through the colosseum with authority. "Welcome to the first trial. I'm assured Cassius explained the purpose of the trials to the participants." My eyes shifted to him, and he gave me a smug smile, which I ignored.

Cassius. It fit him perfectly.

"I seek the best of the best, true fighters and warriors, to retrieve something that has been taken from me, from us. Each trial will test your ability to think quickly, react swiftly, and fight for a spot in the king's special guard—a truly high honor."

The crowd cheered loudly at this declaration. The noise was so piercingly loud that I wanted to cover my ears. We were entertainment for them.

"We will keep track of ranking here." The king pointed across the arena to where a giant leaderboard suddenly appeared, high in the sky. It illuminated all fifty names of the participants. Mine was near the bottom in bold red letters. Underneath my name were two names written in white. The two men who died earlier today. Why was my name at the bottom, because I was a woman? My darkness swirled in my chest with irritation. Did they think I was the weakest here?

"At the end of each trial, the bottom 10 will be dismissed from the competition until we have only the top ten participants left, who will go on to the final task. If it is completed, all who survive will be granted a wish."

"Too bad you'll be out after today, little dove."

I ignored the burly man next to me. Out of all the participants, though, he was the one closest to me. Instead of giving him attention, I let my thoughts focus on Sybil and the twins. I needed to do this for them, for all of us locked away like criminals in Exile.

"Your first task is to retrieve the object from the center of the ring and make it out of the arena." He said it as if it were simple, but there had to be more than that. The king's eyes locked on mine, and he gave me a friendly smile that widened when I glared at him. "Remember, we'll be watching, so don't use magic in this trial or you will be disqualified."

The ground started shaking as soon as the words left his mouth. Large mountains lifted out of the ground around us in place of the colosseum. The light surrounding us was replaced with near-complete darkness as day shifted into night in an instant. A moonlight glow surrounded us even though the moon itself could not be seen. Trees, larger than any I had ever seen, surrounded us, eliminating any chance of us escaping. They created a circular barrier, letting us know where the task would take place.

A bright, glowing red light drew our attention to the middle of the meadow. As we watched, a small stand appeared with a tall glass vase on top of it. The vase seemed to be filled with glowing red stones, and I realized what we had to do. There must only be enough stones for forty of us to get. Anyone without a stone would be eliminated.

I glanced up at the leaderboard looming in the sky above us. I wanted to see my name move to the number one spot. My feet stayed rooted to their spot though, as doubt filled me. It was too easy of a task. There was obviously something the king was not telling us. No one else moved either. Everyone was standing still, anxiety etched on to their features. Nobody wanted to make the first move. At some point, someone would have to go and reveal the true nature of the task in front of us. I just needed to be patient.

CHAPTER 8

I tried to focus on the illusion of the landscape we were in. It wasn't real, but I wouldn't know that if I hadn't seen it build itself around us. Whoever generated this magic had outdone themselves. My first thought was that it was elite magic, but the king of Crimson would never allow that. It must be a spell or something, from a witch, maybe?

I risked one small step into the taller grass to test what would happen. Perhaps it was quicksand or something similar. My foot was only met with hard, unmoving ground.

The slight ruffle of movement from others getting restless echoed softly in the eerie silence. My instinct told me to wait, but my competitive nature wanted me to charge forward. I looked around at everybody else but could hardly see them in the faded moonlight.

I turned slowly to look behind me. I knew a crowd was watching us, even if they weren't visible to me. The silence reminded me of Exile. There were no sounds of animal noises or water flowing here. I wondered if this was the same spell that cast the shadow boundary around us. The air was pleasantly cool and smelled like pine trees. I shifted my boots, making my daggers stab my ankles. No one said we couldn't have weapons, and I had a feeling I would need them.

"Fuck this. I'm not scared!" a man close to me yelled. He had only made it one step before horrific screeching had me covering my ears. We could all hear thrashing coming from the trees behind us. Within seconds, the man who yelled was plucked from the ground with ease. I couldn't make out what took him, but we all saw it fly him into the darkness.

My eyes noticed the leaderboard shift as another name appeared below mine in white letters. It was nice to see my name move up on the board, but not at the cost of the man's life. I uncovered my ears as the shrieking died down again. Sweat beaded on my face as adrenaline pumped through me. My heart raced at the sight of what just happened. Something had caught that monster's attention. Noise? Movement? I didn't want to test my theory and be wrong. Maybe it was something else entirely. Damn it.

Nobody was moving or speaking out of fear. All my time in the Forbidden Wood told me to keep my eyes trained on the trees. I didn't want to miss the monster again. Minutes ticked by without anyone moving and no creatures appearing.

After waiting for so long, an idea popped into my head. It was risky, but I couldn't just stand here forever. Leaning down very slowly, I grabbed a rock. My breath caught in my throat as I surveyed the woods again. My movement hadn't seemed to attract anything, though. I slowly tossed the rock into the middle of the arena, aiming at the glass vase. I was hoping the noise of it would attract whatever the creature was.

When the rock hit the vase, all the red stones tumbled to the ground and the sound of shattering glass ricocheted around us. The noise echoed past us into the forest, and the shrieking of the creatures started again. We could hear them thrashing through the trees towards us. I laid on my stomach and watched as winged monsters flew from the trees and toward the center of the arena.

I held my breath as three of the creatures landed near the stones. A small gasp escaped me when one of them turned towards me. It was unlike anything I had ever seen before—a batlike creature, light gray and translucent in the moonlight. Red and black spikes adorned the tops of its wings. Its face was devoid of anything, including eyes, thankfully, except for a large split across it where its mouth must be.

We all knew that the Forbidden Wood held many monsters, but I had never seen one of these in all my years of sneaking around in them. Maybe I had just been lucky enough to never run into one.

Someone across the arena from me let out a startled cry at the grotesque sight of them. Their ears bent toward the man before letting out a piercing shriek into the dark sky. All three creatures took off in his direction, and chaos erupted. Men were yelling and running to escape the arena.

The young fae from this morning with red hair and freckles moved swiftly towards the stones without any noise, ignoring the turmoil around him.

I was impressed at how fast and quietly he moved. Following his lead, I headed quickly towards the stones but stopped by a boulder to ensure I was still off their radar. This was just like sneaking through the shadow boundary and through the Forbidden Wood. It wasn't until I was halfway through the meadow that a deafening crash sounded next to me. A rock rolled past me, hitting the large boulder I was hiding behind. The impact was loud even with men yelling.

When I glanced behind me, the burly man gave me an evil smile. I turned back to continue, but let out a cry as one of the creatures swooped down and grabbed me. Its long claws dug into my shoulder with a piercing cry. A deep, painful sob tore through me before I silenced myself. One of the monsters was manageable, but all of them would kill me.

The creature's ankle was as cold as ice when I grabbed it to steady myself and take the pressure of its claws off my shoulder as we started ascending. I reached for the dagger in my boot, praying to the gods above that I didn't drop it. With the dagger balanced in my hand, I pulled it back as far as I could for power. The blade seemed heavy as I angled it at the monster's ankle. I sliced as far through it as I could, nearly severing it from the monster's leg.

Thankfully, we hadn't made it too far above the ground before it dropped me, but the wind was still knocked from my lungs as I landed on the ground. The air whooshed from me, leaving me gasping for breath as pain shot through my shoulder and back. Warm blood soaked through my shirt, but my attention was being pulled elsewhere as my eyes caught the faint blue of a wisp by the tree line. Even though it had no eyes that I could see, I could sense that it was watching me as it flickered out and appeared next to me in the field. I couldn't explain the feeling of urgency that filled me when the wisp came closer.

I needed to hurry up before the stones were gone or that creature came looking for me again.

Men were still shouting, some using magic to fight off the creatures even though it wasn't allowed. Thoughts of Sybil, the twins, and the mother with her young son who died for no reason plagued me. They were counting on me to stand up and finish this task. The pain that shot through my shoulder took away my breath as I stood up.

By some stroke of luck, the creature had dropped me closer to the stones than where I had been. There were still quite a few, which meant I might still place in the top ten. I grabbed a stone and turned towards the edge of the tree line. My eyes took in the horrific scene unfolding. Creatures had ripped men apart, eating parts of them before leaving to kill another.

Blood splatter covered the tall grass of the meadow. It was an absolute massacre. There was no way only ten would've died here. A quick glance at the scoreboard showed my name in second place, but having a rock didn't secure my safety. Refusing to look behind me at the sounds of terrified men and creatures, I forced myself to push forward. I had seen enough of the chaos in front of me. Task one was almost behind me. I just needed to walk through the boundary. Slowly, as to not draw attention, I began to edge to the tree line. I was nearly there when the wisp cut me off. No one else seemed to notice the blue orb floating in front of me. I opened my mouth to ask what it was doing, but it shifted to the side, making my eyes follow.

The burly fae had trapped the young fae man.

"Give it now!" the giant fae whispered harshly. He was restraining the young red-haired fae by his upper arms. The fae shook his head, refusing to give the stone, his red curls bouncy with the movement. The burly man didn't hesitate to punch the kid in the face. The sound of crunching bones had me turning away.

I continued towards the edge of the arena, reminding myself that that was not my battle to fight. I didn't need to involve myself.

The wisp must have thought differently though, as it stopped me again, clearly wanting me to reconsider. The crunch of the fae's bones made me flinch. I mulled my options over. If the burly man got that stone from the kid, he would definitely make the top ten for this task. I needed the best of the best to actually win so I could win the wish. That kid should be in the top spot with how well he did getting the task done. His stealth was unmatched, and that was valuable.

As I turned to face them again, the burly man grabbed the stone from the boy.

Fuck. I guess I was involving myself.

Grabbing the dagger from my boot, I quickly threw it at the man. He swallowed down his painful cry as my blade buried itself in his wrist, falling to his knees in pain. My dagger was long, so it stuck straight through his wrist on both sides. The stone fell from his hand, and so did the young fae. His body was a heap of blood and broken bones. He didn't move or make a noise, making me worry he might be dead already.

I hurried over to him. I wasn't letting him lose his top ten spot because of that asshole. He was bloodied, and his hand was twisted in the wrong direction. Gods be damned. Grabbing his stone, I slipped it into his pocket.

"Come on," I whispered as I lifted him. He sobbed softly. Thank the stars that he was smaller than the typical male fae.

"Shhh." My eyes darted around, but the creatures were too busy with other contestants to notice his small noise.

"Just leave me. I'm too wounded to do well in the next task," he muttered.

"I'll heal you when this task is completed," I promised. I knew he must be important because the wisp made it a point that I needed to step in, even though it was stupid to involve myself.

He leaned into me as a couple of others ran ahead of us and through the boundary. Damn it. My focus was on getting us through the edge of the trees. We only needed to be in the top ten to receive the most points. When we were almost there, I heard the burly man making his way towards us. He had a stone in his hand, but I was sure he wanted to kill me or both of us.

"This is going to hurt," I warned the young fae.

"Wh–" His sentence was cut short as I shoved him through the barrier. His name shifted up on the leaderboard.

The burly man tackled me through the boundary. The brightness on this side was nearly paralyzing. Pain seeped into every part of my body. I let out a painful cry as my shoulder landed on the unforgiving ground.

"You fucking bitch!" The burly man yelled now that the creatures weren't a threat. His fist connected with my face, and I cried out before I bucked him off me. I stood and kicked him as hard as I could in the face. The crunch of his nose gave me great satisfaction. His reaction was quick, as he swiped my feet out from under me, causing me to tumble to the ground. I didn't care where I was hitting.

My only goal was to inflict as much pain as possible as I swung my fists.

I grabbed his wrist where my dagger embedded into it and squeezed. The horrifying scream he made called to the darkness in my chest, the darkness that didn't let me feel bad for killing others who got in my way. My fire magic simmered in my chest, but I pushed it down. Losing control couldn't happen. His other fist caught me off guard when it connected to my eye. Again, my fire magic surged forward, but I held it in the cage of my chest. The burly man lay under me as we both swung our fists mercilessly before we were torn apart.

Cassius pulled us away from each other. His eyes were black as night as he stared down at the burly man, then shifted his glare to me. The man and I were both bleeding from our faces. Blood soaked my shirt from the shoulder wound. Others had gathered around to watch the fight. I stared him down as he huffed angry breaths.

"I'll fucking kill you!" the burly fae promised. I glanced at the leaderboard and noticed I was above him in spot number four.

"Looks like I placed before you. Does that mean I won the bet?" I said smugly, just to piss him off more.

It worked, and he lunged for me again, but shadows instantly circled us, blocking him from getting close. Cassius and I stood together in his darkness, where no one could see us. My eyes focused on the black, misty shadows that had formed a wall around us. His black eyes focused on me for a long moment before looking over my wounds. I'm sure I looked like hell because my body ached with every small movement.

"You shouldn't have involved yourself," he seethed. "You would have made first place."

"The boy deserved a place in the top ten. He was the best at the task. I want the best of the best in the top ten with me. It's the only way to earn the wish."

"Well, now he's useless because of his wounds," Cassius hissed as he squared himself, like I might punch him. My hands curled into fists. "You wasted your spot to help someone who likely will fail the next challenge. Just worry about your damn self out there."

Why was he so pissed off at me?

"I didn't ask for your opinion on the matter," I argued right back. I had taken a step closer to him, so he knew I wasn't intimidated by him and his shadow magic. I'm sure my fire magic would be a challenge for him. "I know what I'm doing. I'm not stupid."

He stepped closer to me, too, but I couldn't move away because of his shadows. They had closed in around us, not allowing any extra space. His hot breath fanned my face as he exhaled sharply through his nose.

"Look at you!" he breathed. "Look at how much you gave up. You're beat to hell, Thea. How are you supposed to do well in the next trial?"

"Let me out of your shadows," I demanded as I pushed at his chest. I knew what I was doing and what consequences my actions would have. He was just like Kaz, Kai, and Sybil. They all thought I was too impulsive and reckless.

His shadows disappeared immediately, and we stormed away from each other. The contestants were all gathered in a small area, watching as Cassius and I fought. I walked over to where other survivors had congregated.

The king stood on his small balcony. "The trial has concluded. You all demonstrated great bravery and skill today." He turned to the leaderboard. "It appears we lost more than ten participants, so thirty-six of you remain. I want to remind you that killing each other is prohibited between trials. However, you are allowed to use magic now that the first task is completed. I will see you all when the next trial is to take place." His eyes pierced into me as he spoke. Then the magic faded, and we were at the castle again.

I turned to find the red-haired fae. He was sitting on the ground in front of the doors, nursing his broken hand. I hurried over to him. His dark eyes found mine as his body shivered with pain. I leaned down and helped him rise to his feet.

"Come on, let's heal you up." I huffed as we both struggled to move inside. We passed the men's sleeping quarters and headed towards my room so we would have privacy.

I wasn't quite sure how to use the healing magic Sybil gave me, but I hoped I could figure it out. The walk to my room felt more expansive than it truly was. The fae next to me grunted in pain with each step forward. The others had walked by us without offering any help. I thought of tripping the burly fae as he passed but controlled my impulses.

We paused in the hallway, leaning against the black stone walls to catch our breath.

"Most would have just left me," he breathed out in painful breaths. "I wouldn't have blamed you if you'd done the same."

"I saw the way you moved so quietly and quickly. You would have gotten first place if it wasn't for that prick. I want the best in the top ten with me." It was odd being vulnerable towards this stranger. "Besides, that man is a fucking troll. Any excuse to stab him is enticing."

The fae laughed but stopped abruptly, pain contorting his face. I moved to help him to my room quickly.

"His name is Leer, by the way," the boy grunted.

I didn't care what the burly fae's name was. I would still refer to him as a troll until he was eliminated from the tournament.

When we finally reached my wooden door, I turned to look down the hall as I sensed eyes watching me. Cassius stood staring at the two of us disappearing into my room. His face gave nothing away about what he was thinking, but his shadows still furled around him in an angry cloud.

Ignoring him, I walked through the door and helped the boy sit on my bed. The sound of the door locking had me releasing a long breath of relief.

"What's your name?" I asked as I moved towards where he was sitting.

"My friends call me Nev."

"Alright, Nev. I'm not sure how well I'm going to be able to do this," I said honestly. "So, let's get to it."

I could tell he wanted to ask what I meant, but I didn't give him the chance. I inspected his wounds. His hand and ribs were definitely broken. Sybil's magic hummed in the amulet around my neck, eager to be utilized.

Was I just supposed to touch where he was hurt? Nothing happened when I did that. Hmm. I had never seen a healer heal. I hadn't seen anyone use magic before, besides myself and Cassius. I focused hard on his wounds and willed the magic to fix them, but that didn't work either.

This was ridiculous.

"Is something wrong?" Nev asked.

"No, it's just being a little shy," I sighed, grabbing the amulet around my neck, willing the damn thing to show me how to use it. Suddenly, the orange and red colors started to bleed from it and seeped out and across my hand. The colors then traveled into my body, pulsing through my veins with a power I had never experienced before. Nev's eyes widened in shock as the magic ran through me.

Once I could feel the magic in every part of me, I reached out and touched Nev. The power seeped through me and into him. We watched in amazement as his hand slowly pieced itself back together. Then his bloodied face healed before my eyes. Nev stared at me in awe. I could feel my own wounds hurting less and knew it was likely healing both of us at once. The magic glowing in my veins was illuminating small swirls of red, black, and orange on my skin, just like they had in my dream. The marks were so faint though, I doubted that he would spot them.

Nev flexed his once broken hand and smiled brightly at me. As I let go of the amulet, Sybil's magic lingered in my chest with my own. He stood up fully healed and threw a few punches in the air in front of him to test it out.

"Like new," he chuckled. "Thank you." He smiled brightly at me.

"It was no problem."

"You healed up nicely, too." He pointed at my shoulder. I did feel better, but I was exhausted. My eyes were heavy as I sat on the bed.

"Are you alright?" His brows creased.

"I just need to lay down and rest." My words had barely left my mouth before my world went dark.

CHAPTER 9

My eyes fluttered open enough to see who was moving me. Cassius lifted me gently off the floor before laying me under my blankets. How had he gotten here so quickly? I tried to sit up, but he gently laid me back down.

"Easy, Thea," he sighed. "I'm just getting you situated." Nev was pacing by the doorway.

"Sorry Thea, you passed out, and I didn't know what to do," Nev said.

I opened my mouth to respond, but nothing came out.

"You need rest." Cassius was close to me as he spoke, but my eyes were feeling hazy again. "Using magic too much will weaken you, especially if you don't use it often." My mouth opened to ask him why he thought I hadn't used magic often, but the question died on my tongue as my mind fell into the darkness again.

I was stuck in the dark, suspended by time. How long had I been here? Where was here? Nothing but cold darkness encircled me as I looked around. My chest tightened with a suffocating panic.

"Little viper?" *His voice instantly stopped the panic from taking over.*

I turned towards Cassius. As I did, the walls around us transformed from darkness into my room at the castle. He came towards me quickly and inspected me for injuries.

"You look uninjured."

"I healed myself after the trial."

Confusion crossed his face. He stared deep into my eyes as he contemplated something.

"I've never seen you heal before."

"Well, you don't know anything about me, Cassius. You've never seen me use magic."

He nodded like it was true but didn't say whatever was on his mind. He turned away from me and glanced out the window of my room. Standing up slowly, I joined him. It was nighttime in the kingdom of Crimson. The fountains were all lit up, and the water shined red under the lights. It was beautiful. I had always wondered what the red lights were when I admired the castle from the Forbidden Wood.

"The gardens are my favorite part of the castle," *he spoke softly.* "I like to go out there to clear my head and think."

The gardens were peaceful to look at, but my favorite part was the sound of trickling water. He was much calmer in my dreams than in real life. I wondered which one was the real him. He turned to me and froze me in place with his piercing golden eyes.

"You need to watch yourself while you're here. Danger hides everywhere, Thea, and you are the biggest target. If you don't look out for yourself, you'll die." His voice held an angry tone.

"What do you mean?" I asked.

"It will only be more dangerous the longer you stay. The target on your back will only become larger the farther into the trials you make it. There are others that don't want you to succeed."

"Cassius, I'm stronger than you think I am. I can handle it." I paused and turned to him. His eyes held a real concern for me. "You know something that you aren't telling me," I accused.

He didn't deny it. Instead, he simply reached up and smoothed my braid over my shoulder like he had done it a million times before. Before I could question him again, he pulled me to him and hugged me tightly. The gesture caught me so off guard I didn't know what to do but hug him back. He held on for a long moment, then stepped away from me.

"It might be a while until I see you here again."

"What? Why?"

He disappeared from my sight. I moved towards the spot where he was standing and stopped. There was no trace of him except for the lingering scent of forest and rain.

★★☽★★

As I sat up from my dream, I shivered at the sweat dampening my forehead and shirt. I sucked in a heavy breath as my eyes adjusted to the brightness from my window. Cassius was standing at the foot of my bed watching me.

"Bad dream?" He raised his eyebrow at me.

He had always told me he didn't remember me when he woke up. Was that true, or was he trying to keep me at a distance? Did he know me or something about my past?

"How long have I been out?"

"Almost a full day." He cocked his head to the side like he was studying me. Did I miss the second trial?

"I should be up, getting ready for the trial."

"There isn't one today, but you should eat. I brought you some food."

The aroma of the soup and bread he brought to my room made my stomach growl in hunger. I glanced at him and wondered why he was even here and why he was pretending to care about me at all.

"I don't need a caretaker," I snapped at him. His golden eyes darkened for a brief moment before returning to their original color.

"You're welcome," he spoke sarcastically. "Don't mistake this for me giving a shit about if you're alright. It's my job to make sure all the contestants make it to the next trial without dying. It would be boring to watch if only three of you were left standing. I have better things to do with my time than pretend to care about your well-being, so I'll be leaving."

He disappeared through my doorway and out of sight. What a prick. I couldn't trust kindness, especially from someone who protects my enemy.

Those that were kind to me always had ulterior motives. Pushing others away and keeping them at a distance is something Sybil always warned me would make me lonely. But it also kept me safe. She worried that I didn't care about anyone and that I enjoyed being alone. It wasn't true, but I still couldn't let my guard down, no matter how much I craved to find somewhere I belonged.

Who would ever want a monster like me? It was better to push other fae away before they decided I wasn't worth loving and rejected me first. I was frustrated with myself as I ate my food but decided to leave my room and explore the grounds a bit more. I shouldn't feel bad about my attitude towards Cassius. He had been an asshole since the trials started.

I took a piping hot shower and dressed in new clothing that Cassius had probably brought me. Guilt seeped into my mind as I replayed the attitude I had shown him. I guess I could acknowledge his kindness without putting my trust in him.

When I was presentable enough, I left my room and made my way outside. The air was cooler than I was used to in Exile, but the sun shined brightly here and warmed me.

Wisp was waiting for me. I followed it happily, until the soft blue flame tried to take me down the cobblestone road towards the town. I paused, having no intention of mingling with Crimson fae, but the wisp moved back toward me quickly. It stopped only a few feet in front of me before swirling around me. I had never seen it this close before. If I focused hard enough, I could almost see the silhouette of a woman within it. She stopped, and I swear she pointed to the town. I huffed in irritation, and I headed in that direction.

The streets were lively with fae, like they had been when I first walked through them.

A stone bench in a small park caught my eye, so I sat down to admire the happiness that everyone seemed to have here. My past was a mystery to me, but something told me that I wasn't used to this happiness there either.

I had spent so many nights trying to convince my own mind to help me remember what I was missing. Sybil thought it was trauma preventing me from keeping my memories—that I had endured so much pain that my mind made it all disappear forever so I could simply keep surviving. I wanted to believe that, but why was my whole life missing? Why didn't it just take out the part where I was sent to Exile, since that was obviously traumatizing for everyone who went?

A sinking feeling started to form in the pit of my stomach. Maybe my life was just as bad outside of Exile as it was in it. After all, I was fine being alone, and I naturally didn't trust anyone. It seemed like those were traits that I had before being placed in Exile.

My chest grew heavy with a darkness that lived deep within it. Something was wrong with me, and I knew it. A large part of me wanted to know about my past, but at the same time I didn't want to know anything. Wisp moved from beside me and swirled around me like she sensed a shift in my thoughts.

Music started playing somewhere in the town, and I closed my eyes and admired the sound. It was peaceful here. Something about that thought made me feel like a traitor. This is the kingdom of a monster. I shouldn't be out here enjoying myself. Not when Sybil and the twins were living off nothing.

Guilt clawed at me as I stood up. Enjoyment was not something I should get to experience here. I turned towards the castle and started back. I would not enjoy this facade that the Crimson king had made here. This was probably a show he told them to put on.

Fae watched me stand abruptly, and I couldn't place why I felt unnerved by them. They seemed almost happy to see me. No one had seemed to recognize me in Crimson, so I wasn't sure why they stared. Wisp stood in front of me as if to stop me, but I kept walking right into her. A part of me expected Wisp to be hard, but instead she burst into a million small glowing specks as I walked through her.

She didn't appear again.

When I entered the castle's gates, I made a quick turn left towards the gardens. Maybe Cassius was there, and I could ask him why he was such a prick, but if not, I would sit by the fountains to help calm my racing heart. I rounded the tall hedge that served as an entrance to the garden and made my way into the maze of greenery and flowers. I sighed; it was more likely that I would get lost in these vast gardens than for me to find Cassius here.

I headed towards the center of the pathways, where the biggest fountain was, walking slowly to enjoy the scents and sounds here. I stopped at the sound of faint voices floating through the air. Hesitantly, I peeked around the hedge wall. Cassius stood in front of a black stone fountain with another man that had dark blonde hair and a stunning woman. The woman was talking closely to Cassius. I couldn't hear what was being said over the water of the fountain, but it looked serious, judging by their rigid statures and furrowed brows.

The other man stood watching but said nothing. The woman moved closer to Cassius. Her vibrant blonde hair was blowing softly in the wind, and she was dressed impeccably well in a silk white dress. Was this what he meant when he said he had better things to do with his time? Meet beautiful women in the gardens?

My eyes watched as Wisp appeared next to him and instantly turned black. She had never been that color before. I didn't care what he did, but apparently Wisp did. The woman's hands touched him as they spoke, and he didn't stop her. Suddenly Wisp moved toward me as if I was supposed to stop this interaction. My eyes drifted back to them, and I was surprised to see that Cassius had noticed me watching. He smirked like the smug prick he was. I went to leave, feeling uncomfortable because something was obviously going on between them.

"Excuse me. Can we help you?" Her voice held a cold, unfriendly tone.

When I glanced back, Cassius' golden eyes were assessing me, waiting for my reaction.

"I came to speak to Cassius, but it wasn't important."

Her cold blue eyes narrowed on me, and her pretty face contorted with anger. Or was it possibly jealousy? Either way, this woman was pissed that I was here and that I had interrupted whatever they were doing. Cassius' face seemed annoyed by my presence too, but that was usual.

"Do you know this woman?" She turned her hard stare at Cassius. His eyes left mine, and he peered down at her with a smile that didn't match the crabby attitude I always got from him.

"She is just a participant." He dismissed me with the phrase. I don't know why the dismissal pissed me off, but it did. It was clear they wanted me out of there, but I stood where I was, unable to move out of anger and defiance. Her hand gripped his possessively, and my eyes narrowed at the touch. Cassius must have seen a look of disgust or jealousy, because he gave me a knowing smile before stepping slightly away from the woman, so her hand fell.

"Oh, how odd." The woman turned her nose up at me. "A woman participant. How utterly un-lady-like and savage. Although, I suppose I should have guessed by the atrocious clothing you're wearing."

My eyes shifted to Cassius to see if he would tell his guest to quit being rude to me, but it was clear he would do nothing of the sort. The bastard smiled at her comment while staring me in the eyes. My clothing was rags compared to what she wore.

"It's sad a family would send their daughter into this tournament. Did they not have a son, or did they simply want to get rid of you?" She gave me the fakest smile she could. Magic burned under my skin like it might explode. My fire wanted to escape and evaporate this woman in front of me. I could grab my dagger and kill her before she had even stopped fake-smiling at me. My darkness hummed at the thought, as if to tell me to do it. Wisp even flew towards the woman, glowing with black flames of anger. Wisp rammed into the woman, making her shift slightly, as if she sensed the attack. Her blonde hair blew up slightly from the energy being put out by the wisp. Cassius' smile widened like he knew exactly what had happened.

"You should teach your friend some manners, or put a gag in her mouth before letting her out in public." I smiled back at her but spoke to him.

The man beside her was horrified but seemed truly entertained by the exchange. He smiled at me brightly. Cassius' eyes were full of amusement at the reappearance of my attitude. Bored indifference painted my face, but the woman was turning red with anger.

"Do you know who I am? You should be bowing for forgiveness," she hissed.

"If you have to tell someone how important you are, you aren't that important."

The blonde man laughed so loudly that I knew I had struck a nerve.

"Cassius, will you say something to her? This is embarrassing." She started to fake sob as she latched onto his chest. He made no move to comfort her as his eyes found mine. They twinkled with something close to pride as a satisfied smile spread over his handsome face.

"Don't worry. I'm leaving. I've got somewhere to be." Instead of heading for the castle, I turned around and made my way out through the front gates, venturing into the depths of the forest. My fire was raging inside of me, and I needed to let it out somewhere safe. Once in the trees, I began to run. I ran through the thick forest until my lungs burned and sweat beaded down my back. The air was hotter the farther from the castle I got. The wisp was waiting ahead of me in a clearing, floating around as a melancholy gray figure.

I stopped at a pool of water that stood so still, the sky was reflected in it. Gazing at my image cast in the water, I noticed my dark braid was coming undone and my once vivid green eyes were now consumed by swirls of blackness. There was a faint scar running from my hairline over my eye and down my cheek. My skin was literally starting to glow with anger. That woman was so fucking rude, but what pissed me off more was Cassius' dismissal of me. He let her be rude to me and seemingly enjoyed the spectacle.

With that thought, I yelled and sent my fire into the pond. It ran freely from me and came forth like never before. Power pulsed through my body so intensely that I finally realized how much magic I had. Could I burn down the whole forest if I were mad enough? It felt good—too good. This was the first opportunity I had to let my magic out freely. I was always cautious when out of Exile, but I didn't care at this moment.

My power and energy drained quickly as fire exploded from me. I screamed into the sky, hoping it would soothe this unnecessary rage in me. As my fire slowly died, I sank onto the mossy shore of the pond, which was now nonexistent. My fire evaporated the water, leaving dry, cracked mud behind. I fell to my back in complete exhaustion. The bright blue sky was starting to change colors with the setting sun, and the air was cooling off, but I couldn't be bothered to move.

Besides the exhaustion from using my magic, I was tired in general. I had been fighting to survive for so long that it was utterly exhausting just to make it through the day. My thoughts drifted to Exile and how I missed Sybil and the twins. What were they doing right now? What would we do if I freed all of us? Maybe then I would seek out information about my past and who I was, possibly even find my family. If I dared to dream, I hoped that maybe someone who loved me was waiting for me too.

My eyes fluttered closed as the warmth of the fading sun hit my face. Before heading back, I would have to rest. With that thought, I drifted into a deep sleep.

When I woke up, blackness surrounded me, but I found comfort in it. As my eyes adjusted to the dark, I stood. With the uncertainty of the timing of the next trial looming, I knew I needed to hurry back to the castle. In a swift motion, I snapped my fingers, conjuring a ball of orange fire that hovered in my palm, illuminating the darkness that enveloped me.

Attempting to navigate my way back by following my footprints from earlier proved difficult. Distinguishing between my tracks and those left by animals was challenging in the dirt.

A long breath escaped me when Wisp appeared next to me. Her soft blue flame was darker than normal, but I didn't know what that meant. She floated in front of me and led me until the castle appeared in the distance, but as much as I knew I needed to be there, there was a part of me that wanted to be here.

My reaction to Cassius and the woman made me wonder more about who I was before losing my memory. Somewhere deep inside, I knew that I was used to being treated poorly, and the way that woman spoke to me today had triggered a past wound I couldn't remember. The feeling of loneliness had always been a constant, and I was sure there was a deep-rooted wound from my past that caused it.

At times when I sat long enough in the silence, emotions and feelings that felt... familiar to me would bubble up. I knew I enjoyed being alone, and I always enjoyed the silence. Perhaps I was this way because I didn't have a family or someone that loved me. But whenever I thought that way, something would nag at me in the back of my mind like it knew that wasn't true. The same nagging feeling happened every time I thought of not having a family too. Someone out there knew I was gone; I was sure of it. The true question was, did they care?

The sound of horses running at a fast pace stopped any more thoughts from forming. I smothered my flame, doubtful that they had seen me, but the wisp still floated by me. Would they see her? No one had seemed to notice her before, so I doubted it. Cassius was hard to miss as he led them in my direction. Even in the darkness, I could see that his shadows surrounded him.

My feet froze where I was as they halted in front of me. Cassius' horse was so large and black that it was hard to tell where he stopped, and Cassius began.

"Where have you been?" he snapped with so much venom that I took a step away from him.

"Out," I retorted. "I wasn't aware we had a curfew." The wisp swirled around Cassius as if she were happy to see the smug bastard. Her color shifted in front of my eyes from dark blue to a vibrant, dark green.

His face pressed into a concerned look, and he turned to look behind himself.

"Is there someone out here with you?" he asked suspiciously.

His eyes narrowed on me when I shook my head. "Then what are you looking at?"

My eyes shifted from the wisp to Cassius, and I didn't look at her again.

When I went to walk around him, his shadows wrapped me in a vice and held me in place. Using them, he plucked me off the ground and set me on his horse with him.

"Put me down," I demanded.

Ignoring me, he settled me on the saddle with my back pressed to his front, his shadows holding me tightly so I couldn't jump off.

"Am I a prisoner now?"

Still, he ignored me. His arms wrapped in front of me as he grabbed the reins. The horse took off in a dead sprint for the castle. I struggled in the death grip of his shadows for a moment before giving in and relaxing, but Cassius remained angry and tense against me. I wasn't sure why he would be so mad, unless he was angry with how I talked to his friend earlier.

I refused to apologize for my behavior. He should be the one to apologize. The warmth from his chest slowly seeped into me, and I shivered at the contrast from the cool night air. He pulled me in closer to him and wrapped me in his cloak. Night and rain and forest were all I could smell.

As we got closer to the castle, I was the one who became tense while he seemed to relax. Cassius and I were so close that I became hyper-aware of my every movement. My ass was practically in his lap. Had I ever been this close to a man before? I grew increasingly tense with every bump and jerk the horse made. If anything, he didn't seem to notice how I bounced on his lap, or he found me atrocious enough that it didn't affect him. His grip tightened around me, holding me flush against him. The position only made the friction more intense.

Cassius leaned forward enough that his lips brushed my ear so he could whisper, "You're killing me, little viper. Relax."

Hearing him utter that nickname had me forgetting about our bodies moving together.

"What did you just call me?"

Turning my head as far back as I could without snapping my own neck, I glared. Our mouths were almost touching as he stared at me with his angry black eyes.

"Little viper." Cassius' eyes drifted slowly to my mouth.

"Why did you call me that?"

"It fits you." He shrugged. "You carry the viper-handled dagger everywhere." His eyes moved from my mouth to looking past me to the castle we were next to.

Little viper is what dream Cassius called me, not real Cassius. Maybe he did remember me from dreams. Why would he lie about it though?

"I can walk from here." I struggled as his shadows still held me hostage. The horse stopped abruptly, and he dismounted before grabbing me and setting me on my feet. His eyes held unspoken words as he released me from his magic, and I turned toward the castle without a glance back.

The guards parted as I stormed through the halls. That man was frustrating beyond words. How dare he manhandle me and be in a bad mood towards me.

When I got to my room, I locked the door and stared out the window to the gardens. Wisp was there dancing around the fountains in her dark green form. I tried to ignore her, but couldn't help but wonder, why was she so damn happy?

CHAPTER 10

I watched as the shadows moved under the crack of my door and up to my handle. It made the softest clicking noise as Cassius unlocked it. I pretended to be sleeping when he opened the door. The night had passed without dreams or visits from Cassius, just as he had warned me. Even in the silence of the room, his footsteps weren't heard. If I *had* been sleeping, I wouldn't have noticed he walked close to my bed.

"Good morning."

Sighing, I opened my eyes and met his golden ones as they stared down at me. Without another word, he turned away from me and sat in the small chair near the corner, watching me like I was in trouble.

"My door was locked for a reason."

"You think locking your door will keep me out?" He leaned forward so his elbows rested on his knees. "I can reach you no matter where you try to hide from me."

His smile was wicked as he moved his hand to release shadows towards me. The dark cloud skimmed over the floor and up my bed, covering my body. If he was trying to scare me, it wouldn't work. The shadows were warm as they twisted up my leg and thigh. He didn't stop there. They kept moving upward over my torso before wrapping around my neck and wrists. Cassius had pinned me to the bed without effort.

"If you're trying to scare me, it's not working."

He stalked towards me and sat on the edge of the bed, staring at me. There was something in his eyes I hadn't seen before. The coldness of the room had me shivering as his magic slowly pushed my shirt up, stopping at the bottom of my breasts.

"You look quite nice like this, Thea." He gazed over my face before his eyes slowly traced down, seeming to take in every part of me. Cassius' golden eyes swirled with blackness as his gaze lowered until he had seen every inch of me. I could practically feel the trail his eyes made over my body. My breath caught in my lungs as our eyes collided. Cassius' jaw was tense as he watched me. What was he thinking about? Did he like what he saw or not?

"Cass-" I stared, but he seemed to pull out of whatever trance he was in.

"Where were you yesterday?" he clipped.

That's what this invasion of privacy was about?

"Why does it matter?"

"No one saw you after your little outburst in the garden. A few rumors were going around. One was that you left the trials to go back home, and the other was that you were meeting a man in town. So, since you came back, I assume it is the latter."

I couldn't focus on what he was saying after he called the garden incident an outburst from me. My eyes burned with anger, and I knew the moment he saw them change color from my magic. He sucked in a deep breath before an impressed smile curled his lips.

"You're lucky I didn't have an actual outburst after you let that woman speak to me that way. So, if you think that was an outburst, you are very mistaken."

"From what I've seen you do, I thought you were able to handle a bad attitude on your own," he smirked at me. "Unless you wanted me to save you, Thea? Do you want to be the damsel in distress?"

"You are the last fae I would ask to save me."

Something close to a frown tilted his lips before he put up his indifference towards me.

I glared with as much hostility as I could. "I went to the forest to blow off some steam after your *friend* was rude."

Looking over at me again, his eyes slowly traced over my pinned body.

"Alone?"

"I'm done answering your ridiculous questions. Did you sneak into the living quarters of the other participants and pin them to the bed?"

He gave me a big, genuine smile that caught me off guard, and my anger simmered down slightly. He was too handsome for someone I had no business liking, and he was also a complete prick.

"Were you jealous, Thea?"

I scoffed.

"You are so full of yourself."

"Admit to me that you didn't like that woman talking to me or touching me, and I'll let you go."

"Fuck you," I seethed. He would never know how much the sight of her and him pissed me off.

His face softened as he watched me. Why was he looking at me like that? I wanted to look away from him, but he watched me like he...cared. Why did it feel like we had done this before? He lifted his hand and brushed the hair off my forehead softly.

"How long are you going to pretend that you hate me?" Sitting on the edge of the bed, his hand reached for my wrist, tracing a pattern I couldn't see.

"Why did you come in here?" I whispered.

His face turned hard the moment the question slipped past my lips. He tensed as he stared at me. There was a war going on behind his eyes, but I didn't understand why.

"I shouldn't have come," he sighed as if conflicted. He rose to his feet and released his hold on me. A shiver ran through me as his shadows dissolved into nothingness.

"Cassius..."

"It'd be best to interact as little as possible. After all, you hate me, so it should be easy for you."

Before I could form a response, he walked out of my room. I stared at the door for a long moment, thinking he would come back in, but he didn't. Something deep in my chest had twisted at the tone of his voice, but I ignored it. Why was I disappointed that he didn't stay?

When I got to the dining hall, the men were already eating. Before I sat down, I needed to ask Cassius why he was acting so damn weird toward me. So instead of sitting with Nev, I headed straight for him. His golden eyes watched my every step towards him before they swept across the rest of the room.

"I want to know why..."

"How many times do I have to tell you, Thea? I don't want or need you warming my bed. Stay the fuck away from me." His voice boomed in the quiet space.

The chattering in the room stopped as my cheeks burned with intense embarrassment. What the fuck was his problem? His face was cold with indifference. I glanced over my shoulder to see all the men staring at me as Cassius humiliated me. This guy was such a fucking asshole. When I turned back to him, he seemed to wait for a reaction, but I couldn't think of anything to say.

There was a hint of surprise on his smug face when I just nodded softly and turned to sit next to Nev and some blonde-haired guy I hadn't noticed before. Cassius gave me a smug smile before he left the cafeteria. Ignoring the stares and whispers, I started to eat my food, even though what just happened left me nauseous. My mind swarmed at the way he had treated me. It was like he was trying to piss me off.

"Everyone was worried about you after no one saw you yesterday," Nev said to break the tension. "This is my friend, Haden."

"It's nice to meet you, Thea." Haden stood and gave me a polite bow. The gesture was odd, but it was better than gawking at me.

"It's nice to meet you as well. A friend of Nev is a friend of mine." I smiled at him. Cassius had returned and stood near the wall by the main doors of the dining hall, watching me. It was easy to pretend I didn't notice him as I focused on Nev and Haden telling stories from home.

"We should ask her," Haden whispered. Nev's eyes widened.

"Ask me what?"

Nev glanced up at me nervously, and I wondered if I was really that scary to make him act this way.

"We were thinking that maybe the three of us could form an alliance." He looked around before leaning closer. "Everyone else is forming them, and we heard a few wanting to ask you." That was a surprise. Most of the men seemed to stay clear of me.

"We don't even know what the trials will be. How can we form an alliance?" I asked as I ate my food.

"Well, it's more like... if we can help the other out, we will," Haden said. "Of course, when it comes down to it, it's each of us on our own. But would it hurt to help each other out if we can?"

"What place did you finish in the last trial?" I asked.

"Seventh."

Top ten. Maybe it would be good to have a little reassurance during the trials. If we could work together to finish them faster, it would only work in my favor.

"Ok, sure." I shrugged.

Haden's face beamed brightly at me before standing up and leaning across the table to hug me tightly. I gave him a small pat on the back as Nev laughed. Cassius turned and walked out of the dining hall as I sat back down.

Nev, Haden, and I spent longer in the dining hall than anyone, and we speculated what the next trial could be. They had ideas from being dropped in a body of water to being locked away in the darkness. They were all foolish ideas to me. The uncertainty of what the next challenge would entail consumed me, but I was certain that their assumptions would be far off. Whatever awaited us would undoubtedly be something none of us could have anticipated. The king would make sure of that.

"I heard we get to use our magic in one of the trials." Haden smiled. "That's what past contestants have said."

This news didn't make me happy. Sybil had said fire magic was unheard of and it would probably lead to them knowing I had elite magic.

"That would be helpful," Nev agreed.

"What magic do you have, Thea?" His expectant stare pierced through me. Something in the way he watched me told me to conceal my abilities.

"Healing," I lied. Haden's jaw tensed, as if he wanted a different answer. I wondered what he had expected me to say when his friendly smile came back. Then again, maybe I was just being paranoid.

"What magic do you have?" I asked, switching the attention from myself and back to them.

He set his hand on the table, and frost moved across the surface. Interesting. Shifting my attention to Nev when he smiled before his eyes shifted to a bright blue. The lights in the dining room shone so bright I had to close my eyes. Light magic.

My eyes shifted around, wondering what kind of magic everyone else held. It was likely that some didn't have any magic at all.

"I wonder when the next trial will be," I sighed with impatience. "You would think that it would move quickly."

"The king just likes to keep us guessing," Nev sighed as if he were bored.

"Well, I'm going to town," Haden said as he stood up from the table. "You guys are welcome to come if you want."

We got up and followed him into the hallway, where Cassius stood with a group of other guards. He didn't look up at me or give me an ounce of attention. When we passed them, I could feel his eyes on me, but I didn't bother looking back. When we got to town, Nev and Haden led me to their favorite places. They had grown up in the kingdom of Kizar and visited the Crimson kingdom often with their families.

The town was quieter today. Not as many fae lined the streets. It was peaceful as the sun shined brightly on us as we wandered along the cobbled roads. I smiled as I watched a young boy lift his hands, causing a gust of wind to smack into himself. His parents clapped with pride as he used his magic. Another fae held up one finger, twirling it, making a vine grow up the side of the wall in a flash. Dark, crimson-red flowers popped up all over it. As much as I hated to admit it, this kingdom was beautiful, and it made me feel terrible that I didn't hate everything about it.

"Why does Crimson let other kingdoms join in their trials, but not Cerithia? Why not just have only Crimson fae participate?" I asked.

"Well, I can only assume that if Crimson wants the final task to be completed, then they need to allow other king-doms to participate, needing to gather the best skill from wherever they can find them. Only taking Crimson fae would be a disservice, as they may not have the fae needed to complete the task," Nev explained with a shrug.

"But if that were true, then why not Cerithia?" I asked again.

"Crimson and Cerithia have been enemies for the nearly three hundred years I've been alive, and I'm sure much longer before that," Haden responded. "They hate each other. I think the final task will have us doing something to Cerithia."

"Makes sense, I guess."

When the sun started setting, we dipped into a small cafe for dinner instead of going back to the dining hall. The cafe was quaint with dim lighting and old wooden furniture. We took a small table by the window. It was empty except for two other couples, but they were too deep in their conversations to notice us.

Once dinner was in front of us, Haden turned his attention to me. That uneasy feeling came back. A sense of running away invaded me, but he wasn't talking to me or saying anything. Why wasn't Nev noticing this awkwardness?

Nev seemed completely oblivious to us as he joyously ate his food without a care. My eyes shifted back to Haden. He was still staring at me, but before I could say anything, he turned away. I started considering if it would be smart to back out of the alliance with him. Dinner was silent, and Nev was no help at all with the awkwardness.

"It's amazing, isn't it?" Haden smiled.

"What?"

Haden's eyes shifted to Nev for a short moment. Something told me to not give him a reaction because that is what he wanted from me.

"The food."

He was toying with me. Nev still didn't do anything until Haden stood up, and even then, he just smiled at me like he usually did. My instincts were telling me that something odd was going on. All I knew was I wanted to get away from Haden.

A fae with gray hair approached our table and gave me a welcome distraction. "Dinner is on us. Go out there and kick some ass in the trials." We all thanked him as we stood. When we stepped out of the café, it was eerily dark and quiet. Wisp had appeared close by me, but she was dark red this time, floating between me and the guys. They had started talking, but I was too uneasy to pay attention to what it was about. My heart beat wildly with apprehension and the overwhelming desire to leave Haden's presence as we got back to the castle.

"I'll see you later." I was desperate to say my goodbyes and be away from him.

"Don't be ridiculous," Haden said with a smile. "I'll walk you to your room." Wisp exploded into a powerful red flame between us. She didn't like him either.

"That's not necessary," I said as nicely as I could muster, but started backing away from the two of them and edging towards my room.

"Haden's right. You should have him walk you to your room. There are some dangerous fae here, Thea."

I wanted to tell him that I thought Haden was a dangerous fae, but that wasn't possible. Nothing was going to change their minds, so I hurried past them without another word. The hallway was dark and silent as we moved quickly. When I got to my door, I turned to him, standing too close. I took a step backward.

"Thanks. Goodnight," I said weakly before turning to open my door.

He grabbed my arm before I could manage it, though.

"I'm glad you decided to form an alliance with us."

"Let go of me," I said, struggling to wrench my arm free.

"I'm not the enemy here, Thea. You can trust me." His expression said otherwise. "You do trust me, right?"

"Haden, you're hurting me. Let go." His smile only grew more wicked the more I struggled against him. Frost moved over the sleeve of my cloak. I noted the wisp shift from red to dark green as fear gripped my chest.

"Is there a problem?" Cassius stood ten feet away in the shadows. I hadn't heard him, and apparently neither had

Haden. His frost disappeared as he plastered a friendly smile onto his face.

"Just saying goodnight after hanging out with my girl."

"She's not your girl," he snapped back.

"Or yours apparently." Haden glared as some unspoken conversation passed between them.

Cassius shifted his eyes to me before focusing on Haden again, his mouth in a hard-pressed line. After a moment of tenseness, Haden lifted his hands in a sign of defeat and stepped away from me.

"I'll see you tomorrow, *friend*," Haden said, a hint of malice to his voice. Before he made it a few steps away, Cassius hissed his name, causing him to halt. He and Cassius stared each other down.

"If you touch Thea like that again, I'll rip the arms from your body."

His possessiveness had me holding my breath. Haden glared at me from behind Cassius. "Somebody sure is possessive over something that doesn't belong to them." Cassius' jaw clenched at Haden's jab, but he didn't respond. When Haden's footsteps disappeared, Cassius fumed at me.

"You shouldn't be alone with any of these men. First, you had Nev in your room alone, and now Haden."

"Haden was right. You do sound possessive." I crossed my arms over my chest. He didn't respond. "You should probably leave then, since you're a man and I'm alone with you."

His eyes darkened. "I don't count. You never have to worry about your safety with me. None of these men can be trusted with you, so stop being alone with them. If you need something, come to me, little viper. I'm the one you trust."

"You told me to stay away, Cassius. Which is it? You can't have it both ways. Either you want me around or you don't want anything to do with me."

Cassius' golden eyes traced over my face as his lips pressed into a thin line. He turned quickly and disappeared down the darkened hallway without a response. I stood watching him, trying to process his words. The incident in the dining hall replayed in my mind. Conflicting feelings of liking what he said and despising what he said warred inside of me.

Meanwhile, Wisp danced around him as if she was happy to see him, and I wondered whose side she was really on.

For hours I lay in bed that night, tossing and turning, trying not to think about why he said what he did. Eventually, I tossed the covers off myself. Nothing was going to work, and I wouldn't be able to sleep until I spoke to him. I got up and immediately went to find Cassius. I would make him tell me exactly why he said what he did.

My eyes scanned the darkened hallway as I made my way down it. There were too many doors down here to know which one was his.

"Looking for something?" When I turned, a guard was watching me closely.

I sighed heavily as the words left my mouth. "Where is Cassius' room?"

The guard smirked, and I rolled my eyes at his assumption. "Keep going straight. It's the third door on the right." I turned and moved quickly. My fist pounded on his door. When he didn't answer, I kept pounding without stopping. This asshole would wake his ass up and tell me what his problem was.

Suddenly, his door swung open violently. Confusion crossed his face when he saw it was me, before a playful smile appeared. All thoughts evaporated when he raised his hands high on the door frame, gripping it, fully displaying his bare chest. It glistened from the shower he must have been in. Water dripped from his dark hair and down his tattooed chest. My eyes drifted lower to the towel wrapped snuggly on his narrowed hips.

"See something you like, little viper?"

"No," I seethed at him as my eyes snapped up to his.

"Liar." His smile widened. "If you wanted to see me naked, all you had to do was ask." The horrified expression he saw on my face made him chuckle softly. My eyes tried to drift back down his chest to admire the tattoos, but my mind made me focus.

"Did you want to come in?" He raised his dark brow at me.

"Are you seriously flirting with me?"

"Depends." He cocked his head to the side as he watched me carefully. "Is it working?"

"What the fuck is your problem?"

Letting out a long breath, he finally answered after a long pause. "A lot actually, so be more specific, Thea." He stared at me, and his eyes darkened as they drifted over the oversized shirt I was wearing before meeting my gaze.

"I want to know why you said all that shit in front of everyone. Then you stick up for me with Haden. Do you hate me or something?"

"Or something," he muttered so softly that I knew he didn't expect me to hear him as he turned his head away from me. He ran his hands over his face, and my eyes watched all of his muscles ripple at the movement. "Do you really want the men here thinking that I'm feeding you information about the trials before they happen? Because that's what they think is happening. You spread your legs for me, and I will give you information. Saying that today was a good way to stop the rumors. You're welcome."

"Why would you care if they said that? We both know that's not true."

The muscles in his jaw clenched. Cassius was clearly trying to be careful with his words, and it only made me more curious.

"Because maybe I don't want you to get unfair treatment from them. Maybe," he stepped towards me, "I don't want others thinking I slept with you. Maybe," another step, "I just like knowing I can get under your skin. Or maybe I'm giving you a *real* reason to hate me." I had to tilt my neck back to meet his eyes as he stood too close.

"What do you mean, a *real* reason to hate you?"

"I've done nothing to you, little viper, so why do you look at me like you hate me so fucking much?"

"Because I do," I breathed.

"Liar." He leaned down so he could stare me in the eyes. "Is that what I should call you from now on? My little liar."

My heart pounded quickly at the way he stared at me. I did hate him, but I couldn't tell him about Exile. There was no way I could tell him that he served my biggest enemy. His golden eyes swarmed with blackness as he waited for my answer.

"You're my *enemy*," I whispered. Black shadows swarmed behind him with an angry tension.

"Who filled your pretty head with these lies, my little liar?" Something flickered in his eyes before he sighed heavily. "You can keep trying to convince yourself and everyone else that you hate me, but no one believes that bullshit. Even you don't believe it."

"I'm not trying to convince anyone."

"Why are you here in the middle of the night then, if you don't care?" His captivating eyes pinned me to my spot. He was right; there was no reason good enough to be at his room in the middle of the night. "It's because you care what I think about you. That doesn't sound like something my *enemy* should care about."

My fists clenched as I held in my retort.

"I just wanted answers, but if this is the game you want to play, then I'll play it with you." Disappointment filled his eyes.

My heart was beating too rapidly to think of something to say. This was getting too dangerous, so I turned to leave. Cassius called out to me in the dark hallway, making my feet pause.

"When you're ready to admit the truth, you will be on your knees begging for me. The longer you make me wait, the more begging I will demand from you."

CHAPTER II

Startled by the relentless pounding on my door, I sat up in bed, questioning if I was caught in the grasp of a vivid dream. As the pounding persisted, I gathered my thoughts and quickly dressed myself. When I mustered the courage to open the door, to my surprise, there was no one in sight. Intrigued, I cautiously peered into the hallway, only to find an empty corridor with no signs of anyone nearby.

Well, I was already awake, so I decided to stretch my legs and headed outside to the garden to get some fresh air. I glanced at the guards that were gathered in the hallways. My eyes immediately scanned for Cassius, but he wasn't around.

"Looking for your boyfriend?" Haden asked with a friendly tone, but I knew better. I hadn't even heard him come up behind me. Instantly I had an uneasy feeling form in my stomach, but I ignored him. When I didn't answer, he chuckled. "Tell me, Thea. I'm curious. Does the captain of the guardsmen trade you trial secrets when you spread your legs for him?"

My fire magic instantly began to rage deep in my chest. He wanted to get a rise out of me, and I wouldn't do it. Continuing to ignore him, I sat on the edge of a beautiful black stone fountain. My heart raced in my ears as Haden sat close by. The sound of the flowing water helped ground me and kept my magic from surging forward.

"You alright?" Nev looked genuinely concerned for me when I turned. I hadn't heard him either. My focus was not doing well today.

"I'm fine," I lied as I swiped my hand into the cold pool of water.

In the grand scheme of things, Haden wasn't important. What he thought about me wasn't important. No sooner had I started relaxing though, the ground began to shake and the blinding light that had surrounded us in the first trial suddenly reappeared. It shined so brightly that I shut my eyes tightly.

When the light dimmed, we were back in the arena again, only it seemed bigger than before. The amount of fae watching was at least double what it was last time. My eyes immediately found the king of Crimson, and next to his side was Cassius. He didn't look at me, so I turned away.

"Then there were thirty-six left!" The king bellowed. "Welcome to the second trial!"

The crowd roared so loudly that I plugged my ears.

"Today's trial will be something we've never done before."

The crowd of fae in the stands quieted at this news. We waited impatiently as the king waited to speak again. His eyes gazed around at the spectators before landing on me. Cassius was watching me closely, as if he expected me to have some kind of reaction to the news the king was about to announce.

"The contestants will be going to the Forbidden Wood!"

A collective gasp spread like fire through the spectators, then through the contestants. It seemed like I was the only one who didn't seem too bothered by this. Cassius gave me a slow smile, like I reacted exactly how he expected. The whole crowd was silent with... fear. Tension filled me.

What would we be doing in the Forbidden Wood? What if someone stumbled into Exile? Could I go see Sybil and the twins? Maybe, but would Crimson be watching? My eyes moved around the participants, and I saw that they fidgeted with worry. I was sure the stories of the Forbidden

Wood had been drilled into their heads since they were young.

"All of the contestants will be dropped into the forest and must either survive the night or survive until six are eliminated or forfeit. We want to see who can think and adapt in harsh, unpredictable environments, who is clever enough to survive against the many monsters of the wood."

The crowd didn't clap or become excited at this declaration. My eyes paused on Haden, who was watching me curiously. I was the only one here who didn't look worried, but I had done this plenty of times. If anything, the Forbidden Wood was less scary than others made it seem.

"I forfeit!" My head snapped to the side to see one of the men bow as he forfeited his spot. What a coward.

"Anyone else?" The king gave the contestant a look of disapproval. When no one else spoke, he continued, "Magic may be used, but you may not kill each other."

My heart beat in my chest as my eyes drifted to Cassius. He was wearing his signature black guardsman uniform, but all I could picture was droplets of water running down his muscles from last night. Cassius' smug smile made me snap out of my staring. Whatever the king had spoken to us had been missed by me. Suddenly a table of weapons appeared in front of us.

"You will each pick a weapon, plus any that you have on you already."

We all moved quickly to the table. My eyes were focused on the bow and arrows. Just as I went to grab them, Haden snatched them. He gave me a cruel smile before walking off. When I peered back at the weapons, there was only a small knife left. Sighing, I picked it up. At least I had my daggers.

"Best of luck. We'll be seeing some of you soon," the king announced. My eyes found Cassius as he mouthed *"my little liar."*

I didn't have time to glare at him before we were instantly enveloped in a darkness that I knew all too well. We were in the Forbidden Wood. The air was chilly, enough that I lifted my hood up over my head. The others were moving around too much, but I knew better. They were being too loud. I laid down on my stomach and waited. It only took a few short minutes for a monster to come crashing through the trees.

I watched a small, animal-like creature run at one of the contestants. I expected the contestant to be eaten, but instead the man shot something towards the creature. The animal froze in place. The contestant must be Haden.

The flickering blue light of the wisp caught my eye. She twirled around a tree, trying to get my attention. Scanning the other contestants walking away from me, I stood and hurried towards the wisp. She kept moving farther and farther away from me, but I followed her, knowing she wanted to show me something or keep me safe. Moving away from where the other contestants were had been my main goal anyway.

We weren't allowed to kill each other, but I wasn't stupid. I knew that they would try and have a monster kill me. The plan was to stay away from all of them. Wisp stopped, and I immediately knew what she had been leading me to. A tall oak tree stood in front of me, one that I recognized immediately as the one marking the entrance to Exile. I walked to it quickly before I saw the oversized 'X' carved into it. My chest tightened as I realized how close I was to home. I never thought coming back to Exile would feel exciting. Sybil and the twins had been on my mind, and knowing they were alright would bring me comfort. If only I could have brought them some food.

Turning, I glanced around to see if anyone was watching me, and then I jumped through the boundary. I collapsed immediately onto the ground of Exile as pain gripped me. Gods, I didn't miss this fucking pain or the hot sticky air, so hot that I gasped as it filled my lungs. I knew I couldn't stay here long. They would notice I was missing. Hopefully, nobody witnessed me jump.

Quickly, I stood up and ran to our home. Without knocking, I barged in and shut the door before turning. Sybil and the twins stared at me in shock. Then all of a sudden Sybil burst into tears at the sight of me. The twins just gaped. I thought she was crying because she was happy to see me, but as I took a step towards her, she spoke. Her words made me freeze in my tracks.

"She didn't make it!" she wailed. The twins seemed to understand whatever she meant by that, but I didn't. "Now we have to be in this hell hole another year."

"Thea," Kaz frowned. "You're back."

"No." I frowned at a sobbing Sybil. "We're doing a trial in the Forbidden Wood. I just wanted to check in."

Sybil stopped crying immediately and stood. What did she mean by stuck another year? Why not say forever? Something in my mind felt like it was trying to claw its way out of the depths of forgotten memories but never surfaced.

"You didn't fail the trails?"

"No?" I glanced at her oddly. "I would probably be dead if I failed."

Sybil nodded and peered over at the twins oddly. They all looked at me in a way that confused me. They were definitely keeping something from me.

"What did you mean stuck for a year?" I asked. The twins glanced at one another briefly before looking at me.

"Well, if you failed, we would be stuck."

"Yeah, for forever, not a year." My eyes narrowed on her as all of my suspicions came crashing back down around me. "What aren't you telling me?"

Kai was the one to stand up and try to approach me, but I held my dagger out so he couldn't step too close. He frowned at me as I pointed the blade at him in a fighting stance.

"We won't hurt you."

"You all have been keeping something from me, and I want to know what it is," I demanded.

Sybil took a step towards me, but I moved my dagger to keep her back. Her blue eyes held sadness I had never seen before.

"All you need to know is that we are on your side," Kai whispered.

"No, not good enough," I growled. "Tell me or I'm leaving."

No one said anything, and I realized that I was no longer safe there. My emotions were swirling inside of me as I ran out the door and back towards the border, worried that they would try to keep me from leaving. Sybil demanded that the twins stop me, but I didn't look back. My lungs burned in the thick, hot air. The twins were faster than me, but I was so close to the boundary. Kaz was the one to finally tackle me to the ground. I landed a punch to his face, and he tumbled off me. I crawled towards the boundary, but Kai grabbed my leg and yanked me back. They both stood over me, glaring down at me.

"Thea, we aren't your enemy," one of them snapped.

"You guys know more than what you've said to me. I can't trust you." I slowly crawled back from them and closer to freedom. When they looked at each other, I stood and ran, but right before I fell through the boundary, Kai and Kaz yelled, "Captain, wait!"

But it was too late. I was through the boundary when the wind knocked out of me once again. I laid in the flowers while I waited for air to return to my lungs and stared at the stars. Why the fuck had they called me Captain? Maybe I had misheard them. Tears filled my eyes as I went over what had happened. I had been so excited to see them, and after only a few moments, I had been running for my life. Why were they lying to me? Even as the air returned to my lungs, I lay there. Something in my mind wanted to break free but it couldn't, and it made me cry.

What was wrong with me? The wisp was dark blue as she moved closer to me, but I didn't stand up. She didn't seem to care as she floated close by and waited patiently for me to get up. Eventually, I stood. I didn't want to be too close to Exile in case anybody else was watching me. Wisp led the way through the woods, and I hardly watched around me for any sign of a threat.

I should have been paying attention because I would have seen Wisp turn the darkest shade of black in warning. But I had been so preoccupied with everything that I didn't see Leer until it was too late. When I met his gaze in surprise, he sneered at me.

"We can't kill each other," I reminded him.

"I'm not going to kill you."

Before I could defend myself, he threw some sort of powder in my face. My eyes burned painfully, and I dropped to the forest floor, trying to rub it away. My skin felt like it was being stabbed by a thousand tiny pinpricks.

"But I can make it so you're an easy meal for monsters," he laughed. "You're going to be very tired in a moment. At least you don't have to be awake when the monsters eat you."

My eyes cracked open when I felt something wrap around my ankles and wrists, forcing me on my back. Leer's eyes glowed green as the roots of trees wrapped around me, making it impossible to break free. He was doing this with his magic.

"Have a good nap."

The darkness of the night helped him disappear, and his laugh faded with him. Suddenly, the tiredness he talked about hit me. My eyes were fuzzy as I saw some sort of movement, but a moment later, I realized it was Wisp, along with several others. They were circling me, almost as if they would protect me, so I stopped trying to fight the darkness and gave in to the exhaustion.

★★☾★★

An odd noise caught my attention, and I opened my groggy eyes. The forest was orange and yellow from the sunrise. I went to stand up but stopped when I remembered Leer had trapped me here. Dark clouds were moving over the pretty sunrise as I lay on the forest floor feeling weak.

My eyes scanned the woods as heavy rain began to soak me. It was becoming dark as the rain made it gloomy and difficult to see. Something moving on the ground and coming towards me quickly caught my attention. My fire magic didn't surge forward, even though I tried my hardest to call it. A creature was crawling towards me, making hissing and snarling noises. It had thick brown fur and long, sharp horns that would kill me if it stabbed me. It was on four legs, but it was maybe only knee height. I had never seen one of these before.

It was small, but the razor-sharp teeth it snapped towards me told me it would rip me apart. One of the wisps floated in front of me, and the creature stopped immediately, staring at the bright blue flame. As soon as it did, though, two more small creatures popped out of nowhere. They seemed faster than the last one. They both screeched as they headed towards me. Without a wisp to distract them, I braced myself for the attack.

The closest one launched at me, landing on my chest. The scream I let out as his teeth dug into my shoulder, tearing my flesh, shook the trees around me violently. Suddenly, the creature was ripped from me by a black flamed wisp. Warm blood spilled from the wound, and I worried the smell of my blood would attract more monsters. My eyes closed tightly as I searched deep within myself for my magic. It floated in my chest, not moving, so I tugged on it.

When I did, it exploded from me in a blast that ripped trees from their roots and incinerated my attackers. My hands lifted into the air as the heat from my fire magic warmed my skin. It rippled across me in small orange flames, burning through Leer's magic and setting me free.

The wisps and the small creatures were gone when I tried to stand; my legs gave out, so I resorted to crawling. Why hadn't I been pulled from the trial? If the sun had been rising when I awoke, that meant that I survived the night. Shouldn't I have been pulled? The pain from my shoulder intensified as blood dripped down my arm. There was too much blood coming from my wound. Those little shits had the sharpest bites I had ever seen.

A long while later, I saw the wisps floating in the trees near me. They were all black, as if they were angry. My eyes focused on the black castle in the distance. It would take me days to crawl there. I tried summoning Sybil's healing magic, but I was too weak to use it.

"Thea?" Grabbing a dagger from my boot, I held it out to the Crimson guard, who appeared from behind the trees. His eyes widened with shock.

"Captain!" The man bellowed so loudly that I covered my ears. A moment later, dark shadows swirled in front of us, and Cassius stepped through them in his black uniform. The normal golden color of his eyes was gone and replaced with pure black. His focus was on the guard before he pointed to me. When he saw me, Cassius' body went rigid.

"Little viper?" He breathed as he kneeled down, not caring that I had my dagger drawn. "You're alive." There was a tone of relief in his voice.

My body shook violently from the cold, or maybe from the fact that I had lost large amounts of blood. Either way, I couldn't respond to him as he lifted me into his arms and stepped into his warm shadows. Dizziness overtook me as we stepped from the shadows to reveal the front of the castle. Cassius burst through the doors and was met by a group of fae made up of contestants, the king, and other guardsmen.

"Thea?" I thought it was the king that sounded confused.

A commotion followed us as he hurried through the castle with me in his arms. Suddenly I was on top of a table with my shirt being ripped from my shoulder.

"Fuck." Cassius muttered as he inspected the wound. "What bit you?"

I explained to him in small, gasping breaths what type of small creature had bitten me. He cursed softly and rubbed the hair gently from my face as pain coursed through me. Sweat formed a layer over my entire body as I shook violently.

"Their bites are venomous. You need to heal yourself before it kills you."

"I c-can't."

"You can," he said confidently. "Close your eyes and feel for the energy you need to heal yourself." I tried, but it was futile. When I opened my eyes, Cassius leaned down next to my ear. "Take it from me if you have to. Don't be scared. You won't hurt me."

My eyes found his when he leaned back. Did he know what lived inside of me? He reached forward, grabbing my hand tightly in his, and nodded. I closed my eyes tightly and sensed his powerful shadows surging around him. Once I knew where it was, I pulled on it, tugging it into me to fuel my own magic. His shadows rushed into me and swarmed in my chest with so much energy that my own magic expanded. Cassius' hand squeezed mine as I opened my eyes.

"Good girl," he whispered as he dropped my hand and left the room. Why was he in such a hurry to leave?

I didn't have time to ponder his abrupt departure. I knew I needed to hurry. The venom was burning through my veins like wildfire. Reaching deep inside of myself, I combined the new magic present in my body with Sybil's magic, not making a show of grabbing the amulet because I no longer needed it. Once I used it, it had somehow become a part of me. It was present now. I was present now, along with Cassius' powers as well. The darkness inside me hummed at the new shadow magic I now held inside of my chest.

I was collecting magic inside of me and keeping it as my own.

With all of this magic combined inside of me, I began to feel the burning sensation die down. After only a few moments of focusing, it stopped completely, leaving me lying on the table gasping for air in exhaustion.

I had only discovered I could take others' magic as my own a few years ago when I almost died in the Forbidden Wood. A creature had been lurking close by the boundary, and I hadn't noticed it until it was too late. As I had laid on the forest floor bleeding out, the darkness in my chest had crossed into Exile and stole Sybil's magic to heal myself. When I realized what I could do, I was too horrified to tell anyone. Whatever the darkness in me was, it wanted more. It practically whispered into my mind to take it all from them, to drain magic from everyone.

I was a monster, and I knew it, but Cassius seemed to know too, which had me worried that I would be killed as soon as I stood up and left the room. How could he possibly have known, though? This ability went beyond elite magic. This was something that should never have been possible.

It was disgusting.

Evil.

I sat up on the table and rolled my shoulder to test it. It felt good. I was relieved, but also scared. I knew that I was in danger. Surely Cassius would tell the king they had an elite magic holder present. The king would probably execute me in front of his entire kingdom as a spectacle and example.

The window in the room caught my attention, and I wondered if I should just jump out and try to escape before they killed me. Before I could decide to flee or not, the door burst open, and shock ran through me as the king walked inside, alone.

"I'm glad to see you didn't die, but I need to know what happened because you did not come back when the trial ended, and you should have."

I was too stunned to speak. Why wasn't he condemning me to death for what I had just done? His dark eyes stared at me with no disgust or malice in them, which was confusing. I wondered if he was just biding his time until the guards came and took me away.

Finally, I found my words. "It was Leer. He disabled me with some kind of powder that knocked me out and took away my magic. That's why I was hurt so bad. He left me defenseless in the woods."

The king seemed to retreat in thought, but only for a moment. "Very well. I'm going to assume whatever Leer threw at you also prevented magic from pulling you from the trial at its conclusion." The sad smile that appeared on his face didn't comfort me. "Let's go." His crown tilted towards the door. Adrenaline spread like fire in my veins. The darkness called to my mind, telling me to take advantage of this opportunity and just kill them all before they turned on me. I could see the cluster of men waiting in the room beyond. My eyes scanned the group of contestants waiting with Cassius.

Before I could process what was happening, the same bright light that signaled the start and end of the trials began to shine brightly all around us. I closed my eyes and covered my ears as the sudden cheering of the crowd boomed so violently that I couldn't hear the darkness in my own mind. As I slowly opened my eyes, the light dimmed, allowing me to see how many fae were gathered.

The first thought that hit my mind was that they were going to execute me in front of all of them.

My mind began to race as the king took his place on the balcony, smiling broadly at the loud cheers.

"Thea lives!" The king exclaimed, and the crowd roared to life again. Confusion spread through me at their gestures. They were happy. "But unfortunately, we are left with a new issue. One contestant must be eliminated, so we will allow a challenge for the final spot in the top thirty."

"I'll challenge!" Leer's voice was easy to recognize.

The crowd quieted down as his voice bellowed around us.

"Leer, I thought you might." The king gave him a pointed look. "Who would you like to challenge?"

"Thea," he smirked at me. The other contestants watched each other oddly, like they didn't understand something.

The king nodded ever so slightly before turning to Cassius, whispering something. Cassius' eyes found mine before his jaw clenched tightly.

"Then you have a fight. Take your stances."

A small, white circle appeared in front of us on the ground. We both stepped in and waited on opposite sides of it.

"You will fight until one of you cannot fight anymore, be it by death or by forfeit." Cassius was the one to speak this rule.

"Oh, you may use magic if you wish." The king said it nonchalantly, as if just tossing that fact out there. Leer sneered at the king and then at me. My darkness swarmed through me at the news. It wanted me to take from Leer, kill him, crush him with our power. No one here had seen my fire magic though, and I didn't want to use it if I didn't need to. It looked like I didn't have much choice but to hide it, along with Cassius' shadow magic, leaving me with only the healing magic they already knew I had.

"Begin."

Leer instantly ran at me, not wasting a second, but I quickly dodged his attack, then stepped in and kicked the back of his leg as he passed me, filling his eyes with rage as he fell to the ground. His eyes changed to a bright green as he stood, and he lifted his arms, as if summoning something. I looked around, not knowing what to expect. Suddenly, vines materialized out of nowhere and snaked their way into the circle we fought in. They wrapped around my feet as I tried to move, but I couldn't leave the circle. I couldn't go anywhere though; the vines held me in place. Nature magic again.

"Healing magic won't help you escape this, will it?" He laughed as the vines squeezed my legs so tightly, I thought they might break. The more I moved, the harder they clamped down on me. I attempted to grab for my daggers, but he caught my hands in his vines without lifting a finger. Laughter escaped him as he walked towards me and stopped in front of my face.

"I feel kind of bad at how easy this was, Thea. How embarrassing will it be for you to die in front of the whole kingdom within minutes of the fight beginning? On the other hand, it will only make the others fear me like they fear you." He slapped me with a backhand so hard that my head snapped to the side at the force of it. "I'll have to find someone else to torment. Perhaps Haden or Nev?" I struggled against the vines, but it only caused them to curl around every part of me but my head. Leer had turned to the crowd and pumped his arms into the air like he had won.

Idiot. No one from the crowd cheered in his favor.

"If you let me go now, you live," I muttered. This made him and some of the others laugh. "Is that a no?" I asked him.

"That's a fuck no," he said with a laugh.

"Alright, but remember that when you're on your knees and I'm about to kill you."

My fire had been waiting for me to give it control, to let it consume me and save me. It was instinctual. Closing my eyes, I took a deep breath to control the urge to completely set it free. I didn't need to let all loose. It would be reckless and put everyone in danger. I only needed a little bit of it. When I opened my eyes, revealing red and black swirls of color, Leer's smile instantly disappeared.

Fire appeared in my hand. It spread slowly from my fingertips and down my legs, burning the vines as they went. Leer stepped back only for a moment before trying to strike back with his magic again. This time, it was the roots of the trees coming for me. Dodging them was easy with just a flick of my flame towards them. The heat made them retreat instantly. Fear overtook Leer's eyes as he realized he made the wrong choice of challenging me.

He backed away, but I was too angry to stop. The way he had treated me when I got here and the way he was so willing to kill me fueled my anger. Lifting my hands in front of me, I summoned a ball of fire. It was time to end this. Just as I was about to vaporize him, he fell to his knees in front of me, his hands up in supplication. The sight of him on the ground made me smile.

"I forfeit," he said quickly. "Forgive me, Captain. This wasn't personal."

The phrase caught me off guard. "What do you mean?" I asked as the ball of fire disappeared from my hands. My darkness evaporated immediately.

"Please forgive me." He bowed his head and refused to look at me. Why was he asking for my forgiveness?

Desperate for an answer, I practically begged, "Do you know who I am?"

"Leer has forfeited!" the king proclaimed.

The crowd roared with cheers at the news, but I was still focused on what Leer had said.

"Leer, who am I?" Before he could answer me, a group of guardsmen approached, and he was taken away without saying another word to me. Peering around at the other contestants, I noted that they all stood in shock. So much for keeping my magic hidden. Strangely, the king was smiling at me as he raised his hand to silence the crowd.

"What a lovely display, Thea. The top ten contestants will be joining me and my family for dinner tonight in the great room. The rest of you will have a special dinner in the dining hall." With that, he turned away from us. Suddenly, the ground began to shake, and the colosseum crumbled around us. The blindingly bright lights appeared again, and when they disappeared, we had been deposited back in the hallway of the castle.

The other contestants all stared at me as I made my way to my room. Fear gripped me, and I barricaded my bedroom door behind myself as soon as I entered. Exhaustion plagued me as I sat on my bed. Using my magic always weighed on me, but I was suspicious about the king's lack of anger at seeing it and worried about why he wanted us to go to dinner.

Was I going to be killed because they figured out that I held elite magic? Was fire magic elite, or was it the darkness in my chest that made me elite? Either way, Cassius knew my secret, and I was sure that sealed my fate.

CHAPTER 12

The loud bang of my door barricade crashing to the floor woke me up. My dagger was in my hand and against the throat of my intruder within a moment.

"Easy, little viper, or I might think you're flirting with me." Cassius' eyes twinkled with amusement. I lowered my dagger with a heavy sigh.

"The barricade is there for a reason." I sat on my bed. He stood still like he might spook me if he moved.

"This is for tonight." He tossed a heap of fabric at me and watched me unravel it to reveal a silky, emerald green dress. While it was undeniably beautiful, dresses weren't my thing.

"No, thanks," I said, tossing it on the bed next to me.

"You need to dress the part, Thea. You can't show up in your boots and bloodied clothing. The king expects effort to be made." He peered at the dress and then me. "Besides,

I thought if I got your favorite color, you might not fight it as much."

"How did you know this is my favorite color?"

"Lucky guess." He sighed heavily, like I was getting on his last nerve. "It matches the cloak you wear, so I figured you'd like it."

"Fine, but I'm not happy about it."

"I didn't think you would be," he said, giving me a pointed look.

I averted my gaze to the stone floor of my room as he stood there, not saying anything. I was still worried that I would be kicked out of the tournament or killed for my display of magic earlier. Could I trust him to warn me if I were in danger?

"It's just dinner, Thea. Whatever you're worried about, I can assure you it is not on the agenda."

How could he read me so easily? Maybe I wasn't as closed off as I thought. It was kind of nice not to always feel trapped in my mind with no one seeing my struggles.

"Will you be at dinner?" I asked.

"Yes."

"Then I will see you shortly," I said, dismissing him. He gave me a slight smirk and nod before leaving my room. A weird feeling washed over me every time he left. A part of me I didn't understand wanted to tell him I was a liar because his presence brought me comfort, but I didn't understand the feeling. I shook my thoughts of Cassius away and focused on something else.

I couldn't help but think that Sybil would adore the beauty of this palace as the colorful sunset illuminated the room. My mind pushed away the thought of Sybil. Our odd encounter still weighed heavy on me, but I couldn't process what it meant.

I prepared a scalding, hot shower to wash away the blood and dirt from today's trial as Leer's words echoed through my mind. Did he truly know who I was? There was no way for me to ask him what he had meant now that he was gone. I would add his odd behavior to the list of things I didn't understand.

After struggling for minutes trying to tame my wild curls, I opted to keep them down. I wasn't good at dressing up or making myself presentable because there had never been an occasion to in Exile. The emerald dress matched my eyes almost perfectly. Surprisingly, it fit me well, almost like it was made for me. The silk was soft against my scarred skin. I sighed and looked at my reflection. I didn't know where most of these scars had come from. It was one of the reasons I always dressed to cover my skin. Everyone liked asking questions, and I never had the answers.

My fingers inspected the long scar over my heart. It was almost red in color and stood out amongst the others. Maybe that's why this dinner was so worrisome.

What would I say if they asked about my past? Could I tell them that I didn't remember? Or was that suspicious? I drew in a deep breath to calm my wild heartbeat. Why did going to this silly dinner feel more difficult than the trials themselves? Probably because I wanted to murder the host of the dinner. I would have to sit and listen to him talk, probably about himself. The thought made me want to skip it entirely, but I knew that wasn't an option.

"Might as well get this nightmare over with." I slipped on the heels that Cassius had snuck in here. I assessed myself in the mirror. My dark curls suited the neckline of the dress and helped hide my elite magic mark behind my ear. The dress did fit my form, but I felt exposed and uncomfortable. Everyone in attendance would be able to see every curve and muscle. Every scar.

I felt anything but confident in my appearance, but I exited the room anyways and headed down the darkened hallway. The guys laughing and yelling in the dining hall as I passed made me wish I could be there instead.

The sunset illuminated the hallway with stunning oranges and yellows reflected through the stained glass of the windows. It was magical with the dark red flowers growing on vines across the stone walls. I had expected weapons and armor suits to be the choice of decoration, but I was absolutely wrong. It was comforting to see such beauty in this nightmare of a castle. I made my way to the royal dining hall but stopped outside when I could hear the other guests talking. I glanced into the large room and saw everyone was already there.

This room was far grander than any other part of the castle I had seen. The table was made of beautiful wood that would easily seat all the guests in attendance tonight. The room itself was bright, with a crystal chandelier hanging above the table. In contrast, the walls were draped in dark red velvet. It was beautiful.

"Ah, there is our guest of honor." The king smiled and bowed his head to me.

It seemed like an odd gesture for him to do, but I ignored it. "Sorry I'm late," I apologized, curtsying respectfully.

"A woman is never late. Everyone else is simply early. My wife taught me that soon after our courting began."

His dark eyes seemed friendly as I walked toward the only open seat at the table. Cassius stood and pulled my chair out before pushing it in for me. Golden plates and silverware sat in perfect position in front of me.

"Thank you." My eyes met Cassius as he took his seat next to me.

He gave me a short nod as if he didn't want to acknowledge me at all. Haden was across from me, with Nev at his side. I didn't know the names of the others, except Tagon, who was seated at the far end. The king sat with his wife next to him. She was dressed far fancier than I was, and I realized Cassius was right. I would have felt like a troll had I shown up in my combat outfit. I would have to thank Cassius later for the dress.

My eyes shifted to the younger-looking royals sitting with us. Two boys who were much younger than me sat close to their mother. Their looks mirrored hers with red hair and bright blue eyes. They didn't resemble the king at all, with his dark eyes and hair. The last child was a girl. She looked at me with a big smile on her pretty face. It caught me off guard to see her staring so openly at me. Her hair was a light brown, and she had dark eyes that matched the king's. She was likely a few years younger than me, but it was hard to tell. A confused smile spread over my face, which only made her smile bigger.

Next to her was a man older than the king, and he was openly glaring at me. He wore a fancy outfit, but he didn't seem like he fit in with the royal family. The blue of his eyes was unforgiving as they pierced into me, looking at me like I was disgusting and shouldn't be sitting here. He must have realized he was staring when my eyes met his. He scoffed silently and ran his long fingers through his white hair before turning away from me.

"Shall we eat?" the king asked. The servants bound through the wooden door loudly, making me jump as they placed plates in front of each of us. The food smelled so heavenly. The trial had exhausted me even despite having slept through most of it. Once the servants departed, we all started eating. I cut off a small section of the huge steak that had been served and nearly groaned at the flavor of it. This may be the best meal of my life.

"Good?" Cassius whispered.

"Amazing," I confirmed. He chuckled softly.

"So, Thea, you held out on us," Haden spoke, not fully masking his irritation with a fake smile as he cut his own steak. "You said you had healing magic, not fire magic."

He held my stare as I looked at him. He was trying to intimidate me with his glare, but it wouldn't work.

"Everyone has their secrets," I said simply, popping a chunk of steak in my mouth to stop the conversation.

"I'm just saying it's like we belong together. Fire and Ice." He winked at me then turned his stare to Cassius, who was glaring at him. Nev peered at his friend with a confused look. He obviously hadn't seen him act this way before.

"What else are you hiding?" The older man I didn't know spoke to me, casting the same glare as Haden. I gaped at him confused, the steak turning into ash in my mouth. "Do you have other magic?"

"No," I denied, knowing that the other magic I held was elite magic. It was the reason I carried this mark behind my ear. Perhaps the fire magic was elite as well, but it was nothing compared to the darkness that I hid away from everyone.

"Sure," he scoffed.

"Who are you?" I asked him as I continued eating.

"I'm Lavtan, the king's advisor."

When I went to open my mouth, Cassius' hand squeezed my leg under the table in warning. I stared at him, confused, and he gave me a pointed look, silently telling me to shut the hell up. It annoyed me, but I listened. Cassius didn't move his hand away from me for a few long moments, but no one could notice with how close the seats were.

The king spoke up from his end of the table. "Thea, I was truly impressed by your abilities today. I must admit, I was surprised when Cassius said a woman was fighting in the trials. They haven't had much luck in the past, but you are truly a sight to watch."

I searched his eyes for mockery or malice but found none. He was being truthful with me. It was an odd feeling to receive such high praise from the man I loathed, a man I wanted to kill.

"Yes, quite a sight. Who trained you?" Lavtan asked.

"A boy from back home."

Cassius' fingers tightened on my leg slightly before pulling away completely. I watched him, but he just stared at the king, as if they were communicating with each other without uttering a single word. I wondered if that was somehow the wrong thing for me to say. A silence fell around the table, and the tension inside me continued to mount.

A few of the other contestants spoke about their families and such, but I didn't pay much attention. Cassius turned slightly away from me, like he didn't want to be close to me anymore. Suddenly, I lost my appetite and just wanted to be excused but knew that was unlikely.

I pushed the food around with my fork until the plates were cleared. A small piece of white cake with berry filling was placed in front of each of us as the silence continued. Gods, this was painful to endure. I ate my dessert solely so I could be done with this dinner.

"So, Thea, this boy from home, is he a friend or boyfriend?" the king's daughter asked, smiling at me, but let it drop after her eyes shifted to Cassius, who shook his head to stop her. Her eyes bugged out slightly before looking back at me, as if I hadn't seen their whole exchange.

"Kai and Kaz are friends," I answered but gave no other details. She gave me a big, satisfied smile before continuing her dessert.

When I finished my cake, everyone else was just finishing up as well. Cassius still didn't look at me though and acted as if I wasn't there at all. My hands sat in my lap, and I was squeezing them together in anxiety, my nerves feeling frayed. My eyes glanced at the doors, wishing I could go through them now.

I must not have been hiding it very well, because the king asked, "Are we boring you?" He chuckled lightheartedly.

"No, I'm sorry. I'm just exhausted." The tightness in my chest was worsening. My breathing was almost unbearable because of the panic coursing through my veins. I needed to get out of this room before they saw how worried I was getting.

"Of course," he sighed. "You had quite a trial. We will have dinner again soon."

He stood along with everyone else as they said their pleasantries. Cassius stood but said nothing to me as he said goodnight to the others. Taking the hint, I left without a word to him. Not even the beautiful decorations in the hallway could distract me from the onslaught of nega-tive thoughts I was having about myself, which seemed to amplify with each step I took.

Once I was back in the safety of my room, I ripped the dress and heels off. Why did I constantly feel like I was doing something wrong? It felt like they were all judging me, but I wasn't sure if that was real or my own thoughts fighting against me. Cassius was the main reason I felt like this. I had upset him somehow, and as a result, I had made everything so awkward for everyone.

These insecurities plagued me constantly, like a soft voice whispering how insignificant I was. Like I always did or said the wrong thing. There were times like this that I wished I could remember my past, because this wasn't about Cassius. It was about being too familiar with this feeling. It was the fact that I knew someone had made me think this way about myself.

Or maybe I do mess things up, and I really am the prob-lem.

I changed into my regular clothing, slipping on my boots so I could get out of here and clear my head. I grabbed my cloak, passed through the darkness of the cas-tle grounds, and headed towards the woods.

The moment I stepped inside the trees, all the thoughts running through my head quieted. The woods gave me peace, but it was fleeting. It didn't take long for the panic to fill my chest again. All the horrible things I believed about myself came crashing back into my mind.

Tears plagued me, and I let them fall as breathing became harder for me. I was dying. I had to be. My breaths were small and shallow as I fell to my knees in the clearing. Calming myself had always been difficult when I was this overwhelmed.

"Little liar." Cassius was standing directly in front of me when I opened my eyes again. Seeming to register that something was wrong, he kneeled, lowering himself to eye level.

"You need to slow your mind down," he whispered as his hands came up to cradle my face. My short breaths worsened as I tried to tell him I couldn't, so I resorted to shaking my head.

"Do you feel me touching you?" His thumbs brushed across my jaw and lips as I nodded my head yes. "Good. Focus on my touch until you feel your breath coming back to you. Match your breathing to mine."

His hands lifted mine to his face, and I opened my eyes to watch what he was doing.

"Touch me, little liar." His husky voice shot through the fog of my mind. My hands gripped his face like he had done to me only moments ago. The stubble on his jaw scraped my fingers as they slowly curled. Cassius' hands rested on my thighs, squeezing slightly as he watched me. His eyes fluttered closed as I traced his lips. All the doom I felt in my mind was receding. I focused on him and only him until my heartbeat began to slow back down, and my breathing didn't feel labored from panic.

Once my mind slowed down though, I found a new reason to breathe heavily as my hands explored him freely.

His dark hair slipped through my fingers as I ran them through it, gripping it softly and tugging as I went. Cassius' lips parted as a low hum of approval escaped him. His hands slowly began to skim over my body, and I mimicked his touches. Cassius was all hard muscle under his clothing. My hand stopped over his heart, feeling how intensely it was beating. I continued my exploration, cupping his face again. My thumb rubbed along a small scar on the soft skin of his cheek.

"Do you feel better?"

"Y-yes," I breathed heavily. But neither of us stopped touching the other. Cassius' hands came back up to my face, tracing my bottom lip with his thumb.

My eyes focused on him before closing tightly so I could concentrate on how good his touch felt. His soft breathing seemed impossible to match, so I just stayed focused on his hands. I shivered as he cradled my face with one hand and ran his fingers along the jawline with the other, pushing my hair back where it had escaped its braid. They moved down my shoulders and to my own hands, squeezing them tightly. My thoughts slowed slightly as I focused on his exploration of me.

"Open your eyes, Thea," Cassius demanded, and I obeyed immediately. His eyes ran over my face again before he leaned down and pressed his lips to mine. It caught me so off guard that my mind immediately forgot my worries and instead focused on how it felt so good to kiss a man that I shouldn't be.

My hands gripped his wrists, and he moved his head so he could deepen the kiss. All the reasons not to do this left me when the faintest groan vibrated from him. Something feral snapped inside of me at the noise. I pulled him close to me, leaving no space between us. Cassius' mouth dominated mine as his hands ran over my body, tugging me roughly against him. He gave me one last hard kiss before suddenly pulling back.

He stood up and backed away from me. I watched him from my kneeling position on the ground. My stomach clenched tightly with lust when I saw how disheveled he was.

"Now crawl to me, little liar." A sexy smile curled his lips. My heart hammered at his demand. "Crawl to me and tell me what a liar you are. Then maybe I'll keep touching you like you so desperately want me to."

Gods above, how true those words were. My body craved for him to come back and worship it, but I couldn't force myself to do what he demanded. He sighed angrily as he stalked towards me, his big hand tangling my dark braid around it so he could force me to look up at him. He leaned down like he would kiss me, and my traitorous body leaned up to meet his.

But he stopped an inch from my mouth and smiled wickedly.

"Look at how much you want me, my love." His nickname for me instantly shot lust through me again. "Be a good girl and tell me the truth. I want to hear this pretty mouth of yours tell me how much you want me."

I opened my mouth, but the words died on my tongue.

"Say it," he demanded. "Put us both out of this misery." The words were a soft plea.

When I didn't say anything, he tilted his head, and his eyes drifted to my lips. His frustrated growl died in the quiet space as he released me, walking off without another word. I watched the edge of the forest to see if he would come back, but he didn't. When the shock of him touching and kissing me lifted, an overwhelming need to feel him, touch him, and kiss him hit me. His kiss had obliterated me. It had ripped through all the reasons I had to hate him and tore through the little defenses I had against him. That kiss had made me feel something. It made me feel wanted. Seen. Whole.

I raced through the woods and towards the castle as quickly as I could, determined to find him. Nothing could deter me from Cassius. He called to me.

He called to my darkness.

My mind blocked out anything that would stop this from happening. There was one goal, and that was to feel Cassius again. It was like his kiss had awakened something I never knew I needed. When I got to the castle, I hurried to his room, not bothering to knock. The door banged off the wall at how violently I opened it. Cassius was shirtless, leaning against the wall across the room with a seductive smile on his handsome face.

"What took you so long, my little liar?"

I closed the door behind me and locked it, then fell to my knees before him. His eyes darkened as they followed my movement.

"Clothes off," Cassius demanded. I didn't hesitate as I slipped my clothes off, leaving my small black camisole and underwear on. Then, I crawled to my enemy slowly, loving the way his chest rose and fell quicker the closer I got. His hands fisted tightly at his sides as I stopped in front of him.

I kneeled before him, looking him in the eyes as I told him, "I'm sorry I lied to you. You were right. I don't hate you. Please, I want you to touch me."

The shadows swarmed from him, caressing my bare skin, and I shivered at the contact.

"Not good enough. Convince me, my love."

I licked my dry lips as I reached up and ran my hands over his bare stomach, making it clench when my fingernails scraped his muscles.

"Please touch me, Cassius. I'll do anything you want me to, but please touch me."

His eyes deepened to pure black as he stared at me, touching his bare skin. I smiled as I peered at him.

"I'm yours," I said. "Use me how you want. Put us both out of this misery. Make me forget that I'm supposed to hate you."

My yelp echoed across the room as he grabbed my wrists, yanking me up so his mouth could devour mine. Cassius' hands ran down the length of my body, gripping the back of my thighs and lifting me effortlessly as he pushed me against the wall. His hard length rubbed so perfectly against me that I couldn't stop the noises falling from my lips. Cassius slid down the strap of my camisole and leaned down to take my nipple in his mouth. His tongue flicked over it teasingly.

"Please, Cassius," I gasped, begging for more.

He groaned as he set me on my feet and kneeled in front of me. Cassius ripped my underwear off me and tossed them to the side. He lifted my leg and threw it over his shoulder as his mouth found me. My fingers gripped his dark hair as his tongue circled and his fingers plunged into me at the same time. His tongue replaced his fingers. My hips moved across his hot mouth, chasing the orgasm I so desperately wanted. Cassius ran his tongue up my needy center to my clit.

"Good girl. Take what you want from me, Thea. It's all yours," he whispered before sucking me into his mouth once again. The sight of him on his knees, giving me everything and taking nothing for himself, made pleasure rush through me. My eyes clenched tightly, trying to hold out a little longer because this was the heavens and stars in the form of pleasure. His fingers plunged into me as he sucked me into his hot mouth, letting his tongue flick over my clit.

"Fuck, Cassius. Please. Please." The moan that tore from my throat was violent as I rode out the orgasm against Cassius' face. My fingers gripped his hair tightly to ensure that I drew out every ounce of pleasure I could from him. He hummed his approval against my needy clit before giving me one last lazy lick and pulling back. He stood and kissed me, letting me taste my arousal on his tongue.

But when I grabbed his trousers, he swatted my wrists away and stepped back from me.

"What are you doing? I want more." I breathed heavily.

"I know you do. Which is why I'm making you wait. Because you thought it was okay to lie to me for so long. Consider it a punishment." He leaned in and kissed me again, hard and deep. When he pulled back, he licked his lips once more, giving a small growl of satisfaction. Then he turned and disappeared down a hallway, leaving me standing alone in his living area.

CHAPTER 13

Two days had passed since I had given in to Cassius, and I hadn't seen him once. He had to be avoiding me, or at least that's what my brain had convinced me of.

Unfortunately, I had bigger things to worry about at that moment. Like, who the hell was pounding on my door so violently? My first thoughts were of Cassius, but I dismissed that. He would've probably barged right in here. I got up from my bed and dressed quickly as the relentless pounding continued. When I ripped open my door, the princess stood there, frightened.

"Prin–"

"Somethings wrong," she spoke frantically.

"What do you mean?" I asked, following her frantic steps towards the main doors of the castle.

"Cassius went on a mission for Father. Something about scouting Kizar and Cerithia, but he hasn't returned yet."

"Well, maybe he just decided to stay," I suggested.

"No." She turned to me with wide eyes and pale skin. "You don't understand. One of the men rode back on Cassius' horse, talking about an attack. We don't know if the rest are alive or dead."

Desperation bloomed in my chest. Cassius couldn't be dead. He had to be fine. He had shadow magic, for fuck's sake.

My eyes closed tightly as something tried to claw its way out of the depths of my mind, but as usual, it failed to reveal itself. Urgency to go to him consumed me. Nothing else mattered in this moment except finding him.

"Where's your father?"

"He's outside." She continued to walk but paused and turned to me. "The guard that came back died from his wounds. If anyone can save Cassius, it's you."

I wanted to question why she was so confident that I could save him or would even want to, but my mind kept wandering to Cassius, and visions of him hurt or dead flashed through my mind, plaguing me. The dark magic inside of me was expanding as the overwhelming feelings took over. I barely knew this man, so why did I care so much?

When we stepped out of the castle doors, the castle grounds were being overrun by Crimson guards. Guardsmen were lining up, armed with weapons, and the king was speaking frantically to Lavtan. My eyes scanned the line of guards for their captain out of habit, but I stopped myself when I realized how ridiculous that was.

Lavtan and the king both turned to us at the same time. Relief was clear on the king's face when he saw his daughter, but then it turned to worry.

"Father?" she asked.

The king was clearly trying to remain as calm as possible in the face of crisis, but he couldn't quite conceal his frantic emotions when he realized what his daughter had done. "Verenna, you told Thea?"

"She is our best chance of getting Cassius back," Verenna implored.

"No," Lavtan argued. "This is none of her business." All the clanking and movements from the guards stopped at Lavtan's words. His eyes narrowed on me. Rage warred inside of me at his statement, but I didn't let it consume me like I normally would have.

"Lavtan, we both know that is far from the truth." The king's anger seemed to erupt as he turned to face him, towering his nearly six-foot-three frame over Lavtan, who was shorter than me. While the king may not have been happy with his advisor's words, they held some truth. It wasn't my business, but still, no one would stop me. Stepping forward, I reached for a weapon from a guard, but Lavtan grabbed my arm.

"What are you doing?" he scoffed. "You have the trials to worry about."

I ripped my arm from Lavtan's grip and turned to the king. "Will I miss a trial if I go and help?"

The king's eyes filled with a blend of thankfulness and pride. Cassius needed help, and we both knew that I could be the difference between him being saved or killed.

If he wasn't already dead, that is. My heart sank at the thought of him being gone, and the feeling of dread consumed me no matter how much I tried to stop it. I could feel my eyes shifting color under the overwhelming emotions I was having. I wasn't doing this to help the king; I was genuinely concerned for Cassius, no matter how much I didn't understand it.

I barely knew the man, and even though it was ridiculous, I would not take no for an answer—even if it came from the king. I *had* to go to Cassius.

"I will suspend the trials until you both are back." Pausing for a long moment, he spoke again. "Thank you, Thea. You didn't have to offer, but I'm so thankful you did."

"Here." One of the men handed me the reins of a black horse, and I recognized it as Cassius'. "His name is Onyx."

"I'll need these too," I said, grabbing the bow and quiver of arrows from the rack of weapons nearby.

"Do what you must to bring him back, Thea," the king implored, tucking the princess to his side.

I nodded and followed the group of men on horseback heading into the forest. My heart pounded with worry and panic. There was no denying the pull to Cassius I had felt from the moment I saw him, and he definitely acted the same... at times. Maybe it was the fact that he had been in my dreams for years that caused me to have an unhealthy attachment to him.

He was kind of my friend. A friend that devoured me like I was dinner, but a friend nonetheless. I could be worried about a friend without it being more than that.

There were at least thirty guardsmen in our group. Not trusting them, I rode towards the front so I could keep a lookout for anything, calling on the habits I had built up in Exile to keep me safe. Between the bow and arrows I grabbed and my viper-handled dagger, I was confident that I could take out any possible threats. My only concern was how Cassius and the rest of the men were.

We had been riding through the forest for quite some time when the leader of our group slowed down. The forest ahead of us was so thick that the sunshine hardly penetrated the treetops, causing the temperature to drop drastically. No animals could be heard either, and the eerie feeling surrounding us was inescapable. Thank the gods, I had thought to grab my cloak when Verenna came to me. I shivered in the cold and pulled it tighter around myself.

The horses could only make it through the trees in a singular line because the trail was small and overgrown with vines and plants, which made me nervous. All strung out like this; we were a perfect target.

My eyes scanned around us in the dark. There wasn't much to see through the thick trees. I wondered how much longer we would have to ride when suddenly the lead guardsman halted. He turned to us to say something, but at that moment, an arrow pierced his throat and silenced whatever he was going to say.

The men instantly broke into battle formation at the attack. Jumping off the horse, I disappeared into the thick woods, protecting myself from any more arrows that might be fired.

As I took cover, men in gray-colored uniforms emerged from the woods and launched their attack on the Crimson guards. I couldn't stay here and help them. I needed to find Cassius.

Dark blue flames caught my attention. Wisp was trying to get my attention. She waited for me to come towards her before she moved. We snuck far around the battle and walked deeper into the forest, where the attacker must have come from. It wasn't long before we came to a clearing where more uniformed men were stationed. The light from a small lantern allowed me to see at least six of them, but I knew there could be more.

A tall man with dark skin stood off to the side, laughing with another man at something nearby. I tried to see what they found so funny, but the man was so big that he blocked my view. Silently, I crept towards them through the darkness of the woods.

Once I skirted in the shadows towards the man, I saw them. Cassius and three others were tied up on the ground, thankfully alive. They sat in a circle with their backs together, their hands and ankles bound. The bonds looked like a type of barbed metal, which I had not seen before. Whatever they were made of it must be powerful because Cassius wasn't wielding his shadows. Wisp went forward and floated near him, her color now black with anger. I couldn't tell if they were alright, but I could see that there was blood on the white rags tied to their mouths.

"We need to be ready. The fighting has died down, and they might be coming for them," one of the guards standing opposite the meadow whispered.

"Let them come. They can't cross the barrier we have," the man with dark skin boasted.

He had a protection barrier around them. Shit.

I hoped that the same thing that allowed me to cross the boundary from Exile would allow me to pass through this one, too. I guess I was about to find out. I would wait for a moment when they were distracted before making my move.

"Are you sure it will hold?" one of the men questioned.

"Of course. Besides, we have the captain of the king's guard, and we can negotiate a great deal for him. Or we can kill him," he chuckled. "I haven't quite decided what sounds better."

My eyes shifted back to Cassius and the guards. They all moved slightly, and a sigh of relief left me. Cassius' eyes looked around, as if searching for something, and stopped where I stood. Could he see me? He stared blankly right at me, but he gave me no indication that he saw me.

I paused to watch the group I came with stomping toward us, but they stopped at what must have been the edge of their protection spell with weapons drawn. I watched them step forward only to be stopped by an invisible shield as the men inside the barrier laughed.

"Pathetic," one of them muttered.

"Let's keep them waiting a little longer, shall we?"

This was my moment. To my great relief, crossing didn't hurt like I thought it would. Cassius' eyes immediately found mine, and he shook his head no, but it was too late. I was here, and I wasn't leaving without him.

"Well, well, well, look at what we have here. How did you get through?" The man in control of the barrier asked as I appeared in front of them.

"Give me the Crimson guards, and I'll let you all go."

"A woman?" The man sounded surprised. "I think you'll tell me how you crossed the barrier. Then I'll kill you quickly."

"Give them to me, now." Adrenaline was pumping so fast through me that my body trembled. When they laughed, my darkness whispered into my mind to kill them. It had hoped they wanted to fight.

"Drop the bow on the ground."

I allowed the bow to hit the ground, a plan quickly forming in my mind.

"Grab her," the man demanded.

"It's just a woman. She isn't a threat, so why are we wasting our time?" someone argued. The man shot him a hard look that silenced him.

A man about my height and slightly bigger than me approached. When he reached for me, I lunged, kicking the back of his knees and pulling his dagger out of the sheath on his hip. I pressed the blade hard into his throat.

"I'll kill him," I threatened. "Last chance to give me the men."

The man in charge looked between me and my captive before his blue eyes found mine.

"Then kill him. You will still have five others to overtake."

Smiling, I slid the blade through the man's throat and shoved him to the ground. The others gasped in surprise. It only took a moment before they recovered their wits, and the second one charged with his sword, but I had anticipated it. Grabbing the dead man's sword, I blocked the high attack and kicked the man backward. The next man came and grabbed me from behind.

I used my body weight as leverage and pushed backward, making us both tumble to the ground, his body cushioning my fall. Rolling off him, I stabbed him with the sword. I heard the next man coming and grabbing my bow and arrow. When I turned, he had thrown a dagger, and before I could dodge it, it sank deep into my thigh. Adrenaline pumped through me so hard that I didn't feel the wound at first. I released my bowstring, and my arrow buried itself into the eye of the dagger thrower. Three down and three to go.

I watched to see who would be next. The tall man stood back and watched me with curious eyes. The next man was more cautious as I lifted my bow. Only he wasn't my intended target for this one.

Shifting my bow at the last second, I shot at the man in charge. He moved out of the way, but the arrow had lodged itself in his arm. One of the men tackled me to the ground. My bow snapped in half as it fell from my hands. He punched me several times in the face before grabbing the dagger in my thigh and twisting it. A loud, painful scream ripped through my throat.

It was the pain that brought forth my fire magic without permission, instinct kicking in for self-preservation. Concentrating on the man holding me down, I focused on his chest. He stopped immediately and tried breathing, but my fire had already started burning him from the inside out. I smiled as he stared at me in horror, until his eyeballs popped and flames came out of the sockets. Pushing him off me with little effort, I stood.

"Your magic works inside the barrier." The tall man's body tensed at the realization.

Glaring at him, I took a step forward. My vision pulsed with a red hue as my magic hummed through me. I lifted my hands and saw small black flames moving across my skin. He glanced at the men that were tied up and the back to me, with a smug smile on his face.

"Why would a woman, who is not a member of the king's guard, show up here to fight?" He paced slowly back and forth in thought. "Perhaps one of the prisoners is important to you?"

I made sure not to look at Cassius and kept my face as emotionless as possible. When I didn't give anything away, he chuckled.

"Which one are you here for?"

My flames burned higher in my hands, and the man watched me like I was the most impressive thing he had ever seen.

"Answer me, or I'll kill them all with one look."

I wondered if he was bluffing or not; I couldn't be sure. My eyes glanced at Cassius, who was staring at me in a way that I couldn't read. He was struggling against his restraints, but it wasn't helping him be freed.

"Ah, the captain then?"

The man turned his focus to Cassius, who immediately began screaming as the man's eyes glowed brightly. I couldn't see the magic he was using to hurt Cassius, but his muffled yells were all I needed to hear before shooting fire in the man's direction. He dodged it easily, but it was only a distraction to shield Cassius. My darkness surged forward as it searched for magic I could pull from. It pulsed violently, telling me to take and kill. I could feel the barrier magic nearby, and I focused on it, pulling it into me and then focusing it on Cassius. My magic coalesced and surrounded both him and the other guards sitting next to him on the ground, but no one else would know what I had done as the barrier was invisible.

"All this trouble for the captain? He must be good in the sack, huh?"

He was trying to get a rise out of me, but it wouldn't work. There was nothing more that could make me feel angrier or more possessive of Cassius. He glanced at him, readying to launch his next unseen attack.

Only this time nothing happened, and he looked around, bewildered. My lips formed a sneer when he finally turned his attention back to me.

"How did you do that?"

My stance widened as I grabbed the dagger from my thigh, ripping it out quickly, and flicked it at the only other man guard left. It landed in his heart before anyone could process what was happening. When he dropped to the floor, dead, the tall man gawked at me.

"More men will come," he threatened.

"Then I'll kill them too." I was out of weapons, but he didn't need to know that.

"All for one man?" he scoffed. "That's a weakness. That is something that will get you killed."

My sight shifted to Cassius, who watched me with pleading eyes. He *was* my weakness, and though it made no sense, it didn't make it any less true.

"Stupid girl. Would he have done the same for you?" Would he? I doubted it. My mind faltered for a moment, and that was all the opening he needed to knock me back with his magic. I landed on the ground with a grunt. There was no time to process the pain because the man had immediately run at me and had lifted me by my braid with little effort.

I jabbed my fingers into his eyes, and he dropped me immediately. I kicked him with all the force I could muster and made him tumble back, but he caught himself before falling over completely. He charged at me and took us both to the ground. He was strong, but I was definitely faster, and I proved it as I wiggled my way out of the hold he tried to put me in. My legs wrapped around his neck as he leaned over me, holding him where he was. I punched and punched at him, landing blow after blow on his head. Desperately, he grabbed my thigh wound and squeezed it.

"Fuck!" My legs loosened their hold on him and grabbed me by the neck, slamming me into the ground over and over.

"You used my magic to shield them," he muttered. "How did you do that?"

Turning my head to the side, I revealed my elite magic mark. His eyes found mine.

"That is more than elite magic." His hand squeezed my neck tighter, and I couldn't breathe. My legs thrashed around, trying to desperately get away. Cassius was trying to yell through his gag somewhere behind us.

The man stared at me, and a look of understanding passed over his features. "My gods, it's you. You're the woman from the prophets telling."

Confusion filled me as his eyes reflected terror. His hands squeezed harder, making my eyes flutter closed.

"I must rid our realm of your evil."

When I opened my eyes again, my fire magic exploded out of me, flaring out in an orb of flame that consumed us both. I lost myself in that flame for a moment, my eyes closed in the ecstasy of release. When I opened them again, the man on top of me was burning. He released me and rolled in the dirt, attempting to douse the flames. The swirls on my skin glowed as I stood to watch the man's skin melt from his body. He had stopped rolling around, succumbing to his fiery fate.

The smell of burnt clothing and skin made my stomach churn. As soon as his eyes turned vacant, the barrier keeping the king's guard out vanished, and the men immediately rushed to free the captives. I hurried over to Cassius and fell to my knees, struggling to get the metal barbs off of him without ripping his skin more. Once he had a hand free, he ripped the gag from his mouth.

"What the fuck were you thinking? He could have killed you!"

"That's a weird way to say thank you, but you're welcome." Puffy breaths escaped me. Cassius pulled me to him in a tight hug, and I clung to him as he stood with me, lifting me effortlessly. Not that I had much energy left to stand on my own. My muscles screamed in protest, and my vision was foggy at best. Using so much magic had drained me.

"I got you, little viper," he whispered.

"There's men coming towards us!" one of the guards yelled.

"I need you to stay awake, Thea. We might need your magic to get us out of here." He lifted me up onto his horse before climbing on behind me. He turned me, so I was facing him in the saddle, straddling his lap. Our faces were mere inches apart. His arms slipped around me so he could grab the reins. I slipped my arms around him to hang on.

"We need you to watch behind us and use your magic to repel the enemy if they get too close."

I nodded, and we took off on horseback. I watched over Cassius' shoulder, and before long, men dressed in gray uniforms burst through the tree line on horses. Cassius' arms wrapped around me tighter as he urged the horse to go faster. A flame appeared in my hand when I saw them ready their arrows. As soon as they launched them at us, I used everything I could muster to send a shield of fire behind us. Most of the arrows incinerated in the fire, but a few snuck through. One of them headed straight for us, but I reacted fast. Quickly, I pushed Cassius backward, so he laid his back on the horses. The arrow shot into my shoulder.

"Fuck!" I screamed. Blood poured from the wound when I yanked the arrow out.

He sat back up and urged Onyx to go faster and faster. I didn't have time to succumb to my pain as two riders flanked behind us. One readied an arrow and pointed it at Cassius. My darkness tore out of me and to the man, wrapping him up. The darkness squeezed the man, making his body explode. The other man stopped chasing us after he witnessed the man explode from my magic. The men in gray uniforms stopped as the forest thinned out, almost like they weren't allowed to follow us onto the Crimson kingdom's territory. The wound hurt with every bump we hit.

"Damn it, Thea. Why did you do that?" he snapped.

"It would have killed you!"

His face was angry as he pulled me into his chest and held me tightly for the rest of the ride. I buried my face into the crook of his neck and allowed the exhaustion to take over.

Sybil's healing magic couldn't be found inside my chest. But I had nothing to pull from. Pain radiated through my entire body. Flashes of bright orange light followed us, and I knew it was a wisp, but not the one that was always with me. Then I noticed several others following closely. Maybe I had lost too much blood and was dying? Why could I see these colorful flames that floated around and no one else could? The castle bell chimed as we arrived, indicating our arrival.

All of the contestants and the royal family members were outside the castle when we got back, staring in awe as we rode in. Breathing in Cassius' familiar rain and forest scent helped distract me from the pain.

"Heal yourself," Cassius demanded.

"I can't. I used all my magic up," I whispered. "Why are you so angry with me?" Tears pricked my eyes at how he acted towards me. I had risked everything for him.

He didn't answer. When the horse stopped, he handed me down to Nev and Haden. Cassius turned to the king, who was approaching quickly.

"Cassius, we're so relieved you're alright." He held out his arms like he wanted a hug. Cassius stood still and said nothing. The king's smile faltered when he saw me. I was beaten to hell and bleeding profusely from my shoulder.

"Cassius..." The king started, but Cassius didn't let him finish. Shadow tendrils twisted and crept along the ground in his anger. His eyes turned completely black with rage.

"How fucking dare you." Even at a whisper, his voice held so much authority and rage that I shrank away from it. "Out of everyone you could have sent, you sent her?"

"She volunteered," the king said beseechingly.

"Then you should have told her no. What part of 'I don't want anything to do with her' do you not understand? Keep her away from me. That is all I asked of you. You could have sent anyone else in her place, and it would have been a better choice."

I felt everyone's stares and could sense their pity and embarrassment as I stood there, bleeding on the castle grounds. I felt stupid and pathetic because I cared so much about a man that I barely knew. I risked my life for him because an uncontrollable need to save him had fueled me. I thought he felt the same. Obviously, I was wrong.

The words spoken by the tall man earlier rang in my ears. *Would he have done the same for you?* No, I guess he wouldn't have. Embarrassment painted my cheeks. I must look so pathetic and weak in front of all of them.

"Cassius!" the king snapped. I'm sure others didn't speak to him in this manner, so there was no way he could allow Cassius to. His eyes shifted back to me, and Cassius' black eyes followed. I stood still, not sure what to say or do. Gods, he must be so uncomfortable, and he had every right to feel that way. Just because he had flirted and touched me didn't mean anything. The familiar feelings of never doing anything right crept up. Cassius didn't speak. He looked more pissed off when he caught my eye. He sneered towards me before he climbed on Onyx and left.

Tears streamed down my cheeks as I slowly stumbled away. Again, he had humiliated me in front of everyone. I had only just made it inside the door of the castle before Nev lifted me and carried me the rest of the way. Crying was the last thing I wanted to do, especially in front of Cassius. I would not appear weaker than I already did. Nev sat me on the bed as Haden came into my room with warm water and rags.

As soon as Nev looked at me, I lost my battle to keep my tears at bay. Sobs wracked through me. Nev frowned and squeezed my hand tightly in reassurance.

"What a fucking prick," Haden scoffed. "Look at you. You did this to help him, and he threw a tantrum about it."

"Can you heal yourself?" Nev asked.

"No. I used too much magic. I'll have to try tomorrow."

He nodded but didn't leave. His hands grabbed the sleeve of my shirt and ripped it from where the arrow had entered.

"We need to get this cleaned up, and then you can rest."

"I need to shower," I said, sitting up.

"While you do that, Haden and I will find some salve to help it from bleeding."

The hot water stung my wounds as I leaned my head against the side of the shower and closed my eyes tightly. How could he say all those things in front of everyone? My heart ached at the thought that he had requested for me not to be near him.

I wondered what I could have possibly done to make him hate me so much. He was the one always seeking me out and starting conversations with me. I numbly watched the dirt and blood circle the drain. When my legs started shaking with exhaustion, I got out and dried off. Glancing in the mirror, all I could focus on were the bruises and cuts covering my face. My body was already starting to form deep purple blotches as well. I looked away from my reflection, feeling completely disgusted with myself.

I pulled on an oversized shirt and crawled into bed. A moment later, Nev and Haden walked in with a small container of paste. Nev sat on the edge of the bed without a word and applied it with a surprising amount of gentleness. He finished with a bandage and wrap. I dressed the wound on my thigh myself, without looking up at their worried eyes.

"Thank you," I said to them both.

They gave me sheepish smiles full of pity as they left. I stood and locked my door, barricading it as best as I could. Then I laid down, facing the window, and stared out at the stars, wishing I didn't have to ever see Cassius again.

CHAPTER 14

My eyes stared at the crest on the wooden door. I turned towards the darkened hallway, but Cassius wasn't in my dream with me. I shook away the disappointment and turned back to the marking on the door. It was in the shape of a shield being held up by two golden dragons. It had an 'A' at the center with swirls of silver and blue around it. The shield itself had been divided into four sections. One held small trees within it, one held a set of crossed arrows, stars were scattered across another section, and in the last one, a blue flower that I did not recognize.

It was a stark contrast to the Crimson kingdom's crest, which was gold with a phoenix sitting upon a skull, illuminated by rays of sunlight, and two swords crossed behind it. Of course, the emblem was wreathed with vines of red flowers.

My hand started to trace this unfamiliar crest, but the door opened before I could finish. I walked in, half expect-

ing to see the same scene I had the last time, but this time it was very different. I was watching a memory of myself again, standing in the center of the room dressed in a blue guardsman uniform. The faceless man who had been in my dreams before was standing in front of me.

"So once again, you didn't do what I asked you to do."

I stood stoically without saying anything at first.

"Such a disappointment, but that's nothing new, is it?" he sighed, and his voice was tinged with annoyance. Hurt contorted my face.

"We did the best we could, but they seemed to know we were coming."

"Then improvise, Thea. I'm trying to help you find your place here, but you make it so difficult to keep you around because you never do anything right."

I swallowed hard as I watched myself take those harsh words. Why wasn't I saying anything?

"I will do better," I promised.

"I doubt it," he scoffed. Again, I remained silent. "I detest the fact that I can't rely on you. You promised me your best effort, yet this is mediocre at best. Now, get out of my face."

I turned and hurried out of the room. I accompanied my dream form down the darkened hallway, but I couldn't see any details about where we were. My mind liked to fuck with me.

I paused when we stepped out of the building we were in and into blindingly bright light.

"Saddle up. We're heading out," I demanded.

"We just got back," another guard groaned.

"I said saddle up. We didn't complete the mission."

"Thea, you don't have to prove anything to him. He gets under your skin to push you into reckless behavior for his own benefit." I watched as my dream form glared at the man who said that to me.

"Kaz, we don't have time for this. Saddle up. It's an order."

Kaz? He turned around, and I nearly fell backwards when I saw Kaz, my Kaz from Exile, mounting his horse. He looked pissed, but it seemed to be directed more towards the man who had talked to me poorly. My eyes shifted to Kai when he walked over to another horse nearby. Of course he would be here. Those two were never far apart from each other.

"Heading out again?" Kai asked with confusion.

"Our mission is to find as many elitist magic holders as we can. We can't stop until we have completed it." I spoke coldly and galloped away with Kaz and Kai on my tail.

◻◻◻◻◻

Quickly, I sat up in my bed and sucked in a deep breath. What the fuck? Kaz, Kai, and I knew each other. Why had they always said they didn't know me? My heart beat rapidly, and sweat beaded on my forehead at the memory of the dream. Why were we the ones gathering elite magic holders, and who the hell was treating me that way?

I begged the gods to give me back my memory. When nothing came back to me, I reluctantly sat up and got dressed. Still, no magic stirred inside my chest. I must be too weak to use it still. Maybe after food and more rest, I would feel better, and that could be possible, so long as the trials didn't happen today.

All the talking and laughter died down when I entered the dining hall. I could feel everybody's eyes on me, but I didn't look at them. I gathered a heaping pile of food and turned to find Nev and Haden. Only it was Cassius' golden eyes that I found. He was standing across the dining hall from me. Immediately, I glanced down but could feel him watching me. I could barely stand being this close to him, and since he said he didn't want to be near me, I made the only logical choice.

I headed out the door and went straight back to my room. I would eat and rest there until I could heal myself. The silence was unbearable as I ate an uncomfortable amount of food before falling asleep again.

When I woke up, I was sweating profusely once again. I couldn't remember my dream this time, but my heart thudded rapidly like I was scared or had been fighting.

Enough time had passed that the sun was going down, so I stood and tried to heal myself again, unsuccessfully. Sighing heavily, I struggled to stand up and pull my boots on. Like earlier, everyone was watching me as I got my plate. I turned and saw Nev and Haden at our table. My eyes flicked over to where Cassius stood against the wall talking with another guard. I looked away before he saw.

"Where the hell have you been?" Nev frowned.

"My room, taking another nap after breakfast. I'm just so exhausted." I took a bite of the sausage, and my stomach growled. I was somehow still ravenous, even though I had eaten only a few hours ago.

"That was two days ago, Thea," Haden said softly. "We tried to check on you, but you moved a bunch of shit in front of your door."

Two days? I hadn't woken up once in that time frame. I thought they must be kidding, but their concerned faces proved otherwise.

"Thea, we were worried you died in your room or something." Nev frowned at me. "Glad that wasn't the case."

"Are you sure that was two days ago? I didn't wake up at all, and I still feel exhausted. I didn't miss a trial, did I?"

"The king announced that they were suspended until you were healed." Haden's eyes cascaded over my face before glancing away at the sight of my wounds. I knew I looked horrible.

"Still no healing magic?" Haden questioned.

"I tried when I woke up, and nothing happened."

My eyes drifted to the table next to us when they all laughed while staring at me. My eyes drifted over each one as they whispered about me. Anger simmered in my chest, but what bothered me more than that was the embarrassment I still felt. Nev and Haden turned to glare at them.

"You got a fucking problem?" Haden snapped. When had he become my protector?

"We were just saying that we understand why you formed an alliance with the whore. It must be nice having your own personal slut in the games," one of them yelled loudly. The whole room erupted in laughter. My eyes stayed on the table so I wouldn't give them the satisfaction of seeing me upset. I could only imagine the rumors that had spread about me after Cassius' outburst.

"We teamed up with her because she can combust your body with just a look, asshole," Nev snapped.

"Hey, Captain!" one of them yelled. My attention turned to them as if they were calling to me but then shifted to Cassius, who was just staring at the table talking about me. "Was Thea that bad of a lay that you ordered the king to keep her away from you?"

Cassius' eyes shifted to me, but I didn't look at him. My eyes stayed focused on the man who apparently felt brave today. "I'm taking it that she's a lousy lay."

"Damn, Royer!" One of the men sitting at the table remarked.

Cassius didn't do anything to defend me, and I hadn't expected him to. Nev and Haden stayed silent as well as I stood up with my plate, planning to go back to my room. Before I could make it to the dish station, though, I felt a clump of soggy food collide with my shoulder. The guy that was talking the most shit started laughing.

"How does it feel to be humiliated in front of everyone? If you were wondering, we all think you're pathetic."

My plate hit the floor with a loud clatter as my fire began to burn wildly in my chest. Seeing red, I charged at the man, who immediately stopped smiling. Cassius' shadows instantly formed a shield between us, but I sent a mist of fire out that burned through his shadows. Then, I sent another round of fire mist after the man who had insulted me and wrapped him up in it. His smart-ass remarks disappeared as I stalked towards him. Before I could reach him though, Cassius' shadows pulled me away, forcing me to release the man.

"Stay the fuck out of this," I snapped at him in warning.

Out of nowhere, the man ran at me and tackled me to the ground. His fist connected to my face, but I welcomed the pain. At least it was different than the humiliation I was constantly feeling. Bucking my hips up, I rolled us over, gaining the upper hand. I punched and punched until, out of desperation, he grabbed my arrow wound.

We both tumbled backward as the shadows separated us again. My eyes snapped toward Cassius, who was staring at me with what seemed to be a soft plea. I was in no mood to be nice though, and once again, my fire mist shot out at him, forcing his shadows to scatter.

Not anticipating my strength, Cassius was slammed into the wall at the force of my mist. Then, I turned to Royer and began slowly stalking towards him. My skin was swirling in reds and oranges, and the fiery mist was gathered around me, bathing me in its heat. I smiled as his body trembled. I raised my hands before me, collecting the heat and the flames into a rolling ball of fire. Once it was the right size, I released it and slammed it into the man. He flew across the room, coming to a halt inches before he would have hit the wall—thanks to Cassius' shadows. His clothes were smoking, and his skin was blistered. He threw his hands up in defeat as I moved for him again, so instead I turned towards Cassius.

"Thea, calm the fuck down," he demanded.

"Scared of me?" I snapped.

"I would be stupid not to be," he said. His answer stopped me in my tracks. My eyes scanned the room and saw only terrified faces looking back at me.

"No one else wants to make comments?" I asked the room, only to be met with silence. "You're all fucking cowards." I narrowed my gaze at Cassius, who had his shadows ready to come at me. "And you're the biggest fucking coward in here."

Hurt flicked across his features. Sybil's healing magic surged forward and healed me as I fled the castle.

"Thea!" a voice called after me, but I kept going. I ran until I couldn't anymore and found that I had wound up in town. Catching my breath, I surveyed the quaint black stone structures, and my eyes locked on a charming book-store. Eagerly, I made my way inside, and there, behind the wooden counter, an elderly woman greeted me with a warm smile.

"Good evening, dear. I was just about to close up."

"Oh," I breathed. "I was just wondering if you have any books about family crests from the area."

She gave me an odd look before a smile returned to her face.

"I'll be right back." She disappeared into the back, and I breathed in the smell of all the old books surrounding me, letting their familiar, musty scent calm my troubled soul. My heartbeat slowed as I relaxed, and I was finally able to push my emotions back into their cage. She came out a few minutes later holding a red leather-bound book.

"This has a bunch you can look through."

"How much?" I didn't have much, but hopefully it was enough.

"You're Thea, from the games?" she asked. When I nodded yes, she gave me a friendly smile. "Keep it. Free of charge. You've been very entertaining to watch."

"Thank you." I smiled and headed outside. It was dark now, and hardly anyone was on the streets. I looked at the castle in the distance and wanted to be anywhere but there, so I wandered through the desolate town with my book in my hand. My mind flashed to Kaz and Kai from my dream. Part of me hoped it had been a dream, something made up, but deep inside I knew that wasn't true. My best friends had lied to me. They had acted as if they had no idea who I was and watched as my frustration grew and depression deepened because of it.

Betrayal tugged in my chest as tears welled up in my eyes, but I refused to let them out. I would search this book until I found that crest from my dream in it. I needed to know who I was before all of this; I needed to find my place. Maybe this crest would lead me there because, clearly, I couldn't trust anyone I knew, and today's fight had proven that everyone was terrified of me. That's what I wanted, what I needed to stay safe, but at the same time, I also felt like a monster because of it. Cassius was scared of me, too. The thought was unsettling, but I knew I was better off by myself, without any emotional attachments to anybody. Maybe I always would be.

After hours of wandering aimlessly through town, I headed back to the castle, expecting it to be quiet because it was so late. But when I walked towards my room, I could hear the other contestants laughing. Cautiously, I walked past my room and down the hall, where I saw lights. When I glanced around the corner, the men were in a room I hadn't been in before, some sort of mess hall. And they were all drinking. Their cups filled were with amber liquor as they boisterously laughed. The room was small compared to the dining hall and reeked of a strong drink. Most men stood in groups chatting instead of sitting in the wooden chairs, their drunken energy keeping them animated and lively.

They all quieted down when they saw me, though. Royer sat, all bruised and burned, at one of the few tables available. The guards were also in the room, including Cassius, who already had his shadows ready in case I got violent. I grabbed my amulet and extended my hand toward the guy I had beaten up. Orange and red swirled out from my open palm and towards him, surrounding him in a red haze. He flinched and threw his hands up, expecting more pain. But instead, his wounds disappeared instantly. Confusion marred everyone's face. Good, I hoped that threw all of them off. They all acted as if they knew me, as if I were some violent, unpredictable monster. That should get them talking about me for a different reason.

Without a word, I turned and headed for my room. Cassius' loud footsteps let me know he was following me, but instead of acknowledging him, I put up a wall of fire mist around me.

"Thea," Cassius spoke sternly, but I didn't respond. I walked into my room and locked the door. It only took a moment before his shadows moved under the crack of the door to unlock it. I was ready for that though, and I used my fire mist to create a barrier that he wouldn't be able to get through.

"Thea, let me in," he demanded. "Please."

Ignoring him was difficult, but he was not getting near me right now. I couldn't allow him to use my feelings for him against me. Embarrassment and hurt coursed through me. I didn't know how he could humiliate me in front of everyone.

"I know you can hear me," he tried one last time. When I didn't respond or allow his shadows to unlock the door, I heard him walk away. Sitting in the middle of my small bed, I started looking through the book of family crests, hoping it would lead me somewhere better than this place full of liars.

CHAPTER 15

The next morning dawned clear and bright, but my bed was far too comfortable for me to leave it, so I laid there for a while, enjoying the peace as I stared at the ceiling. For a long time, nothing motivated me to get up and get dressed, but I eventually felt the need to stretch my legs. Slowly, I made my way toward the dining hall but ended up walking past it. I followed the hallway until a set of metal doors caught my attention. When I shoved against the cold metal, they opened to reveal a stunning room full of flowers, vines, and fruiting trees, all covered with a delicate glass roof. Once inside, I let out a calm breath, determined to stay relaxed. The sun beamed through the glass above me, warming my skin and reaching deep into my tense muscles. It was the most sun we had seen since my arrival, and I wanted to soak it up as much as I could.

I laid my cloak in the middle of the conservatory so I could sit on it and relax in the middle of all the plants. My nose filled with floral scents as I settled in a spot. I closed my eyes, allowing calmness to wash over me. This was by far the best room I had seen yet. My eyes fluttered open as my body warmed in the sunlight. Faintly, I could hear birds singing outside.

"We need to talk." Cassius' voice interrupted my relaxed thoughts and instantly ruined my peaceful escape.

"No, we don't." Turning completely away from him, I continued admiring the hundreds of flowers in various shades of color. He gave an irritated huff at my reaction. "In fact, I'm staying away from you, like you requested of the king. So, leave me alone."

"We should talk about this before the trial."

"Why? Because I could die? At least then you wouldn't have the burden of being around me."

I could tell that I had struck a nerve as his shadows suddenly exploded around us, swirling so we could see nothing outside of them.

"You're a child," I huffed.

"You actually think I would want you dead? So I don't have to see you?" he asked incredulously.

"That's exactly what I think." Glaring at him, I stood up. "You made sure everyone in this fucking castle knew exactly what you thought of me. You humiliated me again! You were cruel to me." My voice faded out, betraying the ache in my heart.

His eyes bore into mine for a long moment. He reached forward to touch my face, but I stepped away.

"Stop trying to confuse me. You can't act all gentle and tender after everything that you have said and done. You made it crystal clear what you thought of me. So, I'll keep my distance just as you requested." I flicked my hand up, and my fire mist appeared, radiating from me and easily overpowering his shadows, freeing me instantly.

"Thea, gods damn it. You don't understand. This is for your protection, not because I hate you or don't like you." He grabbed my arm and forced me to look at him. "There are things you don't understand."

I was used to nothing making sense to me, but this just seemed like he was being cruel. I pulled my arm from him.

"Well, you're doing a bad job at staying away from me." He swallowed hard as he glanced away.

"Trust me, I know. But staying away is for the best." He sounded as if he was trying to convince himself more than me.

"I don't understand why you acted that way. Especially after we..." I glanced at him. "It made me feel used, like you got what you wanted from me, and now there was no reason to be near me."

Something close to pain or sadness crossed his features, and I immediately wanted to take back my words. This was all too confusing. I knew I should hate him, but I also knew I'd forgive him right then and there if he asked me to.

"If I could take back what I said, I would," he said, frowning. Then he stepped forward quickly to catch me off guard, pulling me to him in a tight hug. It felt oddly like a goodbye. When he pulled back, he crushed his mouth to mine and held me against him tightly, as if he was scared that I would move away. Cassius' lips were demanding, and my knees probably would have given out had I been able to process what was happening. I didn't even have a chance to kiss him back before he pulled away. My heart was beating wildly in my chest as a strange warmth spread through my veins.

Cassius' eyes were the lightest shade of gold I had ever seen in this moment. That damn tugging started in my chest as I looked at him. I wanted to pull him close to me and not let him leave, but I was still hurt. He must have been feeling the shift in energy too, because he just stared at me for a long moment before reaching out and smoothing my braid over my shoulder.

"Your safety is all I care about. We need you to win the trials, Thea."

"Why don't you just tell me what's going on? You're obviously keeping secrets."

Instead of giving me the answers I so desperately wanted, though, all he gave me was a chaste kiss.

"Forgive me," he whispered. "I don't want to fight with you, and truly, my words were not meant to hurt you. I was angry with the king for putting you in harm's way."

"Don't do that to me again, even if it wasn't your intention. I'm still hurt by what you said, but I don't want to fight with you either."

"I promise." He smiled. "I have to go help the king. I'll see you shortly."

I watched as he walked away without a glance back, the warmth disappearing once I couldn't see him anymore.

Sitting back on my cloak, an odd sense of discomfort replaced the warmth I had been feeling as Cassius' words returned to me. I wondered why so many fae seemed to be keeping things from me.

I was distracted from my inner thoughts though, as clouds moved in and took away the sunshine. Rain started pouring down so violently that it was hard not to admire its dark wrath, and my chest relaxed to the sound of it pelting the glass roof.

Suddenly, the castle began shaking and crumbling around me, letting me know the third trial was beginning.

The bright light didn't bother me as much as it had previously. Instead, my focus was drawn to the riotous cheering and hollering from the crowd. The colosseum was absolutely packed with spectators this time. My eyes immediately found Cassius.

I scanned over the other contestants. We were in a small group this time. Nev stood by me as we waited for the king, who stood from his throne and walked to the edge of the balcony to announce what was going to happen.

"Welcome to trial number three!" The crowd boomed with applause. My eyes focused on Cassius as he watched the king give his address.

"This trial is group-based. You have all been assigned to a team consisting of five participants. Your goal is to get through the maze."

As soon as the king spoke about it, the maze's mammoth black walls tore up through the ground beneath us, cleaving the ground in two. The walls were at least twenty feet tall, solid black, and made of a glossy stone.

"Each team will start at a different section of the maze. The first team to get to the center and grab the stone will win the trial. The next team to enter the center will get second place, and so on and so forth. Only one teammate is required to make it to the center, as it is most likely that some of you will not leave this maze alive. Magic is allowed, and you may do whatever is necessary to win."

The crowd roared at the announcement. They loved a good fight.

"Lavtan will announce the teams, and you will have two minutes to discuss a plan with them before your time starts. A word of caution: the maze is dangerous, and traps are everywhere. Things are not always as they seem."

Lavtan stood, and his eyes stared right at me with a smug look on his face.

"The teams have been selected, and they are as listed!"

Everyone looked up where he pointed in the sky, and our names all shuffled into six groups of five. I found my name and glared at Lavtan. He had me placed with no one in the top ten. My eyes drifted over the other groups. Haden's team had four of the top ten on his. Nev had a decent team as well. Mine was definitely the weakest. I sighed but gathered my team quickly.

"What magic does everyone have?" I asked.

"I can shift," said a man named Kace. His hair was dark, and he had pretty, dark blue eyes that seemed impossibly bright against his dark skin.

"Great. Can you shift into anything you want?" I asked.

"No." He sighed and shifted into the smallest-looking animal I had ever seen. It was the size of a mouse. I wasn't sure how that could help us, but I wasn't about to make him feel bad.

"Ok, that could be helpful. Everyone has seen my healing and fire magic."

"I'm Zade, and I don't have magic." He was tall and appeared strong, which could be useful. "I'm a guardsman though and can fight."

"I have this." The smallest guy on our team lifted his hands, and everything metal lifted into the air. His light brown hair was long and shaggy, and he was at least a foot shorter than me. "The name's Riven."

"I have water magic," a man named Adrel said.

"We have a lot of different magics that will be helpful," I said, trying to find the positives.

"We have the shittiest team. All of us are low ranking," Riven scoffed. "Well, except you."

"That doesn't matter. Only one of us needs to make it to the center, and we all win. How should we do this? We can all split up to cover more ground, but it will make us more vulnerable to other teams. Or do we all go together?"

"Let's split into two groups to cover more ground but not leave us completely defenseless against the other teams we will run into," Kace suggested.

"I'm fine with that. Is everyone else?"

They all nodded. Riven insisted on being paired off with me, and the other three grouped together.

"Alright, you guys stay focused and pay attention to traps. If something seems off, it probably is." I looked around at my scared companions and took a deep breath as the crowds around us started a countdown of the last few seconds. My eyes found Cassius right before the countdown ended, and a foggy haze enveloped the edges of the arena, blocking everybody from our view. No other teams were around us either, as the king had promised. As the noise faded, an opening appeared on the wall of the maze in front of us. We walked forward together, then looked at each other and nodded. Without hesitation, the group of three went to the right, and we went to the left. It was so quiet compared to the noise of only moments before that it gave me chills as we walked quickly but cautiously.

Riven walked slightly behind me, which I didn't like. Sensing he was purposely trying to follow me, I slowed my pace only for him to mirror my actions. Obviously, he wanted me to lead so any traps would get me first. It was a clever tactic, but I hated others walking behind me.

"Did you hear that?" he whispered, but I hadn't heard anything. I shook my head and kept walking. "We should wait a minute," he suggested. "I thought I heard someone nearby."

"We don't have the luxury of waiting to see what it is. We can handle whatever is waiting for us," I said confidently.

This answer irritated him, and he glared at me before brushing past me, shoulder-checking me on the way by. I opened my mouth to tell him off but thought better of it. We didn't need to be distracted or alert others to where we were. He took a few steps, but I pulled him back quickly.

The ground where he had been walking fell away, and he started sliding into the dark pit. I pulled on him, but he was heavier than I was, so I started being dragged towards the crumbling ground as well. What was I doing?

My fire mist exploded around us and lifted him with ease out of the hole. I laid on my back, completely out of breath, next to him.

"Thanks," he said with a snappy voice. What the hell was his problem?

"Next time I can just let you die if you want to keep being an asshole." I glared.

We stood up and backtracked to take another way we passed up earlier. The black walls of the maze only made everything harder to see. We walked in silence for what seemed like many hours but was likely less than one. We hadn't come across any other traps, so I knew it was only a matter of time.

Riven refused to say anything when I asked him which way he would like to try, so I stopped asking and just went with my gut. Where the hell was Wisp? Her and her friends would be helpful right now. We both paused when we heard footsteps approaching somewhere in front of us. When we turned the corner, a member from another group was walking by himself. Before I could say anything, Riven had thrown a dagger, killing the man.

"What the fuck?" I hissed. "Why did you do that?"

"Don't be so weak, Thea," he spoke as he passed me to grab the dagger from the man lying dead at his feet. "Don't pretend like you care about anyone but yourself. We all know you're a monster." He wiped the blood onto his long sleeve before putting it back in its sheath.

"What is your problem? I didn't ask you to come with me."

He ignored me and kept walking. After only a few steps though, a loud clicking noise alerted us that something was happening. We looked around to see that all four walls were now slowly closing in on us.

"Great," I muttered. We ran to the walls, pressing and pushing against them in the hope of stopping them from closing in on us. Nothing we did worked though.

Fear gripped my chest as the walls continued moving. I was pushing against different sections of the wall when I heard a sudden clicking noise, and the walls seemed to freeze where they were. I looked at the ground where my foot was pressed. I lifted it, and the walls began moving again.

"It's some sort of pressure plate or button," I yelled to Riven before I grabbed the arm of the dead man and dragged him to the hidden button. His body weight was enough to stop the walls from moving anymore. After a long moment of waiting, a part of the wall opened, allowing us to leave the death trap. I peeked out of the doorway first, making sure there were no surprises waiting for us, and then cautiously walked through the door, only to be met with an arrow whizzing by my head before embedding itself into the wall. I released a shaky breath and thanked the gods; I wasn't two inches to the left. The booby traps were everywhere here.

Riven took a cautious step forward, but nothing happened. We made our way down a short hall until the maze split into two directions. Riven immediately led us right, even though I wished to go left. He was confident and walked without caution, almost as if he knew where the traps were.

When we turned the next corner, a wall rose up behind us, refusing to let us leave the way we came.

This couldn't be good.

I grabbed Riven when he went to walk forward, but he shrugged my hand away.

"Riven, this seems like we should take it slower," I cautioned.

"It's fine."

When he stepped forward, though, several giant axes swung like pendulums from one side of the walkway to the other. Great. He lifted his hand to use his magic, but nothing happened. I watched him try again, but again nothing.

"It's not true metal," he sighed. "Try burning them."

With determined steps, I moved towards them and unleashed my fire magic, only to find that nothing happened—no damage had been inflicted at all. They still swung in tandem as they had when they first appeared.

"I guess we will have to go through," I sighed.

"After you," Riven scoffed.

Rolling my eyes, I stepped forward. There was enough space between them that I could stand without being hit by the next one. It would fit Riven just fine too, since he was small in stature. My eyes studied the axe-like pendulums for a moment. They were slightly off in timing, so

I waited until the first one swung back before stepping forward. The second one swung directly in front of my face.

The speed of it caused a puff of wind to blow my braid back. I waited again before stepping in between the next two. This wouldn't be hard as long as I paid attention to the timing, but it was unnerving to have blades swinging so quickly on both sides of me. I wanted to turn to see where Riven was, but I couldn't without my head getting cut off.

My steps were calculated as I moved through the blades four more times until I got to the end. I turned to see Riven stepping through the last one right after me. He had followed closely. This time we didn't have an option to choose which way to go. We could only go to the left. It seemed to be getting darker the farther we went.

Something moved behind us. Riven must have heard it too, because he stopped instantly. Summoning a ball of fire to my hands, I used it to illuminate the dark so we could see what it was. A huge black creature was at the end of the hallway where we had just come from.

It looked like an oversized cat, but it had four eyes and fangs that hung far out of its mouth. It snapped its teeth towards us, revealing how sharp they were. Suddenly a loud scream from somewhere in the maze ricocheted off the walls. It was followed by a horrifying crunch of bones, and my mind imagined flesh tearing from the victim. Shaking the image away, I focused on the creature in front of me.

The creature's eyes were completely white, and I wondered if it was somehow possessed. It stomped its front paw on the ground, dragging its sharp claws against the hard stone and causing small sparks to light up its face. Its ears pinned back before it released a loud snarl towards us. As soon as it started running our way, I cast a fire shield in front of us, but our relief was short-lived as the creature stepped through the flames unphased.

"What the fuck?" Riven muttered.

The creature's fur was on fire, and it didn't seem fazed at all. We watched as the flames moved over its fur, charring it and only seemingly making the creature stronger. He lowered his head and began slowly stalking towards us, the ground smoking where each burning paw touched the ground. His ears were laid back, and his teeth were bared. A deep rumble of anticipation was emanating from his throat as his muscled, flaming form came towards us. We ran in a dead sprint down the corridor.

"We can't see shit. Thea, use your magic to light up our path."

A long stream of fire shot out along the wall. It only showed a long hallway. We kept running, but the creature was gaining on us. Suddenly, another scream echoed through the maze, making the hair on my neck stand.

"Riven, jump!" I warned as my fire showed the floor missing in front of us.

We both jumped into blackness, as if leaping into a void, hoping we didn't just jump to our deaths. We only fell for a few seconds before slamming into the hard ground. Both of us tumbled and rolled before finally slamming into a wall. We were both hurt, but we didn't have time to waste.

"Let's go." I stood up and held my hand to help him, but he swatted it away. His rudeness was getting worse, but at this point I didn't have time to care.

My magic lit up the space around us, and I saw only one way to go forward. Hopefully, that meant that we were almost done. At this point, I wasn't even sure how long we had been in here. It had felt like time had stopped moving since we started the trial. We hadn't even run into any other teams, which I thought was odd. Scanning the tops of the walls, I wondered where Cassius was watching me from. I knew he was there somewhere; I could sense him.

After a short walk straight forward, the maze guided us somewhere. The walkway here was wider than it had been anywhere else. I sucked in my breath as I noticed that down the path, there was a faintly glowing red light.

"Do you see that?" I asked Riven. "Maybe it's the end of the maze?"

When Riven didn't answer, I turned—only to see him glaring at me with a dagger in his hand.

"Unfortunately for you, you won't be getting to the end of the maze." The smile he gave me disarmed me with how much hatred it held.

"We're on the same team. We all get the points." I backed up towards the red light. Riven followed me with the dagger pointed at me.

"This isn't just about points, Thea. There's a bigger game being played here, and the only task for me is making sure you don't place in the top ten. Did you know that if you kill one of the top ten contestants, you get their points?"

"Who told you that? I doubt that's true," I scoffed. It sounded like something Leer would have made up just to get others killed. "Why me? I haven't done anything."

He laughed maniacally as he stalked slowly towards me.

"You are a monster," he hissed. "The prophet's vision told us that, but can you imagine what would happen if you got your wish granted?"

"You don't know what my wish would even be," I snapped back.

He gave me a knowing smile. "You and all your disgusting friends would be freed."

My heart sank. How could he know where I came from or what I wanted with my wish? What did the fae in Exile have to do with this prophecy? He was the second man to tell me I was the center of a prophet's proclamation. What had this prophet said that I was going to do? Both men that referenced it had called me a monster or evil. The part of me that knew I was dangerous worried that they were right, that I should be feared and hated.

"There is a whole group of men in this competition whose only purpose is to prevent you from getting that wish, Thea, bonus points if we kill you."

"I don't even know who I am!" I said frantically. "Maybe the prophet you mentioned saw visions of another woman."

He shook his dagger at me as if to say no.

"The prophet named you specifically." He cocked his head to the side. "Deep down; you know you're a threat to everyone, so let me end this here. Then, maybe these stupid trials can stop once and for all."

His words didn't make any sense. "Why would the trials end if I died?"

"It must be so blissful to not remember what you did or who you are. You destroy everything you touch!" His eyes flashed with a burning, hot rage. He took a deep breath and closed his eyes tightly, as if trying to reign himself in.

"Riven, whatever the prophet said can be changed. If the prophet predicted I would do something bad, then I can choose to stop it, but I don't know what it said."

"None of us can ever trust you. You proved that the last time we gave you a chance, and you used it to disappear with all your disgusting elitist friends."

With every small bit of information he told me, the more confused I became. I was running out of time. He knew more about me than I did, and I had no argument against anything he was saying.

"Riven, I'm not evil."

"Liar!"

I realized that nothing I said would change his mind about me. I lifted my hand up, but he saw my move coming. Without him moving a muscle, he used his magic to throw the dagger, staking my hand to the wall of the maze. A loud sob escaped me and ricocheted around us as I turned to remove the dagger, but he used that moment of distraction to drive a different blade into my stomach. The dagger I had pulled from my hand fell to the ground as I slid down the maze wall.

My body was in shock, and I couldn't do anything for a few long moments. When I tried to take a deep breath, the blade cut deeper into me, forcing me to only take shallow breaths. I went to grab Sybil's healing amulet, but he stepped forward and ripped it from my neck, putting it in his pocket.

Even though I didn't need the amulet, I still couldn't feel her healing magic. My eyes stared up into the blackness above us.

This was it. I was dying, and so would everyone in Exile. Blood filled my lungs, making me cough it out. Cassius was going to see me die today.

The dagger in my stomach had sunk almost all the way through me. I couldn't even feel my fire magic trying to surface to try and help, which only increased my panic.

Wasn't death supposed to be peaceful? This was a nightmare. Pain seeped into every part of my body as I sat against the maze wall, slowly bleeding out.

"Looks like you'll fail this tournament, just like you did in all the others. Let's hope you won't be back to try again."

He turned his head to the side at the sound of others moving in our direction before chuckling softly.

"I hope you have a painful death, Thea." Then he set off towards the red light. Thankfully, Haden's team was the one coming around the corner.

"Thea?" Haden kneeled. Conflicting emotions flickered across his face. "You guys go ahead. I'm going to stay with Thea," he demanded of his teammates. "I'll be right back. I'm going to find something to help move you to the stone, so you'll be pulled." He turned and hurried around the corner. I just lay there in confusion, not understanding what I did to deserve this.

I looked up and saw that Kace's small, mouse-like form was headed straight for me. He was bloodied when he transformed back to his fae form.

"Thea, what happened?"

"Riven," I whispered. "You need to get to the red stone and win this."

"Can you heal yourself?" he asked. I shook my head no. He glanced at Haden's team closing in on the stone. "There's no way I'd be able to outrun them or outfight them."

He was right, but I needed to get out of here, and the only way that would happen was if we finished the maze. Dying in this dark hellhole was not an option. Kace looked defeated.

"Help me up," I demanded. I had a plan.

"You shouldn't move."

"I'm dying anyway, but damn it, I'm not dying in this fucking maze." He stared at me like I was crazy as I slowly stood up, feeling the blade cut into me more with each movement. "Shift. I'm going to throw you toward the stone. When you're close, shift back and grab it. If you get to it first, we'll be pulled from the maze, and you won't have to fight. Even if you don't get the stone, we'll be pulled because you made it to the end."

"Okay," Kace agreed as he shifted into my hand. He was small, but I didn't know how far I could get him to the stone.

"You got this, Kace." It was the only encouragement he got before I threw him as hard as I could. Pain sliced through me at the movement, and his small body disappeared into the darkness as he left my hand. My eyes never strayed from the red stone, watching Haden's team closing in on it.

"Please work," I whispered to the gods. Suddenly, Kace's body appeared in midair as he shifted into his fae form, slamming hard into Haden's teammate. The two knocked the pedestal over and caused the stone to go sailing through the air, landing on the ground and skittering across the floor. Both men immediately recovered and went running after it, fighting to get to it first.

I could only make out their silhouettes, but I couldn't make sense of who was who. My eyes became hazier the longer I stood there. Finally, after a final scuffle, one of them lifted the stone into the air. A sudden rush of dizziness passed over me, and I was once again pulled into the bright light of the colosseum. My eyes focused on Haden's teammate, who held the red stone.

We hadn't won.

But it didn't matter because I was dying. Riven was standing off to the side, but he immediately made a beeline for me as soon as he saw me. Kace was close by him, bloodied.

"You couldn't just fucking die!" he hissed, his light skin turning a dark shade of red. "Well, good thing the trial isn't completed," he sneered as he grabbed another dagger. Before he could do anything though, I pulled the one from my stomach and threw it at him as quickly as I could. It embedded itself into his forearm, making his other dagger fall to the ground, which only pissed him off more.

I fell to my knees as the effects of losing too much blood took over. My eyes closed, waiting for the final blow to kill me, but it never came. When I opened them again, Haden had just driven a blade through Riven's heart. I tried to rasp out a thank you, but the world tilted, and I fell face first towards the ground. Something caught me before I hit it. My eyes fluttered open when I heard a voice yell.

"Thea!" Cassius' voice boomed so loudly in the colosseum that the ground shook. Everything else was dead silent.

Had everyone left? Cassius slid to his knees next to me as his shadows slowly lowered my head to his lap.

"Thea?" He sounded panicked. I should have felt it too, but I didn't feel anything at all. "Open your fucking eyes!" he demanded.

I cracked my eyes open slightly.

"It's alright," I murmured.

"Heal yourself, damn it."

"Riven took it." He looked at Riven's dead body, and his shadow tendrils moved quickly to retrieve my amulet. It was in my hand a moment later, not that I needed it to use her magic. It already lived inside of me, but it didn't matter because there was nothing for me to use to fuel it.

"Heal yourself, Thea. Come on, I'm not losing you again." His voice sounded so broken.

My body was so weak, though, that I had nothing left to give. I couldn't even feel my fire magic, which was always at the surface, ready to explode. My head shook no as a slow, agonizing darkness crept in.

"I'm dying," I whispered as silent tears trailed down my cheeks. "I can feel it coming."

"No," Cassius declared. "How do you use this healing amulet?" He grabbed my face and lifted my head so I could gaze at him. I turned my head so he could see my elite magic mark behind my ear.

"Any elite magic can power it?" he asked. My head wouldn't move to answer him, but suddenly he was lifting me up and running.

"Move!" he yelled.

Then, everything went dark.

CHAPTER 16

*D*ying was weird. I was suspended in black nothingness, but I felt peace for maybe the first time in my life.

It was nice, until it wasn't.

A small, faint light in front of me caught my eye, and I slowly floated toward it. When I got to it, I saw that it was a wisp with blue and purple flames. Reaching out, I touched her, causing her orb of light to explode into millions of pieces.

Sudden brightness filled the darkness I was suspended in. Flashes of fae appeared before me; some I didn't recognize, and some I did. A moment later, the images slowed down, and I could make out more of the faces. I saw Sybil, Kai, and Kaz, but they weren't in Exile. They were standing by a stunning gray castle, smiling at me.

Then it flashed to Cassius. He walked into a small room dressed in his armor. His face was hard and cold until he turned and locked eyes with me. Then a bright smile appeared on his face before he disappeared.

The crest I saw on the wooden door appeared in front of me in a bright flash of light. Then I watched myself standing there, as if looking in a mirror. Only my reflection was wearing a blue guardsman uniform with that mysterious crest on it.

Had I been a guardsman? What was this? Some sort of life flashing before my eyes before everything goes dark and I die? Only these "memories" I didn't recognize. I had never seen Cassius in his armor before. Sybil and the twins all said they didn't know who I was, so why did I have memories of seeing them somewhere not in Exile?

The image shifted to a man and woman standing with two children. I recognized their hair and clothing from my dreams. They were the void-faced fae I had dreamt about.

Only now could I see their faces clearly. The man was tall, a bit heavier set, with graying, dark hair and a beard. His eyes were bright green, like mine. The woman at his side was very short with long blonde hair. Her face was pretty with her dark eyes, but she looked miserable.

The kids looked like them. Both of them were girls, with blonde hair and dark eyes like the woman. But they were tall like the man. Their clothing looked expensive, so I guessed they were nobility or royalty. They each wore the mysterious *crest on the chest of their clothing. I took a step forward but stopped when I saw another version of myself standing off to the side, watching them with hurt in my eyes.*

They all turned away from me and ignored me as they left the room.

The vision flashed to Cassius again. We were both in a field, wearing armor with our weapons drawn. Both of us were panting and covered in blood as he took off my helmet and stared at me.

Then all the images were gone, and darkness obscured my sight again.

"Thea?" Turning, I saw Cassius again, standing in the darkness.

"Cassius?" Confusion coursed through me.

"I'm sorry," he whispered before he reached out and pushed me back, causing me to fall backwards through the darkness.

□□□□□

I sat up and sucked in a deep breath. A room full of eyes shifted to me. I looked around the chamber, expecting it to be mine, but it was much nicer. The room was huge and had two big windows that seemed to take up the entire wall. The bed I was in was three times the size of mine, and I had dark green blankets covering me.

"Thea." Cassius rushed over to my side and sat next to me on the bed. He grabbed my hand, but I pulled it away. His brows furrowed at the movement, but he didn't try to grab it back. The king and a few others I didn't recognize were watching me.

"How long was I out for?"

The king spoke first. "Four days. We were worried you wouldn't wake up."

When I looked back to Cassius, a sense of familiarity washed over me. Were those my real memories? Did he know me before? Uneasiness filled my chest. Why was everyone lying to me?

"What's wrong?" He frowned at me.

"I'm just confused and tired." I didn't feel sure enough to tell the truth. The more I learned about myself, the more deceit I saw from those around me.

"Riven said a lot to you before he stabbed you. What did he say?" Cassius was tense, and his eyes filled with worry. He was not telling me something. Everyone around me seemed to know me more than I knew myself.

"I don't remember. Something about my points." Another lie. A noticeable relief washed over him and the king. I wondered if it had been a mistake to come here at all. I should have stayed in Exile and found a way to free everyone from there. Why was everyone so fucking cryptic and misleading? Maybe I was a monster, and they didn't want me to remember that.

"That's all he said?" Cassius asked, eyes wide with skepticism. His shoulders were slumped as if he knew I was deceiving him.

"I'm sure he said more, but I just don't remember anything else. I was trying to think of how to stay alive."

Cassius nodded as his golden eyes scanned over me. He didn't say anything, but then again, he didn't have to.

"I'll be back in a moment," he assured me, but his words brought me no comfort. He and the king disappeared out of the room, and then the other men followed. I stood up as quick as I could, which was really quite slow considering my recent injuries, and went to the door hoping to sneak out, but I paused when I realized they hadn't actually left.

"She's lying to me," Cassius whispered.

"Cassius, she may not remember. What Riven did was traumatic, and he truly might have not said anything to her." The king sighed. "She seemed genuine when she said she didn't remember."

"I know her better than anyone, and she's lying straight to my face. He either told her something or she's having more memories. It's just like last time."

Last time?

"It's not like last time, Cassius." The king was angry now. "We don't know anything, and it would be stupid to make assumptions. For now, all we can do is trust her and what she tells us."

"I'm not assuming. I know Thea, and she is not being truthful." Cassius didn't sound angry. He sounded sad. "I can't keep doing this year after year."

"You can, and you will. You heard what the gods said. She's done so much better this time around with Sybil's magic. Besides, I know you'll do whatever you must to save her."

My heart pounded in my chest.

Cassius *had* been lying to me.

The king was lying to me.

Everyone was lying to me.

I couldn't bear to hear any more, so I went back to bed and curled up under the blanket. When I heard them come back in, I pretended to be asleep. I couldn't look at anyone without more confusion consuming me. Everyone knew who I was but me. If Cassius cared, then why was he keeping things from me?

"Thea?" Cassius whispered. I didn't move and kept my breathing steady. After a long pause, I heard him shuffling around before the bed dipped and he crawled in next to me. He lifted the covers and pulled me close to him. The warmth of his body lulled me to sleep quickly.

□□□□□

I abruptly woke up, startled when Cassius moved next to me. Within a split second, he had me pinned to the bed with his knife at my throat. His eyes were black as night as they bore into mine. His breathing was short and choppy, as if he were in a fight.

His hand wrapped around my neck as an angry look took over his face. Was he sleeping? Despite my body urging me to, I didn't fight against him. It didn't seem like he knew who I was. My heart thudded rapidly in my chest at how vacant those black eyes were.

"Who the fuck are you?" he hissed as he gripped my throat tightly and his body pinned me below him.

"It's me, Thea," I choked out.

A look of confusion passed over his angry face. He pushed the blade of his knife harder against my neck in warning.

"That's not possible," he hissed. "Who are you?"

"Cassius, please. It's me," I whimpered as silent tears streamed down my face from the fear coursing through me. What was wrong with him? Lifting my hand slowly, I moved the tips of my fingers along the stubble on his jaw. He shook his head back and forth slightly, like he was chasing away bad thoughts.

His eyes were still completely black as he stared at me. He set the knife down and grabbed my jaw tightly in his hand. He turned my head to the side before moving my hair out of the way so he could see my elite magic mark. I heard him let out a long breath from his nose. My eyes squeezed shut tightly at the amount of force he was gripping my jaw with. He turned my face back towards him, and I watched his eyes move over me slowly, as if making sure it really was me.

"Are we in a dream?" he whispered.

"No."

"You're really here with me?"

"Yes."

His grip on my jaw lessened, but he didn't let it go as his mouth suddenly descended onto mine. Cassius' body kept me in place, not letting me move at all. His lips dominated mine, almost angrily at first. The longer he kissed me, though, the lighter his grip became. His hand moved from my jaw to the side of my neck to pull me closer to him. His tongue brushed against my lips, and I welcomed it as a deep groan vibrated from his chest. Cassius broke the kiss only to press kisses down my neck and back up to my elite magic mark.

My whole body hummed at his touch, like it had been starved from it forever. My hands moved to his dark hair and pulled it so he would find my lips again. Cassius slid his hand down the side of my body to grab the back of my knee and wrap it around him. I could feel how hard he was as he thrust forward, grinding against me and hitting the perfect spot.

"Cassius." I groaned at the sensation.

"Thea?" He sat up quickly, and I was greeted by his golden eyes, which were swimming in confusion. He stood up and turned his back to me, breathing deeply and holding his head for a moment. Then he straightened up and said, "That shouldn't have happened."

His words smothered any warmth his touch had brought to me only a moment ago. I swallowed hard as he seemed distraught that he had touched me. He stopped his pacing and glared at me with no emotion.

"I should go."

I hesitated at his words. He didn't seem angry, but something like regret flittered across his features.

"I'll go," I said, throwing off the covers and standing up.

Tears welled in my eyes as I grabbed all of my things that I could see. I quickly ran in the general direction of my room as my emotions threatened to escape me. How could he be so upset when it felt so right to touch him? Why was he so angry with me when he was the one who kissed me?

I didn't understand why I was so upset by this. Cassius should mean nothing to me. Why did he matter? He was keeping secrets from me. I shouldn't care that he wanted to get away from me. It should have never gotten this far to begin with. When I turned the corner to head down the hallway to my room, I collided with a hard chest, making me fall back onto the floor.

"Are you alright?" Nev frowned at me. His eyes cascaded over my bare legs and the black shirt of Cassius' I was wearing. Disgust contorted his features. Red flames caught my eye as Wisp appeared next to Nev. She quickly put herself between Nev and I, which allowed me to slowly crawl backwards from him to escape whatever danger Wisp felt I was in.

"I'm fine," I lied. "Sorry, I was just heading to bed since I'm feeling better."

Nev just stared down at me with disdain painted across his face. He had never looked at me like this, and I was uncomfortable. My instincts were telling me to get up and run, but this was Nev. He was my friend. Nev reached into his pocket, but I couldn't see what he grabbed. Wisp flashed immediately to black, and I backed myself up against the stone wall.

"I am sorry about this," he sighed before opening his palm and blowing some sort of dust into my face. My eyes stung so badly that they immediately watered up. Abandoning all of my things, I stood to run, but he grabbed my hair and pulled me to the stone floor so hard that the wind left my lungs. I gasped for air as I struggled to fight him, but he was easily overpowering me. I couldn't figure out why my one friend in this competition had turned on me.

I opened my mouth to yell, but no noise came out. He grabbed my wrists and wrapped barbed metal around them, causing them to bleed as the spikes dug into my flesh. The pain was so intense that I sobbed as he lifted me up and carried me outside. Thankfully, the night was cold against my skin. Cracking my eyes, I could see the soft red glow of Wisp following us.

"Please," I whispered as I tried to figure out where he was taking me. I attempted to summon my fire magic, but I couldn't feel it anywhere.

"Your magic won't work with these cuffs on," he snapped. "I wasn't planning on taking you tonight, but I guess when the opportunity presents itself, you have to take it," he laughed.

"Why?"

"You're going to pass out here in a moment, Thea. We'll have plenty of time to talk when we get home."

I tried to ask him what he meant, but blackness clouded any sort of control I had over my body. My eyes fluttered open and shut as I fought unconsciousness. The last thing I saw were the treetops above us in the night sky before I lost my ability to fight anymore.

CHAPTER 17

"**W**ake up!" Nev clapped his hands loudly in front of my face. My head pounded as it tried to chase the fogginess away, allowing bits and pieces of what happened to come back to me. Peering up at Nev from the ground, I tried to spit out the rag he tied into my mouth, preventing me from speaking. Wherever we were was much hotter than the Crimson kingdom, and I didn't particularly like it.

My arms burned with a sharp pain. Nev had wrapped the magic cuffs from the tips of my fingers up to my elbows while I'd been passed out. The sharp barbs punctured my flesh, making it bleed.

"Good morning. I was worried that I accidentally killed you with the paralyzing powder." Nev's boyish looks had vanished. The man who stood in front of me now looked like a crazed lunatic. His eyes were empty voids as I squirmed with discomfort. His red hair was sticking every which way, and his clothes were dirty and soaked in sweat, as if he had been through hell.

"That worked out better than anything I could have planned," he gloated. He pulled the gag from my mouth, which was so dry I could hardly breathe without it being uncomfortable.

"I don't understand. You were my friend."

"I was never your friend," he scoffed, like that was the stupidest thing he had ever heard. "You were entirely too easy to trick."

My head pounded so violently that I squeezed my eyes shut to find relief. Dizziness combined with the intense heat made it difficult to focus on anything when I opened them again.

I tried to find my voice again. "I saved you."

"You did," he conceded. "Thanks, by the way. If you hadn't, I wouldn't have been able to carry out my assignment of making sure you disappear from the trials."

"You're one of Riven's men?" I asked him in order to gauge his reaction.

Nev stepped towards me suddenly, with wild anger in his eyes. He lifted his hand and slapped me across the face so hard that I fell over. I squeezed my eyes shut at the pain of rocks and sticks stabbing me.

"Riven was a moron." Nev sat me back up before going over to his bag and grabbing an apple. He sat in front of me and ate it. "Riven was just a small pawn in the game. I'm a bigger player than he was ever going to be. He talked too much."

"Are you going to kill me?"

He took a bite of his food before glancing off to the side and seemed lost in thought for a long moment.

"No. My assignment was to make sure you stayed alive and to get the king and Cassius to leave the castle to find you."

"They won't come for me," I huffed. "They couldn't give two shits about a participant in the trials." I lied. Their conversation that I overheard made me think that Cassius and I had a history beyond the trials.

Nev threw his head back and laughed so loudly that birds flew from the trees. I watched him as he quieted down and stared back at me with a raised eyebrow.

"You actually can't remember anything?" He sighed, annoyed. "They would burn down the realm to find you, Thea, and not because they care about you, but to keep you from getting into the hands of the kingdom of Cerithia."

"Cerithia?" Something in mind wanted to know why everyone in Crimson was so weary of Cerithia. "Why is everyone so damn secretive?" All this cryptic bullshit was getting old.

"Well, you'll know who they are again real soon." He shot me a satisfied smirk. "Do you realize how many fae have died because the Crimson kingdom refuses to give you back to who you belong to because of the prophecy?"

It was starting to feel like everyone knew about the prophecy except for me. I glared at Nev, wishing I could light him on fire. The darkness that lived deep in my chest hummed alive. I could feel it clouding any rational thoughts I might have.

"The Crimson kingdom is the one you should hate. They are the enemy!"

"I never said they weren't," I snapped back.

"No, but you crawl into Cassius' bed and sleep with a man who single-handedly destroyed the alliance between the kingdoms of Crimson and Cerithia, a man so ruthless he would kill anyone for his own benefit. The man is a fucking psycho, and you just look right past it and fuck him anyways."

"It's none of your business what happened between Cassius and me."

"He has a reputation as a cold-blooded killer. A liar. A thief. An evil soul disguised with a pretty face to help him trick those around him, and you fell right for it...again."

"Again?" Confusion clouded my thoughts.

"It doesn't matter. What matters is that we freed you from the Crimson kingdom so that you can return to the kingdom of Cerithia, where you belong."

As soon as he said I belonged there, I got angry, but I didn't know why. The darkness that lingered inside of me was clawing its way out. Who was I supposed to believe? The Kingdom of Cerithia had sent a group of men to make sure I didn't complete this tournament. Riven had tried to kill me because of it. Now I had Nev sitting before me, acting as if Cassius was the one to blame.

Cassius was keeping secrets, but so was everyone else. We were all liars, but there had to be a truth somewhere. I looked up to the bright sky and wished for some fucking clarity on the matter.

I needed more information to piece together all of this. Maybe Nev could give me just enough to understand. "Riven said you guys didn't want my wish to come true."

"We don't." He looked at me skeptically, as if I had more thoughts about this. "It would be the downfall of the kingdoms."

"You guys don't even know what my wish would be," I argued.

"We know what it will be. Why do you think the Crimson kingdom wants you to win the trials so badly? Because you disappeared with all the elitist magic holders, and no one can find them. Everyone wants the same thing." He stared at me for a long moment. "Your kind needs to be controlled before they kill us all, and the only way to do that is with you."

"Elite magic holders aren't fucking monsters."

"Keep telling yourself that, Thea."

He stood up and glanced into the thick woods we were on the outskirts of. I watched him gather his bag of belongings. Great, we were moving again. He poured some more of that powder in his hand, but I couldn't fight against him as he blew it into my face. At least this time I closed my eyes so it wouldn't hurt as much. Fighting would be pointless, so I closed my eyes as he lifted me. His heavy footsteps lulled me into a deep sleep.

□□□□□

"Thea?" I turned around. Cassius stood in his room at the castle. He seemed distraught. "Where are you?"

"We're in a dream," I whispered. I wasn't used to seeing him here anymore.

"Nev took you. Do you know where you are?"

"I thought you didn't remember things from dreams?" My eyes narrowed on him.

"It was for your protection, little viper. We can talk about it when I get you back. Now, where are you?"

I hesitated to tell him anything. Who could I trust? Nev was carrying me tied up through a forest, but Cassius had never hurt anything but my feelings. Both were liars, though.

"We're headed into the thick forest that I rescued you from, but he wants you to follow," I warned him.

Cassius watched me and took a hesitant step forward, but I stepped backward. The outburst in his room still played fresh in my mind. I was tired of the back and forth with him. He halted when he saw me step away.

"If I could tell you what I know, I would," he sighed. "I can't, Thea. Not until the curse is broken. Not until you re-member everything," he said in a pained voice as he watched me, looking like he wanted nothing more than to pull me close to him. I was also in pain, mostly over the fact that I couldn't remember why we were this way with each other.

"So, you have been lying to me, keeping who I am a secret? You and I know each other, right? That's why I feel this way about you without hardly knowing who you are." I was angry now.

"I tried to stay away so it wasn't confusing for you, but I'm not doing a very good job at it. I just wanted you to do well in the trials this time."

"Because I've been in the trials before? Riven and Nev have both told me. Nev says I shouldn't trust you, that you are a fucking monster, that you broke the alliance between

two kingdoms, and that you kill mercilessly. He said that I fell for your shit before and that I was doing it again. What happened the last time I was in the trials?"

"The kingdom of Cerithia always made sure you didn't place in the top ten, and you always disappeared back to where you were hiding before we could follow you and help free you." He was angry as he spoke. "Last year, you made the eleventh spot, so we were hopeful that this would be the year that you finally made it."

Cassius had announced at the start of the trials that this was the seventh year. Had I participated in each one of them? If I had, why hadn't Sybil or the twins said anything? Confusion plagued me again. It was like I was living someone else's reality.

"I've competed seven times."

He looked confused as to how I knew but confirmed my guess.

"Why do you want me to win the trials so badly?"

"Because you need to steal the witch's bloodstone from the kingdom of Cerithia, and you need a group of men to help you. We have sent others to try, but they aren't powerful like you. They need your magic to guide them. My family cannot set foot on Cerithia territory without starting a violent war. If you can get the stone though, it will give you back your memories and help save our kingdom."

His family? My heart thudded in my chest as I stared at him. How had I not noticed before? He looked similar to the king of Crimson. Except for his eyes, Cassius' eyes were a stark contrast to the king's. This was why the king was so worried about his return when he was taken. Cassius was the prince of the Crimson kingdom.

"You're the prince?" A sense of tension filled the small space.

"Yes," he nodded. "I know it looks like I'm keeping secrets from you and trying to disguise things, but I truly cannot tell you because of the curse. No one from the Crimson kingdom can speak of it. I want nothing more than to tell you everything. I've spent seven years trying to bring you back to me. I wait each year for the trials because I can see you again, even though you don't remember me. And I'll keep doing it every year until you remember every detail about us. I will never give up on you."

"Why am I cursed?"

"I don't know. If I knew, I would tell you."

My head hurt with everything I had learned. How could I still not remember anything when Cassius had just given me so much information?

"Why do I dream of you? I've dreamt of you for as long as I can remember."

He gave me a smile.

"I'm part dream stalker from my mother's side. I needed to see you, even if you didn't know who I was. So, I went to your dreams to visit."

A tugging feeling overwhelmed me, and I looked backwards as if someone would be there. I tried to shake the feeling away, but I couldn't.

"I'm waking up." I turned to Cassius. He stood staring at me, his body tense with worry.

"Can you use your magic?"

"I have magic cuffs on." I could feel myself being pulled from the dream. "We're not that far into the forest."

Before he could respond, though, I was ripped from the dream.

□□□□□

My eyes squinted in the brightness of the sunlight. I was sitting on the ground again, and once my eyes adjusted, I could see that Nev was seated at the side of a small stream in front of us. He sat there, staring at the water for a long time before turning back towards me.

"Oh, you're awake?" he asked, seeming confused.

When I didn't respond, he just shrugged and continued doing whatever he was doing in the water without acknowledging me again. I scanned the forest for anything I could free myself with, but there wasn't anything. The gag was back as well, so I couldn't speak. The sound of the creek running made my mouth feel even drier. The sun beamed down on me, making me sweat even though I was still only in Cassius' shirt.

A few minutes later, Nev returned, looking triumphant as he held a fish in his hands. He built a small fire, and I watched as he skewered the fish and roasted it slowly. My stomach growled loudly. I was so famished.

"If I ungag you, will you not ask a million questions?" he asked, skeptical of my ability to follow through on the request.

I nodded yes. He still didn't seem sure of my answer, but he untied my gag anyway. I sucked in deep, desperate breaths, but the air was so hot that it didn't make me feel any better.

"I need water."

Nev sighed in annoyance but grabbed a bottle next to him and held it up to my mouth so I could drink. It was cold and crisp and tasted so good against my parched tongue.

"Are you going to feed me?"

"Yes," he said grudgingly. "I have to keep you alive. Besides, walking this far to the Cerithia territory is taking longer than I thought it would, so we need to rest here for the night."

I didn't say anything at this announcement. My eyes scanned the woods again as I waited for Cassius. I knew without a doubt that he would come for me. Even though he pushed me away, I could see the want lingering in his eyes when he stared at me. Obviously, he warred with his feelings for me, but I don't think he or the Crimson royal family would let what Nev did slide. He had already gone directly against the rules of the tournament.

The black wisp caught my attention as she floated close by with several others. Something about their presence calmed me, but I wondered why their flames were black. My darkness hummed at the sight of them, like they called to it and were trying to beckon it to release. The darkness slowly crept through me, like it was preparing to attack. I wasn't sure it would get past the magic barbs on me though.

"Why are you so quiet?" Nev asked.

"You told me to not ask questions," I reminded him.

"Yeah, but you literally never do what you should."

"Well, I want food, so I'm keeping my mouth shut. Maybe after dinner I'll pester you with questions."

Nev looked at me from the other side of the fire. His eyes were nothing close to the friendly guy I had been friends with at the trials. How could he have been so convincing?

Maybe I was gullible, and everyone knew that, so they had preyed upon that weakness.

An unnerving feeling hit me when I realized everyone knew more about me than I did. I would think that being told things about myself would trigger my memories, but it hadn't. I knew there were still huge pieces of my life missing.

And then there was the matter of the witch's bloodstone.

Nev startled me out of my thoughts when he sat in front of me with the fish. He took a bite before feeding me one. We did this in silence for a long time. The fish had no real flavor to it, but it tasted so good on my empty stomach. And anyways, I had survived off of less before. Nev didn't leave when we finished, and I knew something was coming.

"Do you know something?" he accused.

"What do you mean?" I bit out. "I've been tied up and dragged through a forest by a deranged lunatic. It's not like I'm having conversations with others out here." I hoped that my attempt to make him feel stupid would work and he wouldn't interrogate me the way I wanted to interrogate him.

He studied me closely. "You're oddly quiet."

"Because you won't answer any of my questions anyway, so what's the point of talking? Should I beg you to let me go?"

"I never said I wouldn't answer any questions. You just need to ask the right ones."

Again with this cryptic shit. I wanted to roll my eyes and spit at him.

"Why don't I have memories?"

"You were cursed," he answered without hesitating. "After the prophet spoke of you being the downfall of kingdoms and wiping out those who didn't feel the same about elite magic, someone felt the need to erase your memories so you couldn't remember whatever your plan was."

"Who would do that?"

"No one knows." Nev seemed genuine in his response.

"When did this prophet predict I would be the fall of kingdoms?"

"Seven years ago. You are a monster, Thea. The prophet's telling told us that. You will crumble kingdoms. You will kill kings. But the question is...what kingdom will you be a monster for? You could burn the whole realm down if you wanted to." His eyes glanced over me. "Seems fitting."

"That doesn't sound like me," I argued.

"You don't even know who you are, so how can you be sure that it was not your intention before the curse was placed?"

His question struck a nerve, and I went quiet. He was right. What if I was this destroyer of kingdoms? What if I planned on burning down the realm around me? The darkness I held inside made itself known as I struggled to convince myself I wasn't a monster. If Cassius knew the prophet's proclamation and it was truly that bad, he would not be trying to save me. He would want me to die if I was the cause of suffering. If I were to threaten his family's kingdom, he would not let me live to see the day that the proclamation came true. I stared at Nev for a long moment.

"So, the kingdom of Cerithia will kill me when I get back to it?"

He shook his head. "No. You are a valuable fae to have when on the right team. But you will have to choose which kingdom your loyalty lies with—Crimson or Cerithia."

"But I'm a threat to both."

"No, you're a threat to all the kingdoms that you are not loyal to. The thing with you, though, is no one can trust a fucking word you say because you burn bridges just as fast as you build them. No one wants to take the chance of releasing you from the curse if they don't know that you are fighting for them."

"So, what about the other kingdoms? Don't they want me, too? This seems to be a fight between only Cerithia and Crimson."

"Yes, they do want you. All of them are desperate for you to pick them to fight for. Most kingdoms are terrified of you. You could take down armies of enemies with a flick of your wrist if you wanted. You are the most feared fae the realm of Elloryon has ever known. Long ago, the realm was ruled by a single family. Then a terrible war divided it into five territories: Akecia, Crimson, Kizar, Cerithia, and Falgon. Crimson and Cerithia are the worst of enemies, though. The other three territories stick to themselves for the most part. None of them are strong enough to get between Cerithia and Crimson to steal you away."

There was nothing to say because I wasn't sure what to ask at this point. All the kingdoms wanted me for one reason. Yes, they were all terrified of me, but if I was with them, then they would be safe from me. The more I learned about myself, the more I sounded like a monster. Swallowing the hard lump in my throat, I tried to keep myself from getting upset. I didn't want to be feared.

I was trying to free a whole group of fae for fuck's sake! How did that sound like a monster? Maybe because elite magic holders were monsters. I wanted to shake away that feeling, but it stuck with me. Maybe us being locked away had kept harmony for all the kingdoms. Maybe it was better for me to be a prisoner since every kingdom only wanted to use me as a weapon anyway.

Is that what Cassius wanted from me, too? The realization that I was only a pawn in this shifted something deep down inside of me. The wisps all seemed to burn bigger at this shift, like they sensed it too.

No one cared about me. The only reason anybody wanted me around was to hold me over the heads of others as a threat, a weapon. A feeling of dark numbness consumed me. This was definitely not the first time I had reached this conclusion. Maybe going to Exile had been done to keep everyone safe. Why should our realm live in fear of me? My mind shifted to a memory that broke free from the curse.

I stood in the castle hallway of the Crimson palace. I could hear the king and Cassius talking in angry whispers.

"You need to do whatever you can to convince her to choose us, Cassius," the king demanded. "You're running out of time."

"How am I supposed to tame a monster!" Cassius hissed back. "Thea will always do what she wants because no one

can control her. Why do I have to be the one that has to do this?"

The king spoke so softly I could barely make it out. "You'll get her to pledge her loyalty to the Crimson kingdom, or you won't get your throne when the time comes."

"Fine," Cassius snapped. "I'll keep pretending like I care so much about her. At least she was so starved for someone to love her that I barely had to put effort into it. Pathetic."

"Well, make sure she believes you actually care about her and don't completely despise her. That should be easy if she is that desperate for anyone to show her some attention. Gods above know her family never wanted her either."

I ran back to his room and sat numbly on the bed. I had never heard Cassius speak so poorly of me.

He thought I was a monster. He thought I was pathetic. Just then the door to his room opened, and he walked in wearing a big, genuine smile. My heart couldn't understand how he could put on such a good show for me if he truly hated me. Cassius pulled out a bunch of the most beautiful flowers I had ever seen before from behind his back. He kneeled on the floor between my thighs and pulled me to him for a hard kiss.

All I could think about though were his words. What was he thinking about every time he touched me or kissed me? I'm sure disgust filled him. Was he thinking of someone else? My heart cracked under the weight of betrayal that his words made me feel. I truly cared for him, and I thought I had finally found something real, someone who could love me, someone who saw past the elite magic I held. I thought Cassius loved me.

"What's wrong, little viper?" he asked, frowning that his gift hadn't gotten the response he expected.

I wanted to tell him off. I wanted to tell him that I had heard every word he said about me, but a bigger part of me didn't want him to stop pretending. I wanted to pretend like he loved me. I wanted to pretend the smiles and the kisses were real.

I really was pathetic.

I hated myself more than ever before. I wished so deeply that I wasn't a monster. I wished I was worthy of a love like Cassius. His words had broken me more than years of my family's outright disgust for me had.

"Nothing," I lied. His hand brushed my braid off my shoulder. Cassius' golden eyes stared at me like he truly did care.

"I missed you today," he spoke softly.

All I could think of was how unworthy I was of even this fake affection he showed me. Who could love someone they were terrified of? Cassius had made me think that I could be normal, and I never would be.

CHAPTER 18

I shook my head back and forth to get rid of the memory. I didn't want to feel this way, but it was too late. That darkness seeped through my flesh and bones, wrapping every part of me in black numbness. Heartbreak threatened to crush me, but I let the darkness take away that pain. Everyone in my life had molded me into the monster they thought I was.

"What's your problem?" Nev questioned. When I smiled at him, he visibly shifted away from me. "Your eyes are black," he whispered.

"I just realized that you're probably right. I am a monster."

Confusion took over his features as he inched away from me. Suddenly, I heard footsteps crunching through the nearby undergrowth. I peered into the forest line and saw Haden walking towards us. As soon as he saw me, he stopped immediately. His eyes shifted to Nev and then back to me.

"What the fuck is wrong with her?" Haden asked.

"She got extremely upset, then her eyes turned black, and those marks appeared." Nev sounded worried. I inspected my still-bound arms and saw that red, orange, and black swirls had crawled up my skin. It felt hot as it moved over me, almost as if it were burning me. It crept up my back and around my neck, where it settled into my mind. It practically whispered its approval of letting it take over me. *I've missed you. Let me take the pain away. I will make them suffer.*

"What took you so long?" Nev snapped. "You were supposed to bring horses."

"The castle is on lockdown. Cassius is losing his shit. He killed a guard this morning because he wasn't at his post last night to prevent this. He wants her back."

The thought pissed me off. He was still pretending to care about me. Would I ever be anything to anyone except a pawn? The darkness clawed its way deeper into my flesh and bones. Marking and tainting any shred of hope I had left that Cassius didn't think I was a monster.

"Well, let's hope he follows us." Nev sneered at me, and I made a noise that was so animalistic it had him retreating immediately. The pure terror on his face made me laugh. "She's lost her fucking mind."

I felt caught between the only Thea I could remember and the desire to turn into a complete monster, just like everybody thought I was. The pathetic Thea was locked up deep inside of my chest now, and I could barely feel her trying to cut her way out of the darkness that had consumed me. I was tired of trying to show others I was worthy of basic decency. They were not going to use me and think I'd be too stupid to notice.

The conversation they whispered amongst themselves was not of interest to me. Nev headed over to the river again with his back towards us. Haden looked at me oddly as he slowly made his way towards me. I watched him like he was prey. He surprised me when he kneeled in front of me. Haden glanced over his shoulder to Nev to make sure he was busy. Haden's eyes met mine before frowning.

"What's wrong, Thea?" he whispered. "Cassius is almost here."

I didn't say anything.

"Did you hear me?" Haden whispered. "Nev is expecting the Cerithian kingdom to come first, but Cassius will be here shortly."

Could I trust Haden to have my back now, when he had so clearly detested me earlier? I contemplated his true intentions but wore a look of indifference. How could I believe anything anyone said to me? Haden had been cruel before, and now suddenly he cared.

"He can't reach you here. You're on Cerithia lands, so I'm going to try to get you back into the thick woods where Crimson borders it, but I need to take care of Nev first."

He wanted me to respond, but I didn't care. All of these men making such a fuss over keeping me, like I was a shiny toy to possess, was disgusting.

"She's got to take a piss. I'm going to take her over there." Haden called out to Nev. Nev turned to us, brow furrowing in deep thought.

"I'll come too. She looks like she's gone complete fucking psycho monster-bitch."

A terrifying chuckle escaped me at the name. Haden looked at me strangely, hesitating for a moment before he bent and picked me up, holding me tightly against him. He carried me through the forest for a moment before setting me down next to a tree. My eyes watched the edge of the forest though, seeing all the wisps gathering at the edge of Cerithia and Crimson lands. They floated in vibrant colors, watching and approving of my monster form. Haden's eyes roamed over me oddly, like he couldn't understand what he was seeing, but I was merely being the villain, just like I had been told.

"Thea, I can't help you if you don't tell me what's wrong," Haden whispered. Nev had disappeared behind a thicket of trees in front of us.

I remained silent as his hands gently unwrapped the barbed cuffs from my ankles. I didn't even feel the pain that it should have caused me. Few thoughts went through my mind as I watched Haden be as softly as he could. Dozens of wisps had now gathered in the woods around me. It was as if my darkness called out to them, and they all shifted to black flames to answer it.

Nev hadn't taken me far past where Crimson and Cerithia bordered each other. Cassius said he couldn't cross into Cerithia, so my best guess was Nev had to stay close to the border so that when Cerithia came, they could kill him or take him hostage since he couldn't cross over.

Haden's eyes suddenly shifted to behind me, and I knew it was Cassius and the guards without turning around. They had finally arrived to save me, or was it to recapture me? Haden held his hand up in warning to them, then pointed to the thicket of trees where Nev had disappeared. Before anybody could make a move, though, a bright flash of light blinded us. Nev must have anticipated them coming and set off some sort of magic. I closed my eyes and stood still until the flash of light burned out, but the guards and horses who hadn't predicted what would happen stumbled around, still blinded.

"What the fuck is on her?" Cassius barked at Haden. "Get the cuffs off of her arms."

Haden worked quickly to free my hands from the magical barbs. Then his eyes shifted from me to Cassius.

"Come on, little viper. Let's go." Cassius held out his hand for me while still on top of his horse, but I remained where I was, glaring at him. The blackness of my eyes startled him, and the colorful swirls displayed on my skin didn't help ease him.

"What's wrong with her?" he questioned Haden.

"When I showed up, she was like this. She hasn't said anything to me."

Moving past them, I headed towards the thicket of trees that Nev had entered. When Haden and Cassius tried to stop me, I just put a wall of fire mist up between us, stopping them from coming any closer to me than I wanted. When I entered the tree line, Nev was standing there like he knew I would come for him. When he realized my barbs were off though, his smug face dissolved into sheer terror.

"And you said you weren't a monster," he spat in disgust.

Without thought, the tendrils of my fire mist moved from me and along the forest floor. Nev didn't stand a chance. As soon as he realized what was happening, my magic had him locked in a vice. He tried to summon his light magic, but he wasn't able to. My darkness had robbed him, draining his magic completely from him. It seeped into my fire mist and settled in my chest with the others, completely transferring from him to me.

Slowly, I stalked towards him, his eyes watching my every move. I circled him, like a predator hunting their prey, my eyes watching the guards and Cassius to be sure they didn't interfere. They all stood there watching what was unfolding. Cassius' brows furrowed in confusion as he looked at me. He thought I was a monster, so he was getting a monster. I would be their villain.

"Please." Nev struggled against my grip in vain.

"Please," I said in a mocking tone. "Not so tough when I'm uncuffed, are you?" I purred.

"I can tell you everything, but you can't kill me."

When I laughed, it didn't even sound like my own laugh. It was dark and sultry. It only took a few steps to reach him and make him squirm even more.

"I already know everything I need to. I'm a monster, and everyone wants to trap me," I whispered quietly, so he was the only one that heard me. "I guess this is the part where I embrace the prophet's telling and burn the realm down around me. Kill the kings and whatnot." I turned and looked at Cassius, feeling hurt and betrayal bubbling up. "But I think I'll start with you, *friend*," I spoke loudly so Nev could still hear me as I turned and walked away.

I let my fiery hold on him heat up until his flesh began to sear. Flames erupted on his clothes and spread quickly, melting them into his skin. His screams echoed through the forest so loudly that the birds flew away as my fire consumed his body.

I smiled in satisfaction, feeling my darkness purr in happiness. The guards watched me in horror as I came towards them, my skin swirling and a fiery mist of shadows enveloping me.

This new-found power was almost intoxicating. Killing Nev had been easy, and I didn't even lift a finger to do it. The wisps circled around us, a frenzy of excitement.

"What horse do I get?" I asked casually.

"You can ride with me," Cassius said.

"I don't think so," I hissed at him. "As you can see, I don't need saving or help." One of the guards handed over the reins of a tall, pure white horse, save for a black marking that covered half of its face. As the rest of the men scurried to their horses, Cassius grabbed my arm and pulled me back to him, so we were eye to eye. His hand brushed the hair from my face gently.

"Thea, what's going on?" He looked so genuine and caring. It made me sick that I had fallen for it over and over again.

"You don't like the new look?" I scoffed in a fake offense.

"Why are you acting like this? I don't like it."

Laughter bubbled out of me. "Well, I don't like the little show you've been putting on for me. Pretending to care about me so I'll pledge my loyalty to your kingdom was a good move, though." I ripped my arm away from him. "I've got a trial to win, so let's get to it."

"I didn't fake anything," he argued. "Whatever Nev told you is a lie."

I spun quickly to face him, pure malice dripping in my voice. "He didn't need to tell me. I saw it myself. My own memory has no reason to lie to me, Cassius. You think I'm a monster; I heard you say it. You are disgusted by me and only pretended to care so you could get your throne."

"Thea, that's not true. Why are you remembering false memories? Did Nev manipulate you?"

"Nev was a moron," I scoffed. "I saw and heard you talking to your father. I know that he put you up to using me, and you reluctantly agreed. It's just like I've always been told. The Crimson royal family is nothing more than a bunch of lying cowards."

Jumping up on my horse, I left him standing there with his mouth open in shock and rode off towards the Crimson castle without waiting for them. I thought the horse would spook from me, but she acted as if my darkness didn't bother her at all. The guards fell in behind me, and I urged my horse to run faster, my hair whipping around in the wind as we broke through the thick forest tree line and into a meadow. I could hear another horse coming up to us, and I knew it was Cassius, but I didn't bother acknowledging him.

He didn't try talking to me or stopping me as we rode, so I just let my horse give me her full speed. I only slowed down once we reached the outskirts of the Crimson castle yard. Cassius rode next to me, the tension rising between us with each silent moment that passed.

When we arrived at the castle, a whole group of guards, contestants, and the royal family stood smiling. Until they saw me, that is.

I jumped off my horse and headed towards the castle doors, not bothering to acknowledge any of them. The king stepped in front of me though and waited for me to look at him.

"We are so glad you're back, Thea."

"Why? Because you wouldn't want me in the hands of another kingdom? Would you be too scared that I would burn the realm down, starting with all the cowards that live in this castle?"

He took a step backward and glanced at Cassius in confusion before he returned his gaze to me. The sadness in his eyes took me aback momentarily, and I wondered if I was overreacting. He looked as if he was truly hurt by my words. But I had to stay strong. I couldn't let them in and crumble my resolve of the truth I saw.

I reminded myself that they only saw me as a power pawn. The weakness I carried of wanting love, of wanting to be seen as someone worthy of love, would be my downfall. I didn't need anyone.

The other contestants' whispers about me reached my ears, asking why I looked the way I did. I ignored them and kept my gaze on the king, waiting for his response.

"Thea," Cassius snapped in a warning. I knew I was being blatantly rude to the king and in front of others, but what did it matter? They wouldn't kill me; they needed me more than I needed them. So, I turned to him, ready to fight.

"Yes, *Prince* Cassius?" I barked out his title with so much venom. "Did you have something to say, or were you just going to keep lying to my face?"

Not a single murmur could be heard in the crowd. Cassius looked at me with disappointment.

"Please, stop," he begged quietly. "You don't know what you're talking about."

"Thea, you've had a traumatic experience. Let's get you inside to rest." The king patted my shoulder gently.

"Here's an idea. Why don't all of you cut the bullshit?" I yelled towards the crowd. They all looked at me how I wanted them to, like I was unhinged, like I was the monster they had all been warned about.

Cassius grabbed my arm and shoved me past the king, dragging me with little effort down the hallway towards my room. I gave him a smug smile when he looked at me as he shoved me into my room and shut the door. His eyes were as black as mine now, his shadows forming around him in an angry cloud.

"Why are you doing this?" he said softly. "We're the only ones that care for you!"

I scoffed, standing my ground.

"You're allowed to be an asshole to me, but I can't do the same," I bellowed. He frowned at my words. "I remember things from time to time, you know. That is why I am doing this! A memory returned to me, and I saw you and your father arguing. He was commanding you to trick me into thinking you cared for me! So I would be loyal to the Crimson kingdom! Admit it. I'm just a pawn in this fucking game. You said I was a monster yourself. That I was pathetic because I was so starved for attention that you barely had to put effort into tricking me."

Recognition flicked across his face, and with it, any doubt left in my heart, any hope that I was wrong, disappeared like smoke in the wind.

"You don't have the whole story," he said gently.

"Did you say those things or not?" I glared.

"Yes," he whispered.

"Get out."

"Thea, that isn't the full truth. We–" I cut off his sentence before he could finish it by shoving him, hoping he would shut up with his lies.

"Leave!" I yelled so loudly that the walls of the castle shook.

"Please don't do this," he begged. "I can't lose you again." He looked as if I was breaking his heart. Good.

"You never had me to begin with," I hissed, hoping that if I said it with feeling, I would believe it myself.

"Damn it! Would you stop?" He took a step towards me but stopped when I started to clap loudly.

"What a great performance, Prince Cassius. You truly are convincing at playing the whole caring guy act, but I'm not interested. After these trials, I hope I never see you again."

His black eyes turned a dim gold at my words, and his angry shadows dipped low to the floor in hurt. Cassius opened his mouth to say something, but he shut it and looked at me like I had slapped him in the face.

"You can't mean that," he frowned.

"I mean it." There was a little voice in my mind begging me to stop, that I was going too far, but I *wanted* him to hurt, needed him to hurt. "I hope my memories of you will never come back. I wish I had never met you."

With those words, his whole demeanor changed. He went from the fearless captain of the king's guard to looking like a hurt and vulnerable child. He stared at me like I had said the worst thing I ever could. Part of the fire raging inside of me dimmed at the complete devastation on his face. His eyes looked over me one last time before he turned and left my room without a word.

As soon as the door shut, I could hear a commotion out in the hallway, but I stood frozen in my spot. My eyes caught my reflection in the mirror of my bathroom, and I stared at myself. My dark hair was in wild curls from the horse ride, and my green eyes had been replaced by the darkest black I'd ever seen, but what caught my attention most were the tattooed swirls along my arms and up my neck.

A monster, that's what I looked like. I turned away from myself and sat on the bed. I rested my face in my hands as I tried to calm the rage within me. He had been lying to me the whole time.

I knew I shouldn't be feeling bad though, because I wasn't falling for it anymore. Cassius' devastated face flashed back into my mind. I tried to shake the memory of it away, but it wouldn't go. As I paced back and forth, his words plagued me.

I can't lose you again.

CHAPTER 19

All eyes landed on me as I arrived at the cafeteria the next evening. I had skipped breakfast after a restless night. Every time I would fall asleep, Cassius' devastated face was there to haunt me. The talking died down when I entered, just like I had expected it to, just like it always had. Haden stood near Cassius at the door, but I didn't let my eyes linger long enough to see their reaction to me.

The tattoos still glowed on my skin, but my eyes had turned back to green at some point of my night's fitful sleep. My cloak was the only protection I had from their terrified glances. I loaded my plate with a bunch of different foods, and I headed out of the dining hall, opting to go sit in the sun outside instead of rotting away slowly in my bed.

I decided on the fountains in the gardens as a suitable spot for my lunch, and I twisted through the tall hedges until I found my favorite one. It was made from white marble and had small black stones embedded within it. Beautiful flowers had been artfully carved into it, with the water flowing from their centers to rundown into a pool full of brightly colored fish.

I sat on the wide edge and faced the fountain, tucking my legs under myself. The water trickling down drowned out any overthinking I was likely to do, unlike in the silence of my room. Slowly, I ate my food and watched the sun set far off in the distance. Part of me didn't understand all that happened yesterday. It was like I hadn't been in control of myself. Maybe that was part of the curse? All I knew was that I had been an asshole to everyone.

But they deserved it, right? At least that is what I kept telling myself. But something, like an itch in the back of my mind, wouldn't let it be. Cassius had said I didn't know the whole truth. Would knowing the truth even make a difference? There had still been times where he had acted as if I was a disgusting, pathetic beast. But if that was how he really felt, then why did he truly look so shattered at my words?

My exhausted mind was trying to make sense of a puzzle that I didn't have all the pieces for. The trials needed to be my focus, not all of this confusion. If I could get my hand on the witch's bloodstone, then I could get my memories and free all of Exile.

The soft sound of approaching footsteps pulled me from the confusion in my mind. I waited until they were closer before pulling my dagger out and turning so it was pressed hard into their throat. Haden didn't move other than to lift his hands to show me that he wasn't here to fight. I lowered my dagger but stayed ready to attack. He slowly sat on the edge of the fountain.

"I helped save you. Why would I go through that trouble just to hurt you now?" he asked, looking offended.

"You think I trust you or anyone here? You were an asshole since the day we were introduced, and your best friend kidnapped me. Why should I believe you don't want to hurt me?"

"I did at first, when I was working with Nev. He had approached me and told me why he was actually here, and I agreed to help because he was a long-time friend. Cassius caught on to who we were though, and I was easily persuaded to change teams after that night I walked you to your room. He came to find me and almost killed me because he knew I was working for Cerithia. The deal was that if I protect you, I live, and so does my family." He looked at the water of the fountain. "Cassius assigned me to keep you safe. That is my only job now."

I wasn't sure what to say to him anymore. Cassius only wanted to protect me because they wanted the witch's bloodstone and to keep me as a weapon.

"You scared the shit out of everyone yesterday," Haden sighed heavily. His eyes found mine, but he did not seem disgusted or scared of me now.

"Good. I want them to be scared of me."

"Well, you achieved that." His jaw clenched as he contemplated his next words. "Cassius isn't scared of you."

"I don't care what he thinks of me." It was a lie, and I knew it.

Haden smiled like we had been friends for a long time, and he knew I was a liar. I looked away from him to try to conceal my true feelings. Something deep in my chest felt relieved that Cassius wasn't scared of me.

"He said he's seen you like that before."

Frowning, I glanced at Haden. Cassius had seen me be a complete monster more than once. He would know I was completely unstable with my emotions.

"How upset is he with me?" I heard myself ask before I could stop it from being spoken.

"Not at all." Haden sighed and stood up. "Whatever you said yesterday completely destroyed him, but he's leaving you alone like you wanted. He just wants you to be happy, Thea."

Haden's words made my doubt about my actions creep up even more. I had hoped he would tell me that Cassius was fine and didn't care how I treated him. That would have supported my thoughts that he didn't care about me or what I thought. But what did this mean? That he cared for me just like he said he did?

"I can't imagine the position you're in," Haden said softly. "To have others know more about you than you do would be unbearable for me. But you can't keep pushing everyone away, thinking that they are your enemy. At some point, you'll have to pick the side you trust the most. What is your heart telling you, Thea?"

He wasn't expecting me to answer. I watched him look around the gardens before he finally settled his gaze on me.

"There's a dinner tomorrow night for all the contestants left. You should probably find a dress." He gave me a weak smile and left. Standing there staring at the water of the fountain, I knew that Haden was right. I couldn't keep pushing others away, worried that they were the enemy. There would be no one left to be on my side. Or maybe that was for the best. All I knew for certain was Cassius had admitted to saying those things about me.

My chest squeezed uncomfortably at the memory. I need to forget about that for now. Grabbing my plate, I took it back inside the dining hall so I could go find a dress. I paused when I heard Cassius and Haden.

"How is she?"

"Confused." Haden sighed. "Wouldn't you be?"

"Does she hate me?" Cassius whispered.

"I think she wants to, but there's something deep inside her that remembers you and won't let her."

Neither one of them said anything further, so I turned the corner and ignored their stares as I set my plate in the wash area. I still had my cloak on with the hood up, so I used it to my advantage. My eyes fell on Cassius who was openly staring at me. He looked like he hadn't slept well at all. Looking away from him, I decided to head into town and find a dress to go to a dinner that I didn't want to go to.

The weather was not as nice as it had been at lunch, but I still enjoyed it. Dark clouds moved over the Crimson kingdom and lightning lit the sky above. The stone roadway changed to a dark color when the rain wet it. I breathed in the smell, a smile on my face. In Exile, it didn't rain. My eyes closed tightly as I breathed in again. I loved this weather.

The town streets were empty when I finally arrived. The cafes, though, were full of fae laughing and enjoying each other's company during the storm. My destination was a seamstress shop I had seen, and I was hoping it was open. Luckily, the door was open as I approached, probably to let in the cool breeze. When I entered the shop, an older woman welcomed me. Her dark eyes were friendly, and her white hair was styled immaculately.

"Thea," she said warmly, like we were old friends. "What may I help you with?"

"Uh..." My arms wrapped around myself.

"You're well known around here." She smiled before concern flickered over her face. "Because of the trials, of course."

"Right. Of course. There is some fancy dinner tomorrow, so I'll need a dress. Something cheap if that's possible." I looked around at the beautiful and exquisite designs she had, worried that there was no way I'd be able to afford anything here. These dresses weren't my style either, but I wasn't sure where else I could go.

"The prince said you might show up here for clothes from time to time. He said the royal family will cover the costs." She smiled again. I must have let the confusion I felt show on my face because she rushed to explain herself. "The prince made it clear that if you need anything from town, we are not to charge you for it. He will cover the costs. He seems very fond of you."

She smiled again as I felt my cheeks redden, then urged me to follow her towards the back of the shop.

"My name is Ophelia."

"Nice to meet you." I gave her a small smile and relaxed.

"So, I'm assuming this is dinner with the royal family?"

Nodding in response, I looked around at all the different fabrics and dresses she was currently making.

"Well, then we better dress to impress." She sighed as she looked through her heaps of fabric. She brought different colors over to me and held them against me. "Black or white?"

"Black."

"The prince's favorite color," she said, giving me a knowing look. That wasn't why I chose the color, but it did make me smile slightly at her blatant remarks. The real reason I had chosen black was because I was terrified to wear white and ruin it with a stain.

She guided me to a room where she took endless measurements of me as I stood in front of the many mirrors. I zoned out at one point, and I didn't realize anything was happening until I felt a shift in the energy around me. I looked around and was instantly startled to find myself standing in front of a mirror back at the Crimson castle, as another memory escaped its bonds in my head and came forward to be seen.

□□□□□

Cassius walked up behind me as I stood in a sheer night-gown. His eyes met mine in the mirror, and he smiled at me as his arms wrapped around my stomach, pulling me flush against him.

"What are you thinking about so hard in here, my love?" He whispered into my ear before kissing the soft skin below it.

"Mostly you." I smiled back when he looked up, just enough to catch my eyes in the mirror.

He gave me a knowing look before tugging me harder against him.

"You miss me today?" he teased.

I could hardly think about anything though, as his mouth moved against my skin and his hands teased me. My eyes closed, and I let my head fall back onto his shoulder so he could have better access.

"Yes," I whispered. "I missed you."

He gave me a noise of approval as he slowly lifted my nightgown up to expose everything up to my stomach. His hands were rough from hard work, but he was gentle as they slid over my stomach and inched closer and closer to where I actually wanted him. He chuckled softly in my ear when I pushed my hips forward so he would get there faster.

"Look at how pretty you look like this."

I opened my eyes to our reflection in the mirror. Cassius was still in his black uniform, but my nightgown was sheer and white. His hands held me tightly against him as he held up my nightgown to expose me. His eyes were glowing gold, and mine were bright green. My hand reached around me and found his hair.

I turned my face, and his lips crashed into mine with so much pent-up want and need. I turned in his grip as he grabbed the back of my legs and lifted me. My legs wrapped around him as our kiss grew wild. His tongue forced its way into my mouth as his hand grabbed the back of my neck and forced me to stay still. I had hardly realized we were moving until he sat on the edge of the bed, so I was straddling him.

His hands lifted off my nightgown as my fingers fumbled with the buttons on his uniform. I tore it off of him, and my hands immediately ran over his muscled arms and chest. His tattoos swirled around every inch of him. I still caught my breath every time I saw them. Cassius was so fucking handsome. He pulled back slightly and looked at me.

"Gods, you're beautiful," he whispered and gave me a soft kiss as my hands ran through his hair. He looked at me again with a slight smile. "I thank the gods every day that I found you, Thea. That you're mine, and no one else can have you."

My heart raced in my chest at his words. His finger softly traced my face.

"I'm only yours, Cassius, forever," I whispered before his mouth crushed into mine.

□□□□□

Ophelia turning me for measurements startled me out of the memory. My heart was pounding so fast I thought she would notice. She continued to hum and take measurements without noticing my flushed cheeks or racing heart. I could practically feel the ghost of Cassius still touching my skin and kissing me deeply. He had looked like he genuinely cared for me, not like he thought I was a monster. So, which was true?

Ophelia smiled up at me as she finally finished taking measurements. "Well, darling, I should have this done tomorrow afternoon. Swing by a few hours before dinner."

"Okay. Thank you, Ophelia." Throwing my cloak back on, I lifted my hood as I left the store. It was still raining, and the clouds had blocked out nearly all the light as I followed the cobbled street back to the castle. My mind flashed with the memory of Cassius and I. The wisp was following me again, but she was pure black, so she wasn't helping me see anything in the dark.

I froze in the rain just outside the castle door for a long moment, stuck in the way he kissed me, touched me, and looked at me—even those pretty words he said. I shook my head to clear it and headed inside. Dinner had already been served, but I went to get my plate, hoping I wasn't too late.

When I walked into the dining room, it was empty. Damn it. My stomach growled loudly as I noticed Cassius stalking down the hallway towards me. His eyes were glued to mine, and I could instantly feel the heat in my cheeks as I looked at him. He could remember all of it—everything that had happened between us. Did he walk around plagued with these memories all the time? Cassius could remember every kiss, every touch, every word spoken.

Did it haunt him the way this single memory haunted me? He was still openly watching me, and I wanted to say something to him, but I didn't know what to say. I had been cruel to him, but he had been the same to me. My mind flashed to him kissing me again. He wouldn't kiss me like that if he hated me. Would he?

"I set a plate of food on your bed, just in case you're hungry." He spoke when I passed him. My feet stopped instantly at the sound of his voice, but his didn't. He kept walking down the dark hallway until he disappeared.

CHAPTER 20

"You know most ladies aren't keen on this sort of thing." Cassius smirked at me from the other side of the white circle on the ground. My smile grew bigger.

"If you're scared of me, just come out and say it," I said. He gave me a wonderful laugh in return. My eyes took in all of the happiness on his face, his pretty eyes shining brightly at me, for me.

"You don't scare me, little viper."

Giving him a big smile, I lifted my sword. He lifted his at the same time but brought it back down with a sly smile on his face. His eyes looked over me slowly.

"You want to make this interesting?"

"Sure." The tip of my sword rested in the dirt.

"Every time we earn a point, the other takes off a piece of clothing."

I glanced around the wooded area we had snuck off to so Cassius could help train me. My eyes shifted back to him with a skeptical look.

"You scared, my love?" he taunted.

"No." I gave him a fake glare. "You've got a deal."

He gave me a smirk as he lifted his sword again. I followed the movement, and we both charged at each other. Cassius was better with a sword than I was, but I gave him a challenge at least. My movements countered his high blow, but he was too quick for me to shield the next one. His blade stopped an inch from my chest.

"Point," he said, smiling brightly as he watched me lift my shirt up and over my head. Cassius showed no mercy as he charged at me again, but this time I expected it. Shielding the blow, I grabbed the dagger from my boot and stopped at his throat.

"Point," I whispered before pushing up on my toes to give him a hard kiss. He grabbed his shirt and tossed it away. My eyes lingered over the way his muscles rippled with every movement.

"Are you distracted?" he chuckled.

I glared at him and headed straight for his chest with my sword. He knocked my first blow and my second. Our swords tangled in front of us in an 'X' pattern, our faces inches apart. Cassius smiled as he leaned in to give me a teasingly deep kiss.

"If you forfeit, I'll make it worth your while." His eyes gleamed with amusement, but I just scoffed as I broke my sword away. He moved towards me quickly, and I didn't have enough time to pull my sword up. His blade stopped an inch from me.

"Point."

I huffed as I slipped off my shoes.

"Shoes?" he groaned, disappointed. "I was hoping the bodice was next." His eyes stared at me with a hunger I recognized all too well.

"Are you distracted?" I mocked him.

He smiled as he replied, "Yes."

"Good." Wasting no time, I struck, but he knew it was coming. This time we sparred longer, each of us fighting desperately to be in the lead. I dove away from him, but his sword followed me, stopping just short of impaling me.

"Point," he spoke, out of breath. Reaching the blade forward, he cut my bodice, causing it to split into two pieces. I stared at him boldly and watched his eyes turn dark. His tattooed chest rose and fell in deep breaths. Cassius tossed his sword down.

"You win," he muttered as he stalked towards me. I was tossing down my sword as his mouth descended on mine, *his hands cupping my face roughly so I couldn't pull away, not that I wanted to. I undid his trousers as we kissed, then stepped back so he could rip mine off my legs, not even giving me time to undo them properly. Our next kiss was more frantic, more needy. He shoved his trousers down only enough to free himself before lifting my leg around his waist.*

He slammed into me. The sound that fell from my lips echoed in the forest around us. Cassius' throaty groan made my body clench with lust.

"Fuck." He growled as he walked us backward. When my back hit the cold stone wall, I gasped and wrapped my arms over his shoulders, giving myself the leverage I needed to make him go deeper.

"Always so wet for me, little viper," he said, his eyes gleaming in approval. "That's my good fucking girl."

Fuck, fuck, fuck. My fingers dug into his hair as his hips hit me perfectly with each thrust. Was it possible to die from great sex? Unintelligible things were falling from my lips.

"Please," I begged, but didn't know what for.

His hand moved up my body and to my throat, where he gave me a little squeeze. His mouth started to descend onto mine, but he stopped an inch away. His hot breath fanned my face as he squeezed my throat perfectly. I tried to move forward to steal a kiss, but he held me back.

"*Cassius, please,*" *I whimpered. I was close. I needed to feel his lips on mine.* "*Please.*"

"*Fuck, I like when you beg,*" *he smiled. He leaned forward and gave me a small, teasing kiss. I growled my disapproval, and he just smiled wickedly.* "*I like those pretty noises you make, Thea, noises that belong to only me.*"

I loved it when he spoke to me like this, like he worshipped everything I did. It only pushed me closer to the edge. His mouth kissed my jaw softly just to tease me some more.

"*Cassius,*" *I warned as I closed my eyes tightly.*

He hummed against my jaw in response. I ran my fingers up through his hair and yanked him to my mouth. This time he didn't fight it. His mouth was dominating, his tongue stroking mine. He was giving me exactly what I needed to fall into my orgasm. My legs tightened around his hips as a moan ripped through me violently.

He pulled his lips from mine, muttering in my ear, "*Let me hear what I do to you, my love.*" *My orgasm ricocheted through the forest around us. My hands gripped him tightly as his thrusts increased. Cassius buried his face into my neck, biting down on my flesh as his orgasm followed.*

"*Fuck,*" *he hissed. His hands squeezed my flesh so tightly I knew I would have bruises. We stayed like that for a long moment before he loosened his grip on me and looked at me. His eyes had gone from black with lust to bright gold in satisfaction.*

Giving me a soft, lingering kiss, he set me gently on my feet. The smile he gave me was infectious as he lifted my cut bodice from the forest floor.

"So, I just need to get naked to beat you in a fight." I smiled shyly towards him.

He chuckled softly and said, "Gods, I love you," before leaning forward and catching my mouth with his.

ⵧⵧⵧⵧⵧ

My bed was soaked with sweat when my eyes shot open. The needy ache between my legs made flashes of Cassius and I course through my mind. Missing so many memories, I hadn't known if I had been with a man yet or not. But there was no question about it now.

Gods, I love you.

His voice echoed through my mind. Cassius had loved me. I couldn't deny the way my memories portrayed us. We seemed happy. We seemed genuine before. No wonder Cassius was devastated when I said those things to him. He remembered us like *that, happy and in love*. He still had all the memories of us being together, and I was sure that wasn't always a good thing. Who wants to remember a love like that when it cannot be returned?

Shaking my head to clear my thoughts, I forced myself to get up and shower quickly so I could hopefully get some food, but it was difficult to know what time it was because of the dark clouds looming outside. I realized I had forgotten my cloak, but instead of turning around to retrieve it, I hurried to get what I thought would be breakfast, but it ended up being lunch.

I had slept longer than usual, which I attributed to the overcast gloom of the storm. The other competitors' eyes lingered on me more than they had yesterday. The colorful swirls of my magic still tattooed my skin, although they had faded slightly. My cloak had prevented anyone from noticing before, but they all saw it now. Oh well, I suppose they would have noticed tonight at dinner anyway. It was better to get the shock out of the way now.

I turned around as soon as I had my plate and instantly locked eyes with Cassius. His were dim gold today, and they refused to look away from me. My cheeks flushed hot under his stare, and he must have noticed because he raised his eyebrow as if questioning why I was having this reaction. I broke eye contact and hurried towards my room so I could hide until dinner, but Cassius' footsteps following me stopped me dead in my tracks. I turned around and saw that he had stopped at least five feet away from me, keeping his distance from me like he thought I wanted.

"I'm supposed to tell all the contestants that there is a dinner tonight that is mandatory," he said, voice completely void of emotion. That was my fault, and I didn't like it. "You'll need a dress."

"I went to see Ophelia yesterday, and she insisted on making one."

A flicker of something passed over his features as my eyes drifted over his face—lips that kissed me, spoke pretty words to me, hands that touched me. Swallowing down the overwhelming memory and feelings of us, I looked back at his eyes. I could see that he wanted to say something more, but he gave me a curt nod instead before setting off down the corridor. Staring at his back, I hoped he would turn around. When he didn't, I went into my room in disappointment and sat on the bed.

I ate in the deafening silence. In Exile, I didn't have much of a choice for the silence, but I had never enjoyed it. I felt alone here, even more so now that I was getting a glimpse of what Cassius had been to me in my past. Part of me was thankful I couldn't remember all of us while I was in Exile because that seemed like it would be torture. My chest squeezed tightly. If Cassius had loved me once, then it was him who had been tortured for years by his memories. How painful it must be for him to remember that love and to watch me compete, being that close without me remembering him. We needed to talk tonight at dinner. I was still cautious of what he had said about using me, but the other memories were making that seem harder and harder to believe.

Time moved unbearably slow as I browsed my book of family crests until I thought it was an appropriate time to go see Ophelia. I grabbed my cloak and slipped it on before heading to her shop. The rain hadn't started again, and I hoped it wouldn't until I was back at the castle.

Ophelia's face lit up at my arrival. "Perfect timing: I just finished! Come, come." She ushered me into the back. I stopped immediately as the dress came into my view, still on the mannequin. I looked at her and immediately got anxious. She expected me to pull off that look?

The dress was stunning. It was black with a corset-like top and a long, loose skirt fitted with a long slit up the right side. It didn't have any shoulder straps, and the back had wonderful silver chain detailing that exposed my skin and would hold the dress tightly to me.

"It's stunning," I breathed. "But I'm not sure I can pull it off."

"Oh, nonsense." She brushed away my ridiculous thought with a wave of her hand. She pulled me forward to a pair of silver heels so I could see them. I didn't bother asking how she knew what size I was because I knew what her answer would be. Cassius had told her.

"Let's get you ready. I figured you may need some help with your hair and makeup." She gestured towards the small table with different products across it. A sense of relief washed over me as soon as she offered.

"That would be wonderful." I smiled and sat down. She busied herself right away and began undoing my braid.

"I think having your hair up will look quite pretty," she spoke softly as she lifted my hair to give me an idea. My eyes closed as she worked on my tangled curls. Ophelia was gentle, like she did this all the time. She had lit candles in her small shop that reminded me of fresh flowers.

After a short time, I opened my eyes and was impressed by the reflection that stared back at me. My normally wild hair was in a fancy updo with little silver accents that would match the shoes and back of the dress. Admiring Ophelia's work, I turned my head from side to side.

"You work miracles." I laughed. "I've never been able to tame my wild curls."

Ophelia's smile was almost motherly as she looked at me in the mirror. She patted my shoulders before coming to sit in front of me.

"Have you done this with me before?" I whispered.

Her eyes looked surprised at my question. She gave me a big smile in return.

"A very long time ago," she admitted. "You said the same thing back then that you just said now." Her eyes zoned out for a moment, like she was remembering our earlier exchange.

As Ophelia began applying my make-up, she told me how she and her husband had come here from the kingdom of Cerithia many years ago. Her husband had been sick for a long time and ended up passing away, leaving her on her own. They didn't have any kids, but she still had many family members here to help keep the loneliness away. I just relaxed and listened to her chatter away, and before long she was done.

I gazed at the mirror in front of me and hardly recognized myself. Ophelia hadn't overdone the amount of makeup, but she knew how to highlight my best features. My eyes were bright and vibrant green against the dark smokiness of the lid, and my lips were a dark, sultry red that made them look plumper and more feminine. I couldn't believe how soft and scar-free my pale skin looked.

"You'll take their breath away," she said as she met my eyes in the mirror. "You better get your dress and run along for dinner before this rain starts up."

Standing, I felt an overwhelming sense of tenderness for this woman in front of me. I wrapped my strong arms around her tightly, and her frail ones held me tightly back.

"It's been quite some time since I've had one of your wonderful hugs." I noticed the tears gathered in her eyes as she pulled back. "Let me get the dress packed up."

She moved around me and neatly put the dress in a bag with the heels. I gave her one last thanks as I left and hurried back towards the castle. Dinner would be starting soon, and I still had to figure out how to get this thing on. When I locked the door to my room, I turned to the dress sitting in the bag on my bed and approached it as if it would attack me.

When I pulled it out, I was surprised at how soft the fabric was—some sort of silk. I held it against me and glanced in the mirror. Sighing heavily, I started undressing. What if this looked absolutely horrific? This was meant for a lady, and I was not anything of the sort. Standing nearly naked, I stared at the dress, trying to determine how I could get in it.

Ophelia had made it to hug me so perfectly that I had to fight to get it over my ample chest. I struggled so much to slip into it that I felt like I had run up a mountain once it was on. I even jumped up and down to test if it would flash my breasts to everyone if I moved wrong. I was pleasantly surprised when they stayed put, and not only that, but Ophelia also had to have worked some magic because they were tastefully out on display. I turned and admired the chain accent, but I hadn't realized how much of my back was going to be exposed. This dress took it to a whole other level.

After slipping on silver heels, I stood in front of the mirror and took in the whole look. It was incredible. I could barely recognize myself. My heart was pounding in my chest. Would Cassius like this? Would he tell me how pretty I looked? I moved my right leg forward, exposing the slit that ran up to my hip.

I felt pretty.

I grabbed my dagger and tied it to my upper thigh, not trusting anybody here enough to go unarmed. Sucking in one last deep breath, I summoned my courage and headed out of my room. I could tell by the eerie silence in the dorms that the other contestants were likely already there. My nerves were in full force as I walked through the castle, thinking of how much of me was exposed. When I heard the soft chatter from the king's great room, I took a moment to catch my breath. My heart slammed violently in my chest, and my stomach churned in anxious excitement at the thought of Cassius' reaction. After all, his was the only reaction I cared about.

The room had been decorated in the same over-the-top zealous details as last time. It still took my breath away, even though I had seen it all before.

"Thea, my dear, you look marvelous," the king called from where he stood. No one was seated. Instead, they were all standing as if waiting for me to arrive. At the king's words, everybody turned to me and stared with surprise. I gave him a small smile as I moved towards Cassius so I could sit where I had last time. I was crushed though, as Cassius hardly spared me a glance. His eyes only looked at me briefly before instantly turning away. I tried to keep my face set as the excitement I had felt for his reaction died slowly in my chest.

It was then replaced by irritation when I saw who he had turned to talk with. The stunning woman from the gardens was glaring at me; they spoke to each other. I didn't know she was back in Crimson.

"Let's be seated," the king said, gesturing to the seats.

The woman practically shoved me out of the way when I went to sit next to Cassius.

"Cassius wants me to sit next to him." She batted her pretty blue eyes at me. He looked at me and then at the woman before pulling out the chair for her to sit in.

I glanced around the table and saw an open seat next to the man who had been in the gardens with them that day.

Walking around the table, I sat in the seat directly across from Cassius, but I didn't bother looking at him.

"You look absolutely stunning." The man next to me smiled brightly and seemed friendly. He shared similar features as the woman, and I wondered if they were siblings.

"You look good for a savage," the woman across the table scoffed. My eyes glanced up at her, and I could see Cassius staring at me and the man.

"I see they let you out in public without gagging you first," I retorted.

The king spit his wine back into his glass as he choked, and Haden chuckled from down the table.

"You may address me as Princess Flora," she snipped out her title like I gave a shit who she was.

"I will do no such thing. You are not my princess."

Her eyes glanced at the man who sat next to me like he was supposed to stop me from saying such things. He just shrugged his shoulders with a soft chuckle.

"You started it, Flora."

My eyes glanced at Cassius, who was looking at me with an odd expression. His gaze shifted from me to the man next to me before he pressed his lips into a thin line of disapproval. I rolled my eyes so he could see. He had let *her* take my seat next to him, so he couldn't be irritated by this.

The king's advisor, Lavtan, began talking to the table about future events coming up at the castle and how everyone should be so excited. In all honesty, I tuned out most of what he said. That is, until Lavtan mentioned finding Cassius a wife and hoping Flora would be at the top of the list. As soon as he said those words, my insides coiled in jealousy. He didn't belong with a woman like that. He belonged with a woman who could fight and hold her own. Didn't he?

I felt eyes shift to me at the announcement, but I refused to stop staring at the wine glass in front of me. I put on my best face of indifference because Cassius hadn't refused the man's idea. The woman was a stark contrast to me. Maybe she was what he wanted to settle down with. She was a princess for fuck's sake.

"Lavtan, you know Cassius' opinions on marriage," the king said disapprovingly.

"I do not think Flora and I would make a good pair." Cassius glared at Lavtan. "I have no desire to marry her."

Flora's scoff had my eyes shifting to her. A smile escaped me at his declaration. "Then why am I here, Cassius?" She ground out.

"I don't know. I did not invite you, Flora." Cassius sighed heavily before his eyes finally looked at me. "My guess is Lavtan invited you, just like he did last time."

Flora was fuming as her pretty eyes glared daggers at her plate of food.

I realized then that the man next to me had shifted closer to me at some point. His thigh pressed up against mine, and I shifted so he wasn't touching me anymore. I grabbed my wine and sipped it but paused when the man's hand rested on my exposed knee. Immediately I shoved his hand off, but he grabbed me again and squeezed so hard I nearly cried out at the pain.

No one noticed what was happening because Lavtan was still talking about Flora and Cassius merging two kingdoms without caring that Cassius had already rejected his idea. I reached below the table and yanked his hand away, this time pulling his fingers back so forcefully that he had no choice but to remove his sweaty hand from me. I stood quickly, my chair making a foul noise on the floor, halting the conversations around me. I glanced down the table and noticed there was an open seat next to Cassius' siblings.

"Thea?" the king questioned.

"I'm going to move to the end of the table," I muttered softly.

"Nonsense. That's where the children are seated," he chuckled.

"Well, I would rather be in the company of children than be seated next to a pig who can't keep his hands to himself." I laced every word with venom as I glared at the man next to me.

"Caleel?" the king questioned. "Are you making Thea uncomfortable by touching her?" I glanced at Cassius, whose eyes now swirled with blackness. His dark tendrils of shadows slowly crept towards us.

"Does it matter?" Caleel scoffed. "Women who dress like that are hoping to catch the attention of a male like me."

"Excuse me?" Cassius stood up and slammed his palm down on the table, making everyone jump at the clanking of the dishes. "If you touch her again, I will cut off both of your hands and send them to your parents." Caleel looked to Cassius and then at me.

"Sorry, Cassius, I didn't realize she was your whore." Caleel smirked as he got up, drawing his sword. Within a second, he had it out and held against Cassius' throat across the table. Before Cassius could move though, the king stood up with his hands raised.

"Now, now, let's not make any rash decisions," the king pleaded.

Caleel smiled at Cassius like the smug prick he was. I stood there watching as he pushed the sword harder into

Cassius' neck, causing a droplet of blood to run down from the tip of the blade. Cassius stared at Caleel with his fists tightly at his sides. Flora was frazzled as she watched it unfold. Possessiveness unfurled in me when I saw Cassius bleed, and a deep need to protect what was mine overtook me. Using my foot on the chair Caleel had scooted out, I slid it so hard into the side of his legs that he lost his balance with the sword.

He caught himself on the table, but I was already moving behind him. Before he could stand up, I grabbed a fist full of his hair and pulled it so hard that he was staring at the ceiling. My dagger pressed to his throat, and I noticed that Cassius was watching me closely.

"Drop the sword," I demanded. When he refused, I moved my dagger and slammed his face down into the plates on the table, shattering them. The room was dead silent besides Caleel's heavy breathing and small whimpers of pain. He dropped the sword as I yanked him up by his hair again. My blade pressed harder into his throat. My eyes shifted around the room to horrified looks. No one dared move or say a word to me.

"If you ever point a weapon at Cassius again, I will fill our dinner bowls with your blood and send only your head back to your kingdom." I hissed loudly. "Now apologize to him for cutting him."

Cassius stood there watching me without moving a muscle.

"I'm sorry, Cassius," he whimpered like the coward he was.

"Very good," I mocked him. I spun my dagger in my fingers a few times and then brought it down hard, stabbing his hand to the table. His pained sobs mixed with the gasps of the other diners and echoed around the dining hall. "That's for thinking you can touch something that doesn't belong to you."

I grabbed my dagger and yanked it from his hand before wiping his blood on the shoulder of the nice jacket he wore. Stepping forward, I let my leg fall out of the slit of my dress as I put the dagger back into its place. Cassius' eyes stared openly at my exposed leg. Any gold that had been present in his eyes was gone, replaced by an inky blackness that I was getting to know well.

"Caleel and Flora, your time visiting is over. You are not welcome back," the king hissed. "I should have your head for daring to hurt my son."

They scuttled away out of the room, and I held my head high as I looked around. Haden was smiling brightly at me like it had been great entertainment. My eyes shifted to Cassius, who stood angrily by the table. The dark tendrils of shadows swirled around him. No one said anything.

His eyes looked me over one final time before turning and walking out of the room. I followed him without thinking. He must have heard me though, because he stopped dead in his tracks but didn't turn towards me.

"Cassius-" My words were cut off.

"Do not follow me," he demanded. "It's you I am trying to escape from."

I hated that I didn't know if his warning was malicious or not. He likely hated me after everything I had said to him, and I couldn't blame him, not after I had seen us in a new light with the returning memories plaguing me. Maybe I should apologize, but my throat caught any words that might have escaped. He was deathly still, like he was listening for my decision to either leave or try to come to him.

"Go enjoy dinner," he spoke softly before turning and walking down the darkened hallway. But I wasn't hungry, and I most definitely was not going back into that room after what had just happened. I hadn't even wanted to come to this dinner in the first place, and the only reason I did come had just walked away from me. He couldn't even stand to be in the same room as me. Gods, I must have looked psychotic to act so possessive and jealous during dinner. With my emotions threatening to overwhelm me, I turned quickly on my heels and went to my room. As soon as my door shut behind me, I tore the fancy dress from my body. I tossed it and the shoes away from me as if they were the reason I was upset.

I had hurt him. I had said mean and nasty things to him. I had no right to be upset by his dismissal of me. He probably hates me now. *Gods, I love you.* His voice echoed in my broken and useless mind. I laid down to try and sleep, but I was too preoccupied with what memories would plague me once I did. Would it show more happiness, or would it show me nothing? I stared at the dark ceiling and let the tears slowly leak out of my eyes, knowing that I was not going to get any rest that night.

CHAPTER 21

I sat on the edge of my bed, staring at my daggers. Then my eyes shifted to the bow and arrows that still sat in the corner from when I saved Cassius. What I needed was to disappear for the day and be alone. I had to try and make sense of this jumbled mess inside of my head. If that was even possible, I snorted to myself. How could I piece together a puzzle when I had less than half the pieces?

I couldn't. The only thing I could do was rely on the words of others to understand my own life, and I struggled with that. I struggled to trust anyone who tried to be friendly to me, and now I had to trust that they would be honest with me. My chest clenched with uncertainty. Would I ever know the full truth of any of this? I wanted to believe Cassius and everyone else here, but I wasn't a fool and understood how easily they could manipulate me if they wanted.

My clothes itched as I slipped them on. These walls and thoughts were suffocating me slowly. Opening the door to my room, I peeked my head out slowly. I saw no one, and not a sound could be heard. I knew it was so early that most people would still be in bed, but the complete silence of the castle unsettled me. I hurried to the front doors and closed them softly behind me, then crossed the yard to the stables. Once inside, I looked around and spotted Onyx, Cassius' beautiful black horse. Smiling, I approached him slowly with my hand out, allowing him a chance to recognize my scent. He nuzzled my palm and allowed me to stroke my chest for a moment, then stayed calm while I saddled him. I led him through the yard and had just jumped into his saddle when I heard the castle doors bang open behind me, causing my head to whip around.

Cassius emerged with three other guards. Perfect timing. He stood conversing with his fellow soldiers, looking around the yard. His words stopped abruptly though, as he spotted me on top of his horse. He took a step towards me, but I flicked the reins, and his horse darted into the woods, leaving Cassius behind. As he ran, I leaned far forward so the branches would not hit me, and my cloak flew freely in the breeze behind me. Onyx wouldn't take any directions from me, ignoring my pull on the reins and cues to turn. I didn't know where the horse insisted on taking me, but he seemed to have his own destination in mind.

I turned my head when I heard galloping behind me to see that Cassius was coming up behind us. The horse he rode was white as clouds and didn't fit him in the slightest. I smirked to myself at the sight of the ill-fitting horse and his big frame. I turned forward, not seeing anyone else following me. Onyx slowed to a steady trot before a clearing emerged.

My breath caught when I realized where we were. There was still a white circle on the ground, but it was overgrown with grass and shrubs. My eyes peered to the left where the stone wall stood, unchanged from the memory of Cassius taking me against it. The horse had brought me to where Cassius and I used to train together. Obviously, he had made this trip many times before. I turned when I heard the other horse reach the clearing and saw Cassius arrive. He stopped and clambered off his mount awkwardly, his size making it hard to dismount. He walked up to me, his feet crunching in the gravel, and yanked me off the horse, placing me down in front of him. His shadows curled behind him like black wings, and his eyes swirled with irritation.

"What are you doing?" he hissed. "You stole my horse?"

"I would have brought him back," I sighed. "Why did you follow me?" I breathed heavily, trying to show my annoyance.

"You snuck out of the castle at an ungodly hour and stole a horse. I was making sure you weren't trying to leave the trials."

His black shadows bowed slightly in defeat as he said what worried him. His eyes swam with emotions that I should have been able to read but couldn't. I didn't even trust myself enough to believe the thoughts going through my head. Cassius' hands still gripped my arms as we stood there staring at each other.

"I just wanted a day to myself," I whispered.

"You didn't come back to dinner last night." It was a statement, but a question lingered within it. I looked away from him and towards the horses behind him.

"I only went to that stupid dinner so I could see you," I said defeatedly. Tell him the truth, I told myself. Tell him what you've been seeing about the two of you. "And you were too busy with Flora, and after she left, you didn't care to stay. You ran from me."

I gave him a hard glare, but his eyes held no distaste or malice. They softened as he listened to my reasoning.

"You said you hate me, yet you protect me from a man with a knife to my throat. You tell him if he ever harms me, you will send his head back to his kingdom. You get jealous when they mention me taking a bride. I don't know what you're thinking inside of here," he pointed at my forehead. "I left dinner, but I came back. I just needed to not be near you for a moment."

He stepped past me and rubbed his hands down his face in defeat. The wisp was dancing around our horses in her dark green flames. She hadn't been around lately, or maybe I had been too stuck in my own head to notice.

"Your possessiveness and desire to protect me were too much. It's torture to have you act like you care for me, but also hate me just as much." His eyes shifted to me, and I watched as they turned dark.

"Well, now you know how I feel," I answered back. He frowned at me but didn't say anything for a long moment.

"I left so that I could collect myself, because all I wanted to do was slide my hand up the slit of that dress and show you how fucking good we are together. It is killing me that you might hate me, Thea, that you don't remember us. I pray to the gods I don't believe in that you will find your way back to me, because I can't do this without you. I don't want to do this without you."

His eyes stared into mine. "I'm lost without you."

My heart beat hard in my chest because Cassius looked so... heartbroken. His pain made my body ache. Something inside of me felt the same—the part of me still lost somewhere deep in my forgotten memories, the part of me that remembered him.

"We've been here before," I whispered and moved my hand around the white circle where we sparred in my memory. His eyes didn't move from mine. The tug that I felt deep within me when he was near me pulled tightly in my chest, like it wanted me to go near him. I took a step forward.

His chest heaved in short puffy breaths as his hands clenched into fists to his sides. "How do you know that?"

"Sometimes I have small flashes of memories, little moments about you and me." Admitting it felt good. "We trained here. You were so playful with me, so different from that first memory I had of you."

Sadness flickered across his handsome features again. He glanced around the clearing and focused on the wall for a moment, and I wondered if that was the first thing that he thought of too. How many times have we done that here?

"So, I guess I just need to get naked to beat you in a fight?" A smile tugged at my lips as I repeated my past words to him. His head snapped to mine quickly at recognition of the phrase.

"You remember that?" His voice was strained.

"Yes." I nodded. "You've been haunting my every dream and waking thought since I said those horrible things to you. I wonder if my heart is trying to help me understand who you are to me and how good we were together, because it remembers even if my mind doesn't."

He stepped towards me without hesitation.

"I've missed you so fucking much," he whispered as his fingers moved the hair from my face gently. "I thought it would kill me when you disappeared the first time. Time slowed to an unbearable pace, and I felt so empty that I thought my heart would shrivel and fade away without you. Then I heard you calling out to me as I slept. I thought I had completely gone mad without you, but I followed your voice, calling out to me softly in my dream. I realized it was you, but you didn't seem to know who I was, so I was content just watching you. Just being near you would have been enough to live out my life."

"I could never understand why I felt safe when you were in my dreams. I never said anything. I was too scared that you would leave and not come back." I admitted. His hand cupped the side of my face, warming it as the chill from the storm still lingered.

"But you still said those horrible things about me," I whispered so softly I didn't know if he had heard.

"Your curse keeps me from telling you too much information. It's a form of punishment for me and you." His golden eyes shifted between my green eyes as he frowned. "I'll try to tell you, but I don't know how much I can say."

I nodded in understanding.

"My father and I had intended for others to hear that conversation, not you, but you always were good at sneaking out and when I asked you to stay." He chuckled softly. "Someone was feeding Cerithia information from our castle, and we were worried that they would tell Cerithia that you were no longer a prisoner, so we tried to make it seem like you were unwanted by us. We thought we could hide..."

His words were cut off suddenly, and I frowned when he tried to speak again, but nothing came out. He groaned in pain when he tried again. I hurried to him, trying to heal him with magic, but it did nothing to ease him. Cassius held up his hand as if to say he needed a moment. I watched him carefully as he finally took in a full breath.

"Prisoner?"

"You started as a prisoner here." He watched me for a reaction. Flashes of the dying guardsman muttering my name outside of Exile flashed into my mind. It made sense now how he knew who I was. "Not that we could contain your powers. You and I had a history before that, and you didn't remain a prisoner for long."

"What kind of history?" My heart was pounding in my chest with all this new information. I wanted more. I wanted everything. He gave me a wicked smile that made my stomach clench with anticipation.

"A history that got us into this mess." Cassius' smile dropped. "We were born as enemies and actually tried to kill each other before I finally took you as a prisoner. Raised to hate each other but destined to love one another."

I paused at the information. So, if we were born enemies, then I must be... Cerithian. Fragments of the puzzle in my mind started piecing together.

"How did that happen if we were enemies?"

"I can't tell you. I've tried already," he sighed, irritated.

"And what is your involvement with the elitist magic holders?" It was a question that had plagued me every day for as long as I could remember. Who was responsible for Exile?

"It is forbidden to talk about. The curse will hurt me if I even try to mention it. I tried the first year you came back for the trials, and I was bedridden for three days."

So many thoughts and questions swirled in my mind that I didn't know what to ask or what to say. This was more than anything I could have thought—so complicated. I was in love with my enemy, and he was in love with me too. We had caused this curse and mess. The kingdom of Cerithia must hate me.

"Let's continue this conversation at our favorite place." He grabbed my hand and helped me onto his horse before climbing on behind me. The white horse with a half-black face followed us.

"She's yours," he whispered. "Her name is Kaida. You probably hurt her feelings when you took my horse instead." I looked at her as she followed next to us contently. She had been the only horse who hadn't been spooked by me when Cassius and his men had saved me from Nev. Even in my dark form, she had seemed unbothered.

I noticed that Wisp was following closely, still with her dark green flames. She was happy.

Cassius led the horses through the thin forest for a little bit before a clearing welcomed us. A field of flowers greeted us on top of a knolly hilltop. Beautiful shades of red and orange blanketed the grass as we climbed down from the horse. I rubbed the face of my horse to apologize for not taking her. She gave me a nudge as if to say it was ok.

Cassius grabbed my hand and led me toward the cliffside. My eyes took in the sheer drop and the waterfall that cleaved the landscape, booming with a power that rattled me to my bones. Its water was so blue that it gave the illusion that the sky was falling over the cliffside. Mist formed in the sunlight, creating multiple rainbows in the ravine. My mouth gaped open at the beauty of this hidden place. Cassius squeezed my hand tightly.

"There are some perks to you not remembering anything." He smiled softly at me. "I get to witness all the firsts again—the first kiss, the first look of lust, the first look of our favorite place. You and I are the only ones who know of this. We found it by accident, and your face was in awe of it, just like it is now."

"It's stunning." I smiled at him.

"You haven't smiled like that in years." The weather here was colder due to the waterfall. I tugged my cloak around me tightly, and Cassius pulled me closer to him, so I was tucked under his arm.

"When I lived in Exile, I had always been so lonely. It didn't matter who was around me; I felt incomplete. I prefer to be by myself most of the time, and I always thought it was because I was so lonely in my past. Now I wonder if it's because I wanted your company. I felt lonely because no one else could compare to you. Even in my dreams, I felt less lonely with you lingering in the shadows. Maybe my heart knew that I wouldn't feel better until you were near me again."

Cassius was still for a long moment, and I thought maybe I had said too much. But it was true. I felt lonely every time I watched him walk away from me or didn't see him. His presence alone could ground me, heal me, and tame me.

I stared up at him when he didn't say anything back and met his golden eyes. He was watching me with a strange expression on his face, almost like I had hung the stars in the sky, and it made me suck in a breath at the sight of him. Then he leaned down, kissing me softly for a moment, before he lost his restraint. With a growl, his lips dominated mine, and his hands pulled me to him. I molded myself against his body as if we were two pieces that fit perfectly together. His tattooed hands cupped my face as his mouth devoured me, and his tongue danced with mine, teasing me.

All I could think about was how hard he felt against me. I pulled him to my mouth so that he couldn't pull away. He only groaned in approval as I pushed harder against him. His shadows burst out around us like they couldn't help it, but then I realized my fire mist was tangling with them as well. My cloak hit the ground as soon as I untied it. Cassius stared at me surprised, but before he could object, I pulled my shirt up and off. I needed him now. His eyes cascaded over me slowly, but frantically.

"Remind me how good we are together," I demanded. It was the only encouragement he needed. My cloak lay beneath me as Cassius lowered us to the ground, then he tore his shirt off, flinging it away in his hurry. His warm skin glided against mine as he kissed me deeply. I tore my mouth from him so I could see his face. He kneeled back as I sat up and ran my fingers over his tattooed chest. He was perfect.

A wide smile spread over his face when I couldn't keep my hands to myself. My hands stopped their exploration when I noticed something entwined in the dark swirled tattoos. It was a dark green 'T' tattooed above his heart with a viper coiled around it. My eyes watched as his smile faded.

"My little viper," was all he whispered in response. I grabbed him and pulled him back on top of me. Need flooded my body as his hands moved over my skin as if he had missed just being able to touch me. I hadn't worn a bodice, so his hands squeezed my breasts before he kissed down my jaw to my chest. The stubble on his chin scrapped my skin, setting it on fire with need. I focused on the darkened sky above us, my heart beating wildly as his warm mouth closed around my nipple. The teasing flick of his tongue made me moan into the echoing of the waterfall. Every touch was addictive, making me want more.

I could feel him smile against me as he moved to the other nipple to tease it. My hands tangled in his dark hair as he touched me, like he knew what I needed more than I did. His hand slipped into the band of my trousers, and he hummed his approval when he realized how wet I was already. My hips bucked up to meet his fingers as he grazed my sensitive body. He looked up at me with black and golden swirls in his eyes, his thumb circling my clit.

"You always were so ready for me, little viper," he purred while tugging my clothes off. Lying naked in a field full of flowers with Cassius looking at me like I was the prettiest thing he'd ever seen was a dream. His eyes turned completely black as he admired me. His shadows moved over me, warming where they caressed. "You haunt me, Thea. The way you feel, the way you taste, the noises you make are my undoing." His fingers gently caressed my skin as his eyes softened.

His words wrapped around me as his hands smoothed over my thighs before he tugged me by the hips down to where he had freed himself. My fire pulsed violently through me with anticipation. I could feel my eyes burning as I caught sight of us. Pausing when he caught my fiery eyes, he smiled so brightly that I felt my heart squeeze with something more than lust. He *liked* my fire and power. He didn't think I was a monster.

"As much as I would love to savor this moment, I can't control myself, Thea." Cassius looked at me as if to say he couldn't stand not being inside of me at this very moment. His hand stroked down his cock as he stared at me.

"Please," I choked out.

He leaned forward onto his hands on either side of my head, caging me in with his tattooed muscles. I could feel him teasing me. I lifted my hips, and the tip of his cock sank into me, making him let out a soft growl at the small sensation.

He pulled back out before sliding into me in one fast, swift movement. A sound fell from my lips that couldn't be drowned out by the waterfall. Pure pleasure pulsed from me.

"Fuck," Cassius hissed as he waited a moment. "The memories of us don't compare to this," he whispered. His mouth found mine, and he thrust his tongue inside of it, trying to be inside me in any way that he could. I moaned against him, causing his hips to pick up the pace until he was almost slamming into me. There was nothing gentle about this. All the years of pent-up tension were releasing from Cassius. His tattooed hand came up and squeezed my jaw tightly as his mouth dominated mine, his tongue circled mine in the rhythm of his thrusts. He pulled his face away so he could watch mine as I fell completely apart beneath him.

"Such pretty noises, Thea," he groaned possessively. "All for me."

"Yes." I breathed, nearly choking on it as he slammed into me at a pace that would surely kill me.

"Mine." It was so soft I nearly missed it. My stomach clenched tightly as my orgasm crested at the sight of him losing control over me. "Fuck, you look so fucking perfect under me, my love." My fingers dug into his flesh, yanking him down to me, and my legs tightened around him as my orgasm exploded through me, releasing a fiery mist into the sky above. My eyes tightened as pleasure like I had never felt before ricocheted through me, turning me inside out. A cry from deep inside of me tore loose, drowning in the noise of the waterfall. He had buried his face into my neck, biting me roughly before he leaned up on his hands and watched my face as his hips slammed into me, chasing the pleasure he desperately needed. His eyes locked onto mine.

Leaning back, he grabbed my hips, moving me so fast against him that I was quickly climbing into bliss again. My mouth fell open, but nothing came from it.

"Again," Cassius demanded, as if he could feel I was holding out a little longer. "Let the forest around us hear those screams for me. I want the whole realm to hear you, Thea. Let them know who you belong to."

His voice, his words, his urgency were my undoing as the most feral scream ripped from my chest. I couldn't hear anything but his name being called into the sky like he had asked for. The only thing that drowned me out was the growl of pleasure that fell from him as he found his release with me. I swore I felt the ground beneath us shake at his power. For that one raw, primal moment, everything felt right, like I was exactly where I was supposed to be. I didn't want it to end.

CHAPTER 22

Cassius collapsed on top of me. Our breathing was frantic as we lay in a heap of pleasure in the field of flowers. He rolled off of me but pulled me to him, so I was lying naked across him, feeling the thumping of his heartbeat as it calmed down. as I sat up to look at him.

I shoved him onto his back so I could straddle him. His black eyes stared at me, taking in my every move. His hand came up and brushed my wild curls away from my face. My vision pulsed with a red haze, letting me know my eyes were still the color of fire.

"So, that's how good we are together." I smiled.

He nodded and gave me a sly smile in return.

"How long has it been since we've done this?" I looked down at him as I traced the 'T' over his heart.

A look of sadness crosses his beautiful features. "Six years. The first year you came to the trials, we reconnected, but you didn't know who I was in the slightest, and you were eliminated before the second trial."

I saw his wheels turning in his mind like he wanted to ask or say something, but he wasn't sure if he should.

"Just ask whatever you are thinking." My voice wavered, worried it would be something bad.

"Six years is a long time. I wouldn't be upset if there had been others besides me." It wasn't a question, but he wanted an answer.

I shook my head no.

"Up until a few days ago, I assumed I was a virgin."

His laugh filled the air around us. I swatted his chest, and he smiled up at me with deep emotion in his eyes.

"There's been no one else for me either."

I wasn't going to ask because I didn't want to know if someone else got this when I wasn't here to give it to him.

"A virgin, huh?" He tried to hide his smirk as his hands gripped my hips softly. "Was it a shock to see those memories of us?"

"Yes." I looked away from his face, trying to hide the emotions bubbling up, but he turned it back. "I don't want to forget this again."

"I don't want you to, either."

"How do you do this every year, knowing I won't re-member you?" I traced the 'T' on his chest again, as if I could burn it into my memory.

"Your mind might not remember me, but your heart does, and that is enough for me. Every trial you've come to, you've sought me out, asking questions about me, staring at me a little too long, smiling at me, and finding reasons to be near me," he confessed. "It's like the curse couldn't take your desire for me away from you, and it shows me with every little thing you do."

"But you wanted to stay away from me this time."

"I've never tried to actually stay away from you before, and I thought it would help you not to be so distracted by your feelings for me that it would keep you from doing anything reckless—like save me from those men in the forest. But obviously it didn't work."

Something shifted into place in my mind.

"That's why you were so upset that I had come to help you. You didn't want me to get hurt and not compete in the trials." He nodded, leaning forward and kissing me softly. "When I heard you were missing, my mind went crazy, like I didn't have a choice but to go to you. No one could have stopped me." Pausing, I watched his face soften at my words. "Why did you tell me to leave your room?"

"I was still so scared that I would lose you again. I'm sorry for making you feel that way, for saying what I did, and for making you think that I hated you and wanted you away from me." His eyes looked up to mine. "I thought it was a dream when I woke up to you in bed with me, but then you were actually there. At first, I was confused. But honestly, I felt that I needed to keep you away from me so you wouldn't focus on me instead of the trials. It has happened before, and I didn't want to chance it happening again. I figured I could hold off until you were done with the trials, and then we'd have a lifetime together."

The rain started falling around us, cutting off our conversation as we hurried to get dressed. Cassius pulled me onto Onyx with him, and Kaida followed closely. He wrapped one arm around me and his other handheld the reins as we darted through the forest. I laughed as it soaked through our clothing, and his arm holding me squeezed me tightly.

"You did always love the rain," he said from behind me. I turned my face towards him and smiled brightly before crushing my lips to his. The horse slowed down as Cassius' hand dropped the reins so he could pull me closer. He twisted me so I was facing him, my legs straddling his hips. The horse kept walking at a slow pace as Cassius' hands tugged my hips, so I was rubbing against his hard length.

"Home, let's get home first," he groaned as he grabbed the reins and urged his horse to go faster. I kissed him softly before moving down his jaw and neck. He let out a soft sigh as I moved my hips slowly against him, teasing him. I smiled when his fingers tangled in my hair and pulled me back so he could find my mouth and devour it with his.

He held the kiss for the whole ride back and broke it only because the horses walked into the stables. Cassius practically dragged me to the castle doors before stopping, as if he had a sudden thought.

"Stay with me in our room."

Our room.

"Yes."

He gave me a lopsided smile as he dragged me through the castle hallways. We passed the room I had been to before then walked up a long spiral staircase I hadn't seen. When we reached the top of the stairs, I saw separate living quarters from the rest of the castle. There was a large living area with a nice kitchen and dining room off the side. It was mostly decorated in forest greens. I couldn't admire much about it as Cassius dragged me quickly to the left. When we entered the last door at the end of the hallway, I froze. I had been here before. The mirrors I had been standing in front of in my memory were to the left of the giant four-poster bed frame. The bed had beautiful dark green bedding and accents in off-white.

"You like it?" Cassius smiled. "You should. You picked out everything in here," he said, lightly chuckling.

"I had a memory of us here not that long ago," I replied. "I was standing in front of the mirror, and you had come in being extra flirtatious."

Cassius' eyes shined a bright gold, like he was happy to know I remembered something else. The look had my heart racing with deep emotions.

"You told me you thanked the gods above that you found me."

"I still thank them, even if I don't believe in them like I did before," he whispered. Cassius paused before he continued. "I prayed to gods I don't believe in, and I begged the stars above that they let you choose me to love, Thea. That has been my only prayer since I first laid eyes on you."

I was the one to move first. My strides towards him were swift. As soon as my mouth touched his, he had me up in the air so my legs could wrap around him, and we fell to the bed in a messy, chaotic heap. Our clothes were flung to the floor like we hadn't touched each other in years, even though it had only been minutes. I had never felt a burning need like this.

Cassius slid to the floor to kneel between my knees. His hands undid my boots, my daggers clanking to the floor. His smile was contagious when he met my eyes. He gripped the waistband of my trousers, and I was naked with one swift pull. His rough hands ran over my thighs before gripping them to spread them, so I was completely exposed to him.

I knew I should feel embarrassed or nervous, but he looked at me like I was a sight to behold. Sitting up on my elbows, I watched as his head descended. My legs threatened to close tightly when he ran his soft tongue along my pussy. When he knew I would keep my legs open for him, he let go of them and ran his fingers over me before plunging them into me as his mouth licked and devoured me, making me moan loudly into the space of our bedroom.

My hands gripped his hair as he wrapped his arms around my thighs and hauled me against his face completely. His tongue shoved into me, hot and demanding.

"Cassius," I warned.

"You wanted me, my love, so you'll take everything I give you." That was the only warning he gave before I came with a breath-stealing orgasm. I had fallen back on the bed with my hands tangled even into his hair as I held him in place. As my hips moved across his mouth and tongue, I was greedy for more as I came. Cassius was crawling on top of me before my orgasm finished, his lips swollen and glistening from me. His tongue assaulted my mouth in the same fashion as it had my clit.

I lifted my hips up to get him to slip into me, but he just smiled against my mouth as he pulled far enough away that I couldn't. A frustrated sigh left me.

"So eager, my love?"

My heart pounded at the nickname he called me. As if he could hear its beat pick up the pace, he stopped smiling. His hand ran up my stomach until it was over my heart.

"This is my favorite thing—hearing this, feeling this beat in your chest for me."

I didn't know why tears sprang into my eyes as he felt my erratic heart beating, but it seemed important that he said that.

"I like it when you call me that," I confessed.

"My love?" Cassius smiled when I nodded yes. He leaned down and kissed me softly, his tongue dancing lazily with mine. He wasn't rushed. Cassius was controlled and calculated in every move, every caress of his hands. He pushed his hips into mine and filled me at a deliciously slow pace. I could hardly catch my breath when he finished pushing completely inside of me. His forehead rested on mine as he slowly pulled back and then filled me again. He was savoring this. I wanted to savor this moment, but I wouldn't remember it if I didn't complete the trials. Tears sprang to my eyes at the thought.

Cassius shifted us and rolled so I was sitting on top. His hands gripped my hips tightly as I lifted and sank back down on him. His eyes stared at mine.

"Tell me what you're thinking," he whispered.

"That I don't want to forget this. That I don't know how I ever could forget any of this when it feels so right." I moaned when he yanked me down hard.

"You look so pretty sliding down my cock, Thea." He groaned when I picked up my pace. His eyes glanced down to where he slid into me. "Fuck." He threw his head back onto the pillows and watched my face.

"What are you thinking about?" My hands splayed over his tattooed chest as I slowly sank down his impressive length.

"How much I love you." He didn't miss a beat as he spoke, but I stopped moving. "This is one of those firsts that I don't mind having again." He smiled at whatever my face looked like. Cassius sat up so we were face to face and kissed me roughly. My hips moved quicker against him. Cassius' hands squeezed my flesh tightly as I rolled my hips into his at a relentless speed. My orgasm was teetering on the edge of release.

"Quit holding out on me, my love, let me hear you," he whispered into my ear like a sweet caress. My arms wrapped around his shoulders and yanked him into me as my orgasm ripped through me. Cassius gripped me tightly as he roared into my neck and found his release. Our cumming together was so intense that I could hardly hear myself whimpering as my orgasm died down.

"Fuck," he groaned softly as we both tumbled backward on the bed.

We faced each other, both of us breathing heavily. I felt so peaceful, so whole. His fingers traced over my face like he wanted to draw me into his mind so he could never forget.

"Was it always like this with us?" I asked.

His eyes sparkled with amusement.

"After you finally admitted your feelings for me, yes." He laughed softly as he continued. "After we stopped trying to kill each other, it turned into this." His hand gestured to the bed and us.

"I don't understand how we jumped from trying to kill each other to sleeping together." I smiled at his happiness. "Did I ever come close to killing you?"

"Every time we met in battle, you nearly killed me." His hand sat on my hip lazily, like he just needed to touch any part of me he could.

"Why didn't I kill you?"

"You wanted to fuck me more." Cassius laughed loudly when I smacked his chest. "I can't tell you why, but someday you'll remember."

"So, you liked me first?" I wanted to know more about our history. Anything he could tell me would never be enough to satisfy this hunger I was feeling for more of him and us.

His eyes flashed black before turning gold again.

"Yes." He smirked like he was remembering fond memories. Gods, I wondered what it was like to remember all of them. "You used to be so mean and acted so disgusted at the thought of me, but I could see the lingering stares. You could have killed me in those battles, but you didn't. It became like a teasing game, and I was not going to lose it. You consumed my every thought and want. You still consume them."

"Weren't you worried about me being your enemy?"

"Not really," he said with a shrug that was shockingly carefree. "I just needed you, and that's all I thought about for years after I first saw you."

"Years?" I sat up and stared at him. "How long have we known each other?"

He lifted his hands like he was counting. "A long time," he answered back.

His fingers made small circles on my naked skin as he watched me. My eyes darted around the room at the simple but tasteful design. It did look like something I would have picked out and decorated.

"The trial is tomorrow," he whispered. "We held it off as long as we could because I wanted you around longer, even if you hated me."

I nodded in understanding at him. The final trial before I was to travel to Cerithia and get the witch's bloodstone to break the curse and be able to stay with Cassius. And to free everyone in Exile.

"The sooner I get it done, the sooner I can free everyone from Exile."

"What's it like there? You've never said anything about it."

"Horrible," I said. "There are no more animals to hunt. The creek ran dry. It's so hot and eerily silent." My eyes glazed over as I remembered the years of living in Exile. "I can break free of the boundary and get what I can, but it hurts every time I leave."

A flicker of something crossed his face as he broke eye contact with me. He grabbed my hand and held it tightly.

"We know you can break free. I've sent men into the woods to track you when it gets close to the trials, but I had to stop because you kept on slaughtering them."

"Everyone in Exile believes Crimson is responsible for locking us away."

"Why do they think that?" His eyes flashed black in anger. "Do they not remember either?"

"I'm not sure anymore. They were acting oddly towards me before the trials."

"That's why you kept saying I was your enemy." His whisper was so quiet that I nearly missed it. "Hopefully you'll never have to go back. And if you do go back, maybe this time we can find you and break you free."

"I doubt you'd ever be able to find Exile; it blends in like it's not even there. There's a large oak tree in the middle of the forbidden wood. You can't miss it; it's the only one in the whole woods and stands taller than any other tree. It's marked with an 'X'. That is the start of the shadow boundary around Exile."

He rolled onto his back and pulled me to his side as the blankets draped over our naked bodies. I wanted to keep asking questions, but exhaustion clouded over me. I closed my eyes and listened to his heartbeat, letting it lull me to sleep with Cassius holding me against his body.

CHAPTER 23

The next morning, I was woken to Cassius awaking with a start, jerking up in bed as if trying to escape a bad dream. He stared down at me for a moment, reassuring himself that I was still there, and smiled before kissing me.

"As much as I'd love to worship you some more, the trial will be starting shortly. You should get dressed—unless you want to do it naked." A playful gleam shined through his eyes.

"Maybe it will help me against the others like it does with you." I chuckled but stopped when his face lost its humor, remembering how important my performance would be today.

Reluctantly, I stood up and got dressed. I stared in the mirror, watching Cassius do the same, donning his black guardsman uniform. The tension radiated off of him, and he didn't look at me. He hadn't said anything for a long moment, so I walked to stand in front of him. His eyes finally looked at me, and I saw how dim in color they were.

"I'll be alright, Cassius."

"This is where you fell from last time, not making it to the top."

"Was it something I did?"

"No." He frowned. "You were distracted by Cerithia men. You disappeared before I could say anything to you."

"But Cerithia can't compete?" I questioned.

"No, they can't, but they are clever at sneaking into the trials. Which is what happens each year, no matter how diligent we are in stopping them," he sighed.

"Well, I won't get distracted this time. Besides, I'll expect you to ravish me as a prize for making the top ten, so that's a good motivator." I smiled up at him when his eyes flashed black momentarily. He leaned in and kissed me hard while holding me tightly to him. A knock on his door had us breaking apart so he could answer it. Two guardsmen in red uniforms stood at the door to tell Cassius it was time to go.

I waved at them when their eyes went wide as they spotted me in the room. They avoided my eyes like they would be crucified if caught looking at me. Cassius said something to them before they left, and he turned to me and held out his hand. Stepping forward, I slid my hand into his. I didn't look back in the room to admire it because I would be back shortly.

We walked hand in hand into the hallway where the dining hall was. The remaining contestants gazed over at us as we walked towards them. They must have been told to get ready for the final trial, too. Haden's eyebrows shot into his hairline when he saw us. The guardsmen stood waiting for Cassius to give orders. When Cassius stopped at his spot, I kept walking, but he pulled me back and gave me a hard-lingering kiss.

"Come back to me, my love," he whispered.

"I will." I turned to the gaping faces of contestants and guardsmen. Haden gave me a grin so big I could feel my cheeks blushing.

"This is the final trial. So, let's get it over with." Cassius spoke while staring straight at me.

At his words, the ground began to rumble around us, but no one yelled or screamed. We were expecting it this time. We all stood as tapestries and walls shredded into nothingness. Suddenly, the bright light of the colosseum blinded us as the crowd cheered at us. Twenty of us stood in a group waiting for the king to step forward onto his balcony. When he did, Cassius stood next to him with his golden eyes watching me. The crowd roared at the sight of the king for quite some time before they quieted down. He was dressed in Crimson red from head to toe, and his black crown sat upon his head of dark hair. How had I never realized how similar he and Cassius looked?

"The final trial!" He boomed as the crowd tore into a new frenzy. My eyes never left Cassius as he watched me closely, giving me a small smile as the noise died down.

"You have all been impressive to watch. This trial, though, is the most difficult to get through and will likely take the lives of several of you." The king's eyes flicked to me momentarily before continuing. "Those that succeed will be placed in the top ten and will travel to Cerithia to return the witch's bloodstone to our kingdom. For six years we have tried and failed. No one has returned alive."

The tension from the crowd was palpable. Looking around, I tried to make out the faces watching us, but with the bright light shining from behind them, I couldn't.

"The next trial will be a recreation of the fates of those who competed before you and died. When the bodies were returned to the Crimson kingdom, a seer performed a sacred ritual that revealed how each of them died. We have created a magical simulation that will test you against the six deaths they faced to see who can come out of them alive."

We have to survive six death traps. Six. The number seemed like so much in this context. I understood the reason for the task, but what if we all died trying?

"Once you have escaped a simulation, it will put you into the next until you have completed them all. You will be rated mostly by who can actually get through the task. If more than ten emerge, the fastest ten will get the points. Once the simulation starts, we cannot stop it until it completes the entire series. It's very likely that less than ten of you will be standing at the end of it."

No one cheered at the news.

My eyes glanced at Cassius' stoic face, and I knew we were both wondering if this could be the last time we saw each other. I would do this for him, for us, and for Exile. I gave him a bright smile to show him I could do this and to assure him that he didn't need to worry about me.

"You may be in the simulation at the same time as other contestants. You may choose to work together or not, and magic is to be used. Best of luck to each of you."

Haden sighed heavily next to me. My eyes remained locked on Cassius as his figure slowly faded away along with the colosseum.

We were all standing in a field. It was black as night, but we could make out the silhouette of trees around us. My eyes tried adjusting to the darkness. There was a small break in the forest where the light shined through it. We must be heading there. Pointing to the light, Haden looked and nodded, but none of us moved.

I wondered what was lurking around, waiting for us to move or make a noise. Those creatures from the first trial flooded my mind. Nothing seemed to be watching us or lurking in the field. As soon as I took a step forward, a snapping noise broke through the ground and echoed around us. Suddenly, the land below us shook so violently that it split into two. Haden slipped, but I grabbed him quickly and hauled him back up. A shriek sounded from the crevasse that split the ground into two. Shit. Large, winged creatures flew from the ground and straight into the air. We all held our breath to see if they were noise-sensitive like those other beasts. They started barreling towards us, though. They knew we were here.

"Run!" someone yelled, and everyone scattered towards the light in the trees.

I saw one of the creatures descending on me, but I shot my flames out in front of me, burning it before it grabbed me. They were fairly small but could kill us with their long, sharp talons. I gawked at the small, translucent-skinned beast on the ground. It had ears, eyes, and a mouth that held thousands of tiny razor-sharp teeth. Someone screamed, but it was cut short as a creature ripped into his chest. I stood horrified, watching as his insides spilled out of him onto the ground.

Don't get distracted, I told myself.

I could incinerate all of them with my fire magic, but it would likely drain me for other tasks. I saw that Haden was struggling with a creature, but he launched his frost into the night sky and froze it solid. The monster instantly dropped and shattered into a million pieces when it hit the ground. We were running as fast as we could. Grabbing Haden's hand on the way by, I yanked him along with me. He would survive this with me. Another shriek from the creatures put me on high alert.

They were headed straight for us. I pushed Haden as hard as I could to the left, and he tumbled out of range of the creature's claws. The beast scratched my shoulder, gouging it deeply, but I kept running. My ears rang as I heard another contestant's yell cut short. Focus. Focus. Focus. The light in the trees was getting closer and closer. We were almost there.

Haden was quick on my heels. When a creature swooped for me, I stumbled, freefalling into the black depth of the crevasse. My mind went blank in terror, and I didn't know what to do. All I could think was that I failed Cassius and Exile...again. The free fall had my hair whipping around me, and the wind whistled loudly in my ears. How long would I fall before the ground caught up to me? I closed my eyes tightly so I wouldn't see my end coming. A moment later I realized I was not falling; I wasn't moving at all.

When I opened my eyes, my fire mist was circling all around me in a cloud of fire, but it was twisted through with dark shadows. I felt the darkness in my chest hum with power as I was lifted towards the darkened sky above me. Apparently, my magic wouldn't let me die so easily. Thank the stars above because I had thought my end was here. Once I reached the top of the crevasse, I could see Haden looking over the edge as if he had been watching me fall to my death. My magic lifted me above the rim and laid me gently on the ground, so I was staring up at Haden. A creature swooped at him, but he had frozen it within a moment.

"Thank the fucking stars, Thea. I thought you were dead." Haden sighed heavily.

Taking a deep breath as I lay on the ground, I smiled when I noticed a small animal crawling towards me. It was Kace in his shifted form. I stood and scooped him up in his small animal frame. He wasn't as fast as the rest of us, so I could help him, and he was likely undetectable being so small. My fire burst out in front of us as one last creature tried to stop us, but it was dead before it hit the ground.

Haden, Kace, and I slipped into the light of the trees, and I felt dizzy as the light blinded me. I looked around, not understanding where I was. When the bright light faded, I gasped in surprise. I was in a cage, chained and locked shut with my hands tied in front of me. Haden, Kace, and a few others were in similar cages as well. The walls, the floor, and the ceiling of the room we were in were white with no other markings. As time passed, more contestants kept appearing in the room, also locked up in separate cages. I counted them. Seventeen of us.

We were all looking at each other, wondering what was going to happen next, when suddenly, the room started filling with water. Fuck. Were we going to drown? Our hands were tied as the water filled the room quickly.

I looked at Haden, who was across the room from me and struggling with his bonds fiercely. Kace was already shifting into a small animal creature in his cage. He slipped from the bars and was gone in the blink of an eye. My eyes shifted to the man next to me as the water kept rising. He had been on my team during the maze, Zade. The man held no magic, and I could see panic in his eyes. He would not survive if I didn't help. He tugged on his restraints, but they didn't budge.

My fire bloomed across my skin as the water rose, caus-ing the chains to melt from my hands. But before I let myself out, I held my hand toward the magicless fae next to me and melted the chains from his hands as well. He looked at me in awe as I melted the lock off the cage he was in too. I couldn't let him die. He nodded in thanks before he disappeared. I looked back at Haden's cage but saw that it was already empty. Holding my breath as the water rose above my head, I melted my cage open and left it.

When I opened my eyes again, I was lying on my back. The hot sun beat down on me so fiercely that my clothes were already nearly dry. I stood up and at first saw no one else with me. But when I glanced around, shading my eyes from the hot sun, I saw a group of four Guardsmen standing a short distance away. They all held weapons that were pointed at me. Great. Slipping my dagger from my boot without them seeing, I stood.

The dagger left my hand so quickly that the fae it hit in between the eyes fell dead to the ground before the others realized I threw anything. Once they realized this, though, they launched arrows at me. All it took was a flick of my wrist, and my fire burned them from the sky. One of the men charged me with his sword. Grabbing my other dagger, I moved towards him. I dodged the blade easily and twisted myself behind him, but he was saved as another guard prevented me from killing him with a violent shove.

I turned and fell to the ground when another guard punched me. He moved quickly toward me. Pain radiated from me, making it difficult to concentrate. The man lifted a sword so he could plunge it into my chest. Before he could move, my darkness exploded out of me and wrapped him up. Without permission from me, it squeezed until the sickening noise of bones crunching filled the air.

I stood, stealing the sword from his dead body. I met the next man blow for blow. Fuck, I was not as good with this heavy sword. He swung his blade at me, causing my sword to fall from my hands. Wisp appeared close by, her form burning black. Below her was my dagger. I darted to the left, sliding down on my knees to avoid the guard's swinging sword. I grabbed my dagger and twisted quickly. My blade pierced into his stomach, and he fell over dead. Relief flooded me when I saw the bow he had slung on his back. As I notched an arrow though, a throwing knife lodged into my thigh.

"Fuck!" I gritted out, aiming at the next target and releasing the bow. The arrow flew from the string and hit his shoulder. The pain in my leg made it difficult to focus on anything. Pulling the next arrow back, I shot at the same guard, but he dodged it. Shit. There weren't any more arrows. Throwing down the bow, I ran towards the remaining man as he sprinted at me. The last one was the largest of the guards. He towered over me. His giant hand grabbed me by the throat and slammed me so hard onto my back that the ground shook.

I tried to summon my fire magic, but for some reason, I couldn't. My eyes closed tightly so my darkness could find something to help us. There was another magic lingering in the air. My opponent was using magic to nullify mine. Interesting. I pulled on his magic, bringing it into myself, and immediately felt it coursing through my veins. His eyebrows shot up as I took away his barrier. Instead of using magic, I grabbed the dagger in my thigh and ripped it from myself before slicing it through his throat. The man fell next to me, dead.

Sybil's healing magic mended my wounds as I progressed to the next challenge. My eyes were met with darkness again. I glanced around but couldn't see anything. Cautiously, I took a step but stopped when I felt my legs sinking into something. Mud? The more I struggled to free myself, the more I sank into it. Great. How the fuck was I supposed to use my fire to help me? I summoned my fire mist and tossed it out like a rope, hoping it would catch on something. When it caught around a boulder, I pulled myself slightly out of the mud.

The light where I was supposed to end up mocked me from a distance. I pulled harder as I tried to wrench myself free, but only succeeded in speeding up the process. My mind raced with ideas for how to save myself. Trying to stay calm, I closed my eyes as I continued to sink and searched the air around me for any magic to help me. I felt Haden's frost magic hanging in the air around me. He must have used it recently here. Hopefully it worked. The traces of it were faint, and I had to concentrate to find it. There it was. But before I could pull it to me, my head became submerged below the mud, the panic making me lose my grasp on his magic.

My chest felt like it was being squeezed so tightly that I could hardly hold my breath in, and the effects of suffocation were starting to settle in. I struggled frantically but quickly realized that the more I struggled, the quicker I sank. Doing my best to calm down. I held still, my body trying to preserve the last breath I had taken. My lungs burned with the need to breathe in, and on instinct, my body tried, forcing mud into my mouth and nose. I tried coughing it up, but that only made it worse. My vision was going dark. This was it. I was going to die in a fucking mud pit. My thoughts became sluggish, and my head pounded along with the slowing beat of my heart.

Suddenly, I felt an icy coldness touch my hand above the mud before a large, warm hand wrapped around mine. The force of them tugging on my hand hurt so badly, but

I would take it over dying. Within a moment, my head was above the surface again, and I was spitting out a mouthful of mud and blowing it unceremoniously out of my nose. As soon as my hands were free, I wiped it out of my eyes, trying to see who had saved me. I landed hard on the ground, realizing my body lay on the now frozen mud pit. Rolling onto my back, I stared up at and saw Haden staring at me in worry. Next to me was Zade, the magicless fae, his arms covered in mud from dragging me out.

"Fucking hell, Thea... Are you determined to die today?" Haden spoke in puffy breaths. They both looked exhausted. His words rung with truth, though. I was not doing well in the trials. I was getting too distracted.

"I owe you both," I wheezed. My lungs still felt like I had a pile of bricks on my chest. Haden and Zade helped me up, and we walked across a now-frozen field of mud. When I felt Haden's magic still lingering in the air, I pulled on it slightly, feeling a rush of coldness fill my veins. Shit, this was uncomfortable. Was he this cold all the time? When we reached the light at the end of the field and stepped through it together, emerging into a room where Kace was waiting.

"Thank the gods," he sighed.

"Have you seen anyone else?" I asked weakly.

"No, but I just got here."

The room we were in was small with gray walls and a dark stone floor. There were no windows or any other distinguishable features. As the moments ticked on, a couple of others that I recognized showed up. We didn't have to move for some time, and it was nice to catch our breaths.

Thirteen contestants remained. That wasn't too bad considering we only had two death traps to finish. Without warning, the door we had all come through was sealed shut.

"Well, that can't be good," someone muttered.

Nothing happened at first. Then suddenly, a table full of different foods and goblets of water appeared. A break within the trials? Everyone let down their guard and walked toward the table. We all began drinking the water, but only a small drop had hit my tongue before I threw the cup away from me. The first contestant who downed a large glass of water fell over, shaking and foaming at the mouth.

"Poison."

Shit.

"Who drank some?" I shouted, the panic getting the best of my composure. Everyone raised their hands. A small amount had gotten on my tongue, and the bitterness was starting to burn. The contestant who fell to the floor was dead. Sybil's healing magic forced its way to where the poison had touched me, healing me quickly. The other contestants were starting to breathe heavily, and one of them hunched over, holding their stomachs. I reached for Haden first and healed him, then Kace, then Zade.

"Give me that, bitch." Someone yanked the amulet from around my neck, and it fell to the floor, shattering on the ground below our feet. No. The pretty colors swirled into nothingness. The healing magic was already settled in my chest permanently, but without her amulet, how would she get her magic back? A fight broke out. Haden and Kace had started punching the fae that grabbed me.

"You idiot!" I was so angry that fire burst over my skin, and my eyes shifted to black as I turned my attention to the man who had grabbed me.

Before I could kill him, he fell to the floor, dead from the poison. I glanced around, realizing I had only healed the four of us. We needed ten. I closed my eyes as Sybil's magic surged forward.

"Holy fucking shit." Haden said, backing away from me as I opened my eyes.

I was glowing, but I wasn't on fire. A brightness filled the room as it flowed from me and into every fae still standing, healing magic. All of the competitors were watching me, and I knew they would know my elite magic by the end of this, but that didn't matter right then. Once everyone was completely healed, the glow faded away, but my eyes were still dark. Eleven of us remained.

Before we had time to think, we were all back in the colosseum. The bright lights blinded us momentarily. We all stood in a small group.

"We did it," Haden said as he breathed heavily.

"My love." Cassius' voice had me turning towards him. The crowd wasn't loud, but we could hear them shifting around. I took a step towards Cassius, then paused. How many scenarios had we done? The creatures—that was one. The water was two. The guardsman was three. The mud. Four. Poison was five.

This was a trap.

Looking around, I saw each one of the contestants talking to someone, but I couldn't see anyone in front of them. When I turned to Cassius, he smiled at me.

"You did so good, Thea," he cooed, but his eyes weren't the right shade of gold. I gave him a once-over as a feeling of uneasiness filled me.

I took a step backward, and he clocked the movement. His jaw ticked in anger, but he faked a smile that Cassius didn't normally give me.

"Haden!" I called over my shoulder. "Who are you talking to?"

His eyes shifted to me quickly, like I had broken a trance. His head shook slightly before looking in front of him again.

"Della," he said, a smile breaking across his face.

"Haden, we only did five tasks. This is a trick," I yelled.

"No, she's here." Haden took a step forward toward this invisible woman he was smiling at. Shit. What the fuck was going on? All of the contestants were walking towards the trap when I glanced over at them.

"Thea, baby, it's me." Cassius said again, but I still wasn't convinced by his smile.

My face scrunched at the nickname. It sounded so weird coming from him. It wasn't something he would say. My eyes drifted over him looking for anything else that wasn't right.

"Take off your shirt," I demanded. Cassius stopped and smiled like a predator who was catching his prey. He ripped his shirt off, and my eyes scanned over him. Something had to give away what was going on.

"You want to touch me?" He cocked his head to the side with a wicked gleam in his eyes. I looked over his tattoos and immediately noticed that the green 'T' hidden amongst his black swirls was missing. This was not Cassius. Closing my eyes, I felt for his magic, but it wasn't close to me. It was high above me. I pulled on it, and I could feel his shadows caressing me gently. Cassius. I smiled as his magic willingly came into me, almost gasping as his shadows settled in my veins with my fire.

My eyes snapped open when I heard the scream of one of the men. I looked over to see him being ripped apart by whatever invisible thing was in front of him. My nose crinkled at the fake Cassius, and I realized what these creatures were. They were sirens, showing us our greatest desire. They couldn't hurt us unless we touched them first. Haden lifted his hand as if he were about to reach for someone.

"No!" The ground shook when I screamed. My hand shot out a swirl of fire and shadows, cutting in front of the contestants like a giant wall and hopefully blocking them from their sirens. The man who had touched his was dead. All the contestants looked at me as they shook their heads in confusion.

"They're sirens," I yelled. "Do not touch them."

Haden observed the wall of black and red swirling in front of him. His hand reached out and touched it softly.

"How'd you do that?"

I ignored his question. We'd have time for that later. "Maybe if we're all blocked from them, we can be done with the task." We waited for a few long minutes, but nothing happened. We weren't being pulled from the simulation. Squeezing my eyes shut, I tried to think of what we were supposed to do.

"Maybe we need to kill them?" Kace muttered. "It would make sense. We have to kill someone we want the most."

"Sirens can't attack unless you touch them, so kill them without touching them, and do not fall under their spell again." Haden sighed.

Tossing the magicless fae one of my daggers, he nodded for me to drop the wall.

"I'm dropping the wall," I called out. As soon as I did, my siren, who still stared at me like Cassius would, stood close by smiling at me. His shirt was off, and my mind flashed to touching him, kissing him, holding him. It clouded me with images of us touching each other, and I took a step forward. I heard someone yell in the distance. No, I heard them scream before a horrible noise of flesh and bones being ripped apart. It was enough to jar me from whatever hold the siren had had on me.

Lifting my eyes away, I formed a ball of fire within my hands. The siren didn't falter when he saw it. My eyes shifted to the color of fire as it overtook me. An over-whelming need to protect myself ran through my veins. The real Cassius' shadows wrapped around me as if to coax me and calm me. I focused on the siren in front of me and saw its fake smile falter as a dark glow started forming deep in its chest, under the skin.

The image of Cassius flickered into something horrific. A green-skinned man now stood in front of me, with beady black eyes and qualities that resembled a fish more than a human. The siren couldn't move as my fire burned him from the inside out. Just to make sure he was truly dead, I pulled my hands out in front of me to expand the fire in his chest and watched him explode in front of me.

I turned to see who was still standing, but before I could, I was pulled back to the colosseum. I was somewhat dizzy from using so much magic, but I wasn't nearly as weak as it had made me before. Maybe because I had been using my magic more lately and my tolerance was higher. An arm flung over my shoulder, and I smiled up to Haden. My eyes shifted to see who else was there. Kace. I smiled at him and Zade but frowned when I saw that only three others stood with us.

My eyes shifted to the leaderboard, seeing only our seven names in red. The others had died. The sirens had still gotten them. My stomach sank, but I couldn't think about it. My name was second, behind Haden. I smiled as I gave Haden a hug.

"We fucking did it." Relief overwhelmed me. For the first time, the roar of the crowd comforted me. The weight of the trials slipped off my shoulders because I had a real shot now at getting that wish. I would think about how difficult the final task would be after I celebrated how far I'd come. My mouth was dry from the poison, and mud clung to every part of me, leaving proof of what I had done today.

I was ripped from Haden's hug and pulled against a hard body that smelled like forest and rain. Cassius. The fae watching us roared as he hugged me tightly. He pulled me back, and I saw relief in his eyes. Pulling him down to meet my lips, the crowd roared louder.

"You did so fucking good, little viper," Cassius whispered as he pressed his forehead against mine.

"We have a top seven!" the king bellowed into the colosseum. The group exploded in excitement, louder than they had ever been before. Cassius pulled back and held my hand firmly as the king smiled down at us, and I smiled back. "For your bravery and hard work, we shall have a ball tonight in your honor."

The roaring of the crowd died out as the ground trembled below us and the blinding lights surrounded us once again. When I opened my eyes, we all stood in the hallway of the Crimson castle.

"There is food and refreshments in the dining hall. You will all have clothes sent to your room for the ball tonight,"

Cassius said to us. His hand still held mine tightly. When the other contestants wandered to the dining hall, I turned to Cassius.

"I thought I was going to lose you when the siren showed me in front of you." Cassius frowned.

"His eyes were not the right shade of gold, and he didn't have the 'T' tattoo. I knew it wasn't you almost immediately."

He hugged me tightly and held me for a long time.

"I have to work on some planning for your retrieval of the witch's bloodstone, so I won't see you until the ball. Your dress will be sent to our room."

He leaned down and kissed me possessively. I hummed at the dominance in his kiss, and he smiled against my mouth.

"You used my magic during the trials," he whispered. Not a question, but a fact.

"Yes," I whispered.

"You took some of Haden's, too, when you froze the sinking mud."

I pulled back, glancing over his face to see if he was disgusted that I could do such things. It was unnatural for even elite magic holders. Others should fear me for it. I could use any magic I wanted; it collected within my veins. It made me a monster.

"It's unnatural," I muttered, almost embarrassed. "There is something evil within me, and it wants me to feed on all the magic around me."

His fingers tilted my face to his, but I didn't see disgust.

"Do not be ashamed of your elite magic. I already knew you could take it. Nothing about your powers disgusts or scares me." He gave me a soft kiss. "Let me show you something quickly." Cassius dragged me down the hallway towards my old room. He shut the door before he tugged his shirt off.

"You are worried that we know you have elite magic. You tried to hide it from us because you were told we locked you all away."

My heart raced loudly in my chest. Yes, that is what all of us in Exile knew to be true. His golden eyes pinned me in place as his black shadows swirled around him and then disappeared. I was confused until he turned his head to the side. The left side of his neck held an elite magic mark. Emotions racked my mind. He had elite magic too? His eyes studied me as I stood like a gaping fish out of water.

"You hid your mark?"

"I've had it hidden since the elite magic fae started disappearing. It's habit to keep it hidden."

Stepping forward without thought, I ran a hand over it, and it glowed brightly at my touch. Cassius hummed like he couldn't help himself. I remember how it felt when he ran his finger over my mark, and it felt good, warm. His mark was almost identical to mine; it was just missing one star by the crescent moon.

"Do others here know?" I asked.

"My family and you." Cassius trusted me enough to show me his secret. I leaned up and kissed the mark. He hauled me up and pushed me against the wall as his lips crushed mine. His tongue pushed its way into my mouth, and I groaned when his length rubbed against me perfectly. A knock on the door had him growling, frustrated.

"I have to go." He sighed before setting me down on the floor out of breath. I watched his shadows swirl around his neck and shield his elite magic mark. "Get some rest before the ball. I'll see you there."

He gave me one last kiss and smiled at me before leaving.

CHAPTER 24

I gathered a few of my possessions from my old bedroom before heading to the suite I now shared with Cassius. Our space smelled like night and rain. It instantly soothed me and made me tired. I spent time looking over the simple yet tasteful decor of the small living area. The kitchen was a dark green that reminded me of the forests of the Forbidden Wood.

The couch was a rich dark green too, with a cream-colored rug under it. The living room had black accents that made it look so much like the two of us mixed. There were huge windows carved out in the dark stone tower that overlooked the gardens of the castle. I smiled as I admired the castle grounds from the tower. From here, I could easily spot the wisps dancing in the gardens, all a bright, happy color.

I wondered how long I had before I needed to go to Cerithia. I hoped I would be able to relax for a few days. I wanted to get lost in Cassius for as long as I could. Heading to our bedroom, I set down my things before pausing at the beautiful red gown hanging up. Ophelia must have made it. I headed towards the bathroom but paused and turned back towards the nightstand on my side of the bed. Curiosity pulled me over to it, and I wondered what I had in this room that I hadn't touched for years.

It wouldn't be snooping if it was mine, right? Curiosity overtook me as I walked over to it and opened the drawer. Dozens of dry flowers sat inside with some little knick knacks I didn't remember. I pulled the corner of a paper out from under the flowers. My eyes drifted over the beautiful handwriting.

I'll love you in this life and the next. My soul will always find yours.

-Cass

A love note from Cassius? I smiled to myself as I set the note down and went to take a shower. The bathroom had a large black granite tub in the corner next to a window that spanned the whole wall. It was a dream. The shower was on the opposite side of the room. It was also made from black stone and had shower heads pointed in every direction.

I undressed and crawled in, watching mud and blood swirl down the drain as I washed the grime of the last trial off my skin. Dread filled my chest as I stared at the dirty water circling the drain, a reminder that the hardest task was still ahead of us. I could die. No one had ever come back alive. But I was from the kingdom of Cerithia, wasn't I? What would they do if they saw me? I was sure I was considered a traitor and would be killed immediately.

Shaking the thoughts away, I decided I would give myself tonight before I worried about the last task I needed to complete to get my wish, to break my own curse, and to help the Crimson kingdom. I dried off and lay in the bed, staring at the red dress hanging up, before exhaustion found me and I passed out.

I sat up abruptly, jolted awake by unpleasant dreams of the day's trial.

My eyes burned with tiredness as I stood up to get ready for the ball. I started by doing my makeup with what I found on the vanity, smokey eyelids, and a deep red lipstick to match my dress. I left my hair down but tamed the curls into orderly ringlets as best as I could. Staring at myself in the mirror as I pushed silver dangle earrings in, I thought I looked... pretty. My face and body had filled out since being here and eating regularly. I was curvier than I thought I had ever been. Huffing loudly, I struggled to get into the red dress that was made to fit like a glove. Two pieces of chiffon fabric were clipped together at the shoulders with pretty silver stars and fell over my chest, leaving a deep v-neck that extended all the way to right above my naval, leaving little to the imagination. The pieces twisted in a beautiful design over my hips, then cascaded around my legs, slit all the way up to my thighs. There was barely anything covering my body. My strong legs were exposed from the sides of my hips to the floor.

One wrong movement and the whole room would see my goods. I strapped on the shoes that were set with the dress—a pair of diamond, gleaming heels that twisted and tied up my calf. I trusted Ophelia to know what kind of dress I needed for tonight, but I was showing so much skin. I glanced over myself and admired how well the dress fit me and how it accentuated every feminine part of me. and showed every curve that I had—thanks to plenty of food. I walked to the bed, turned around so I was facing the mirror, and walked towards it.

Gods above— I looked like a filthy fantasy. A smile spread across my face when I thought of Cassius' reaction to me. He wouldn't be able to keep his hands to himself. I realized how different our situation had become since the last time I had dressed up for a dinner celebration. Now I knew Cassius loved me, wanted me. There was no one but me, and that made my smile wider. Never would I have thought this could be my situation. Cassius and these trials had given me a new purpose to keep moving forward. Thank the gods and stars above that he was mine.

I added a bit more smokiness to my eyes to help accentuate the dress's sultry nature. Squaring my shoulders, I left my room and headed down towards where the ball should be happening. My heartbeat thundered in my chest when I heard the voices and laughter of so many fae. Only this time, it wasn't because I was insecure. No, I craved to see how Cassius would look at me. Walking into the room we had eaten fancy dinner in before, I was in awe of the transformation of the space. The table was gone, but new tables lined the room with a huge array of food and drinks.

So many fae filled the room, all dressed in the most beautiful dresses and clothes. My eyes took in all of the gold and silver dripping off any surface they could decorate. The chandelier shined brightly, and beautiful music played and filled the large space. It looked magical, breathtaking. The crowd quieted down as I entered the room, and everybody turned to stare at me. From the skin showing to the color of my dress, I stuck out like a bold red rose in a sea of pastel blooms. I held my head high, finally understanding my self-worth and feeling every bit of it.

The crowd parted, and my eyes met with Cassius' as he sat on a throne at the front of the room. His clothes were the finest I had ever seen him in. The fabric was stark black, with small silver detailing, including the Crimson kingdom's crest over his heart. He wore a crown similar to the king's. It was black, powerful, and decorated with dark green and silver jewels. His eyes locked on mine as the crowd parted to allow me through. He was sitting with such powerful arrogance on his golden throne that it made me smile at him. All of his movements froze as he caught a glimpse of me.

My hips swayed as I walked for him, making his eyes immediately turn black as they watched me. It was easy to forget that others were in the room with us. They all faded away when Cassius watched me, like he physically couldn't look away. I stopped in front of his throne and gave him a smug smile as I curtsied. Before I stood up, he had left his throne and walked down the two granite steps to me. He lifted my face to his.

"Do not ever bow for me, my love." He gave me a soft kiss as the crowd behind us grew louder. "I don't know if I should thank Ophelia or curse her for this dress."

Turning slowly, I let him admire the whole dress.

"Do you like it?" I purred, batting my lashes at him.

His eyes held me firmly where I was.

"Let's see how long we can make it through this celebration before I haul you off to some dark corner and have my way with you."

My face faltered at his words. It was he that wore a teasing smile this time. He grabbed my hand and led me to the middle of the floor, where others danced. He pulled me into him and wrapped his arms around me. I didn't know how to dance, but I knew he was touching me more than necessary.

"You aren't allowed to dance with anyone else. It feels like you're naked against me," he said, fingers tightening against me. I laughed at his possessiveness and laid my head against his shoulder as we swayed to the pretty music. I could feel others watching us, but it was easy to ignore them when Cassius was holding me like he wouldn't ever let me go.

"When I was in Exile, I spent so much time thinking that there was likely no one waiting for me in the realm. I wouldn't let myself even consider it was a possibility because I feared this the most," I whispered, "that I had someone like you, and you were suffering while I couldn't remember anything."

His hand gripped my naked skin tightly on my back.

"I would wait for all eternity if it meant I got to hold you like this for only one night." He kissed my forehead. "I will make you fall in love with me over and over again if need be, Thea, because you and I are one soul in two bodies, and life would be meaningless if we were kept apart."

Tears sprang to my eyes.

In all those lonely nights in Exile, I never would have dared to let myself think I had this. I didn't know I had such love waiting for me. My heart swelled at the sight of Cassius when I pulled back to look over him. He gave me a bright smile that he didn't show often. How did I get this lucky? Even if I never remembered our beginning or my past, I could die being truly happy with what I did know. The song ended, but we danced through another and another. His eyes glanced at something behind me, and I saw his father nod for him to come over to him.

"Work awaits me. I'll be back momentarily." He gave me a kiss, signaling to everyone in the room I was his and not to touch. It was likely enough to keep everyone away from me. The aroma from the food table caught my attention. Everyone was having such a great time. Haden was dancing with a beautiful woman, but he smiled at me like we were truly friends.

An overwhelming feeling settled in my chest. Would I make it back from the last trial? What if Cassius had to endure losing me all over again?

The room suddenly felt too small and too loud, so I headed towards the large black velvet drapes behind the thrones to get a break. I didn't know where Cassius had gone, but I wouldn't be long. Slipping through the drapes undetected, I immediately leaned against the granite pillar. I closed my eyes and took a deep breath. I didn't even hear Cassius when he sneaked in and grabbed me.

"My love, are you hiding?" Cassius had pulled me back into his chest. His lips pressed into the elite mark behind my ear. The dark stubble on his jaw scraped against my skin and sent a jolt of electricity through me.

"I felt overwhelmed," I whispered.

"Hmm, I can help relieve stress," he whispered. "It wouldn't be the first time we snuck back here for the same reasons."

I turned slightly towards him as a mischievous glint met his eye. I just pressed myself back against him in response. Cassius moved us so quickly that I didn't realize what he was doing until my chest was pinned to the pillar. It was cold compared to my too-hot skin. Cassius' big hands ran up the back of my bare legs with a hum of appreciation. His fingers slipped under the thin underwear I was wearing, and he groaned softly into the crook of my neck.

"Such a good girl." He praised me when I widened my stance so he could feel all of me. His teeth grazed the flesh on my shoulder and bit down, and my hips jerked back into him when his fingers circled my clit. His hands tugged me by my hips back into him, rubbing his hard length into me. I should be horrified that only thick black velvet drapes separate us from everyone else, but it only fueled my need to have him now. Cassius' clothes felt rough against my skin when he moved one scrap of fabric to the side.

"This will be fast, Thea. We don't want others to come searching for us."

"Please," I panted. His hands traced my skin before grabbing harsh handfuls of my ass. Cassius let out a loud breath as he undid his trousers. His hand covered my mouth as he sank into me so quickly that my knees buckled under me. Cassius held me between his body and the pillar. My ears rang with the sounds of everyone around us.

"As much as I love hearing what I do to you, I don't want others to hear what belongs to me," he whispered against my ear as he held his hand firmly across my mouth. "So be a good fucking girl and keep quiet."

I groaned and squeezed my eyes shut tightly with every thrust of his hips. My hands tried to grip the pillar, but it was pointless. Cassius stopped just long enough to turn me, so my back was against the pillar. His hand wrapped around my leg and lifted it around his waist before sinking back into me. His thumb ran over my lips, smearing my red lipstick intentionally.

"Fuck." He hissed, and his mouth descended onto mine immediately, swallowing all of my moans. My arms wrapped around him and pulled him so close that he couldn't leave. I tried to pull away as my orgasm tilted on the edge of breakthrough, but he pinned me by my throat to the pillar and didn't let me move.

"Not too loud, my love," he growled before his lips found mine again. I tried to hold out longer, but nothing would have tamed the orgasm that ripped through me. He didn't mind though, as he muffled my noises and kept them for himself. Cassius kissed my neck, his stubble skimming my skin, and groaned his release so softly that I knew no one could hear but me.

We stayed against the pillar for a long moment before he gave me a soft kiss and wiped my smeared lipstick off of both of us. I gave him a lazy smile that he returned.

"I do love this dress." He chuckled softly.

My eyes looked at the crown that still sat on his head. It was weird to see him with it on. He was the next king of the Crimson kingdom. My eyes traced over his handsome face. Everything about Cassius drew me to him like a moth to a flame. An overwhelming urge to tell him how much I loved him hit me like a tidal wave.

"I lo—" I was cut off by a huge explosion in front of us. We were both blown away from the wall and tumbled onto the floor of the room. My ears rang at the force of whatever hit the castle.

"Thea!" My eyes met Cassius as he pulled me up to him. His crown was gone. I could feel my head bleeding as I tried to make sense of what had just happened. Ringing filled my ears, making it impossible to think clearly.

"What's happening?" I spoke frantically as the loud screaming and chaos erupted at the celebration.

"We're under attack." His black shadows suddenly swirled around him, and when they disappeared, he was in his armor. Cassius grabbed me by the shoulders and turned me so that I was facing him. I didn't like the worried expression on his face. "Listen to me, Thea. You need to go get changed, get weapons, and you need to take the others to Cerithia, now."

"What?" I shook my head no. "I don't want to leave you yet."

Cassius' face twisted in pain at my frantic words, but they were true. I didn't want to leave him. I thought we would have days.

"You have to. Cerithia probably got word that you survived the trials and are attacking us to prevent you from coming. If you can sneak out and get there, you'll have a higher chance of getting the stone and coming back to us sooner. We will have a lifetime together after that."

I stared at his terrifyingly handsome face for a long moment before giving him a lingering kiss. He held me tightly as chunks of rubble and castle flew around us. The screaming of other guests increased. Cassius kissed me once more before pulling back.

"How am I supposed to concentrate on my task if I'm worried about you?" I asked quickly.

"I'll visit when you sleep."

"That might not happen at all." I replied, knowing that sleep would be a luxury in the coming days. After a resigned frown, he grabbed my wrist before his finger came up to my hairline, where blood seeped from a wound. Confusion filled me as he wiped it on the inside of my left wrist. Then he wiped blood from himself and smeared it with mine.

A hot, searing pain had me ripping my arm from him with a surprised cry. Red and black mists swirled over my wrist for a moment before vanishing, revealing a mark in the shape of a crown where our blood had mixed. The crown glowed slightly like the swirls on my skin that appeared. It was a vibrant red, as if it had been burned into my flesh, but it no longer hurt. My eyebrows knitted together as I tried to understand the marking. The base of the crown wrapped around my wrist, and the points of the crown moved up my forearm toward my elbow.

"It's a blood mark. It will link us together. I'm not entirely sure how to communicate through it or how much we can. Although I can feel how much you don't want to leave me right now." He frowned.

"How did you know how to do this?" I traced the raised burn of the crown.

"A blood witch showed me once." He spoke so casually, so simply, but I had so many questions that I didn't have time to ask. Blood witches had become extinct with the humans, or at least that was what I had heard before.

Glancing at his wrist, I noticed he didn't have one. "What about you?"

"I can feel it without the brand because our blood sealed together in the mark."

"How?" I asked, confused. Another explosion interrupted my questioning. Fae screamed all around us. I gave him one last kiss instead of waiting for an answer.

"Be safe," I demanded.

"I'll see you soon, my love."

Then he was gone, and I was running through the rubble of the celebration. Dead fae littered the ground, but I couldn't linger to see who it was. I headed up the stairs and changed into my clothing as quickly as I could, twisting my hair into a braid before getting my daggers and bow. I paused before I left though, so I could scribble a note for Cassius down—just in case.

My heart will remember you, seek you, love you even if my mind cannot remember. My soul will always seek its other half.

Love,
Little Viper

I set it on his nightstand and then headed towards the men's sleeping room.

CHAPTER 25

When I got there, only five of them were dressed and ready. Tagon was missing.

"He died," Zade answered as I peered around for the seventh member of our group. Haden and Kace stepped forward. Sadness filled me, but I couldn't linger on it.

"We need horses to sneak out without being detected. Who knows the way to Cerithia?"

"Me and Zade," Haden spoke and pointed to the magicless fae.

"Let's go."

The hallways filled with smoke and rubble as we wove our way out of the castle. Fire burned harshly, making sweat bead on my forehead. A hole had been blown into the side of the castle, so we climbed over the stone rubble and out into the fresh air. My eyes and throat felt raw from the smoke overtaking the castle. Other fae flowed out of the wreckage through holes that shouldn't be there to escape the attack.

We were all dressed in dark colors to blend in with the night. Once we all had our horses, we headed towards the woods, but I stopped and observed the castle being hit by huge balls of fire. The wisps were watching the attack in shades of black. I pulled deep within myself and felt the barrier magic I had taken from the guardsmen who took Cassius in the woods. I summoned it forward and created a barrier so tall and wide that nothing could penetrate it. It illuminated a soft blue where the balls of fire tried to break through.

It wouldn't hold forever, but it would buy them time. We turned and moved into the woods as fast as the horses could take us. A sense of pride and relief spread through me, and I knew it was Cassius through the blood mark. The barrier was working. I smiled as I raced through the dark forest on my horse. She seemed to know where we were headed and needed little direction from me.

ооооо

We covered a great distance after a day of traveling, only stopping to rest our horses. I had known we entered Cerithia lands some time ago because the air was much hotter here, probably because the sun seemed to be out constantly, and their trees did little to offer protection like they did in Crimson. Crimson always seemed to be gloomier, with the sun not making appearances as often. It was sticky and hot in Cerithia, much like Exile had been. My skin balked at the heat. I wasn't sure how to work this damn blood mark, so I tried to feel for Cassius as I stared at it.

It only took him a moment to send relief through it. I took a deep breath and looked around the thick forests of Cerithia. The thin trees were unhealthy, and flowers did not grow on the forest floor, even though it was spring. The birds chirped faintly somewhere in the distance, but nothing near us. It was early morning, and the air was only slightly cooler than it was at midday, but I was thankful for the small reprieve.

"How much farther?" I asked Haden, as we all sat and ate some food they had packed.

"Less than a day," he sighed. "The kingdom is directly in the middle of their lands for protection. We should be there by nightfall tonight."

I nodded as they all stared at me.

"Is anyone here familiar with the castle?"

"Only you," Haden responded. Great. I couldn't remember anything about my time as a guardsman at Cerithia. Maybe being there would help my memory. It hadn't worked at the Crimson kingdom, but I needed to be somewhat positive.

"Well, we can't rely on me remembering anything." I sighed, eating a handful of berries I had foraged. We rested for a short time before heading through the thick forests again. My mind wandered to Cassius and the castle. Hopefully, there wasn't too much damage done.

If Cerithia knew I made it through the trials and attack, they would be expecting us soon. Hopefully, they wouldn't think we would leave so quickly after everything, but I doubted we would get that lucky. No one had ever made it back to Crimson after attempting this mission. Why was everyone so sure that I could? I was so caught up in my thoughts that I didn't notice Cerithia's castle in the distance at first.

It stood on a tall hill above everything else. The walls were made from gray stone and blue flags whipped in the small breeze. My chest tightened significantly at the sight. Was it fear? Or was it because it was familiar to me, even if I didn't want to admit it? Images plagued me in quick flashes.

I saw myself in my blue uniform while in battle, swinging a sword and covered in blood. After that, I saw myself arguing with the royal family, anger and hurt painted across my face. Then I could see myself sitting in a small, dingy room wearing tattered clothing and crying. I felt feelings of deep sadness plague me, as well as extreme loneliness. I shook my head, and the flashes of memories left faded away for a moment, then came back with a vengeance, hitting me like an arrow.

I was smiling at the King of Cerithia as he gave me a small gift. Then I was walking through the forest with a blonde girl my age and a handsome guy. Flashes of the handsome guy kissing me sent a zap of jealousy through the blood mark. Can you see my thoughts? I asked through the marking, not expecting a response. Jealousy still sat in my veins. I would take that as a yes.

Why was I remembering things about my time here already? Maybe because I was from here or at least had fought for the royal family. Did my family reside here? Did they wonder what happened to me? I wasn't sure if anyone did, but I did know that Cassius was waiting for me, and I would be fine if he was the only one.

"We should sleep until nightfall so we can all think clearly before making a move," Kace muttered. We all agreed. There were a series of small caves we had passed, and we turned towards them to make camp. The cave was dark but cool as I laid on my cloak. Why hadn't memories hit me as quickly in Crimson as they did here? Obviously, being in Cerithia had triggered a vast amount of memories, but Crimson had only shown me memories of Cassius. If I truly did live in Crimson with Cassius, wouldn't I remember more? I thought sleep would evade me, but it found me so quickly.

ooooo

Cassius sat on our bed in the Crimson castle, waiting for me to appear.

"Hi," I murmured.

His head snapped up at me before he stood and crushed me into him.

"You're alright." He sighed before giving me a hard, lingering kiss, and I immediately thought of the memories he had seen of me kissing another man.

"You can see my thoughts?" I asked, pulling back.

Jealousy bloomed over his features.

"You sent them barreling down the mark. I didn't know I could until I saw Jesper kissing you."

"I didn't mean to show you. They came out of nowhere. I don't even know who he was."

The tension was palpable for only a moment before it was gone.

"He's an ex of yours. I knew of him, but I didn't want to see it."

"I don't know how to control this thing." I pointed to the mark. Cassius wrapped his arms around me and held me tightly for a long moment.

"Your barrier saved a lot of fae, Thea."

"I wasn't sure it would work." The scent of night, rain, and pine drifted from him as he pulled us down on the bed, so we were both lying together, and I snuggled into his side. We didn't say anything more. We just relaxed in the presence of each other. It wasn't long before Cassius sat up and pulled me along with him.

"It's time to wake up, my love," he whispered as he kissed me. "The witch's stone is in the throne room, highly guarded by men you trained."

Confusion must have taken my features because he offered a larger explanation.

"You were the captain of the Cerithian guard; it's how we met. It's why we were always trying to kill each other." He gave me a proud smile. "You are a great warrior, Thea. Even without your magic, you are clever, smart, tactical, and strong. You are the best captain of any guard the realm has ever seen—a true leader. You just need to believe that about yourself."

Captain. A female captain? I nodded as if I understood, but it was hard to wrap my mind around it. I knew I was part of the guard, but not the captain. It was nice to know I *was successful even without my magic. Cassius' words sank into me. I needed to believe in myself enough to be a leader. I didn't need to wield my magic around to do things well. Cassius gave me a long, lingering kiss. This could be the last kiss I ever give him.*

"Don't ever think like that again." He growled as he pulled away, reading my negative thoughts.

"Sorry," I whispered before kissing him again. He devoured my mouth like it gave him life before pulling away.

"I'll see you soon, little viper."

□□□□□

I nodded as I faded back to the cave I had been sleeping in. I lay there for a moment to gather my thoughts. My fire magic was going wild under my skin. It was ready for whatever we were about to step into. We would do this, but how many of us would come back? I stood up and wrapped my cloak around me, stepping outside the cave.

Walking to the small clearing between all the leafy trees, I watched the gray stone castle in the distance. The large blue flags whipped around in the warm breeze. There was a distinct smell of flowers and sunshine here, where Crimson smelled like forest and rain. A large city sat a short distance from the castle, like in Crimson, but this city looked larger.

Small homes made from scraps of wood and other mis-matched items sat on the outskirts of the tall buildings. It was still pretty but held nothing to Crimson.

The others had started emerging from their spots in the cave. Haden walked up to me as I looked over the land-scape that was nearly opposite of Crimson in every way.

"How's it feel being back here?"

"Odd," I sighed. "It all looks so familiar, but at the same time, I don't recognize it."

Haden nodded as he stared at the castle.

"I've been looking at the landscape. The best thing to do would be to circle wide to the right to the grouping of trees close to the castle and scout the guard rotations before making our way in."

Zade and Kace both came and stood with us. We all just stared at the kingdom of Cerithia in silence before we gathered around to make somewhat of a plan.

"Cassius said the stone is in the throne room and heavily guarded," I said.

"Cerithia is known for their level of skilled guards," Haden spoke softly. "Trained to be ruthless." His eyes moved to me, "by Thea herself."

He hadn't meant it negatively, but I wished to the gods above that they would give me some insight into my own past. I shook away the thought. Cassius said I was a true leader even without my magic, and I believed that. We didn't need my memories. I was a skilled fighter; Kaz and Kai made sure of that.

"If I trained them, then I can beat them," I said confidently. "Someone should stay back just in case something goes wrong so you can get word back to the Crimson kingdom."

"We all go in," Zade said. "Our bodies will be delivered to the Crimson kingdom if it doesn't work out."

I nodded in agreement but felt a tug of despair in my chest. They were all willing to risk their lives to not only get a wish but also to help break my curse.

"I will use my magic to protect us as much as I can, but I do not know what I am capable of." I spoke the truth to them. I had never admitted that I did not know my own magic well. "Sometimes it gets out of hand."

They all nodded as if they understood.

"If I am trapped, if I cannot get out, you will leave me," I ordered.

"We cannot return without you, Thea," Kace spoke. "You are the only one that has to make it back alive. It is our only mission here."

There were so many questions I wanted to ask, but I didn't. Cassius had ordered them to protect me.

We made a plan to split into groups of two to cover more ground and work from different spots of the castle. Zade was with me even though Haden had tried to stop it. I had appreciated them fighting over who was going to go with me, but we didn't have time, so I chose.

We rode swiftly to the castle through the thicket of trees in the outlying fields, splitting up on the way. Zade and I left the horses in the thick forest and moved closer on foot. We set up posts in two leafy trees that helped us see over the large, ten-foot wall surrounding the castle. We waited for an eternity to see where the guards were stationed, but none ever emerged. Something was not right, but we didn't have time to wait. It was nearly nightfall. Jumping down from my perch in the tree, I moved across the large castle grounds first, but no traps awaited us.

The castle of Cerithia embodied everything Crimson didn't. It was made with light gray stone, and the flowers that decorated the outside were lush and brightly colored. No dark colors were anywhere to be found. The blue flags that waved in the wind were the color of the sky, and the crest was gold like the sun. My footsteps faltered as the crest showed me the same one from the wooden door in my dreams. Zade grabbed my elbow and rushed me forward, through the front door of the castle.

We figured it was such an obvious entry point that it would not be an expected move. The gamble paid off, and we were met with no resistance.

Where the fuck was everyone?

Immediately, I took in the foyer that was so white and bright it hurt my eyes. It all felt... familiar. Wisp suddenly appeared to my left, her blue flames lighting the darkened hallway. I followed without much thought; it seemed like Wisp knew where to go. The darkened hallways still seemed bright with their light-colored walls and floors.

The tapestries that hung depicted mostly pictures of the sun and flowers. Beautiful blues, gold, and silver hung from everywhere. I froze immediately when Wisp flashed red in warning and heard a noise down the hallway a moment later. Zade and I crammed ourselves against the wall in the darkest corner we could find. We held our breath as two guards dressed in blue walked past us without noticing.

So, there were guards on duty. This was proving to be more unnerving than we had anticipated. We expected the castle to be on lockdown, but the fact that this seemed almost too easy didn't sit right with me, and I began to think that maybe we should pull out of here. Zade started walking down the hallway again before I could protest going farther.

I stepped out and began to follow him but stopped when I heard the faintest noise behind us. When I turned, the two guards that had passed us were now facing us and had their swords drawn. Their eyes widened in recognition when they saw me. They didn't drop their swords but made no move to hurt us. Wisp rammed at them, causing them to stumble slightly from her unseen force. It wasn't enough to help me get the upper hand, though.

"I don't want to hurt you, but I will," I promised.

Before they could say anything, Zade had knocked both swords from their hands, each of us taking one. The two guards didn't give in easy though, and they both came at us, ready to fight. The guard that charged me was small in stature. His hair was bright blonde, and his eyes were so blue that it was like looking into a summer sky. I was surprised when he shifted his weight suddenly and landed a swift kick to my chest. Pain racked through me as I fell into the wall.

"You're out of practice, Captain," he said, hissing out my title. I flicked my wrist and wrapped him in a fiery mist.

"I don't need practice when I have all this magic," I snapped back venomously. He struggled against the mist, but I walked up and punched him as hard as I could, rendering him unconscious. I hoped he would not awaken until we were long gone. Zade was busy fighting the bigger of the two, and his skills were unmatched by the Cerithian guard. Dodging a punch to the face, he grabbed the guard's arm and twisted it behind his back, putting him in a chokehold and keeping him there until he passed out.

"Let's get moving," I whispered, and we hurried down the hallway. We made turns in the hallways that felt right, but we really didn't have any idea where we were going. I slowed when the wisp appeared at a corner, not moving. We approached the corner slowly, spying more guards sitting outside of a wooden door.

My heart pounded hard as I recognized that it was the wooden door from my dream. How many times had I wondered what this door was, and now I was standing mere feet away? The large crest on the door belonged to the royal family of Cerithia. It had to be the king's throne room. Dread filled me. Why had I dreamed of this door so much? Was it due to the witch's bloodstone being in there? Six guards stood outside this entrance, but how many waited on the inside? I wondered if there was another, less secure entrance that we could use. Gods, I wish I could remember more about this place.

I turned to Zade but was met by the sight of four guards restraining him instead. Realizing he was in danger, I stood up and raised my hands in defeat.

"If you move, we kill him," one of the men sneered. "Move forward."

I heeded his command and turned towards the throne room, where the guards now all watched me and immediately drew their weapons on me. Glancing over their faces, I felt tugs in my mind that let me know they were familiar. These were men I had trained. I was their captain. Fear trickled into my mind, but a calm, soothing emotion spread through me to combat it. Cassius. I tried as hard as I could to push the image of me being caught to him, but I didn't know if it worked. I felt nothing through the blood bond.

"Captain." The guards bowed as I stood in front of them and lowered their swords.

They opened the door and ushered me right in. Their weapons were still drawn, but they weren't looking at me with malice. When I walked in, I froze in place when I saw that the king of Cerithia stood in the middle of the room. In his hand was what looked like a giant red ruby, the witch's bloodstone. The guards shut the door behind me, leaving me and the king alone.

CHAPTER 26

My eyes scanned the room, which was dominated by a silver throne at the front. I tried to focus on the king in front of me though, instead of the over-the-top décor. He was slightly heavy-set and extremely tall. His dark hair was highlighted with streaks of silver, and his eyes matched my own, a dark green that reminded me of the moss that grew in the Forbidden Wood. His crown was tall, gold, and decorated in blue stones that matched the blue robe he wore. He was good-looking, but years of being king had weighed on him and seemed to have weathered him a bit.

His dark, bushy eyebrows furrowed as I stood staring at him. His eyes widened as he gazed over me like he was seeing a ghost. I guess I hadn't been here in seven years at least. He cleared his throat as if he were getting emotional.

"So, it's true. You finally made it through the trials." His voice wrapped around me like an emotional hug. The feelings confused me because I didn't know this man.

He locked eyes with me, and I could see the questions swimming in them. His grip tightened on the red stone in his hand.

"You will not be stopped if you choose to take this stone to the Crimson kingdom." He frowned at me. "You and all of your friends can go back if you choose to."

"I'm supposed to believe that you'll let me walk out of here and give your enemy this stone." I scoffed. Did he think I was stupid? "Why would I ever believe you?"

He took a deep breath and looked over my face in thought.

"You still don't have any memories," he guessed. "Is that why you look at me like a stranger?"

"You are a stranger," I hissed.

Pain, that is what crossed his features, and something deep in my chest tugged at the sight. I pushed away the feeling.

"I thought the curse wouldn't take all your memories. I thought you could recognize your own father, Thea."

Father.

I blinked slowly as my mind tried to process this. An empty void filled my mind as the word ricocheted through it.

"Thea," he whispered and took a step towards me slowly, but I stepped back. "We have missed you so much over the years," the king choked out with emotion. "You have a family, and we love you."

Something deep in my memories called him a liar. I had seen him in my dreams, and he was always so mean to me in them. I only glared back at his comment.

"I know we fought, and I pushed you too hard. I have regretted it every day that you've been gone. I have often wondered if I had shown you how much I did care, if that would have kept you from running into the arms of our enemy."

"What are you doing?" I questioned. "Am I supposed to stand here and believe that you missed me? You want to think that you tried to find me, that you love me, that you want me back? I have flashes of memories, and all of them showed that you left me feeling like shit."

He flinched at my words, as if they slapped him.

"I know, but now we have a chance to try again. For me to right my mistakes and show you that I can be the father you always needed me to be."

"Give me the stone," I demanded and held out my hand.

The king stood, stunned, looking at me like he couldn't believe I wouldn't take his word for it. His eyes filled with unshed tears. His daughter, I had thought images or memories would plague me with this information, but nothing came. Why hadn't Cassius told me this?

"They haven't told you anything, have they? If they had, then you wouldn't be getting this stone for them. You wouldn't choose them over your own father, over your family, or over your kingdom. Did they even tell you who cursed you, or what actually happened?"

"They can't. The curse keeps them from saying too much."

He laughed. This bastard laughed at my response, and it made me so angry. I felt my fire coming forth, and he held up his hands in defense.

"Cassius was always a clever boy; he always had a keen sense of telling pretty lies and finding ways out of telling the truth. I almost wasn't surprised when you told me you loved him. He's a master manipulator, and you were the perfect target—because of me, because you felt you had to settle for that monster. The Crimson kingdom will do whatever it can to be in control and to have all the power. Including lying to you about all of this, about whom, and why you were cursed to begin with. He can tell you, but he doesn't want to because he is still using and manipulating you after everything. After seven years, you still fall for it, and I can't be upset because you have no memories."

I wanted to refute this, to argue with him, but something stopped me. A tickle of a memory somewhere in my broken mind. Was Cassius lying to me? He had told me he couldn't say anything, but he had told me a lot about us in recent days. He had waited until the trials were almost over to tell me anything.

"I can see you thinking it over, which means you know it's possible." The king watched me with pity.

"He took you from me and kept you for himself under the guise of love, but this was always his plan. From the moment he saw you, you were his finale in gaining the most power in all of Elloryon. He wants to overthrow the other kingdoms, and you are the key to power and control Thea. The prophet told all of us. You alone can make kingdoms crumble. You control *everything* because of your magic. You are a weapon, but you can still choose if it's for good or evil. You just have to choose what side to fight for."

A new sense of belonging slipped into place in my mind. My father seemed accepting of my power and abilities. It was the first time that I contemplated my magic being used for good instead of evil. No one else had ever mentioned that I had a choice in this. Sadness filled me as I realized that I had let others dictate and tell me what I was going to be and do without much of a fight. They had treated me like something to be feared, but my magic could do good; I saw this now. I could use it to help others. Maybe I could even change the prophets telling.

"You don't think my magic is... evil."

"Only if you want it to be, Thea."

I turned away from him so he couldn't see the confusion clouding me. I glanced at Wisp for some clarity, but she just floated in the shadows like a white flame. She had never been that color before, and I didn't know what it meant. Doubt swirled in my mind and wrapped everything I knew about Cassius in a dark blanket. His face clouded my mind. He wouldn't do that to me. He wouldn't hold things, like the reason for the curse, from me. Cassius loved me. Didn't he? Everything I thought I knew threatened to crumble around me. I couldn't possibly know the truth of anything on my own. I relied on others, and it made this all impossible to sort. My heart couldn't fathom Cassius betraying me. It wasn't true. I turned back to the king to find that he was holding out the bloodstone to me.

"I know you are confused. I can't even imagine, Thea. So, take this." He handed it over without hesitation. The stone's power hummed through it as I looked up at him, not understanding why he was letting me have it. "Just do me one favor before you cross back over to Crimson."

"Okay," I agreed hesitantly.

"Ask Cassius who is responsible for the curse. Ask him why you were cursed to begin with. He can tell you, so do not let him fool you into thinking he can't. Demand it if you have to. You deserve to know the truth before giving this stone to a side." He pulled me to him and hugged me so tightly, his scent of sunshine, flowers, and fresh air wrapping around me. I could feel my eyes filling with tears, but I refused to let them fall.

I didn't hug him back. When he pulled away, I peered over his face, which barely resembled mine, but those eyes undeniably mirrored my own.

Father.

My father was the king. Cassius hadn't told me that. Cassius hadn't told me anything but happy, pretty memories of us. He had intentionally left out anything bad, and I didn't question it because I wanted to be happy. I wanted to turn a blind eye to the bad times. It didn't even cross my mind to think about asking. He had kept things from me already. He didn't tell me he was the prince or that we knew each other. Cassius only revealed things when he wanted to.

He could tell me things but only told me what would make him look good. The whole kingdom had treated me so well for being the daughter of their enemy, for being the captain of their enemy's guard. Doubt crept into my mind as I turned around and headed for the wooden doors that I had come in. I shouldn't be quick to trust my father, but gods, his words made sense. Cassius hadn't told me the truth about anything until I asked.

"You will always have a spot here in your home," my father called after me.

I didn't acknowledge him. I wanted to say this wasn't my home, but I just kept walking. The guards bowed to me like I was still their captain as I passed. The stone felt heavy in my hand, and a shift of uneasiness had filled me as I walked through the castle and out the front doors. Slowly, I walked towards the tree line where my horse was. The rest of the competitors were all waiting for me with looks of confusion and worry. When I reached them, Haden gripped me tightly by the shoulders.

"I thought they killed you," Haden sighed. "They caught all of us, and then just let us go," he said, confused. I held out the bloodstone, and they all quieted down. "You got it." His shoulders sagged with relief, but I couldn't even summon a fake smile.

My mind was weighed down by what my father had said. I knew he had a motive and wanted me to choose him and the kingdom of Cerithia, but I couldn't shake the words away. They swirled and gripped all my happy memories of Cassius and shielded me from them. This would all be sorted out when I asked him about it. At least that's what I told myself as I climbed on my horse and took off in a dead sprint towards the Crimson kingdom.

I could feel Cassius tug on the bond of the blood mark, and I barely could muster the mental to let him know I was ok. Was I okay? No. Haden had asked me countless times if I was alright. I lied and said yes, but he told me he wasn't buying it. I didn't answer him again. When we rested for the night, I didn't sleep. There was no way I could face Cassius right now. My mind was still processing the things my father told me. I would confront Cassius at the border. He couldn't cross over to me, and it would give me time to think. Besides, my father was following us. I had heard his guards moving in the trees around us as we slept. I would have them to back me up if this went sideways.

Worry filled me from the blood mark. He knew something was wrong, but I didn't even try to respond anymore. I needed someone to tell me the truth, and Cassius would do that. Whatever he told me, I would take it as the truth because I loved him. I woke the guys up at first sunlight so we could get to the boundary of Crimson and Cerithian lands quickly.

"You didn't sleep," Haden observed. "Please tell me what's going on, Thea. I'm on your side."

"Did you know the king of Cerithia is my father?" I scrutinized him, hoping that he would show me a face of pure shock, but he just frowned instead.

"Yes."

"Cassius never told me," I whispered. "He could have told me that at least."

"Thea..." Haden started, but I urged my horse to go quicker, pushing her to a run to avoid any more conversation. She ran so fast that my braid whipped in the wind and became loose. My mind was a foggy haze of confusion, racing with thoughts of Cassius and I. What if everything my father said was true? What if Cassius never loved me, never cared for me, but really was using me? Flashes of what Nev had said when he kidnapped me swarmed through my mind. The memory of Cassius I had regained while with Nev had been awful. He had said such cruel things about me.

Cassius had also said he was trying to avoid me in order to help me make it through the trials, but was that an excuse too? Did he just want to be far away from me because I was just a pawn? He had humiliated me twice, and both times he had given me some excuse that I believed immediately. I should have pushed more, questioned his motives more. Fae in Exile had blamed the Crimson king for our imprisonments. I had fallen for their fake kindness so easily. Shame filled me. I felt like I failed Sybil and the twins.

Or maybe my father was lying. But what did he have to gain from lying? Maybe he didn't want his daughter to serve his enemy. Dread filled my chest, crushing my lungs to the point it physically hurt to breathe.

When the boundary came into sight, my stomach churned with fear. I asked the gods above to let this all be untrue as we came to a large clearing. The boundary between Crimson and Cerithia threatened to swallow me whole as the pressure of choosing settled heavily on me.

They were all there waiting. Crimson's fae and royalty all stood in this clearing to welcome us back. The guys had ridden in front of me through the boundary that divided the land without noticing I had fallen behind. I could feel the bloodstone pulsing in my pocket as if to tell me to ask for answers.

Immediately, Haden went and said something to Cassius and the king. Their gazes immediately darted to me, full of concern as they moved closer. I dismounted my horse and stood twenty yards from the boundary. Cassius' body was tense, and his eyes flickered with something close to worry.

"My love?" Cassius stopped right at the boundary. "What's the matter?"

Our eyes locked, and I could feel it. I could feel that I would never be the same after this. I would either be broken beyond repair or finally whole. Either way, though, I would forever be altered.

This was the defining moment of my life.

"Did you not get the stone?" The stone. He was worried about the damn stone. I pulled it from my pocket and showed it to him. "Then why do you look so... sad?"

I took a breath to steady myself for whatever was going to happen, for whatever he would tell me. Maybe I could even forgive him for withholding the information from me. Maybe it wasn't that bad. Cassius ran his eyes over me as if trying to see if I was wounded.

"Why am I cursed?" I asked softly, but I knew he heard me. His body stilled so slightly that if I wasn't so worried about his response, I wouldn't have noticed.

"I can't tell you." Just as my father predicted. A lie. I just knew he was lying to me. The realm stood so still as doubt clouded my empty mind even more. Please, Cassius, don't betray me like everyone else. Not you. I can't handle you being the one to hurt me, to break me.

"Who cursed me?" I tried a different question.

"Thea, I can't—" His skin paled.

"Yes, you can!" I yelled so loudly that it shook the ground. "Just tell me."

He didn't say anything for a long moment. His pretty golden eyes stared at me like he was trying to come up with a way to tell me something I didn't want to hear.

"She knows you can tell her." The king of Cerithia appeared from the forest behind me. I had felt them following us, but I didn't care. I didn't warn the rest of my team because I had a feeling this was the beginning of the end. Cassius glanced at his father with a look of sadness I had never seen before. Was his father the one who had cursed me, like I had thought all these years? Could I forgive that?

"Tell her who cursed her, Cassius," my father demanded softly.

CHAPTER 27

Cassius stared at me with pleading eyes, and it made me so anxious that I felt tears brimming in my eyes, threatening to escape.

"Who?" I begged. The wisp stood by Cassius with dark gray flames.

"Please, Thea, don't do this. You're so close," he begged.

"Who!"

We stared at one another for what seemed like an eternity. My stomach lurched at the way his body sagged with defeat. The way his eyes filled with regret and remorse made tears silently slide down my cheeks.

"I did," he confessed softly.

As if I had been slapped, I stumbled backwards. No. He didn't do this to me. He loves me. My fire mist burst out of me, and it crept along the ground towards him, wrapping around his wrists, but instead of hurting him, it seemed to caress him. It begged him to be lying. Cassius closed his eyes tightly, like that was the worst thing I could have done to him at that moment—to caress him like he was everything to me, because he *was* everything to me. He fell to his knees as silent tears fell down his face.

Haden and everyone behind him watched me like all of them had known he was the one who cursed me. My magic tightened on Cassius as the truth sank in. That darkness that lived in me clawed its way up my chest. *Betrayal, betrayal, betrayal*—it called out in my mind.

He had lied to us. The darkness wanted to take over to help me from falling apart, but I couldn't allow it. *Kill him. Kill him. Make him pay for what he did to us. For making us believe his pretty words, for being so blind.* The wisps had gathered by the dozens at Crimson's border, all of them a sad, melancholy gray to match how I felt.

"Tell her how you cursed her, what you had to do to her for her soul to be damned," my father demanded with anger.

"Please," Cassius begged on his knees, still bound by my magic. "Thea."

"He killed you," my father answered. "He drove a dagger straight through your heart, that viper-handled one you love so much."

Cassius' lips pressed into a hard line as I fell to my knees. Somewhere far away, my world fell off its axis and stopped moving. My body froze at the statement, but I still hoped that my father was lying. My fire mist jolted a wave of betrayal down it. Cassius' painful sob made me pull them away, but I could see what I had done. I had burned red marks around his wrists.

"But I'm not dead," I muttered to my father. "I'm fine." He was lying. This had to be a lie. My father gave me a look of pure pity.

"Tell me that he's lying, Cassius," I cried out to him. His eyes were so colorless as he looked back at me. My heart thudded inside my chest loudly as I waited for him to refute all of this. All he had to do was tell me my father was lying, and I would run across this boundary and choose him. "Tell everyone that you would have never done that to me." He physically winced at my pleading.

"He's telling the truth," Cassius whispered. The wisps turned black in an instant, then began swirling together like a black tornado. Only they didn't go after Cassius. They charged at me instead. Were they angry with me for believing Cassius? They broke into a million floating orbs when they rammed through me, but I couldn't focus on them.

I shook my head no. "Why are you lying to me?" I cried out. "You love me!"

He simply hung his head in shame. No, this was a bad dream, and I would wake up in the cave. I must have fallen asleep.

"It was a betrayal that ran so deep and was so wicked that it cursed your soul to die over and over again in front of the man you had loved so deeply. The gods themselves came down from the stars to curse you for loving the wrong man. These trials they put on every year to get you out of hiding were just a ploy. You don't need them to get your life back. All you had to do was take the witch's bloodstone and gift it to a side. You weren't meant to die. You were never supposed to be with him," my father hissed towards Cassius. "He just wants you for your power and the stone."

I shook the images out of my mind of Cassius driving a dagger with a viper-handle through my heart. He killed me with my own dagger.

"You've died in every trial but this one," my father continued. "His curse to bear is to watch you die over and over. His burden is to make you fall in love with him over and over again without you ever remembering who he is. Because if he can't convince you that he loves you back, you'd never choose him to gift the bloodstone to—not over your own family."

Cassius was completely broken now, and I was slowly slipping into a darkness so black that I didn't know if I would ever find my way out of it. I felt my own darkness trying to consume me, as if to say it would protect me.

He had killed me. He had cursed me. He had broken me beyond repair.

"The day he killed you, the gods granted him a choice. Either let your soul move to the next world or give you a chance to get your life back. Your magic is special, Thea, and it was never meant to end so quickly. Even the gods did not see the betrayal coming. Your memories were erased each time you died so that you did not have to remember what he did to you."

"That is not why they erase your memories!" Cassius called out to me. "He's manipulating you, my love."

"Then tell her whatever excuse you have." My father glared.

"I can't." He frowned. "Thea, I swear…" His voice faded as my mind raced.

My mind flashed to Cassius resting his hand over my heart a few short days ago. He had made it a point to say it was his favorite sound. But he had apparently ended that sound by stabbing me through the heart. I didn't know how to believe that I had died over and over again. I could hear sobs come from me, but I felt as though I watched it all from outside of my body. How could this happen? He had convinced me he had loved me. Had he pretended the whole time? Nev's words came back to haunt me. *You're falling for it...again.*

Did he ever love me? All of the stories he told me, were any of them true? Everyone's eyes were on me as I kneeled in the dirt and mud, feeling the betrayal as if it were the first time I ever felt it. My darkness erupted so viciously out of me that the noise that ripped from my chest sounded unnatural, and the ground cleaved in two between us from the power behind it. Birds flew from the trees as dark clouds moved over the clearing to match the devastation I was feeling. Still though, the wisps didn't move from Cassius' side.

A sharp, unforgiving pain had my eyes snapping to my wrist where the marking he gave me sat. Only now the crown had a large crack through it. Broken, just like me. Red and orange swirls formed on my skin as darkness covered my sight. Cassius was saying something to me, but I couldn't hear him through the thoughts of betrayal screaming through my mind. The weight of his betrayal was slowly crushing me as I kneeled in the mud, and the truth of everything came crashing around me. Tears ran down my face like rivers, taking all the happy moments with Cassius away with them.

He never loved me. It was all a show. I was just a pawn, like I had feared. If my curse was losing memories, did that mean Exile was a part of it?

"What about Exile?" I asked my father.

"I don't know what that is," he frowned.

"Where I have lived these past seven years. Where all the elite magic holders live."

My father's eyes frosted over.

"That must have been part of the curse," he muttered. "It doesn't exist."

"Thea, he's lying!" The king of Crimson called out to me.

"B-but I've been there. I've lived there with Sybil, Kaz, and Kai. It has to be real."

My father glanced down at me with pity. My stomach lurched at the look, knowing that only bad news would follow.

"Sybil and the twins died, Thea. They can't be in Exile with you because they're dead, and Exile doesn't exist."

My mind raced with flashes of Sybil and the twins. That couldn't be true. It all seemed so...real. Tears blurred my vision as everything I thought I knew was ripped from me. Was part of the curse to make me think I wasn't alone in Exile? Nothing made sense.

"I'm sorry," my father whispered. "I know how important they were to you."

A fog of confusion overtook any ability I had to think. Sybil and the twins were dead. I had died. Cassius killed me. Cassius didn't love me. My father was the only one telling me the truth. He thought my magic could be good.

It was too much to process.

"It was all a lie," I whispered, trying to process it all. Sobs wracked through me as racing flashes of my time with Cassius tortured me. How did I fall so easily for his bullshit when I knew I was never worthy?

"No, it was not," Cassius pleaded.

"You killed me." I tried not to cry, but I was no longer in control of my emotions. "You shoved my own dagger into my heart and killed me. For what, power? To curse my soul? I do not understand."

"Because it had to be done." He said it so casually, like he wasn't talking about ending my life. His face was cold as he looked at me now. He couldn't pretend to care about me any longer, I supposed, like it didn't matter...like I didn't matter. I was a pawn to everyone, and I should have just stayed dead. Cassius' face contorted like he heard every thought racing in my mind. At his declaration, I stood on shaky legs and frowned at him one last time before turning and handing the bloodstone to my father.

"You chose Cerithia," Cassius said in a voice so dark and menacing that it made me recoil from him. "Do not come back to the Crimson lands again, Thea Alzara of Cerithia, born enemy of my kingdom, my crown, Crimson fae, the family of Valeska... of me." He stood and glared at me, his eyes so black I could hardly tell it was him. "I wasted years pretending to care about you all for you to still choose Cerithia!" His voice bellowed so loudly that trees swayed at his madness.

Stop. Please. My eyes begged him.

I could not stand to know it was all a lie. I could not get through this. At least if I didn't hear him say it, I could pretend.

"Stop." My one word plea fell from my lips because the lump in my throat wouldn't allow any other response from me. I feared I would lose myself completely if he kept talking. It made Cassius' dark shadows swirl around him in an angry cloud as he fisted his hands by his sides.

"No." His voice was thunderous in the clearing. He took deliberate steps back to escape me, each one making my chest ache with loss. "You chose them, so I guess you want the truth. How easy it was to manipulate and bend you at my will. I've never had to work so little for something before, Thea. You were so fucking desperate for attention and love that you would have fallen for the first man to bat his eyes in your direction. And I thought I was lucky, blessed by the gods above, that I found you first, before another kingdom could sink their claws into you. What a waste. That is what I will remember every time I think of you."

His shadows circled him in an angry, ominous storm, filled with hate and disgust for me. No one had ever looked at me with this much hatred. This wasn't him pushing me away to protect me. Cassius meant every word he said to me.

Tears brimmed in my eyes as Cassius transformed into a heartless monster. *A waste. Pathetic. Unlovable. Unworthy of love. I should have stayed dead.* My body trembled at the hate in his voice when he talked about me. How could he be my Cassius, the one I loved only yesterday? Everyone behind him stood immobile, like they too couldn't believe how horrible he was being, but they did nothing to stop it. The Crimson king looked at me with pity as I sank onto the ground, curling into a ball so that Cassius' words could not get to me, but they still had.

Please, gods above, let the ground open and swallow me whole. I did not want to be here any longer. I needed Cassius to be lying. He was the only one to make me feel like I wasn't a monster. If he thought I was a monster, then it must be true, and who would ever love something so grotesque as me?

"Look at the pathetic captain of your guard, King Luren. Look at how easy it was for me to weasel my way in and break her." Cassius laughed, and it pierced straight into my heart, obliterating it beyond repair.

Someone lifted me off the ground, and I didn't fight it. Maybe they would end my pathetic existence.

"It's alright, Thea. I've got you."

My eyes stared up into bright blue ones. His hair was dark blonde and his face handsome. The boy who had kissed me in those memories when I first arrived at Cerithia lifted me effortlessly. The wisp's black flames caught my eye as they swirled around me. I didn't know what they wanted from me.

"You can have my sloppy seconds, Jesper, but just re-member how easily I took her from you the first time," Cassius hissed at the man holding me, then tensed with hatred as he watched me being carried away.

"Enough!" my father yelled. "Being a sore loser doesn't suit you, Cassius," he said in a much calmer, composed tone, allowing a smug smile to creep onto his face.

"Who's the loser here? I no longer have to tame that monster you're holding. I don't have to pretend to love her. I don't ever have to touch her again or force lies out of my mouth to make her believe anyone could love her. How could they love a monstrosity like you?" His last words were directed at me and were punctuated to drive home the idea that I was not worthy of anyone, especially the prince of Crimson, who could have whomever he desired.

I was a monster. He thought I was a monster, just like I feared. He had to be completely disgusted every time he touched me, kissed me, or said those pretty lies to me. Did my touch make him feel uncomfortable? Did he think of someone else when he looked at me like he loved me? Was there someone else he loved, someone worthy of him? Did they laugh behind my back because I stupidly thought he could love me when I knew all along that I was a disgusting monster? The thought of every touch and kiss we had shared made me cringe inward with complete disgust for myself. His words shredded through any hope I had that I could be desired or loved by anyone. I didn't even love myself; how could I expect anyone else to?

My gaze shifted to Cassius as his cold, unforgiving eyes glared at me with pure hatred radiating from them. Yet my pathetic heart still wanted him to say he was lying and to come get me, to live in those pretty lies he whispered to me. Everything I thought I knew about my past crumbled around me and painted the true, sad, and pathetic existence I had before Exile.

Unloved now, unloved always.

"I've got better things to do than be here," Cassius spoke as his eyes stared at me. Then he turned around and disappeared into his shadow mist without a glance back. My eyes stared at where he had vanished. Haden, Zade, and Kace stood on Crimson's side, staring at me with confusion. The wisps floated in a white flame. They didn't move from their spot, almost like they didn't know how to process the news either. Weren't they my friends? The clearing was silent besides my sobs that sounded like my heart had been ripped violently out of my chest. The king of Crimson's face was the last one I saw. Tears filled his eyes as I turned away from him.

They had all used and betrayed me. All of them probably laughed with Cassius about how stupid the princess of Cerithia was.

I heard the unnatural growl in the far distance, and it called to my own darkness. Cassius. He must be so relieved to be free from me and to never have to see me again. Never touch me or lie to me; now he could be free to find someone else. Jesper placed me in a carriage with him and my father, and we slowly moved away from the clearing. I could hear them talking, but all that ran through my tainted soul were images of a life Cassius had promised me, a life that had never been possible, a life I didn't deserve but allowed myself to believe in anyway.

My darkness swept through me, quelling my emotions and allowing me to only notice a small ache of the betrayal I was feeling. Would I ever be able to free myself from this pain? I was a monster, and I should have never left Exile. I should never have been born.

But something darker burned below my hurt...rage. Rage that Cassius had used and manipulated me so effortlessly. Rage because I loved a man who only wanted to take something from me. My eyes glanced up at Jesper as he watched me oddly.

"We'll make everyone in Crimson pay for what they did to you." His eyes shone brightly as I nodded in agreement.

Vengeance... My darkness hummed at the thought.

"Don't worry, Thea, you will get your chance for revenge," my father bit out coldly. "This time, you will be the one to drive a dagger through Cassius' heart, if he even possesses one."

SHAY TAYLOR

SUBSCRIBE TO SHAY'S NEWSLETTER FOR UPDATES ON PROJECTS, GIVEAWAYS, AND EXCLUSIVE CONTENT!

WWW.AUTHORSHAYTAYLOR.COM

FOLLOW SHAY ON TIKTOK AND INSTAGRAM

@shaytaylorauthor